Buenos Aires
Broken Hearts Club

The
Buenos Aires
Broken Hearts Club

JESSICA
MORRISON

5 SPOT ●●●●●

NEW YORK BOSTON

This book is a work of fiction. Names, characters, places, and incidents are the product of the author's imagination or are used fictitiously. Any resemblance to actual events, locales, or persons, living or dead, is coincidental.

5 Spot
Hachette Book Group USA
1271 Avenue of the Americas
New York, NY 10020

Visit our Web site at www.5-spot.com.

5 Spot is an imprint of Warner Books.
The 5 Spot name and logo are trademarks of Warner Books.

Printed in the United States of America

First Edition: May 2007
10 9 8 7 6 5 4 3 2 1

Library of Congress Cataloging-in-Publication Data
    Morrison, Jessica.
      Buenos Aires broken hearts club / Jessica Morrison. — 1st ed.
          p. cm.
        Summary: "A debut novel about finding a new life and happiness where you least expect it"—Provided by publisher.
      ISBN-13: 978-0-446-69912-9
      ISBN-10: 0-446-69912-8
          1. Young women—Fiction. 2. Life change events—Fiction. 3. Web sites—Fiction.
      4. Buenos Aires (Argentina)—Fiction. I. Title.
      PS3613.O7765B84 2007
      813'.6—dc22
                                                              2006031876

For Christi, Leanne, Shaun, and Sophy—

my broken hearts club

ACKNOWLEDGMENTS

First thanks must go to my first readers, my mother, Elizabeth Rains, my sister, Danielle Michael, and my almost-sister, Leanne Chapotelle. You slogged through my typo-ridden first draft and returned careful comments that helped make this a much better book. Another great big thank-you to Kerry Morrison. You gave me several things for this book, dear friend, including all the lessons in love and heartbreak I'll ever need.

Thank you, Bill Contardi, my all-knowing NYC agent, for your encouragement and endless patience with this publishing neophyte. Eternal gratitude goes to my editor, Caryn Karmatz Rudy. Your sage suggestions and boundless enthusiasm meant more than you can know.

My thanks to all the friends and family who kept me afloat with their unfailing confidence that I would make something of this little idea I had—especially my dad, Al Hyland, who is also my biggest fan. And thanks, finally, to my friends in Buenos Aires for never suspecting how scared I was to travel there, and for later understanding how scared I was to go home. I'm glad I did both.

The
Buenos Aires
Broken Hearts Club

CHAPTER ONE

I feel light-headed, like all the blood is draining from my face, arms, legs, baby toes. This
might have something to do with the fact that
my hands are pressing against the armrests so tightly my fingertips are turning purple. My entire body is ready to pounce. If that
flight attendant would just get out of my way, I could head back
up the aisle, through that maze of a connecting ramp, past the
gate personnel, and into the safety of Sea-Tac Airport. But she's
struggling with someone's stupid oversize blue carry-on that's
clearly too big to fit in that tiny wire frame at the check-in counter
that tells you when your stupid oversize blue carry-on is way too
big to fit in a plane's overhead compartment. I could try one of
those exits conveniently located at midcabin: two near the front
and two near the back. We haven't actually started moving, so
how far down could it be to the tarmac anyway?

I peer out the window—it looks pretty far down—and the lu-
nacy of this plan hits me. Am I actually plotting my escape from
an airplane just minutes from takeoff? If this moment were happening to someone else, a character in a movie, say, I'd probably be
laughing. It is funny, isn't it? I attempt a laugh, but all that comes
out is a sad little wheeze. No, not funny. Definitely not funny.

The tanned and taut older woman in the seat next to me
glances in my direction. "Afraid to fly, dear?" she asks in a buttery
Spanish accent.

"No," I reply. "Afraid to land."

She looks at me quizzically and, I think, a bit amused. She wouldn't give me that look if she knew what I've gotten myself into. If she knew my pathetic state, she'd be offering me one of those little purple pills she chased with a miniature bottle of vodka a few minutes ago when she thought no one was looking.

Two weeks ago, life was so so so perfect. Flawless. On track. Nobody had it more together than I did. I watched in pity as Gen Xers wandered the streets of Seattle disillusioned and disassociated in their post-grunge, pre-Prada uniforms, desperately grasping their Motorolas and Starbucks as though instant messaging and a smooth Ethiopian roast could fill the gaping holes in their lives. They didn't have a clue where they were going or how they were getting there. My life, on the other hand, was going exactly according to plan, due in no small part to the fact that I had one.

When I was seventeen, I planned my life. The whole thing. Being someone who's particularly good at organizing things, I have to say it was a rather spectacular plan. I didn't just scribble a hopeful list of things to do in the back of a diary or one of those fancy leather-bound journals that cost so much I never understood how people brought themselves to spoil them with Bic scribblings. No, my plan was serious business, and I treated it accordingly. Everything I wanted to accomplish over the course of my life was carefully, deliberately contained in one handy color-coded spreadsheet completed in my grade-twelve word-processing class.

I had always been an orderly child—the kind who has different crayon boxes for each season (use burnt umber in the spring? as if) and took her days-of-the-week underwear very seriously—so it never occurred to me that perhaps planning one's entire life before one can even vote or buy alcohol might be a tad on the ambitious side. I approached the process systematically, as I did all things, drafting version after version until I had it exactly right. My plan was broken into eight manageable ten-year stages. Those ten-year stages were further broken down by major five-year goals, with a list of detailed tasks that would lead to each goal. I'd considered drilling down even deeper, but I didn't want to be neurotic about it. The point was to simply clarify what I wanted and when. It was all there—nothing unrealistic, like be a rock star or discover the cure for cancer, just your typical how-to-be-sure-you've-got-it-all-covered-and-are-blissfully-happy-forever-and-ever life plan kind of stuff. You know, job, apartment, man, kids, house, dog, summer home, volunteer work, crafts, grandkids, another dog, etc.

For years I kept a copy of the plan on my fridge the way other women tack up photos of anorexic models for inspiration. There was one tucked into the back of my day planner, naturally, and another folded into my wallet, in case I lost my day planner. Once I discovered the World Wide Web, I ramped things up a notch and took my plan online. That way I could look at it from home, work, on vacation even, check things off on the go, and quickly print updated hard copies.

I know I can get a little obsessive about it—I know each step in the plan as well as I know every *Sex and the City* plot twist—but if you want to stay on track with your life, you've got to know where the track is, right?

Okay, so not everyone agrees. My friend Trish calls it The Plan, as in "Want to try snowboarding next weekend—or is it not in *The Plan*?" and "I'm not sure if red's your color. Better check *The Plan*." Last year one of my hilarious coworkers with far too much time on his hands posted his own version on the bulletin board in the lunchroom: Become president of the Daughters of the American Revolution, get sex-change operation, take over Canada, knit scarves for the cast of *Cats*, etc. My initially pro-Plan mother thought it was brilliant until she realized that my plan was not exactly like the one she had for me. She found my decision not to have children until my early thirties particularly distressing.

But I knew something they didn't. I had figured out the secret to happily ever after.

Last month, on the eve of my twenty-eighth birthday, instead of wallowing in self-pity or indulging in a quarter-life crisis—on her twenty-eighth, my old roommate Sarah quit her job and moved to Alaska to work as a cook at a logging camp (a logging camp—I mean, who does that?)—I sat back with a glass of wine and the plan (version 12.4) and admired all those happy little checkmarks I'd earned in the past decade:

☐ Get accepted to any—ANY—college out of state. Check. University of Wisconsin. Solid academic program, good social scene, and hundreds of miles from my parents' house. Go Badgers.

☐ Eschew snotty college sorority experience and embrace dorm life à la Felicity. Check. Okay, so my RA didn't look like Noel, but I did make some amazing friends who still liked me when I cut my hair into a pixie senior year.

☐ Lose virginity freshman year to a cute, popular sophomore or junior. Check. Cam Bowers after a kegger. Painful, clumsy, and thank God, fast. I heard Cam got fat and works at his dad's tire company. Still counts.

☐ Try one illicit drug. Check. Pot, acid, X, pot, X, X, X . . . What can I say? It was college. Of course, all that came to an abrupt halt when I woke up one morning wearing someone else's bra.

☐ Get a degree in something non-flaky that might actually lead to a good job. Check. Business admin. So what if my college friends enjoyed their English lit/political science/modern dance classes. They might as well have majored in upselling appetizers for all the good their degrees did them. I, on the other hand, was upwardly mobile.

☐ Get previously mentioned good job. Check. Assistant producer at Idealmatch.com, the fourth largest dating website in the U.S. Worked my way up from researcher. All those dull statistics courses finally came in handy.

☐ Have a one-night stand. Check. Starbucks barista with a Kurt Cobain thing going on. Bonus: still get free Macchiatos.

☐ Buy a pair of shoes over three hundred dollars. Check. Check. Check.

☐ Find adorable apartment in University district, Capitol Hill, or somewhere else really cool. Check. One-bedroom Bridget Fonda-in-*Singles*-esque walk-up with hardwood floors, a fountain in the courtyard, and rent so cheap I felt like I was stealing. (Three-hundred-dollar shoes helped ease the guilt.) Of course, I eventually gave it up to move into a downtown loft with floor-to-ceiling windows and a concierge. So what if the building was kind of impersonal and I never looked at the view. My new roomie trumped Matt Dillon any day.

☐ Meet perfect man. Check. Gorgeous, smart, ambitious Jeff with fabulous downtown loft.

☐ Get engaged. Check. Jeff proposed on Valentine's Day after a decadent meal at the top of the Space Needle, where he gave me a stunning two-carat diamond ring hidden in a piece of cheesecake. My friends would swoon when they heard the story. Like everything else in our one-year relationship, it was pure fairy tale. Could anything but bliss follow?

☐ Have dream wedding. Almost check. Jeff was too stressed working full-time and studying for the bar, but once he was done with that, we'd set a date and start planning (or rather, start putting my wedding-day plans in motion). As long as it happened before I turned thirty, I was fine.

How could I not be? I was twenty-eight and everything in my life was precisely the way it should be. To top it off, Jeff was taking me away for the weekend, I wasn't currently arguing with my mother, and work was great. Being an assistant producer suited me. I spent my days making and enforcing schedules, drafting and checking off lists—it doesn't get much better than that. They liked me, too. There'd been a recent round of layoffs, but I was still there. Better yet, word around the office was that they were going to fill the empty producer spot from inside the company.

I put down my glass of wine and started packing for the trip, trying to focus on all the activities Jeff had planned, but my mind kept wandering back to that job opening. They won't pick you, I told myself. Definitely not. It's too soon. They'll promote someone who's been there longer. According to my plan, I wasn't even scheduled for a serious promotion until thirty. But what if? Or, better question, why the heck not? The big boss loved me. I worked twice as hard as the other assistant producers, rarely ate lunch (except for a fat-free yogurt consumed at my desk between noon and 12:15), and, unlike most of my coworkers, I never, ever showed up to work looking like I was about to start in a triathlon. And I had a plan! When my boss asked me where I saw myself in six months or a year, I had an answer (and an accompanying pie chart). Why not me? A promotion would mean more responsibility (goodbye, yogurt—maybe I could acquire a taste for protein bars?) and more money, but that wasn't what excited me. All I could think about was the plan. Two weeks into stage two, and I'd already be checking off an item! Maybe it was the wine, but it suddenly seemed that things couldn't possibly go any other way. I was going to get that promotion, and twenty-eight was going to be my best year ever.

I didn't even care that Jeff was taking me to the same resort where he'd once taken his ex, Lauren. At first I'd been surprised that he wanted to go back there. Lauren had done a number on him, and I figured the place would be full of bad memories. But I guess guys aren't as sentimental as women are. She was the past, he said. I dug through my underwear drawer and found the white teddy Jeff had brought home a few months before. I tucked it into a side pocket along with the black bra and panties he loved. This was our weekend, and everything was going to be perfect.

Perfect it was, from the beautiful room overlooking the ocean to the bottle of champagne Jeff hid on the beach for our moonlit walk to the pearl earrings he gave me over dinner. When I walked into work the following Monday morning, I was still floating on the memory of it all. As usual, the office was dark and quiet. I liked to start early so I could go over the day's schedule (meetings, industry research, paperwork, bonding with coworkers in the kitchen over espresso drinks, cleaning my desk, scheduling the next day, etc.) before the crowds filed in, the latest garage band cranked out of the office stereo putting its cheap speakers to the test, and the Frisbees started flying. Ah, the Web industry. Never before has so much been accomplished by so many dedicated underachievers. If not for me, nothing would have gotten done in that office, with the exception, naturally, of espresso drinks and spontaneous indoor Ultimate matches. But on this particular morning, I couldn't focus on my e-mail in-box or the list of tasks I'd left for myself the Friday before. I opened Word, intending to compose a letter, but ended up creating a mock business card complete with a new title and new last name.

I could barely hide my excitement when I returned from the printer, a sheet of pretend business cards in hand, to see the big boss waiting at my desk, admiring my wall chart that mapped all current, past, and future projects (color-coded, naturally). She was wearing her gray Armani knockoff, an appropriate suit for a serious occasion, promoting someone, for example. A huge smile broke across my face. I wanted to play it cool, but I couldn't help it. I was already dreaming about getting online and pulling up the plan. Check!

"Good morning," I said quickly, trying to hide the tremor in my voice. My hands were shaking so bad I had to shove them in my pockets.

The big boss turned to face me. "Good morning, Cassie. Glad you're here early. There's something I need to—"

"Talk to me about?" Check!

"Yes. Well. Why don't we go to my office?" She was stammering a bit. What did she have to be nervous about? But then she smiled warmly. I'm just projecting my own nervous energy, I assured myself. And so what if she doesn't look as ecstatic as I feel? She's promoting someone into middle management. Do I really expect the woman to kick off her Prada loafers and do cartwheels? Surely it was enough that she came all the way downstairs to give me the good news herself.

"You bet," I answered, trying not to sound too eager and failing miserably. "Just let me get my notebook."

"You won't need it," she said and started down the hall to the elevator.

I shook my head and smiled to myself. Duh. Star Web producers don't write things down. Star Web producers have people to write things down for them. And make them color-coded charts. And espresso drinks. No, that's pushing it, I decided. No matter how powerful I became, I resolved, I would always make my own coffee. In this state of complete and absolute exhilaration, I followed her down the hallway, rode the elevator, and entered her office. I was so giddy—chattering about the weather while mentally constructing the perfect producer wardrobe—that I didn't notice she hadn't said anything for several minutes, until she spoke again and the sound of something other than my own ramblings made me jump.

"Cassie," she began seriously. I put on my most serious face to match. I am a serious Web producer. This is the face that serious Web producers wear. "As you are well aware, this is a competitive marketplace." She frowned. I frowned back, adding a contemplative nod. "We're slipping into fifth place, and there are a dozen new dating sites coming online every month—"

"None as good as Idealmatch.com," I said.

"Yes, well. If only it were that simple." She took a deep breath and let it out with a whoosh, her cheeks puffing and deflating with cartoonlike perfection. I shifted from foot to foot. All this lead-up was killing me. "Let me say first of all that everyone here has been consistently impressed with your hard work." God, I thought, here it comes. I tried not to smile, but it was nearly impossible, so I settled on a straining grin. "We've seen the long hours you've put in without being asked. You've delivered everything you've been asked to deliver, on time and on budget. Honestly, you're the most organized person I know. You're a perfect associate producer." My grin burst into a full-blown, dopey, big-toothed smile.

"But times are tough."

Wait a second, I thought, did she just say "but"? My brain came to a screeching halt and then started racing backward, sideways, every direction to figure out where this "but" had come from.

"Right now we need visionaries who can help us lead this company. We need people who can make things happen, people who aren't afraid to take risks. And . . ." And? And? "And we don't feel that's your area of strength right now."

My mouth fell open. I couldn't believe it. There would be no raise, no assistant. Some slacker in spandex was going to get the promotion that I had earned. I would be stuck in this stupid job I was perfect at forever. The day couldn't get any worse.

"Unfortunately, with the economy the way it is," she continued, "we can't afford to keep people on just because they're good at their job."

And there it was. Worse. Much, much worse.

My ears started to buzz. The tastefully decorated room began to spin. The big boss stopped talking, reached into her top drawer, and pulled out a manila envelope. It had my name on it in big block letters. This was real. This was really happening. I wasn't only being passed over, I was being fired. "I think you'll find that we've been more than generous, because we like you, Cassie, and we really do appreciate everything you've done here. And, of course, we'll be happy to provide you with glowing references."

I somehow managed to take the envelope, but I couldn't make my mouth move or push air through my lips to form actual words. I wouldn't have known what to say, anyway. I was not going to be a star Web producer. I wasn't even a star associate producer. I wasn't a star anything. Not only would I not be able to check another item off my list, I'd have to *uncheck* something. This was the worst thing that had happened to me. Ever.

That it had happened early in the morning so I could go downstairs and pack up my desk in solitude was at least some consolation. Pitying looks from a bunch of thirty-year-olds in bike shorts would have pushed me right over the edge. As it was, each thing I picked up and put in my sad little cardboard box made me wince. Half-used notebooks. A purple mechanical pencil tagged by a piece of tape with my name on it. Magazine articles I had cut out and organized in a three-ring binder. Hair elastics. Each was a checkmark being erased. I sniffed back tears.

Then I caught sight of something that made me see how ridiculous I was being: my beautiful two-carat diamond ring. I stood still for a moment and looked at that ring as it played with the light breaking in through the blinds. I am something, I thought. I am engaged. That's more than something. That's the most important something. I sent a quick goodbye e-mail to my best office friend, Deb, dropped the manila envelope in my box, and walked out of the office with my head high.

Thank God I have Jeff, I repeated in my head over and over on the cab ride home. Thank God. Thank God. The more I thought it, the stronger I felt. My box of notebooks and hair elastics rest-ing in my lap was no longer a symbol of failure—it was merely a box of things. So Jeff wasn't exactly the most sensitive guy sometimes. He was a busy lawyer, overworked and under tremendous pressure to perform. All I needed was to have him put his arms around me, and everything would be fine. Better than fine. Perfect. Everything was going to be perfect. This was a minor setback. A temporary glitch. A learning experience. A window opening to another turning into a door, or however that saying went.

I certainly didn't need that stupid job, I told myself. Jeff never thought much of it, and clearly, he was right. I'd find something better in no time. It wasn't like I was some hard-nosed career gal, anyway. I'd use the extra time to plan the wedding, get a good jump on things. Item 1: Delete boss from guest list.

The more I thought about the wedding and Jeff, the more I realized nothing had changed at all. Everything that mattered was still on track. I was engaged, in love. Not the kind of all-encompassing love I'd imagined as a child, but a real, steady love. The kind of love a girl can rely on. Jeff, Jeff, Jeff. His very name grounded me. What did girls without fiancés do in times of crisis? I wondered. I didn't even want to think about it. Jeff was the most important thing in my plan—in my life. My mother was right. That one thing was worth all other checkmarks combined.

I tried to keep this thought with me as I pulled an eviction notice off the door of my apartment. It said that Jeff and I had thirty days to vacate. I shook my head in disbelief that things had gotten this far over one neighbor's complaints of imaginary music coming from our apartment in the middle of the day. Sure, Jeff loved his Brahms and Mozart, especially when he was feeling frisky after a shared bottle of wine, but we always kept the volume to a reasonable level. And we both had day jobs, so unless the stereo was possessed, none of it made sense. Several times we'd explained this to the building manager, who said we seemed like a responsible couple and apologized—he was only doing his job. When two more warning letters followed, Jeff had called the management company and straightened it out. We'd laughed it off before, but this formal eviction notice didn't seem funny at all.

I was halfway through the document—what was this nonsense about the complainant having recorded evidence?—when I was practically knocked backward by a thunderous clanging from the other side of our apartment door. It stopped, and the hall was quiet again. Then clanging again, though softer this time.

I put my key in the lock and turned, but the tumblers didn't catch. It was already unlocked. I froze. My heart started to race; adrenaline was flowing. Someone was inside. Robbed on the same day we were being evicted? The odds had to be astronomical. I scanned the eviction notice again. Didn't it say something about the building manager accessing the apartment only with the current tenants' prior permission? There it was, third paragraph, clear as day. Mr. Davidson was a nice man, but how dare he enter our apartment without our okay. It was bad enough that he had let this ridiculous charge escalate into an eviction. I fumed, dialing Jeff's office on my cell phone. Wait till he hears about this, I thought with smug satisfaction. By the time he gets through with the management company, we'll own the building.

No answer at Jeff's office. I'd have to handle this myself.

As I turned the doorknob and opened the door, I was greeted with a third clang. It sounded like it was coming from the living room, or the bedroom, maybe. Sheesh. What was the guy doing in there, anyway? Renovating? I was past the bathroom before I realized that it wasn't random clanging I was hearing. It was symbols crashing together toward the crescendo of Jeff's favorite aria. I followed the sound to the living room, and sure enough, his overpriced, state-of-the-art, wall-mounted CD player was on, with the speakers set to full volume. "Jeff," I called out, feeling guilty about blaming poor Mr. Davidson. If there was an answer, I couldn't hear it over the rising whine of violins. I reached out to turn the CD off, but something stopped me. My stomach tightened. A tingle shot up my spine. "Jeff?" I whispered.

I walked slowly, so slowly, toward the bedroom.

The music was so loud in the bedroom—Jeff had installed the tiny ceiling-mounted speakers himself—that they didn't realize I was there. But I saw them.

Jeff and Lauren in our bed, pale gray three-hundred-thread-count Egyptian cotton twisting around their naked bodies, their legs wrapped around each other, arms flailing with the music as though they were conducting their own personal symphony. Lauren the anorexic cellist. Lauren who'd dumped him three years ago for her bisexual psychoanalyst. Lauren who'd left him with a full set of emotional baggage, from trust issues to the occasional bout of performance anxiety. Lauren whose name he couldn't mention without a disgusted snarl forming in the corner of his mouth. Lauren and Jeff. Lauren and Jeff.

The box slipped from under my arm, suddenly so heavy with all those tiny uncheckmarks, and smacked against the hardwood floor. Despite the music, I swear I heard the box sigh, its contents shifting into a more comfortable state.

"Oh, God," said Lauren, eyes wide and mouth open.

"Oh, shit," said Jeff, much more appropriately, I thought, given the context.

The music paused for a breath before reaching its climax. I didn't say anything. No one moved. The climax came. Boom, boom, boom. (In retrospect, I had to admit that it was impressive the man upstairs had tolerated us this long.) The sound shook Jeff and Lauren into action, as though it would provide cover as they searched for clothing that had been tossed around the floor. The room became a blizzard of naked flesh. I stood perfectly still, the eye of the storm, though I was anything but calm. My entire body trembled. My chest hurt. My mind was simultaneously full of every thought possible and completely blank. Wood instruments, strings, horns, cymbals—the orchestra carried the weight of the moment up into the air and smashed it against the walls. The dresser shook. Jeff's beloved Japanese knickknacks rattled on the shelf above the bed. It was the perfect soundtrack to a life falling to pieces.

While they scrambled to get dressed (with Jeff chanting "shit, shit, shit" almost in time with the music), I ran through my options. At that moment I was livid—would have stormed out without a word if I could have gotten my feet to move—but what about tomorrow or a week from now? How would I feel then? If this had been part of my plan, I might have had some idea of how to react properly. In the absence of a plan, I reasoned, best not to do anything rash.

A strange sense of calm settled over me. Maybe this isn't as bad as it seems, I ventured. I can get past this. We can get past this. People who love each other can get past this. Maybe getting through this horrible thing will make our relationship better than ever. Maybe surviving an affair is something everyone needs to go through. Maybe I should have added it to my plan from the beginning. I never said I couldn't revise the plan, did I? No, I didn't. Revisions are good. Every good plan involves some degree of flexibility. What great document hasn't been amended? The Constitution, the Bill of Rights. Yes, surviving an affair is definitely checkmark-worthy, I decided. As I considered the ramifications of this alteration on Phases Two, Three, and so on (you must always consider the ramifications of alterations on future plan items), Lauren streaked past me, apparently having given up on finding her bra and left shoe.

Then everything went quiet. The CD was over. The front door clicked shut behind Lauren, and we were alone—me, Jeff, and the box. He looked frantically from bed to walls to window to floor to bed again, as though searching for words. I looked at him but didn't speak. If I was going to forgive him, he was going to have to do all the work.

"Oh, God, Cass, I am so sorry." His voice cracked. He stared at the floorboards, but I sensed that tears were coming, that the groveling was about to begin. I straightened my back and looked at him, determined to accept his contrition with the utmost dignity and grace. He is lucky to have me, I thought. He is lucky I have enough vision to see beyond this moment, that I understand that our future is so much bigger than this.

"You can't know how sorry I am," he continued, taking a breath and pulling himself together. "You're great, Cassie. Really, really great. You don't deserve this. And I love you, I do. But—"

"But?" Blood pounded in my ears, inner alarm bells sounding the alert. "Did you just say 'but'?" I wanted so much to sound mad, indignant, though I'm pretty sure I sounded confused, because that's how I felt.

"But." He cleared his throat, picked at the seam of his shirt. "But I'm not *in* love with you."

This wasn't happening. Not happening. Not twice in one day. You're great, but . . . I love you, but . . . Life is perfect, but . . . I could taste salt in the back of my throat. It took all my concentration to hold the tears back. My life was crumbling; that didn't mean I had to.

"Tell me one thing," I said finally, breaking the silence. "Was it something I did?"

"God, Cass." Jeff dropped his head into his hands. "Don't make this harder than it has to be."

"Just be honest with me." The words came out like a squeak, as though a mouse had spoken them. And that was when it hit me: I was losing him, and I was very, very afraid.

He lifted his head and looked at me. "You didn't do anything. Really. I mean, let's face it, you're perfect." The words sounded good, so why did I feel like I'd been slapped in the face?

"Is that a bad thing?"

"No, of course not." He shook his head. "I guess I'm just not looking for perfection."

"Clearly." All the stories he'd told me about Lauren made that fact obvious.

"I know this won't make sense to you, but I need to be with someone who doesn't have it all figured out. I need someone who doesn't make it so easy."

You've got to be freakin' kidding me, I thought. "Are you freakin' kidding me?"

"What do you mean?"

"I mean this isn't the way it's supposed to happen," I blurted out, not so much at Jeff as at the world. "It's supposed to be you and me. Jeff and Cassie. Not Jeff and Lauren. Not you and some stick-thin, neurotic cellist. It's supposed to be me in cream Vera Wang and you in pale gray pinstripes. It's supposed to be a partnership for you and a corner office for me. It's supposed to be a house on the water and a boy and a girl and Christmases at your parents' cabin and Sunday brunches with Sam and Trish and group vacations to Puerto Vallarta every winter . . ." My unlived future came pouring out of me, blending eventually into chest-heaving sobs. Jeff didn't say a word, only sat looking stunned and too scared to speak until I reached the end of my fairy tale.

"I know that's what you wanted," he said. "But I don't think I ever really did."

"So why . . ." I lifted my hand and rubbed my thumb against the diamond's surface.

"I don't know." He looked away, ashamed maybe, and spoke to the floor. "You needed it to happen so bad."

"But I thought . . . I thought." I thought we were in love. I thought we were forever. I thought I was getting everything I'd dreamed about. I didn't know what I thought anymore. My chest began to tighten, my breath quickening. Please, God, I pleaded in my head, don't let me hyperventilate. Not now, not in front of him. I took a deep breath and let it out. I was deflated. There was no better word for it.

"It's for the best, Cassie. Trust me."

"How the fuck can this be for the best?" I shouted. "Please tell me, because I'd really like to know."

"I'm sorry." He lifted his eyes, and I saw instantly that it was over. There was nothing I could do. There would be no revision to the plan. I would not be a star Web producer. I would not be getting married. There would be no Vera Wang dress, no house on the water, no Mexican vacations with all our friends. What was left? I wondered. So much had been stripped away, I wasn't even sure who I was anymore. All I knew was that there was nothing left for me in that room.

"I have to go now," I said the way you end a conversation with a telemarketer, perfunctory, detached. And that's how I felt. Detached from the moment, from my life as I'd known it, from the room in this stranger's apartment. I was floating up and away, and there was nothing to grab hold of anymore, nothing to keep me grounded. I picked up my box of office supplies, stepped over Lauren's wayward shoe, and walked out of the apartment. When I reached the sidewalk in front of the building, I stopped. I looked left, then right, then left again. For the first time in my life, I had absolutely no idea where I was going.

CHAPTER TWO

I'd never felt so completely lost. It was a dry Seattle day, but it might as well have been pouring down rain for the dark cloud that was following every aimless step I took. I must have wandered the streets for hours, my box of office supplies locked protectively under one arm and a blizzard of questions thrashing about in my head. Were there signs I didn't see? Did Jeff ever love me? Was this all really my fault? What did I do wrong? What didn't I do right? What are all those stupid love songs about, anyhow, all those tear-jerking movies? Wasn't love supposed to conquer all? What was so great about love if it didn't make everything perfect? I could have drowned under the weight of all those questions.

Nothing made sense anymore. Nothing was the way it should have been. I'd stuck to the plan, done all the things I was supposed to, and now everything was wrong, wrong, wrong. My life—the life I'd thought I had before being abruptly awakened into my current nightmare—was upside down, inside out.

My life was spilling out onto the road. Well, the remnants of it, anyway. Notebook, purple pencil, butterfly paper clips I'd bought with my own money—it all toppled out of the box that I'd apparently been squeezing tightly enough to rupture. Everything landed around my feet. I stopped, unsure what to do, only vaguely aware of a car screeching to a halt somewhere nearby. I poked at the notebook with a pointy leather toe, kicked lightly at a cluster of paper clips. Even office supplies know when they've outgrown their usefulness, I thought. I lifted the cardboard lid, retrieved the manila envelope, and rested what was left of the box gently on the ground. A car honked loudly. I looked up and saw with a start that I was in the middle of the street. I crossed quickly, and the car roared by, crushing the box under its right tires. There was a slight popping sound, and that was that.

I turned away from the cardboard carcass and found myself at the pier. I'd always loved it down there, especially in the summer, when the shops and restaurants came alive with tourists happily enjoying this Tom Hanks version of the city and tanned locals vying to see and be seen. Now it was empty and gray. I walked to the edge of the wharf. There was nothing before me but cold, dark sea. The end of the world as I knew it.

The reality of the situation began to really sink in. I didn't have a fiancé. I didn't have a place to live. I didn't have a paycheck. I needed a cup of coffee.

I ducked into a coffee shop for a latte and my bearings. I didn't even get to enjoy the first hot sip before my cell rang. Jeff! It had to be him, calling to take it all back, to tell me he was an idiot, out of his mind to give me up. I fumbled through my pocketbook for my phone and caught it at the last ring without checking the number on the display. That was my first mistake. The second was telling my mother what had happened.

"What did you do?" Even through the cell phone static, I could hear the panic in her voice. My mother has some lovely qualities, but I could hardly expect empathy from her in this situation. It's not that she doesn't love me, it's just that she comes from a long line of disappointed women who have passed down hard-won lessons in self-preservation (and oddly small earlobes) to their daughters. She's been married to my sweet, devoted stepdad for over twenty years, but she will always be the woman my father walked out on when I was seven. Security is to my mother what Manolos are to Sarah Jessica Parker.

"Why do you automatically assume that I did something wrong?" The words came out angrier than I had intended, but her criticism was the last thing I needed right now, especially when it sounded a lot like the criticisms circling in my own head. Besides, I needed to be mad at someone within shouting distance, and that was either my mother or the barista. "Let's try being supportive for five seconds. After that you're free to blame me for the world's evils."

"You don't have to snap at me," she said, clearly hurt. "And I don't automatically assume you did something wrong, Cassandra. What I meant was what did you do when you found them?"

"Sorry," I choked out. "I'm just a little . . ." Destroyed. Amputated. Flailing like a headless chicken. "On edge."

"Of course you are, sweetie."

"I don't know what to . . . I can't seem to . . . Mom, what did I do wrong?"

"You didn't do anything. Men cheat. Period. End of story."

"He said I'm too perfect."

"Too perfect? What the heck does that mean?" Now she was the one getting angry, which was possibly the nicest thing she could do for me at the moment. A little parental indignation can go a long way in the right circumstance. Then she took a deep breath and added, "Okay, let's not overreact." And just like that, the old Gwen was back. "We can get through this. Let's give him some time. Maybe he'll—"

"Give *him* some time? He's not exactly the injured party here."

"Of course, sweetie." She put on her best mom voice. "But we've still got some damage control to do. We need a plan."

Her words triggered something inside me, and I couldn't hold it back a second longer. This wasn't going to be discreet. This was going to be Niagara Falls. I cupped a hand over the phone and held it out at arm's length. My mother had begun talking about some woman named Margaret whose daughter had been left at the altar, and I was falling apart at the seams right here in the coffee shop beside a display of oversize, overpriced mugs. The guy behind the counter smiled sympathetically. He couldn't have been over nineteen. This was probably his first job, some part-time work to put a bit of spending money in his pocket while he finished school. He had his whole life in front of him, years and years to get it all right.

I wanted to punch him in the face.

Instead I collected myself, told my mom I'd have to call her back, and finished my latte. The coffee was good and strong, and I felt better—for about ten seconds. No amount of caffeine and soft amber lighting could keep the day from playing over and over in my head. I needed advice from an impartial (nonparental) party. I needed a shoulder or two to cry on. I needed a drink. I called Sam and Trish's office—so convenient having best friends who work together—and asked if they could cut out of work early and meet me at Jimmy's. This was an emergency.

"What's going on?" Trish asked over speakerphone. "Big sale at the Bon?" I started to speak but choked on Jeff's name. All I could manage were several big gulps of air before I broke into sobs. "Hang on, sweetie. We'll be there in twenty minutes."

When I got to Jimmy's, our regular après-work venue, there was no sign of Sam and Trish, so I sat at the bar and sipped on a martini. Jimmy's looked a lot different at two in the afternoon. In place of generically cute, suited guys swigging Heinekens, and PR bunnies spinning on the small dance floor at the back, were scruffy freelancers hunched over their laptops, modern-day cowboys roaming the cyber range. We used a lot of freelancers at my company, and I'd always assumed that to live without any real job security, you had to be either incredibly brave or incredibly crazy, maybe a bit of both. Yet at that moment, sucking back bar coffee and free wireless Internet access, they seemed full of direction. They had project, deadlines, purpose. What did I have? Termination papers, an eviction notice, and a two-carat diamond ring worth as much to me as the beer-stained cocktail napkin stuck to the bottom of my shoe. I threw back my drink and, choosing to ignore the bartender's mixed expression of disapproval and curiosity, ordered a second. The girls would have to catch up.

Halfway through my third drink, Sam and Trish plopped themselves down on the bar stools on either side of me. I hadn't told them anything on the phone, but Sam took one look at my face and threw her arms around me while Trish signaled the bartender for a round. "What did you tell them at the office?" I asked, always amazed by how much freedom they had at the market research firm they worked at.

"What we always tell them," said Trish. "Field research." She passed a martini to Sam and took a big swallow from her own. "Now start from the very beginning."

I took a deep breath and started from the beginning, not sparing even the smallest detail. Sam and Trish listened. The bartender listened. I think a couple of the cyber cowboys might have been listening, too. Most importantly, I was listening. By the time I got to the nineteen-year-old barista, I was more depressed than ever. I'm too perfect. I've got it all figured out. I don't take risks. Could it be that the qualities I prided myself on were actually faults? Jeff's words, my boss's words—it all flashed in my brain like giant road signs telling me I was going the wrong way. Instead of speeding down the fast lane to Success City, I was rolling into Loserville on bald tires and an empty tank of gas.

Sam and Trish stared, looking dumbfounded. I'd never seen them speechless before. Of course, it was only natural that they'd be surprised. If not about the job, then certainly about the guy. They'd liked Jeff. Everyone had liked Jeff. Jeff was very, very likable. Just ask Lauren.

"Unbelievable," said Trish.

"Un-fucking-believable," agreed Sam.

"He's an idiot," said Trish.

"They're all idiots," added Sam.

Trish slammed a hand down on the bar. "Screw 'em all. This could be the best thing that ever happened to you."

I winced. That's what people tell you when something truly, horrifically awful happens. I've said it to pining ex-boyfriends to alleviate my own guilt. I've said it to friends who fell victim to downsizing. Now I was the ex. I was the jobless. I smirked at myself, which seemed to make Sam and Trish feel better.

"That's the spirit," said Sam, giving me a squeeze. Trish took my hand and smiled enthusiastically. I nodded and forced a small smile. They were trying so hard to be helpful, needing me to be okay, that I couldn't possibly tell them I knew it was all bullshit.

In fact, the only thing that made me feel even the slightest bit better came in a ridiculously shaped glass seemingly designed to maximize spilling. Cocktails thinly disguised as martinis for the I'm-not-really-sophisticated-but-I-do-drive-a-Jetta crowd are the best invention ever. I downed the drink in front of me, which may have been Trish's, judging from the look she gave me, and ordered another.

"Maybe you could use a break," said the bartender.

"Look, friend," I began, though it sounded more like "Lick, fren" (those martinis were really strong). I was about to give him a piece of my mind. Who did he think he was telling me when I needed a break? Did he just lose his job, his home, and his Jeff all in the same day? I don't think so. I leaned back, almost fell off my stool, and then tipped forward again, ready to let him have it, but as I opened my mouth, it hit me. The bartender was a genius!

A break. That was exactly what I needed. Not from martinis— from my life. I had worked long and hard to get the right job, the right fiancé, the right apartment, and I'd done it all wearing the right shoes. For over a decade, I ate, slept, and breathed The Plan. Hadn't I earned some time off? You get two weeks for every year in a job, right? With a bit more difficulty than usual, I calculated in my head: ten years times two weeks . . . twenty weeks . . . five months. Heck, let's call it six for good measure.

A girl could do a lot in six months, I figured. A girl could also do absolutely nothing. I could go somewhere I'd never been, spend time by myself. Hello, self. I could learn. Reflect. Get perspective. And, naturally, come up with a new plan. I'd come back six months later from Italy or Morocco or whatever fabulous place, tanned and thin and glowing with inner peace. It was all so Oprah. Maybe they'd feature me in her magazine. Maybe I'd get invited to appear on the show—one of those people who sit in the front row of the audience because their stories aren't quite amazing enough to earn them a spot onstage but are still special enough that you're on-camera and Oprah might even walk down and hold your hand while you tear up. Maybe I'd end up famous, or at least with an endorsement deal for a yogurt company. Maybe I'd even meet someone new.

My brilliant genius bartender was leaning across the bar, waiting for me to say something, his arms folded in that resigned, unshakable bartender way. There was only one thing to do. I grabbed his cheeks and kissed him, a big sloppy wet one, my long-lasting lipstick leaving an optimistic smudge under his nose. He jumped back, blushing cherry red. Sam and Trish laughed so hysterically, I don't think they even noticed me throwing down a couple of twenties and tearing out the door.

The door swung shut behind me, muffling their calls as I stumbled into a cab. There was no time for goodbyes. I was too excited about my new plan to take a break from my old plan so I could figure out a new new plan. I couldn't wait to get started. I'd explain it all to Sam and Trish tomorrow, and they'd understand. How could they not? It was so genius!

"Where to?" asked the driver.

"Any goddamn place I want," I answered smugly. He looked at

me in the rearview mirror as if trying to figure out whether I was high. "Oh, you mean right now." I smiled sheepishly. I couldn't go back to the apartment and there was no way I was going to my parents' place, but other than a last twenty, all I had on me was the credit card that Jeff had insisted I get for emergencies. There'd never been one—until now. "To the most expensive hotel in the city," I commanded. It was the start of a new plan, a new life. Might as well start it with crisp white sheets and room service. The cabdriver smiled approvingly into the rearview mirror and took a left.

We pulled up to the W Hotel on Fourth Avenue. I gave the driver my twenty, swiped a finger under the bottom rim of each eye, sensing smudged mascara, and staggered into the most beautiful hotel I'd ever seen. The walk to the check-in counter was a bit awkward, what with the room swaying the way it was, but the clerk was either too polite or too sophisticated to acknowledge this minor point. She took my platinum card happily and called me Ms. Moore. I felt like a movie star. Despite my lack of luggage, a bellhop escorted me to my room on the fourteenth floor. As I watched the elevator numbers rising, my smile got bigger and bigger. Things were looking up already.

A new plan. The very idea thrilled me to the core, hummed in the back of my mind. I was so young when I came up with the first one. Now I was sophisticated, worldly, twenty-eight, for God's sake. Not that everything on the old plan was bad, not at all. In fact, I was certain most of it was dead on. But there was always room for improvement. Clearly. Like this break thing. Why hadn't I scheduled that in somewhere between first college boyfriend and first non-minimum-wage job? I'd never been to Europe or Africa, or outside of the U.S., for that matter. Major flaw in the plan, that one. And Jeff—what was I thinking? A lawyer with a thing for classical music and Japanese minimalism? If I was going to find my ideal match, I would have to put more thought into it.

No lawyers. No one who spends more on hair products than I do. No one with ex-girlfriend baggage, especially not in the shape of a cello. But what about MBAs who listen to jazz? Divorced doctors who speak Mandarin? I needed criteria. I needed a contingency strategy. I needed to check out the minibar.

A jar of macadamia nuts, two tiny bottles of vodka, and a list of amendments scribbled on hotel notepaper later, and it was time to get serious. The hotel notepaper, though elegant, would get me only so far. Taking a break was serious work. I needed some serious tools. I called room service.

"Good afternoon, Ms. Moore," said a pleasant voice on the other end. "What can I help you with?"

"I need a laptop." I realized as I said it that they probably don't keep computer hardware in the same place they make your grilled cheese sandwich. Which reminded me that I hadn't eaten since breakfast. "And a grilled cheese sandwich, please."

"Certainly, Ms. Moore. They'll be right up." Half a rerun of *Friends* later, I was in full research mode and eating the best eighteen-dollar grilled cheese sandwich in the history of mankind.

God, I love the Internet! With one laptop and one high-speed wireless connection, I found everything anyone could possibly need to plan the perfect life break. Or Life Break, as Trish would call it. There are sites for people planning to travel, sites by people who've already traveled, sites for people who want to help you travel, sites by countries that want you to travel there. There are apartment rental agencies, language schools, hotels, hostels, homestays. There are cost-of-living numbers, travel warnings, vaccination recommendations, literacy statistics, personal an-ecdotes, e-zine stories . . . I bet some people look in a brochure and point to the prettiest beach photo. Not Cassie Moore. If I was going to take a break from my life, I was going to do it right. And the fact that the screen was getting progressively blurry as the evening wore on wasn't about to stop me.

I woke up the next morning to my cell phone ringing. It was my mother, so I let it go to voice mail. My head throbbed "aspirin, aspirin, aspirin." My tongue felt like it was wearing an angora sweater. My phone rang again. Sam. Probably checking in to make sure I'd made it home okay. It rang again; my stepdad this time. Strange, I thought. He never calls me during the day. He must be really worried about me. I'd get back to him as soon as I was finished throwing up.

When I finally checked my voice mail, there were twelve messages, but I never made it past the first one: "Cassie, this is your mother. I just read your e-mail. Is this some sort of joke, or have you gone completely insane? If it's the former, I'm not amused."

E-mail? What e-mail? I went online and checked my webmail, open from the night before, though I didn't remember sending any messages. Please, I prayed, don't let me have e-mailed something sappy to Jeff.

My in-box was flooded with messages, each subject line more cryptic than the next: "I am so jealous!" "Way to go, girl!" "Take me with you . . ." And then I saw the one that really mattered. An automatic response confirming my flight to Buenos Aires. My flight. To Buenos Aires. Confirming my flight to Buenos Aires. Where the heck was Buenos Aires?!

My head began to throb again, but I had a feeling that aspirin wasn't going to help this time. What had I done? How drunk had I been? Clearly drunk enough to do something incredibly stupid, like book a flight to Buenos Aires, but not so drunk that I couldn't enter the numbers of my credit card onto a Web form.

This had to be the worst hangover in the history of the world.

My brain switched to autopilot. I don't want to go to Buenos Aires. I don't want a break. I don't want another martini to come within five feet of me ever. What I do want is to get back on track. I *need* to get back on track. I need a new job, a new apartment, and a new fiancé. Surely there's a way out of this mess. Tickets are refundable. I could send a mass message to everyone saying the whole thing was a joke. Ha, ha. "That kooky Cassie," they'd say and forget all about this in a few hours. Either that, I thought, or I'll shave my head and join a cult in California.

As I roughed out a damage control plan in my head, my cell phone rang again. I dove to reach it before it went to voice mail, certain it would be Sam and Trish, who would tell me once again that everything was going to be okay. But it was Jeff's name on the screen, and my thumb hit the talk button before my brain could veto.

"What the hell is this all about?" Jeff's normally calm and slightly muffled speakerphoned voice was loud and sharp, piercing from right ear to left temple.

"Not so loud, please. Can you talk a bit quieter?" I rummaged through my pocketbook for aspirin. Echinacea, vitamin C . . . bingo.

"No, I cannot," he said even louder. "Jesus Christ, Cassie. You can't be serious about going to Argentina. I mean, Jesus Christ."

Right. Argentina. Buenos Aires is in Argentina. That's South America, right? "I'm about as serious as you are about Lauren." I popped two aspirins and forced them down without water. They left a bitter film in my mouth that tasted a hell of a lot better than my morning-after breath.

"This has nothing to do with that. We're talking about you here." He took a deep breath and softened his voice. "I'm worried about you, Cassie. You're upset and clearly not thinking straight."

"What is that supposed to mean?"

"Come on. Argentina? This is not exactly part of *The Plan*." The words came out so snide. Jeff had always said he was supportive, but whenever he talked about my plan, I thought I'd sensed a bit of a smirk in his voice. I'd assumed I was being overly sensitive.

"Maybe I don't have to do everything according to plan," I said as dryly as possible. I wasn't about to get emotional, not for him. "Maybe I'm not the automaton you've got me pegged for. You're not the only one who can be unreliable—sorry, unpredictable."

"So, what, you're doing this to prove something to me?"

"This might come as a shock to you, Jeff, but not everything in the entire world is about you."

"Look, I don't want to argue." His voice softened. "I'm just worried about you." It killed me to hear those words from him. They cut into me like a knife—a knife I didn't want to extract. "Do you even know what you're getting into? The poverty? The crime? People get kidnapped there, you know."

"Of course I know what I'm getting into." Poverty? Crime? Kidnapping? Oh, God, I thought, my heart starting to race, I can't do this.

"You wouldn't last two days in a foreign country, let alone six months in South America." That did it. Whether or not I could do this wasn't any of his business anymore, was it?

"Who are you to tell me what I can or can't do?"

"I'm just saying it's not Disneyland, Cass. Hell, it isn't even Mexico." Jeff had talked about taking me to Puerto Vallarta once. He'd said we could stay at one of those all-inclusive hotels with a private beach and do nothing but eat quesadillas, drink margaritas, and make love for days. The knife sunk in deeper. I wrenched it out with both hands.

"Well, thank you so very much for your concern, but it's none of your business how long I last. You have no say in my life now." I slammed the cell phone down, but it bounced off the bed and onto the floor with a dull thud. God, I miss real phones sometimes. I looked around the room, but everything had the sheen of major money and the hotel had my credit card number. I picked up a feather pillow and flung it at the wall. It would have to do.

Once my anger subsided, the panic set in.

I couldn't back out now, not after that conversation. I couldn't let Jeff think he was right. I couldn't let Jeff *be* right. Which meant I had to go through with it. "What have I done?" I whispered to myself.

I was going to Buenos Aires, Argentina, South America. Cassie Moore was going to South America. I waited for it all to sink in, but mostly, it hovered at the surface of me. I didn't know how to make it real. I sat dazed at the edge of the bed until the hotel phone rang. Apparently, I'd asked the hotel for a wake-up call, but Jeff had beaten them to it. I dragged myself into the shower, back into yesterday's clothes, and straight to the girls' office.

"For how long?" asked Trish. We huddled in their shared office with the door closed. Sam had run downstairs for lattes, and I'd drawn the visitor's chair up to the corner where Sam's and Trish's desks met. Between sips of coffee, we spoke in whispers like high school girls giggling over rumors and cigarettes in the girls' bathroom. Only there were no giggles, and I was the one about to become rumor fodder.

"The ticket's for six months."

"Oh my God," said Sam.

"And where will you stay?" asked Trish.

"Apparently, I reserved an apartment."

"Oh my God," said Sam.

"And you definitely have to go?" asked Trish.

"I can't back out now. I told everybody. Jeff knows. My boss—ex-boss—knows. I'll look like a total loser if I don't go. This city, my industry, is so small. No one would ever take me seriously again." As I spoke, my leg began to jiggle the way it always does when I'm stressed, punctuating my words with nervous energy. "And Jeff will have the satisfaction of thinking he turned me into a basket case." My other leg got in on the action.

"Oh my God," said Sam.

"You know," said Trish, leaning forward as if she had a juicy secret to share. "This might be the best thing that ever happened to you."

I looked her square in the eye and gave her our we've-known-each-other-too-long-to-bullshit-each-other look. "No, really. I mean it. You hear about these people all the time who experience something really, really brutal—you know, they find out they have cancer or they get a really bad nose job—but they survive it and, voilà, whole new amazing person."

"Yeah, with a bad nose." I wasn't trying to be snarky, only figure out where the hell she was going with this one.

"No—well, maybe. But that's not the point. The point is you learn from adversity." Trish's words sounded ripped from some motivational speaker's script, but her tone wasn't that confident, her sentences rising slightly at the ends with the insecurity of a teenage uptalker. But she was trying, God bless her. I felt compelled to play along, at least a little.

"What doesn't kill you makes you stronger?" offered Sam.

"There you go."

"Maybe you're right," I said, wanting to believe it, wanting to not just sound but feel confident that there might be something to grasp on to in all these clichés. *What doesn't kill you makes you stronger.* Then again, wasn't this the same sort of Oprah thinking that got me into the mess in the first place?

"Remember Cathy Fischer?" It wasn't really a question. Of course I remembered Cathy Fischer. She was Trish's first post-college roommate and our mid-twenties idol. She seemed to have everything together—cool job as a makeup artist, model boyfriend, and a bottomless closet of designer clothes that we assumed she'd gotten through all her fabulous fashion industry connections. Then the creditors started calling. One night Cathy broke down and confessed. She was twenty-seven thousand dollars in debt. The next morning she was gone, leaving unopened bills and empty shopping bags in her wake. We later heard she'd borrowed some money from her boyfriend and run off to London.

"If you're saying I'm like Cathy Fischer—"

"Well . . ." I knew where she was headed. The summer before, Trish had run into Cathy's sister, who told her Cathy was doing great in London, had launched her own makeup line or something. "It is sort of a positive story. In the end." Smiling, Trish leaned back in her chair as if to say, *I rest my case.*

"Yeah. She also declared bankruptcy at twenty-three."

"I'm just saying, maybe things happen for a reason. You can look at this like it's the end of the world, or you can see it as an opportunity."

"To do what?"

"Things you've maybe wanted to try but never got around to. Write, paint, take up the tango . . . whatever you want."

The gauzy memory of my Oprah delusions flitted through my mind. Wasn't there something about discovering my inner brilliance? Or was it peace and harmony? Try as I might, I couldn't latch on. The vodka dreams were gone, and there was only one thing I wanted. "I want to not go to Buenos Aires."

There was a long pause while the undeniable truth of this statement filled the room. Extra-long sips of latte were taken. All the clichés in the world couldn't help me out of this one. Trish shook her head, her forced grin gone. "Never, ever drink and surf."

"Is there any chance that you might want to go? Even just a little bit?" Sam asked hopefully. "You've never really been anywhere, and it might not be completely horrible. You know what they say about Latin men."

"Wouldn't that drive Jeff crazy," I said, smiling for the first time that day. More surprising, I realized there was a teeny-tiny part of me that maybe could almost want to go. Unfortunately, that part was generally accessible only after six or seven ounces of vodka. When I was sober, the idea of traveling across the world by myself scared the crap out of me. With all that had happened, my life being turned upside down as it was, just the idea of being alone in my own hometown was terrifying enough—but, it dawned on me, not quite as terrifying as the idea of running into Jeff and Lauren. If I couldn't wipe Jeff off the face of the earth, maybe this was the next best thing.

"He'll go insane," Trish said with a sly smile. "Imagine all the tortured nights he'll spend imagining you with an Antonio Banderas look-alike. We erupted into a fit of conspiratorial giggles. It felt good thinking of something other than my boyfriendless, apartmentless, jobless state. Oh, God, it hit me, I don't have a job.

"I don't have a job."

"Who needs a job when you've got Antonio?"

"No job, no money. Even if I did want to go—and I'm not saying I do—I can't afford a trip like this. My severance check isn't going to cover me for longer than a couple of months. Oh, jeez." I paused as the weight of it sank in. "I *am* Cathy Fischer." Just when I thought I was all cried out, my eyes filled again and spilled unceremoniously onto the faux wood finish of Sam's desk.

"Okay, let's not panic." Trish, resident problem solver, scrunched her face up the way she always did when she was deciding something important. She leaned forward, touched my left hand, and smiled knowingly. Sam put her hand on top of Trish's, Three Musketeers–style. I did the same with my right hand, not wanting to ruin this sweet *Sex and the City* moment. "No, you goofballs." Trish laughed, lifting my left hand up to my face.

Sam and I ooohed in unison. "Trish," I said, my long-lost smile creeping back onto my lips, "have I ever told you that you're absolutely brilliant?"

In that moment, my hand thrust triumphantly in the air, my best friends by my side, I believed that maybe, just maybe, things really do happen for a reason. Ten minutes later, the symbol of Jeff's undying love was on eBay.

Two weeks later, I am strapped into an American Airlines jet, sharing my story with a kind Argentine woman. I have no fiancé, no job, no permanent mailing address, and, for reasons that are becoming less and less clear as the lights of Seattle become farther and farther away through the oval window on my left, I am headed to South America.

South America. As in not North. As in don't drink the tap water. As in you can't trust the police. As in me rotting in a prison cell, denied food and tainted tap water because I tried to buy fake Fendi from some guy on the street. As in me lying dead in a ditch somewhere, for God knows what reason, my poor parents made to fly down to identify the body and missing a number of favorite televised programs to do so. As in one step away from falling off the edge of the earth.

How did my so-called friends and loving family let me go through with this? Okay, my mother didn't so much let me as choose to believe that I wouldn't go right up until I passed the security point. I could still hear her yelling at my poor stepdad for letting me go when the red-faced customs agent with a chunk of broccoli protruding between two front teeth looked at my ticket and snorted, "Have fun getting kidnapped." As if anything anyone could say would terrify me more than I already was.

"I don't speak a word of Spanish," I tell my sedated seatmate. She nods and smiles sympathetically. "I freckle easily." She tsks compassionately. "I think I might be coming down with something."

She puts her hand on mine, and I ease up on the armrest. She digs in her purse and retrieves the bottle of small purple pills. "Take one," she whispers. "It will make the flying more easy." I've never before taken so much as an M&M from a stranger, but then I've never been en route to Buenos Aires before either. And easy anything sounds really good right about now. I shrug, pop one in my mouth, and take a swig of bottled water.

"You will love Buenos Aires," she says with a dreamy purr.

"The city is magic. You will see. This trip will be the best thing that ever happened to you."

I can't help but cringe a little when I hear these words. "Right," I say. "I'm thinking of having that put on a T-shirt."

She gives me the look of confusion and mild amusement again, well deserved this time. "This is a joke?"

"Yeah. A joke." And it's on me.

But before I can wade any deeper into my self-pity, a velvety Valiumness takes over and ushers me tenderly toward the edge of sleep. I am so tired. The plane takes off, and I feel my body sinking into the scratchy blue fabric of my upright seat. I don't look out the window, can't stand to see home getting smaller and smaller. I close my eyes.

I wake sometime later as the meal cart creaks by, reminding me where I am. I shake a fuzzy head at the stewardess. I'm not hungry, though I probably should be. Food won't fill this hole. I am already homesick. For a blurry moment, I am Judy Garland, and when I lift the thin airline blanket covering my legs, I see red sequined shoes. I try to tap my heels together, but my feet are so heavy, like concrete blocks attached to steel rebar. When I wake again, groggy and dry-mouthed, I am startled to find myself on a dark, sleeping airplane. The buzz of air-conditioning mixes with snores. I check my watch. About ten more hours to go—ten hours and six months. I stare out the window and see nothing but black.

CHAPTER THREE

*W*e touch down on the tarmac with a light bump, and my stomach lurches. I open my eyes and turn as slowly as possible to the window on my left. American Airlines jets. Luggage trucks. Small men in reflective vests. It could easily be Sea-Tac or LAX or JFK. Then, in the distance, I spot what looks suspiciously like a donkey pulling a cart. Yep, that's a donkey, all right. No doubt about it, I am in Argentina. Cassie Moore is in Argentina. There are so many things wrong with this picture I can't even wrap my head around it. My eyes latch on to every detail of the airplane, my safe cocoon for the past twenty hours. The mysterious stain on the headrest in front of me, the dog-eared in-flight magazine, the small TV screen hanging from the ceiling two rows up, even the lit sign for the washroom—it's all comfortingly familiar, and I soak it up as long as I can, desperate to ignore the flurry of excited activity around me as passengers prepare to disembark. One by one, they file out, orderly but impatient to get off.

I am studying the intricacies of the complimentary headset when my friendly drug dealer returns from a final trip to the bathroom freshly brushed, powdered, and lipsticked. "*Chica,* you are excited now, yes?" We are the last two people on the plane, and I want to tell her not to go yet, because once she does, I will have no choice but to get up, grab my bag from the overhead compartment, and step out that exit. But her smile is so kindly hopeful, I have no choice but to nod and smile back. She reaches down and squeezes my forearm, leaving little moons in my skin from her flawless red nails. "I knew! Good. Have a wonderful trip." She collects a small case from under the seat, and I watch her glide down the aisle. My turn.

Exiting the plane, I brace myself for the worst. The flight attendants smile and nod, oblivious to anything beyond upright trays and seatbacks. But I know. According to the six guidebooks I've read in the past two weeks, Buenos Aires is miles and miles of concrete teeming with over thirteen million people, many of them jobless, most of them penniless, all of whom will surely see me as pure U.S.A.-grade evil. I'm not quite sure what the worst would be, though the image of being splashed with red paint comes to mind. At the very least, I'm sure to be harassed at customs. I would shrug my shoulders, but I don't have the energy to lift them. Let the worst begin.

To my surprise, the airport is fairly modern, clean, and free of chickens. In fact, it looks a lot like the airport where this journey began. There is no strip search, no drug dogs. No one even looks inside my luggage. The fact that I don't speak Spanish doesn't matter, since Argentine customs officers communicate in that universal language of dismissive grunts and hand gestures. My passport is swiped and stamped. I am waved here, then there. As I pass each checkpoint without issue, a fresh wave of relief rushes over me. Nothing is ever as awful as you imagine it, I remind myself. Bit by bit, I might just be able to get through this.

And then I leave the airport.

I find a cab outside. The night is clear, the sky tar-black. I roll down the window for air but am immediately chastised. *"Por favor, chica.* No safe," the driver says, shaking his head. "Late, *entiende?"* I roll it back up and stare through the smudged glass. The driver, well intentioned, I'm sure, takes it upon himself to give me a security rundown in broken English. In half an hour, I learn which neighborhoods I should not live in (most), which neighborhoods I can safely walk around in after dark (none), and which cabs are fake and, thus, dangerous (these instructions are vague and only serve to make me scared to be in any cab, present company included). I try to absorb both his warnings and the city whirring past me in the night, a blur of neon and headlights. Hundreds of cars, my cab included, weave around each other with no regard to lanes, and the whole extraordinary scene seems a choreographed dance to the familiar Beach Boys tune coming from the car radio. Together, everything is strange and different and awful and too much. I am not home. I am not a cell phone away from meeting Sam and Trish at Jimmy's. I am not a fifteen-minute cab ride from everyone and everything I know and love. I am on a whole other continent. I don't know what I'm supposed to do here. Worst of all, I don't know who I am supposed to be. There is no plan, and without a plan, there is no Cassie. It's all so overwhelmingly wrong that I have to concentrate on my breathing to keep from hyperventilating. There is no way I am going to make it six months.

So I break it down like any good project manager. I focus on the next few minutes, on arriving at the address on the piece of paper I've been clutching so hard it's already softening. I suspect that the apartment I rented in my drunken state, though nice enough in the online photos, might not be so spectacular in reality, but sleep on the flight was sporadic at best (Valium, shmalium), and the idea of putting my head down somewhere, anywhere, helps get me through the long cab ride. I rest my forehead against the cool window as the cabdriver prattles on, now completely in Spanish. The clogged streets give way to cobblestone roads lined with malnourished trees, and eventually, we thump to a stop.

"You here," the driver says happily.

"Don't remind me," I mumble to myself.

He peeks through his passenger window. "Good house."

The "house" he refers to is a massive yellow wall relieved only by a forbidding wood door, two windows all but obscured by thick iron bars, and several disturbing fissures that run from sidewalk to roof. The website said the suite was bright and had a nice garden view, but the chances of that being true look pretty slim. The only things growing on this sadly sloped, graffiti-stained street are persistent weeds that stretch up hopefully through cracks in the concrete, and stunted trees standing limply every twenty feet or so. Seattle's docks, heavy with rusting ship skeletons and rustier merchant marines, have more greenery.

It's barely been a day, and I miss it so much already. If you get up early enough, you can buy fresh fish, fruit, flowers, pretty much anything, down at the docks. Not that I ever did, but I always knew I could, and now—now I can't. Now those docks are a world away. People who aren't from Seattle don't understand the city. They think we are all Pike-Place-fish-throwing, Kurt-Cobain-mourning, plaid-shirt-wearing coffee addicts. You can't know Seattle's heart and soul unless you walk the streets first thing in the morning, eat hot dogs from a street vendor downtown at noon, hang out in a jazz bar on a Tuesday night, cure your hangover with a 5 Spot Café breakfast. Why did I want to leave, even for a second? I've never wanted to be anywhere else. Besides long weekends in Vegas and that trip after graduation to New York with Trish, I've never given traveling much thought. I don't have wanderlust. Don't even have any real curiosity about other cultures, to be honest. I'm glad they're out there—I just don't feel any need to be out there in them. Seattle in all its wet, sleepy, grungy glory has always suited me just fine. Yet here I am, thousands of miles from where I was and from who I want to be. Instead of salt-worn wood planks solid under my feet, I have a crumbling cobblestone sidewalk mined with dog crap.

If I've set my watch correctly, it's very late, but I have no choice but to knock. While the driver gets my bags, I negotiate sidewalk cracks and crap and locate the door buzzer on the massive yellow wall. If not for the building's cheerful color, I'd swear I was about to check in to a convent. Maybe this is all part of some twisted Argentine plot to indoctrinate young foreign women into the sisterhood—a theory immediately dispelled when I notice a couple of transvestite hookers parked on the corner behind us. One of them smiles at me and says something in Spanish to her/his friend. I smile back and they laugh. Nothing I haven't seen in Seattle, but this one similarity doesn't exactly fill me with comfort. I sigh deeply and shake my head at the few moments when I let myself believe this might not be so bad after all. My finger slowly moves toward the buzzer as my brain calculates whether I have enough room left on my credit card for a room at the Buenos Aires Howard Johnson.

Before I reach a tally, the door swings wide, pouring three squirming dogs and a giggling redheaded child onto the sidewalk. Behind them comes a tiny redheaded woman in a floral-print jumpsuit who throws her arms open at the sight of me and shouts, "*¡Hola!*" She smiles almost as loudly as she speaks. I clearly haven't woken anyone up. "You must be Cassandra!" she exclaims, her accent strong, though different from the cabdriver's.

"Cassie," I say, smiling sheepishly, too tired and discombobulated to feign her level of enthusiasm. At my voice, one of the dogs jumps at me. I stumble back but manage to stay relatively upright. The tiny woman scolds the animal sternly in Spanish—no translation needed—and it runs into the house, followed by the others. None of this bodes well, and I am more apprehensive than before about venturing inside. Is this the Argentine equivalent of white trash? I wonder. The woman looks nice, her small curvy figure and soft curly hair giving her a motherly quality that is highly appealing at the moment, but will her husband be a wife-beater-wearing gaucho? Already paid, the cabdriver slips off with a friendly nod during the commotion. I watch the cab longingly as it sputters away.

"Cassandra, I am Andrea," my host says, pronouncing it An-dray-ah, then throws her arms up in the air as though she has just finished her routine on the uneven bars. "And this—this beautiful chico is Jorge." Hor-hay. The child, no longer giggling, runs behind his mother's legs, peeking out from behind a floral thigh just enough so he can keep one eye on me. I extend my hand, but Andrea ignores it and moves in to give me a bear hug (or a cub hug, in her case) and a kiss on my right cheek. The little boy is dragged forward and back again with her movements, that eye looking up at me all the time, wide with disbelief. I want to tell him I know exactly how he feels. "No handshakes in Buenos Aires, Cassandra. Only hugs and kisses. Isn't it marvelous? Well, let's get you inside. Come, come."

Andrea's English is quite good, which is lucky for me, because her accent is thick and she talks as fast as she walks, even with Jorge hoisted on one hip. I do my best to keep up with her as she shuttles me down a long indoor driveway that houses no car save a tot-sized plastic convertible piled with stuffed animals ready to go for a spin. She slips left through a narrow door in the wall and begins to climb a dark, narrow staircase that seems to unwind endlessly. I catch something about my apartment being the servants' quarters at some point. The rest is a confusing tattoo of rolled R's. Still, it's reassuring to hear so much English in her indulgently maternal singsong tone as she goes through a list of things I need to know, like how to use the key (giant and antiquated, it looks like a prop from a Merchant Ivory film), how to flush the toilet (there's a string dangling from the ceiling; apparently, plumbing is not a national strong point), how not to use the bidet (didn't need to know that), and so on. With her free hand, she makes gestures I can't see about things I only partially understand. When we finally reach the top step, me huffing and puffing and grateful my spinning instructor can't see me now, Andrea unlocks the door, swings it open, and reaches inside to switch on the light, all with Jorge still attached to her hip.

A warm amber wall sconce illuminates a small foyer with floral wallpaper not dissimilar to the pattern of Andrea's jumpsuit, a small rustic wood table, and a narrow mirror with stained-glass trim. "I think you will like it very much. I decorate it myself." Andrea beams proudly. The hallway to our right bends out of reach of the light. I envision a horror of floral wallpaper, floral sofa cushions, floral carpeting . . . I should be so lucky, I remind myself. More likely, I'm about to spend the next six months staring at cracked stucco walls and stained gray Formica. But it smells freshly cleaned—the best thing I've smelled in hours, in fact, between the faint stench of airsickness and the taxi's mix of cigarettes and stale sweat—and at this point that puts Andrea's servants' quarters on par with the W Hotel back home.

"I show you everything now?" Andrea smiles at me expectantly, hitching up Jorge, who buries his face against her neck.

"Oh, no, that's okay," I say a bit too quickly. "*Soy . . . Soy . . .*" I grope for remnants of grade-eight Spanish. Didn't Trish promise it would all come back to me? No such luck. Still, Andrea leans forward and nods, visibly excited by my attempt. "I'm very tired," I say. Translation: I'm about to burst into tears and no one needs to see that.

Andrea is clearly disappointed—and determined. Her frown slides easily back into a grin, and she throws up her free arm like a mad conductor. "Then you come for some tea." It's more statement than question.

Tea? It's almost midnight—I think. "Thank you. Thank you very much. *Gracias. Mucho.* I'll probably just go right to sleep." Translation: I'm going to crawl into bed, fully clothed, lights off, curl into a fetal position, and stay that way until the Jaws of Life pry me apart. I fake a yawn.

Andrea nods understandingly and hands me the key. "We see you in the morning, then. You have breakfast with us."

"Oh, okay. I'll try," I reply, knowing full well that I won't. "But I don't think I'll be getting up early." Not before two or three days, at least. I search my brain for the Spanish words for "depression-induced coma," but my hostess is already letting herself out of the apartment.

"Any hour is good," she sings cheerfully over her shoulder as she shifts Jorge to the other hip before starting back down the staircase. Jorge tucks his face into his mother's mass of red curls, blending their two heads into one impossibly huge Ronald McDonald wig. "We wait."

Then she's gone and I'm standing in the doorway all by myself. I am in an apartment in some strange woman's house in Buenos Aires all by myself. I step back and swing the heavy door shut and fumble awhile with the antique key in the antique lock until I figure out that it's clockwise twice until you hear the click. I leave the key in the lock, grab the handle on my suitcase, and make my way down the short hall with baby steps. It's dark around the corner, but I can make out a bed toward the back of the room. I bang into a stuffed chair of some kind, smash my shin against a coffee table, and tumble, swearing quietly, toward the edge of the bed. It's soft, and as it gives to my weight, the aroma of lilacs wafts up. Maybe it's the sleep deprivation talking, but right now this means more to me than all the luxuries combined in that fancy Seattle hotel that cost more for one night than Andrea is charging me for a month. Could it really be okay here? Could there be some small grace granted to this perfectly stupid American woman who flew halfway around the world to live in a city that she barely knew existed a few weeks ago? I almost don't want to know the answer and feel a small but unmistakable sense of relief when I grope for the small lamp near the bed and can't find a switch. I vaguely remember Andrea saying something about it being on the wall. I'm too tired to get up and look, already sinking, fully clothed, into the supple mattress, into the fluffy down duvet, into the pure, unmedicated kind of sleep I've needed for days. Even if this is as good as it gets, I am grateful for this blessing, however brief it may be.

When I wake up, my head buried under the duvet, it takes a few seconds to register that I am not in Jeff's postmodern-minimalist apartment. Jeff's duvet was thin and dark gray; this one is fluffy and white. I sense light in the room, something Jeff could never tolerate in the morning. I am in Buenos Aires.

I shut my eyes tight and will myself back to sleep, but it doesn't work. I have no idea what I'm supposed to do next. I only know there is no way in hell I am coming out from under this duvet. It's kind of nice under here anyway. I kick my feet out. Pretty roomy, too. I could have my meals delivered, maybe ask Andrea to move a TV under here, and spend the next few months getting fat and watching all those crazy Latin American soap operas I've heard about. If I need to go to the bathroom, I'll have to get off the bed, but I can take the duvet with me. Oh, God. Bathroom. I'm almost scared to think of what that looks like in this part of the world. Wasn't there something about a string? Speaking of which, I really, really have to go. I let go of my duvet fantasy, hold my breath, close my eyes, and poke my head up into the room. I try to prepare myself by imagining the worst. With such a nice duvet, I'm not expecting total squalor, but the memory of the massive crumbling yellow wall and pack of wild canines doesn't bode well. "Here goes nothing," I whisper. I open my eyes—and drop my jaw.

The studio apartment is not just beautiful, it's nicer than any place I've ever lived on my own. It's only one room, but it's huge, with enough space for a living area, dining area, small kitchenette, and this gigantic life raft of a bed I've grown so attached to. Room enough to hide away in for, say, six months. Every piece of furniture looks like something from *Antiques Roadshow*. But not in an old-fashioned way, maybe because the walls are a cheerful cherry red, or maybe because of the black-and-white macro photographs of exotic flowers that hang around the room. Screw the bed. I hop up and run from toile love seat to gleaming oak table to—I slide my hand over wall tiles till I find a light switch—white marble bathroom vanity! Everything is old in the most lovely way, as though this roomful of furniture has aged gracefully in this exact spot for decades waiting for me to arrive. And all of it bathed in morning light flooding in through sheers over wide French doors. I remember—garden view! I pull back the sheers to reveal a large courtyard carpeted in deep green grass and draped with thick, flowering vines. Stepping onto the small terrace, my arms spreading the doors as far as they will go, I inhale deeply from the sweet, fresh air. I feel like Juliet, minus Romeo, of course. But who needs Romeo when you've got a toile love seat and a garden view?

I do, that's who. Even the image of the Eden before me can't compete with that of Jeff and Lauren entwined. I shake my head hard, like a dog shaking off the rain, as if this will set them loose. My Jeff. Gorgeous, successful, great-on-paper, good-in-bed Jeff. Bed. Jeff and Lauren in bed, our bed. How is it possible that weeks later and thousands of miles away, the image of their writhing bodies has grown more vivid? And the sound. I swear I can still hear the knocking of the platform bed frame against the wall. It's so real it seems to be coming from this apartment. Maybe I've finally cracked up. Okay, wait, that *is* someone knocking on my door. It must be Andrea coming to drag me down to breakfast at this ungodly hour of . . . I scan for a clock. Two-thirty. Sheesh. I haven't slept till two-thirty since, well, never.

"Just a second," I call out, looking around the room for my suitcases and wondering which one has my robe in it, until I realize I never undressed last night. I briefly consider whether this might be more embarrassing than greeting Andrea naked, and grudgingly make my way to the door. I attempt to smooth my sweater with one hand and my hair with the other. I'd be perfectly content to hide in this lovely room of hers for the next six months. I could probably even get myself a fairly convincing tan if I hung out on the terrace at the right time every day.

The knocking starts again, louder, impatient. I know she's trying to be friendly, but this is a bit much. "Coming." I round the hall, catching sight of my extreme bedhead and raccoon eyes (courtesy of seventeen-dollar no-smudge designer mascara) in the small mirror. There's the one good thing about being single again, I tell myself as I turn the key and swing open the door: I can look like total crap, and there's no man around to see it.

Except the man at my door, that is. Broad-shouldered, skin the color of a nonfat latte, curly dark hair falling across his forehead. Looking out at me from under his hair are two utterly mesmerizing eyes, deep green like the proverbial grass on the other side. Not exactly Antonio Banderas—handsome, yes, though in an unpredictable, unfamiliar way—and a bit on the short side, but definitely . . . something.

Is this Andrea's husband? But didn't she say he worked in Chile? A brother maybe? Or, judging from his paint-splattered (and snug in all the right places) overalls, a handyman, perhaps. While I rack my morning-fogged brain for the Spanish word for "hello," those impossibly green eyes skim from my wrinkled sweater and khakis to my lunatic fringe and quarterback makeup. I can feel a zit sprouting on my forehead as I stand here. A smile breaks on his face, and it is the most amazing smile I have ever seen this side of a movie screen . . . and then he starts laughing. Really loud. He stops only long enough to say something in Spanish that contains the word *Americana* and prompts him to shake his head at me as though he's remembered some old joke, and then starts laughing again.

I might not speak the language, but I know when I'm being insulted. I cross my arms protectively, feeling more naked than I did when I thought I actually was, and force myself to look him in the eye. "Can I help you?" He might not know my words either, but my tone is unmistakable. His grin disappears. He spurts out more Spanish, maybe more insults or maybe an apology, and looks at me expectantly. I don't want to give him the satisfaction of knowing yet another American has come to Argentina without knowing Spanish, so I stare at him and try to look unimpressed, hoping the expression translates. Cute or not, all I want him to think is that, whatever he's saying or thinking, I couldn't care less. Because at this point I couldn't.

But he laughs again and shakes his head, the way you laugh at a small child who's feigning a fit. Even his dark curls giggle at me. Before I can say something—something that surely would have been quick and witty and biting, which, even if it had been lost on him, would have given me no small amount of satisfaction—he turns and disappears down the spiral stairs. Even back inside, the heavy wood door slammed tight behind me, I'm pretty sure that's him I can hear laughing down below.

Some welcome wagon. I don't want to make a fuss, but I am paying to be here. Whatever the cultural differences, there's no reason one can't be polite. A little common courtesy—is that too much to ask? I'm beginning to realize why I've never traveled before. In a huff, I peel off my clothes, shower off a full day of travel, and shave my legs. In a huff I towel-dry, moisturize, and get dressed in a gauzy summer dress and flip-flops. In a huff, I put on mascara, lip gloss, and a light mist of perfume. In a huff, I repeatedly ram my hair dryer's plug into the unaccommodatingly foreign electrical socket, giving myself a small shock and killing my hair dryer in the process. In a huff, I twist my damp hair into a loose bun. In a huff, I stomp out of the apartment, down the stairs, and up to the enormous double door with an intimidating bronze knocker that leads into the main part of the house. In a huff, I knock. And then, hearing footsteps, I pinch my cheeks and shake my hair free from the bun. Andrea opens the door, child slung on her hip, free hand magically proffering a plate of tiny croissants. Why do I feel so disappointed?

"Cassandra! Fantastic! You come! And you look so beau-ti-ful!" She steps back and tilts her head, sizing me up with approval. I shake my head in protest and attempt to change the subject by saying hello to Jorge, but the second I look his way, he buries his face in his mother's armpit. It looks like she's instantly sprouted a giant tuft of red underarm hair. Andrea doesn't seem to notice as she gestures me inside with the plate of pastries and then through the foyer.

The main house makes my servants' quarters look like, well, servants' quarters. The floor is a dark, gleaming hardwood, the walls a soft, buttery yellow. An enormous oil painting of a man in military uniform stands guard at the foot of a staircase that curves majestically up one wall and out of sight, its wrought-iron railing inscribing the bright airy entrance with delicate black flowers and vines. Directly across on the far wall is an abstract painting on an unframed canvas. It's a flurry of thick strokes, cool blues and electric yellows. I don't know much about art beyond my one long-forgotten art history elective, but I like the painting. To the right are French doors that lead into a small office with a window to the street ("That was the footmen's station," Andrea notes, "when it was the time of horses"); to the left another set of French doors, softened with creamy sheers, opens into a grand salon complete with fireplace and floor-to-ceiling windows that look out to the courtyard. An intricately patterned area rug cushions my flip-flopped feet. A crystal chandelier dangles overhead. Despite Andrea's jeans and bare feet, I feel ridiculously underdressed.

My self-consciousness is quickly chased away by Andrea's warmth. Within seconds I am ushered into her home, seated ceremoniously at a round table dressed with what must be her finest china and linens, and shown an assortment of pastries, fruit, and other morning delicacies fit for a queen. Andrea waits expectantly. "*¿Medialuna?*" She lifts the plate of tiny croissants. Back home, my typical breakfast was a latte on the way to work, but it has been a long time since I've eaten. I put three and a pat of butter onto the small plate in front of me.

"*Gracias,*" I say, the word sounding fake in my mouth. "Thanks."

Andrea lifts an ornate porcelain carafe. "*¿Café?*"

"Please," I say. "*Por favor.*"

As she fills a small cup, the aroma wafts up, and I miss Starbucks so bad it hurts. The particular way of ordering: tall, nonfat, no foam, extra hot. The sound of my quarter hitting the tip box. The tear of the Equal packet. Stir stick and lid at the ready. And then, finally, the heat against the back of my throat, the delicious signal to the rest of my body that it's morning. Except only now it's not hot, milky espresso I taste but the salt of sadness in my mouth. Beautiful furniture and a kind landlady aside, I know with the whole of my being that I won't be truly at ease again until I am home, and the fake smile I'm wearing for my host's sake is starting to get too heavy to hold. Andrea gets up to find Jorge, who has run off after a small gray dog to whom I am eternally grateful.

While she's gone, I take a tentative sip of the coffee, which is surprisingly good, and a bite of scrumptious tiny croissant. I enjoy the moment of calm, take another full sip of hot coffee, and survey the dozens of photographs clustered on a long side table. Many are of Jorge in various stages of growth. Here awed by a clown. There balancing, with the aid of a gentle hand, on a rock by the ocean. Enjoying the attention of a group of old women at a street fair. Sucking his thumb, asleep in a man's arms—Andrea's husband, I assume. He's definitely not the man who came to my door this morning. He looks nice. Tall.

Scattered throughout are photos of Andrea. Some alone—on a beach smiling, in a kitchen laughing—some surrounded by what are clearly travelers, too tan and blond and happy to be anything but on vacation. What must it be like to have so many strangers float in and out of your life, I wonder. To never know what the next airplane will bring your way. For someone like Andrea, this must be an exciting adventure that comes right to her door. Years from now, will there be a side table in my dining room lined with photographs of people I've met here? That might be nice. Of course, if I never leave this house, that will mean a lot of pictures of Andrea and Jorge and the three dogs.

I can't help but laugh at myself. I can't really sit around in that apartment all day and night, however lovely it is—especially not if that incredibly cute, fantastically rude man is regularly wandering about. And there's no way I am going home early. I wouldn't dream of giving Jeff the satisfaction of hearing about that from one of our mutual friends. That leaves me and Buenos Aires and six months to fill. If Andrea's house is any indication, maybe this place isn't completely bad. Just a little rough around the edges, the way even Seattle might look to an outsider. Maybe I can handle another 180 days here. Maybe by the end of it I'll be like Andrea, all smiles and laughter. I take anther bite of croissant. Maybe I don't even need a plan.

Except that I do. Yes, definitely. I really, really do. I can feel my planlessness creeping under my skin like an itch. Denying it won't help. It will only spread out and get stronger, maddeningly so, until I scratch it. As soon as Andrea comes back, I'll excuse myself and set to work. I've got my travel guide, and Sam and Trish gave me a bunch of books on the area as a parting gift. I can start with those to figure out a list of must-see places. There is also that website with a forum that's supposed to have a lot of great info direct from travelers. Andrea confirmed that my suite is wired for Internet, though I'll need to buy a power converter for my laptop.

Ah, there. I'm feeling better already. Thinking about going outside is frightening, but thinking about thinking about going outside I can handle. So long as there's a plan.

Then I notice a picture of *him*. My welcome wagon. Anger starts to rise again until it dawns on me how different he looks in the photographs. Here he's sitting at a café with Andrea and a group of people. They look younger, in their early twenties maybe. They are all leaning in together, shoulders touching, and smiling warmly at the camera. There he's in a crowd with Jorge on his shoulders, looking up and laughing. In another, he stands beside Andrea and the tall man I assume is her husband. He's smiling here, too, but it's not a happy smile. In fact, it looks a lot like the smile I've been putting on for the last three weeks, a smile you wear for the sake of others. It makes me want to like him.

Not everyone makes a good first impression, I suppose. Speaking of which, maybe my own wasn't so great, either. Suddenly, I feel guilty about getting so mad. I might be paying rent, but I am still the foreigner here. But how to make a better second impression? To start, I've got to learn some Spanish, break open that language CD that's buried in my suitcase. Fluency isn't going to happen anytime soon, but surely I can manage to avoid this person until I've learned a few basics.

Learn Spanish. Yes. The decision makes me feel instantly better, calmer. It's another item to add to my plan, I think happily, popping another mini-croissant into my mouth. Pleased with myself, I decide to celebrate with a bit more of Andrea's superb coffee. As I reach for the carafe, I hear someone jiggling the handle on a door behind me. Jorge must have led Andrea on a chase through the entire house. I stand up to help, assuming she'll have her hands full with child, dogs, and probably more food, but before

I can reach the handle, the door flies open. Startled, I step back, stumble over something, and land flat on my butt at exactly the moment *he* walks through the door.

I swallow my mouthful of croissant down hard. I might look ridiculous right now, but I'm determined to keep my dignity. A situation is embarrassing only if you let yourself be embarrassed, right? His eyes meet mine and I try to push out a self-deprecating laugh, but I haven't managed to swallow completely, and bits of croissant fly out of my mouth and onto the front of my dress. Now he's the one who's laughing. You're a guest in his country, I remind myself. This is Andrea's friend or brother, perhaps, and she is a kind woman who has gone out of her way to make you feel welcome. And to be fair, this must look pretty funny.

I can't help it. Anger, residual and freshly brewed, bubbles up. This man has done anything but make me feel welcome. I'm about to give him a piece of my mind when he reaches out his hand. He's not completely devoid of common decency, I see. Part of me wants to ignore his offer, but we're mending intercultural relations here. Very important stuff. I can be gracious. Yes, even an American can be gracious!

I offer him my hand. He takes it and smiles, not at all amused this time—genuinely warm and open. Did Jeff ever smile at me like this? Where did that question come from? I can feel it in my stomach, a tingling warmth spreading out to my fingertips. He lifts me slowly, and I allow myself the fleeting romantic-comedy movie fantasy of our faces drawing closer and closer together until—

There's a loud crash somewhere in the house, followed by a fury of tapping and scratching. We look at each other, eyes wide. He releases my hand and, not quite on my feet yet, I go crashing down once more. My butt is really going to kill later. He blushes and mumbles something in Spanish. An apology? Before I can say anything, he slips back out the door he came in.

The tapping and scratching are getting louder, closer, but I can't seem to will myself to get up. I lie on the floor and wallow in my latest humiliation. Now I've been dropped, figuratively and literally, by two men on two continents. Maybe someone is trying to tell me something. Maybe that whole nunnery thing isn't such a crazy option. As I imagine myself in a habit, something wet smacks me in the head. I reach up to retrieve a damp, fuzzy toy in the shape of a bone. Ewww.

"Jorge! *¡Basta!*"

Andrea, Jorge, and a canine hurricane tumble into the room together through yet another door that I hadn't noticed. I'm starting to feel like Alice in Wonderland. Before I can become the next dog toy, I scramble to my feet. The dogs tumble into the wall behind me, sniff about for a few seconds, and, locating the object of their collective desire, tumble out of the room again.

Andrea swoops Jorge up with one arm. "Oh, Cassandra! Are you okay?"

"Oh, yes, fine." I brush croissant off my front. "All in one piece."

"I'm sorry. I leave you all alone. The dogs . . . You see yourself all the trouble."

"Oh, that's okay. And I wasn't alone. I met . . . uh . . . " The infuriatingly rude Argentine man who has instantly turned me into a bumbling mess. "Um, curly hair?" Well done, Cassie.

"Oh, Mateo!" She claps her hands. "You meet Mateo! My dear friend Mateo!"

"Mateo," I repeat. The name slides over my tongue much too easily. What did I expect? Bob or Joe? He is Argentine, I remind myself. But did his name have to be so damn sexy? I want to say it out loud again, feel the unknown syllables on my lips, but that would be strange, wouldn't it?

"He fix everything for me all the time. He's like second husband." She giggles at the joke, and Jorge joins in.

"That's very sweet of him," I say, imagining Mateo rushing over to screw in lightbulbs, brown muscles rippling under his T-shirt as he twists the bulb . . . What? No, no, no. No rippling muscles. Not sweet. Not sweet at all. I try to change the subject. "Before. Upstairs. He knocked on my door and I opened it." Okay, now I sound like a total idiot.

Andrea looks at me, amused or confused, I can't tell. Then her face brightens with recognition, and she smiles widely. "He's very handsome, *sí*?"

"What? I guess." Am I blushing?

"Good thing you wear a dress today, *sí*?"

"What? Oh." I look down at my dress and feel my face flush a deep hot red. I'd normally pull on jeans and a T-shirt on a day off, and if this isn't a day off, I don't know what is. Was all this for him, a complete stranger who seems to be going out of his way to make me feel utterly unwelcome? "I didn't . . . I just . . ." I give up.

"He is single, you know." She winks at me.

"Oh. Well." I laugh awkwardly, push the idea away with my hands. "Actually, Mateo and I . . . I think we might have gotten off on the wrong foot."

"On wrong foot? What does this mean, please?"

"Uh, we, I don't think he likes me very much."

"Now, that would be very surprising, I think." She winks again and pinches my arm lightly. If she only knew how he'd acted. I'm tempted to tell her that her dear friend dropped me on my ass, but she'd probably construe that into some grand courting gesture. Eager to take the focus off of me, I try to catch Jorge's attention with a big, goofy smile, but he just buries his head in his mother's red curls. Is every man in this house determined not to like me?

"Come, sit. Finish your breakfast."

"Oh, I'm fine, thanks. I'm full. Everything was really good. Thank you so much." I'm still a bit hungry, but mostly I want to go upstairs, peel off this stupid dress, get under the covers, and figure out my next move. Enough of all this Mateo nonsense. No cute Argentine jerk is going to come between me and my new plan. "I should probably unpack."

"Oh, Cassandra, I'm sorry," Andrea says, dipping a piece of croissant in honey for Jorge. "Mateo must do work in your apartment today. I buy new air conditioner. You will want it soon, I think, when summer comes. Maybe one hour, maybe two. It's okay?" Apparently, the cute Argentine jerk *is* going to come between me and my plan.

"Okay, yes. Thank you. That's very nice of you." I'm saying "thank you," but I can feel my face pulling down. I scrape up a smile for Andrea's sake.

"You have big plans for your first day, yes?" How can I tell her that my big plans were to stay inside and make plans? That I would spend the next six months making plans if I could?

"Yes, oh yes. Big plans. Huge." There's that converter for the electrical socket. And a hair dryer. I could get some groceries. I can go for a walk around the block—about fifty times.

"Marvelous. You will have so much fun, I know."

Only when I step through the enormous doors that separate the main house from the old carriage port do I realize that not only do I not have a plan, I don't have my purse. There's no way around it: Mateo or no Mateo, I will have to go into the apartment. I can handle it. In and out. He won't even know I'm there.

Except it turns out that he's the one who's not there. And there it is—an unmistakable feeling of disappointment. I go inside the apartment, find my purse, two city guides, and a translation dictionary without incident. God, what is wrong with me? I don't even know this person. He could have an IQ of 37. He could have a really small . . . shoe size. He dropped me on my ass. He is rudeness personified. I repeat this in my head like a mantra to ward off bad, stupid thoughts, and before I know it, I am outside, locking the front door behind me. As the lock clicks into place, a cool breeze tickles my bare shoulders and sends a shiver through my entire body. That's when I realize one very good thing about Mateo. For a short while, he made me forget exactly what I've gotten myself into.

CHAPTER FOUR

*T*wo blocks up, two blocks left, two blocks down, two blocks right. Head down to avoid the mines the canine population has left for me every twenty or so feet, I walk a square pattern, not so much to avoid getting lost (I do have a map—okay, three) but to avoid feeling more lost than I already do. I realize that this route will take me back to the front door of Andrea's yellow house, but that's about as much excitement as I can take right now.

The population of Buenos Aires is, thankfully, spread out, and the neighborhood—my neighborhood, I suppose—is rather peaceful now that the drag queens have retreated. My occasional sidewalk companions are mostly solitary Argentines moving quickly and with serious intent. It's the middle of the day in the middle of the week, after all, and unlike me, these people have places to go, people to see. At the first stirrings of jealousy, I remind myself to enjoy this rare opportunity of pure, guilt-free leisure—a delicacy I haven't tasted in years. But it's no use. The thought of wandering aimlessly is enough to make me run back to the apartment, Mateo or no Mateo. I need something to propel me forward. I focus on the plug converter and new hair dryer I need. Hardly a checkmark-worthy goal, but better than no goal at all.

I recall Andrea mentioning something last night about a grocery store and other shops on the main street a few blocks over. Assuming I'll find a hardware or electronics store there, I take a sharp turn and cross the quiet street with what feels vaguely like enthusiasm.

Now that I have a plan, short-term as it may be, I indulge in a slower gait, wanting to draw out this feeling of purpose as long as possible. After I buy a hair dryer, what will I do with myself? I push away the question and try not to think too far ahead. Peppered among the more modern concrete apartment buildings are beautiful gems of architecture that assert happier, more prosperous chapters into the city's current story. Strolling from block to block, I am faced again and again with the disparity between what this place is and what it must have once been. One neighbor's house crumbles from neglect as another's stands proud and cared for, a representative of a surviving elite. Some homes have been given up on completely, for-sale signs propped up against boarded windows. Another seems to have been abandoned in a hurry. The upstairs windows are shuttered tight, the front gate left ajar. Three cats loll about in a deep, thick garden overgrown with weeds. Someone started painting the pale blue walls a pretty ballet pink and then gave up a third of the way. There are no ladders or paint cans visible, so I can only assume that the painting stopped some time ago. I stop and stare for a minute, intrigued by the mystery of it. Even in such a state of disrepair, this humbled structure has an undeniable charm. But my curiosity shifts quickly into discomfort. What would make someone stop painting in the middle like that? I don't know why it bothers me so much, but it does. I can't get it out of my mind. It's not the hopelessness about it or the sense of defeat—so many of the houses have that same sad air about them. It's the half-painted wall, the fact that whoever lived there looked forward to a bright future that included pink paint. There must have been much life and love there once. No one paints a house pink if they aren't ridiculously happy. No one stops painting halfway unless that happiness was abruptly taken away. The explanation can't be only financial; unlike the other homes in similar states of disrepair, this one has no for-sale signs. No, inside those walls, someone's life went sideways. I can feel it. And that's when I realize, rather uncomfortably, that if I were a house I would look exactly like this.

I walk on, the neighborhood offering little in the way of a visual salve but much in the way of distraction. A stylish boutique window displays gorgeous leather shoes and handbags—with posh price tags to match, no doubt. I remind myself that a woman with no paycheck has to watch her spending.

Farther down, an old woman sits cross-legged on an old tablecloth, sandwich bags filled with herbs and spices spread out around her. The sun-dried faces of old men on the corner arguing gently over a chessboard contain at once a heartbreaking humility and a fierce pride. When I pass, they tip their heads in acknowledgment but offer no smiles. I return the gesture with as much gravitas as I can muster in a sundress and flip-flops. Stopping at a corner to let a motorcycle pass, I notice the concrete slab is marked with an elaborate emblem and the year 1887. Just ahead on a plain gray wall, artful graffiti calls out against the country's latest president. From this surface view, the contradictions are wondrous. I'm beginning to wish I paid more attention in that Latin American history class I took sophomore year.

One thing is clear: I am out of place in more ways than I can list. Different country? I feel like I've been beamed down from another planet. I don't even look right. In Seattle, my blond hair and mostly black wardrobe were as common as a rainy day. Before I left, I had a ridiculous notion that, with a few subtle tweaks, I could blend right in here. I wasn't about to dye my hair brown (I've had enough life-altering traumas for a while, thank you), but I did bring only the most summery clothes I owned. I didn't exactly imagine a city bustling with women in tiered, multicolored skirts and flowing peasant blouses—okay, maybe I did a little bit—but I expected a bit more Latin flavor. Yet aside from the woman selling spices, everyone here dresses a heck of a lot like the people in Seattle. In fact, despite the warm spring day, most people are wearing pants or jeans, sweaters, and jackets just as they are on my side of the world where it's autumn. And if my sundress doesn't make me feel displaced enough, my blond hair clinches the deal. In a city where the locals look like extras from a Fellini film, I might as well be wearing a neon sign that reads AMERICANA.

The more I walk, the more my shoulders round in. My step becomes heavier and more condensed. I pull my shoulder bag tight against my side. It's a stance I recall from my first day at college when I realized too late that I had gotten my outfit completely wrong (it would take me a few weeks to master the post-grunge, neo-hippie look so popular at the time). I am trying to shrink myself. I know that I can't prevent other people from noticing me, but I can minimize how much I notice me.

As I consider turning around and heading back to the house empty-handed, a young boy tears past me, laughing. He holds an ice cream cone out in front of him like an Olympic torch. Another boy, older, his brother I'm guessing, chases after him. He brushes against me as he passes and stops abruptly. *"Excúseme, señora. Excúseme."* Is it the running or is he blushing? He blurts a string of excited Spanish at me, pointing after his brother, fully unaware that I, the strange, blond, incorrectly dressed woman, can't understand a word he is saying.

"Está bien," I manage, surprising myself more than a little, and I smile. He grins shyly before darting away to find his ice cream thief. I resume my walk, still smiling. My shoulders straighten somewhat. My stride grows a touch braver. Maybe it's not so very horrible being out here in this strange city, because maybe it's really not that strange after all.

This new optimism lasts a whole thirty seconds. Then I turn onto a busy street.

Cars, people, dogs, all loud and impatient and seemingly indifferent to one another, swarm every inch of concrete. Kiosks selling everything from cigarettes to underwear crowd the narrow sidewalk. What was a light and playful wind a few hundred feet to the west is now a gritty gale kicking every loose bit of dirt and pollen into my eyes. Car horns, music blasting from storefronts, and scraps of Spanish conversation flood my ears.

The cacophony of sights and sounds is so overwhelming, I forget for a moment why I've left my safe two-block square. I needed something, didn't I? Something important? As hard as I rack my brain, I can't remember. And while we're at it, why am I here? In this place. What propelled me here? Did I hope for a new home? A new fiancé? A new job? A new life? The questions are harder to bear than the jackhammer that's begun work on the curb to my right.

I wish Jeff were here, his long arms wrapped around me, my face finding that warm, musky nook at the base of his neck. I don't know if I'd say Jeff made me feel safe, exactly—look to men for that, and you're sure to be disappointed, as my mother drilled into me from a young age—but there was the sense of comfort when he was around, a sort of safety in numbers. When I was still living in my apartment near the university but spending most of my time at Jeff's, I came home one Sunday evening to a wasps' nest under construction in my living room. There were no wasps that I could see, but that only meant they were coming back, didn't it? When I called him, hysterical, he didn't hesitate for a second—he came right over and took that horrid thing off my ceiling armed with nothing but an old margarine container and my oven gloves. I stood outside the whole time, certain a hurricane of angry, homeless wasps would return at any moment. With the hive locked up tight in the plastic container and tossed down the garbage shoot, and all the windows in my apartment sealed tight, Jeff whisked me off to my favorite bistro for a pitcher of sangria to celebrate my courage. Later, as we lay spent under his Egyptian cotton sheets, he whispered into my ear, "I like it when you need me." I drew his arm across my chest and curled into him. For the moment I liked needing him.

And now it's just me. No arm, no nook. Those are Lauren's now.

I have to get off this street, away from these thoughts. A block away is a wall of trees that looks promising. I glance at the map, trying desperately to avoid looking any more like an outsider than I already do. There it is, a square of green shining out like a beacon to this weary urban traveler.

The park looks as weary as I feel, but as I enter it, relief washes over me in waves of calm, lush green. Wrought-iron and wood benches bend and buckle from age. Modest statues and fountains have given in to decades of poor weather. And the most amazing thing: cats.

They're everywhere. Black, calico, tabby, orange, spotted, striped, tailless, scarred. They lounge like kings and queens on any still surface that will hold their weight. Around the park's perimeter, people have left piles of cat food, cans of tuna, and other edible offerings. I walk slowly, careful not to scare these tiny citizens, but they clearly have no fear of me. Only a few lift their heads to watch me pass. I am simply one more visitor to their feline haven. My flip-flops beginning to pinch between my toes, I look for a cat-free bench, but such a thing doesn't seem to exist. I ask a Morris look-alike if he minds company, but his only response is a lazy tail flick. I suppose he doesn't speak English. I sit.

It's nice—the cats, the relative quiet, the bit of green. Jeff would like this, I think. Except for the cats. He hates cats. Not big on dogs, either. I love animals. Would we have ended up with birds or fish? I wonder. Not that it matters now. None of it does. All those plans for the future. Didn't they mean anything to him? Didn't I? It wasn't all in my head, was it? There was something real and special there. That week we spent with his whole family at his grandparents' house in Oregon when I helped his mom and grandmother make an enormous Ukrainian feast. I was in that kitchen for six hours. After everyone fell asleep, we drove to the beach and made love on a blanket. Jeff said that he was proud of me, how I settled into his loud, funny family so easily, how I made them fall in love with me. All those Sunday mornings at Sammy's Diner, sharing three kinds of eggs Benedict because we could never pick just one each, telling each other stories from our respective sections of the newspaper. Didn't Jeff tell me once that he knew we were meant to be by the way we did the crossword? And the night he proposed. From the French champagne to the beautiful ring, it was exactly the way I'd always imagined it. He told me he knew it was time to get serious, that all the pieces of his life were coming together. How do you go from that to being too perfect? Am I really too perfect, or is he deeply flawed? Or scared? Maybe it was all bullshit.

I shake my head. Morris looks up briefly and closes his eyes again. What am I doing? I've already been through all of this. I had all the late-night crying sessions with Sam and Trish. I spent countless hours over the last two weeks on the phone screaming at Jeff; I heard all of his weak excuses and even weaker apologies. I moved out of our apartment and into my parents' house. I endured my mother's dramatic silences—her only communication to me coming in the form of increasingly hostile Post-it missives, like the one I found on my toothbrush: *If you get maimed or disfigured in Argentina, what nice American boy will want you?*—and my stepfather's sympathetic smiles. I removed myself from our joint checking account. I sold my beautiful engagement ring. And now I'm here. In a park full of cats. Period. End of story.

But before I can stop it, my heart is off and running. Shortness of breath follows. The sounds in the park are mixing into a low-pitched yet unmistakable buzzing. I close my eyes and dig around for something happy to think about, something that instills a sense of calm. I need a mental reboot. This means pushing out all thoughts of Jeff, which, ironically, used to calm me more than anything. I need something to fill the space he's left inside of me. I can feel my pulse in my neck and behind my knees. My left arm is tingling. Something happy. Something happy. Sam and Trish gossiping over drinks at Jimmy's. No, that makes me miss them. I picture my stepdad, always so calm and reassuring, but that instantly makes me think about my mom—the look of horror on her face when she realized I was actually getting on the plane, her voice shrieking after me, the "what were you thinking" speech I'd be getting if she were here—which is the opposite of relaxing. Come on, Cassie. There's got to be something good to think about. There is always something good. A few weeks ago this would have been easy. There was a list of a dozen things I could tick off to get through a low-level anxiety attack. Now I'm struggling to find one single solitary thing that doesn't send me over the edge.

Everything that made me happy is either thousands of miles away or gone for good.

Just when I'm ready to give up and free-fall into a full-on panic here in the middle of this strange park in this strange city where I'll probably die and be eaten by feral cats, *his* face pops into my head. Mateo. Not the Mateo smirking at me from my doorway. Not the Mateo dropping me on the floor. The Mateo in the photographs, with the smile that's somehow happy and sad, that smile that makes me want to smile back and comfort him, that smile that for a moment makes me forget I am the one in need of comforting. He's the last person I should be thinking about right now; well, the second-to-last person. But I don't want to let go of that smile. It's a small indulgence, harmless, doesn't mean anything. And it works like a charm. Everything else clears away. I can breathe. I am not going to die or become kitty kibble.

Ah, yes, I think, feeling myself again, the electronics store. That means venturing back out onto the street. Maybe just another few minutes or so. It's nice here. With my eyes closed, I could be almost anywhere.

Something soft brushes against my bare leg, forcing me to open my eyes. A small black cat with white eyebrows is twirling herself between my calves. I reach down to pet my new friend, startled by the ridge of spine felt so easily through her fur. She looks up at me appreciatively but doesn't make a sound. None of them does, I realize. I've been sitting in this park spilling over with cats for at least half an hour, and I haven't heard a single meow. Are they that content, or have they simply become accustomed to their own degree of misery? I reach out a tentative hand to my benchmate, who is still sprawled across half the seat, tail flicking over the edge of the wood. He stretches his neck in my direction, then gives up, lolling his head back onto the wood. When I first sat down, I had the childish idea that perhaps I'd stumbled across someplace magic, but open your eyes, and there is a melancholy here that you can't ignore. That might explain why there aren't any couples strolling the grounds, hand in hand. There are at least a dozen people scattered about on benches, and they are each alone.

I've got to get out of here. Stepping gingerly around my little friend, I make my way back toward the entrance. I step into the flow of sidewalk traffic and let it swoop me along, heading south, farther away from Andrea's yellow house. When I feel the panic begin to rise again, I summon Trish's semi-facetious voice: *Fake it till you make it.* Map clutched tightly in one hand, I pump the other, mimicking the determined walk of the urban Argentine. Teenagers, businessmen, grandmothers, children. They all have it. Even kiosk patrons seem to merely slow down rather than stop completely, selecting and purchasing their newspaper, cigarettes, whatever, in one fluid motion. There are no dillydalliers, no aimless window-shoppers. Best of all, I realize gratefully, there is little time or space to be lonely with hundreds of people rushing around you.

It's after four P.M., and I glide along in the throng of commuters and schoolchildren for a good five blocks before I see it. A window crammed with stereos, irons, microwaves, clock radios, and, yes, hair dryers. I've actually found an electronics store! I won't go back empty-handed, defeated by traffic noise and a few troubling memories. My enthusiasm, however, is tempered by no small amount of dread. Now comes the hard part.

Inside the shop, a perspiring middle-aged man rushes to greet me. He offers up a flurry of Spanish to which I can only shake my head. Flash back to fifth grade, when we moved out of our old house and I transferred to a new school midyear. They were way ahead of my old class, and I sat absolutely silent for three whole days until the teacher asked me a math question I couldn't understand, let alone answer. It was like being in a foreign country and not speaking the language. Kind of like this. *"Por favor,"* I say quietly, not even attempting to roll my R's, and point to the hair dryer in the window. But it's too high up, and I could easily be pointing at three different things. The man swabs his forehead with a handkerchief and looks at me curiously. I could mime drying my hair. No, I decide, this is embarrassing enough. But I need that bloody hair dryer. If I don't get it, I will never have a good-hair day again, will never attract a man, will never get asked out, engaged, or married. My future hinges on that hair dryer. *"Por favor,"* I offer again, with more enthusiastic pointing this time. The salesman shrugs his shoulders sympathetically. The other shoppers turn and stare. My eyes feel heavy and hot. Oh no, Cassie. Not that, not here. Keep it together, girl. You're doing fine.

I pull the pocket Spanish dictionary from my bag as discreetly as possible and look up "hair dryer." I am that ten-year-old girl once more, trembling in her chair, admitting finally, eyes planted on the linoleum floor, that she is utterly, hopelessly lost in the math lesson. *I don't know what a fraction is.* "*¿Se-ca-dor del pe-lo?*"

Unlike my new grade-five teacher, who shook her head and tsked loudly, the salesman lights up with a huge smile. "Ah, *sí, sí, sí. ¡Secador del pelo!*" He slaps his hands together and disappears through a door behind the counter. The curious shoppers turn back to their transactions. Seconds later, my damp, grinning salesman returns with a hair dryer in a box. He presents it with a flourish, as if it were a bounty of jewels. And that's all it takes, this stranger's enthusiasm to help an American woman who needs a hair dryer more than anything else in the entire world. There's simply no stopping it. I let loose a sprinkling of tears. "*Gracias,*" I say. "*Gracias, señor. Muchas gracias.*" Somewhere between the next "*muchas*" and "*gracias,*" the sprinkling turns into full-blown sobbing. A fraud, I have my friends and family convinced that I am tougher than what life has thrown me, that I'm a survivor. But I am no such thing. I am, in fact, all raw emotions and seeping wounds. These last two weeks of pretending I was in control, that I knew what I was doing, that Jeff had done me a favor, that I was excited to start a new chapter, it all comes pouring out of me. "I. Am. So. Sorry," I stutter through brief gaps in the crying. "My. Fiancé. Left. Me. For. Some. One. E-e-else."

The next few minutes are a blur. As I squawk out the tale of My Black Wednesday—Jeff, job, etc.—I sense ghostly figures circling about me, feel the light touch of angels on my arms and shoulders. A hand helps me into a chair. Another pushes tissues toward me. Hushed Spanish trickles all around. I hear tsking, but the warm, grandmotherly kind. I am so grateful for it all, even their pity, but I'm also acutely aware of how embarrassed I will feel about this scene the moment I regain my senses. Here's an item I forgot to add to my to-do list: Travel bravely thousands of miles to bare soul to electronics-store patrons and employees who haven't got a clue what you're saying. Check! Is this better or worse than having an anxiety attack in the middle of a park overrun by cats? Hard call. All I know for sure is that none of this was the way this day was supposed to go. Or maybe it was. How is one to know how one's day is supposed to go if one doesn't have a plan? What is wrong with me? Without a bunch of lists, am I truly incapable of functioning? Trish likes to tease me about that very idea, but it's just teasing, isn't it? Life before The Plan was so long ago, I'm not sure. I am sure that I have to get out of here fast.

"*Gracias,*" I say weakly, rising from the chair. "I'm sorry. So sorry. *Muchas gracias.*" How much is the hair dryer? The tag says thirty-five pesos. Thank God I exchanged some cash at the airport. Waiting thirty seconds for my credit card to clear would be unbearable. I grab four ten-peso notes from my wallet, push them into the salesman's damp hands, and rush outside. I clutch the dryer under my arm a little tighter as I head in the direction of the yellow house. Whatever the universe throws at me next, at least my hair will look good.

If I can just make it back to the yellow house, everything will be okay. There is, after all, a lot to do. Bags to unpack, travel books to pore over, lists to make. I should probably call my parents and then Sam and Trish. But didn't Andrea say I need a phone card to make long-distance calls? E-mail will have to suffice for now. I stop and let out a breath. I've forgotten the plug converter I need for my laptop. I'm only a block from the scene of my public meltdown, but, as incredibly kind as those people were, there's no way I'm showing my face there again. Ever. I'll find another store tomorrow. Another store, another chance to humiliate myself. Do I really need the Internet? I could start reading more books and newspapers. And e-mail? I'll single-handedly revive the lost art of letter writing. As great as spreadsheets are, plain old paper sufficed for thousands of years.

The answer to my problem swings open mere inches from my nose. There it is on the door in big block letters: INTERNET and TELÉFONO. I step into the small shop and repeat the second word to the guy at the counter, who reminds me of a doorman at my favorite dance club in Seattle who never smiles. Sam, Trish, and I tell him stupid jokes and flirt shamelessly to see if we can get a reaction, but he's as stoic as a Buckingham Palace guard. The counter guy waves me toward the line of empty glass booths, barely lifting his eyes from the computer game he's playing. His disinterest is kind of nice, like a bit of home. I am tempted to recite a naughty limerick, but I suspect I'd be wasting my breath.

I step into a booth against the window, look up the international code for the U.S., and start to call . . . Who should I call? If I call my parents, I'll have to fake that everything's wonderful or they'll worry. If I call Sam or Trish, I'll end up telling them everything, and that means having to relive it all. I can't do it. My pulse and breathing have finally settled into a normal rhythm. Plus, the idea of Mr. Empathetic at the counter watching me cry is too much to bear.

I call Jeff.

I'm not sure why. My fingers seem to be pushing the buttons, and now it's ringing and I don't have a clue what I'm going to say. Jeff and I haven't spoken, if you can call it that, since I went by our apartment to pack up my clothes. "I've come for my things," I said when he answered the door. He stepped back to let me in, not saying a word, then sat quietly in the living room while I packed. In the end, I took only my clothes. I didn't want anything else, not the things we'd bought together, not even the meager furnishings that I'd brought from my old apartment in the University District. As much as I loved the ebony lamps we swooned over in that swank downtown boutique and the circular area rug I'd hauled home seven blocks from a garage sale, I couldn't bear the thought of keeping anything *she* might have touched. When I'd loaded two big suitcases, three garbage bags, and a laundry hamper full of shoes into the elevator, he came into the hall and said, "Take care of yourself." Not "I'll take care of you." Not "I made a mistake." Not even "I'll miss you." *Take care of yourself.* That's when I finally understood that we were done. I nodded and pushed the lobby button. I held it together just long enough for the mirrored doors to close.

Four rings and the voice mail message clicks on. I should hang up, but I can't seem to manage it. "Hi, you've reached Jeff. Sorry I missed you . . ." He changed the message. Why am I so surprised that he changed the message? It's been weeks. I don't live there anymore. I am thousands of miles away. I sold the engagement ring. What was I expecting? Of course he changed the message. The beep jerks me back to my senses, and I slam the receiver down. If I didn't know what I was going to say when I made the call, I sure as hell don't have a clue now. *Hi, you've reached Jeff. Sorry I missed you* . . . I'm not sure how long I stare at the phone—could be a minute or an hour. It's the strangest sensation to feel as though you are falling, or rather, being pulled down into a hole in the earth, when you are most definitely sitting on a stool in a glass booth in an Internet café in Buenos Aires. I try to conjure up an image of something to calm me, but my mind is blank and buzzing at the same time. A million words and images and thoughts and hopes, but I can't grasp any of it.

There's knocking on the glass behind me. I've been sitting here too long, and I suppose the disinterested young man is now very interested in the crazy woman who spends two pesos on a ten-second call and then sits staring at the phone for hours on end. I would be embarrassed, but I've tapped my quota on that emotion for the day. I fish a five-peso note from my purse and turn to face him with as much disinterest as I can muster.

But it's not the guy at the counter. It's my landlady, smiling and waving wildly, Jorge sprouting from her hip and chewing on a granola bar. I am so glad to see them both.

"Oh, Cassandra," Andrea almost shouts as I step out of the booth. "What happy luck. I'm going to the market now for dinner, and I see you sitting here."

"Andrea. Hello. I was just calling . . . home."

"Oh, marvelous. Your family must be happy to hear from you, *si*?"

"Yeah. Yes. *Si*."

"You tell them how you love Buenos Aires."

"*Si*." I don't even know this woman, but I feel bad lying to her.

"You are done now?"

"Uh, *si*." That's true, at least.

"You come with me to the market, then?"

"Well, I . . ." Market. I imagine open stands of tropical fruit and vegetables, exotic smoked meats and rind cheeses hanging overhead, crooked wood crates spilling over with rustic breads and delicate pastries. I have a kitchen in my apartment. I should probably put something in it—I can't subsist on Andrea's coffee and croissants indefinitely. And I am starting to get very hungry. "Okay, sure. Yes. *Si*."

"Then we go home." Home. That word used to fill me with such comfort. "And you have dinner with us."

"Oh, no, I couldn't." I feel bad—she must get lonely with her husband gone all the time—but I have important things to do. Like organize my T-shirts by fabric and color.

"You have plans? You go out?"

"Oh, no." I want to tell her my plans, but I wonder if they'll translate into "I'm loco." "I just don't want to impose."

"Oh, I thought maybe you have a date." She giggles, and Jorge follows suit. "Maybe with Mateo." Mateo? Why in the world would she think that? Is she teasing me? Does she know that Mateo and I took an instant dislike to each other? If she does, that would have to mean that Mateo talked to her about me. I can only imagine how flattering he must have been.

"Mateo? No. No, no. Nothing like that." I am aware of the rising pitch in my voice. I don't need to look in the mirror behind me to know that I have gone as red as Andrea's hair.

"Then you must come. It is only me and Jorge. We would love your company."

I guess I could squeeze some time from my busy schedule. "All right," I say. "Thank you. That would be nice." I smile at Jorge, who replies by scowling and tucking his head into Andrea's armpit. One of these days, that kid is going to like me.

The three blocks to the market, Jorge runs a few feet ahead of us and then back, ahead and back. This is the movement of someone who feels safe, and it's difficult not to be jealous. As we walk, Andrea does most of the talking. About how the neighborhood has changed in the past decade, about the young people who are moving in and starting businesses, about the older families who lost their savings and are moving out. "Out with the old, in with the new," she says. "Isn't that what you Americans say?" I nod, more than content to listen. Her singsong voice and those delightfully rolled R's nearly drown out Jeff's voice mail recording, which stills plays over and over in my head.

"That was my school." She points across the street to a stern-looking structure with few windows. "Mateo was in my class. All the little girls were crushed by him." She has my attention, but before I can learn more, she's trailed off, indulging in a few silent memories, perhaps.

"It doesn't look like a school," I say, wondering too late if that sounds culturally insensitive. "I mean, I don't see a playground or anything."

"Listen." She stops and looks up at the sky. I'm not sure what I'm supposed to listen for, but then I hear them. Children laughing.

In the city, schools have walled courtyards, she tells me. "For safety." You can't see the children, she says, but you can always hear them. We walk on. She doesn't mention Mateo again.

The market is . . . a market. Bored cashiers stand beside cash registers that pling and chirp. Long lines snake around pillars and displays of sale items. Skinny stock boys skulk around corners, armed with pricing guns and coils of orange stickers. Jars, bottles, and boxes display familiar brands from my favorite peanut butter to the hair color I use. I guess they're called multinational companies for a reason. Oh well, I think, one more thing that's failed to live up to my expectations. Maybe people with low expectations are on to something.

It's easy to hide my disappointment from Andrea, who zips deftly down aisle after aisle, snatching items from the shelves with barely a look. As we move through the store, she keeps a running commentary, pointing out the best brand of fresh ravioli and counseling me on the characteristics of a cheese I've never heard of. This would almost count for an exotic food if it didn't look precisely like the slabs of Edam and provolone beside it. Jorge disappears every few minutes and returns with a can of black olives, a chocolate bar with almonds, squeezable mustard, a bag of red grapes, a baguette that's as tall as he is, anchovy paste. Andrea puts each of his treasures in her cart without breaking speech or stride. Not much of a cook, I drop a few essentials and some treats for snacking into my green basket. (If only I knew where Jorge got that chocolate bar.) When Andrea's cart starts to overflow in the dairy section, we turn sharply and head for the checkout.

On the walk back to the yellow house, I sate my growing hunger with bites from a mini-baguette while Andrea continues with her seminar on the neighborhood. Closer to home, the history gets personal. Each beautiful house I admired this morning has a story, and Andrea condenses them for me as we lug our bags past. Her husband went to school with a girl who lived in the red-brick house on the corner. Set back ten or so feet from the edge of the sidewalk and protected by a black gate adorned with detailed ironwork, this house has a structural disdain for its surroundings. The girl, Andrea tells me, squandered her inheritance long before the economy failed, on a man she met in Brazil, where Andrea was born. "She still lives here, but the number of men who come and go—well . . ." Andrea shakes her head. Down the block is Rosaria's, a modest white building with a weathered red awning. Real estate listings cover its windows. "The woman, she was a famous prostitute," Andrea says, grinning at me. "Now she is one of the wealthiest people in the neighborhood. People like the story, I think. I like her. She is full of life. Always laughing." There are more stories; most are less sensational, but most involve a loss of fortune and dignity. You don't need an A in freshman world history to see that's a common theme here.

As we near the half-painted blue and pink stucco home I passed earlier, I expect a particularly juicy story, but Andrea doesn't say a word. Quite the opposite: She goes uncharacteristically silent. But I have to know. "What about this old place?" I ask, trying not to sound too eager. "Do you know who lives here?"

Andrea stops to contemplate. "This house," she whispers, "this house has a very sad story."

"Did they lose all their money, too?"

"No, something more special."

Jorge, walking on the far side of her, grabs her hand, pulls her down to his height, and whispers something in her ear. "*Sí, amore. Sí,*" she sings back to him gently, swooping her little man up in her arms and giving him a squeeze. He squawks in protest, and she covers his face in kisses. "He is hungry," she says, smiling again. "And so am I. Come. It's dinnertime." As we start again, a light comes on in the pink and blue house, but Andrea is too far ahead to notice. We walk the rest of the way in silence.

"Here we are." Andrea's voice startles me. She unlocks the great door to her yellow house, and the second it swings open, Jorge runs through, shrieking. The dogs appear from around a corner at full speed, and they all disappear into the dark house. Andrea flips on the lights in the entrance. "Dinner?"

"Thanks so much for everything, Andrea," I say. "But I'm so tired, I think I'll go to bed. If you don't mind." The truth is, as lonely as I've felt all day, I'm suddenly not in the mood for company.

"Oh, of course. Of course. You are not used to Argentine hours yet."

"No, not yet." I pass her a bag of groceries.

"I hope it is okay in the apartment," she says as I make my way toward the stairs. "Mateo said he finishes everything."

"Thanks. I'm sure it's great. Thanks again."

Once inside the apartment, I drop my groceries in the foyer and sink into the bed. I should have called my parents. My mom's probably frantic with worry. If only I'd remembered that plug converter, I could have managed a few happy-sounding e-mails. *Hi, everyone, I'm still alive, ha ha. My apartment is gorgeous. I walked the neighborhood today. Met a hundred cats. Bought a hair dryer—very important—a lovely block of cheese, and some cheap red wine. I'm practically a local now!* In its abridged version, it almost sounds fun, doesn't it?

I glance wistfully in the direction of my laptop bag. It isn't there. Oh, God, my laptop isn't there. I rush over and lift each piece of luggage a dozen times. Nothing. I rummage through every article of clothing. Nothing. Jeez, Cassie, think. I swear I left it right here with everything else, but I wasn't in the most lucid state last night. I scan the room, and there it is, sitting atop a desk against the far wall. Funny, I hadn't noticed that desk before. Did

Andrea say something about Mateo bringing up a desk? I don't think so.

Like every other piece of furniture in the room, it's lovely. An antique, no doubt, with a large writing surface and lots of drawers. And that's when I notice the best part of all. Beside my laptop bag and a small vase of purple freesia sits a plug converter. It is an invitation I can't ignore. I plug it in and turn on my laptop, ready to reconnect.

CHAPTER FIVE

You'll have to bear with me. I am no writer. Just an ex-Web producer, ex-fiancée, and temporarily ex-Seattleite who's ended up in Buenos Aires by some bizarre stroke of drunk luck. I am scared, lonely, and consumed by a constant state of dread that I will never find my way back to the life I want. So how did I get to here? That is the question I keep asking myself. Heartbreak? This is more like total devastation.

Just to catch you up—assuming that someone is actually reading this—I lost my job and my fiancé and my home in one day. Then in a moment of temporary (martini-induced) insanity, I booked a six-month trip to . . . where am I again? Ah, yes, glamorous Argentina, where all the dumped and fabulous are going these days. Why, isn't that Paris Hilton over there?

Yeah, right. So far this trip has been anything but glamorous, and I definitely don't feel fabulous. Although my landlady's friend and handyman, M, did make me feel rather fabulous when he knocked on my door my first morning here and welcomed me to his country by laughing in my face. Okay, so I didn't look so hot in my slept-in clothes, and I couldn't understand a word he said, but I was jet-lagged and, kill me, I'm not from here. Of course, he did try to make amends later by dropping me on my ass. Boy, did I ever feel fabulous then. So fabulous, in fact, that now I'm scared to venture outside my suite for fear of running into him in the

house. There's only so much praise and adulation a gal
can take.

But I've got more to worry about than an obnoxious (and,
okay, beautiful) Argentine man who thinks he can get away
with being a jerk just because he gets me the plug converter
I need so I can use my laptop, which is how I'm writing this
blog right now about how obnoxious he is. Speaking of which,
why am I wasting perfectly good cyberspace on him? Back to
the real story . . .

Nearly seven hundred words later, I hit the
publish button. Off goes my very first blog
entry into cyberspace. It feels so good to
write about what I'm going through here—to say all the things I
can't possibly say to anyone back home. If I said these things out
loud to my parents, they would insist I come back immediately
(which I'd be tempted to do but can't if I want to maintain what
little dignity I left Seattle with). Sam and Trish would ply me with
well-meaning platitudes (what else could they do?), and I've had
my share of those recently. The moment I put it all down on the
screen, I am instantly lighter.

No small amount of pleasure is derived from the short rant I
allowed myself on the subject of Mateo's oh-so-warm welcome.
Maybe writing that he's a "stuck-up snob who thinks he's better
than everyone" was a bit harsh, but would anyone blame me for
calling him an obnoxious jerk? What's the harm, anyway? I've
called him M to be on the safe side, not that he's ever going to
read it anyway.

Realistically, no one is. There are zillions of personal blogs like this that no one ever reads, aside from the blogger's mom, maybe. Getting it all out is the important part. And one day when everything is right again, perhaps I'll read through it and laugh. Even at the Mateo bits.

Because I've decided that one day I will look back on all of this with great fondness. To get to that point, I've also decided that Buenos Aires isn't really all that big or all that scary. Admittedly, I haven't seen much of it, and I know that empirically, it is a big city. Enormous, really. And maybe a little bit scary. Okay, totally terrifying, but why should that stop me? After all, Seattle is a large metropolis with occasional muggings and neighborhoods I dare not venture into, but it's my home, and I love it. When I walk through Pioneer Square after the sun has gone down, I always get a good laugh watching the tourists clutch their bags and glance around nervously while they try to decipher the route to Pike Place Market from their complimentary hotel map. Now I'm supposed to turn into the frightened, bumbling tourist? Not happening. So what if it's not safe to hail a taxi on the street here or travel south of certain streets? I'm a born urbanite. I eat, sleep, and breathe city. I dream in concrete and glass. I am big enough for this place. Sure there were a few (five) tough days of adjusting (crying), but culture shock (fear of the outside world) is to be expected. Perfectly normal. Like I told Sam and Trish yesterday via e-mail, it's part of the process. If I hadn't experienced some form of meltdown, I'd be worried something was wrong with me. And I'm fine now. Really. It's simply a matter of putting things in perspective. As suspected, all I needed was a plan.

It has taken four days to set down my goals for this trip, but now that I have, a delicious sense of calm has settled over me. There will be no more anxiety attacks in cat parks or breakdowns in electronics stores for this savvy Seattle gal. Such things are simply not in The Plan. What is in The Plan:

WEEK 1

☐ Start first draft of new plan (includes a list of sights to see before I go home); while working on new plan, it is perfectly acceptable to do little else

☐ Stop thinking about Jeff

WEEK 2

☐ Start travel blog (since I'll be writing all those e-mails anyway)

☐ Stop thinking about Jeff

☐ Eat out in a restaurant

WEEK 3

☐ Enroll in Spanish classes (twice a week minimum)

☐ Research Argentina history online

☐ Take walk around neighborhood and try to go a little farther or in a different direction each time

☐ Get Jorge to like me!

☐ Make an Argentine friend (Jorge doesn't count)

☐ Stop thinking about Jeff

And so on and so forth right up until the day I leave, when Andrea will take a picture of me to add to the collection on the side table in her living room. On that day I will be very sad to leave, I've decided, but (as clearly stated on page four of the spreadsheet) I will mostly be excited about the next phase of my life that can finally begin the moment I touch back down in Seattle.

Of course, I haven't started my plan for that phase yet. Creating an itinerary for this six-month digression is one thing. Constructing a whole new life plan is another. One thing's for sure—this time around, I've got to be way more careful. I left far too much to chance when I made the first plan. At nineteen, you think in broad strokes, and that's exactly where I went wrong. Perfection is in the details. A serious life plan takes meticulous strategizing, fine-tuning, and, I've come to learn, a few contingency plans. But I'm working it all out in my head, and the bones of it are there. Soon the fleshy shape of my new and improved life will be as clear as the color-coding on a spreadsheet.

Until then I'm committed to making the most of my time here, of which remains 175 days and thirteen hours. I know because I've fashioned a rudimentary countdown calendar from a stack of Post-it notes. Each morning I pull off the top one to reveal the current date and how many days I have left. Yesterday I started to feel a little anxious about how big a stack of sticky yellow paper all those days added up to, so I pulled it apart into seven small piles, and I feel a whole lot better. A stack of twenty-five Post-it notes doesn't look so hard. *I can do this. I am already doing this.* Each morning, hands clasped around a mug of Earl Grey, I groggily contemplate that first thoroughly manageable square of yellow papers and recite this with as much conviction as I can muster. It has become my new mantra.

This morning the I'm-okay-you're-okay portion of my day is cut short when Andrea drops by to tell me the language school where her friend works has a beginners' course starting in about two hours. "This is good news, *si*?" How do I explain that I wasn't even planning on researching classes until the day after tomorrow, never mind starting one today, to this kind woman who is grinning at me expectantly, thinking herself immensely helpful.

"Well, actually, I—" I stammer out a pathetic protest, but she shakes her head and hands me her cordless phone.

"You talk to Elena."

In impeccable English, Elena tells me either I come today or I'll have to wait three weeks for the next start date. "We are the best school in the city," she says confidently. "And the teacher is very good. The students love her." I know I can't put this off until my second month. There must be a thousand Spanish classes in this city at any given time, but this is Andrea's friend, and she does speak perfect English.

"Okay," I tell her, and then, balking slightly, add, "Maybe."

Elena gives me the address. It's downtown.

"Downtown? Oh." I hadn't planned on venturing that far out for another three weeks, but did I really expect to find a language school right around the corner? Careless oversight. "That's a bit far, isn't it?"

"No, it's easy," Andrea interjects from the doorway. "You take the subway," she says happily, pushing a map book at me. Is it my imagination, or is she trying to get me out of the house? I catch her eyes roaming from my pile of empty ravioli packages bursting from the garbage can in the kitchen to the rudimentary Post-it-note time line I've created along one wall to the state of my pajamas, which have yet to find the laundry room downstairs. I suppose the apartment has adopted the look of a hermit's cave in the last few days, and I'm not doing too shabby a job at the role of resident hermit. It's just that I needed to concentrate on my plan. Oh, jeez, is that a Post-it note stuck to my knee?

"Can we expect you today then, Cassandra?" Elena asks. Is it too late to back out? Would anyone buy it if I said I had a big day planned already? I peel the wayward sticky from my pajama bottoms, a move that isn't going to help me convince Andrea I had intended to go anywhere other than back to bed with my laptop. Of course, I am a grown-up. I can say no. And I do have things to do. I do have a plan, dammit. A few weeks isn't too long to wait, really. I can accomplish loads of other important things in that amount of time, with or without Spanish.

But then I remember Mateo shaking his head at me in the doorway, the easy laughter at this mess of an American who can't speak the language. That feeling of utter ignorance is not something I want to experience again anytime soon. The last time I saw Mateo in the house, twiddling with the light switch in the front entrance, I ducked behind the giant ficus tree and then shimmied my way back up the stairway before he could see me. I was in desperate need of milk for yet another cup of tea, but, caffeine cravings be damned, I wasn't about to let him make me feel stupid again. I waited for almost two hours, watching TV that I didn't understand, until it was almost dark. Only when I heard voices and then the closing of Andrea's heavy front door did I venture downstairs again. Not exactly my crowning moment, and not a scenario I want to repeat. And hadn't I once vowed that the next time I saw him, I'd have the last word?

"Sure," I tell Elena before I can change my mind. Where the confidence in my voice comes from, I can't say. "I'll see you soon. Thanks." I hand the phone back to Andrea, who claps her free hand to my shoulder and gives it a squeeze before she goes.

So now I've got three city maps and a transit map spread out on the bed. Downtown Buenos Aires. Why do the maps always gray out the downtown? Are they trying to make it look more foreboding? No need. I am still getting used to the main street four blocks from here, venturing more than a few blocks onto its frantic sidewalks only when my supply of ravioli runs low. It's probably not all that bad, I tell myself. I'm overreacting, falling victim to the worst travel tragedy: prejudice.

I consult my main guidebook for a bit of reassurance.

Downtown Buenos Aires, or Microcentro, is a loud,
hurried mix of businesspeople, students, shoppers, and
street vendors all vying for space on narrow sidewalks
shaded by soaring modern towers. If you don't like
crowds, avoid Florida, a pedestrian street where shopping
is a full-contact sport . . .

Okay, I'm not overreacting. Downtown Buenos Aires is going to eat me alive. I try not to think about it, to focus instead on planning my trip. Red, green, and blue subway lines weave their way across the transit map. I need the green line. I think. Six blocks to the nearest subway station, five stops, and about three blocks to the school. I can do this, I think, marking the school's location on each map and highlighting the corresponding paths with a yellow marker. I am already doing this.

If I'm going to sit in a classroom again after all these years, I'm going to take it seriously. I throw on a pair of khaki pants, white button-down shirt, and comfortable black flats. I brush my hair back into a low ponytail and skip all but mascara and blush. Into my knapsack go four maps, one guidebook, a brand-new notepad, a fresh stack of Post-its, three pens, a pencil, a yellow highlighter, a bottle of water, what I hope is an Argentine protein bar, and an apple. Swinging the bag over my shoulder, I take one last look at myself in the mirror and laugh. It's an absurd sight, to say the least, this twenty-eight-year-old woman from Washington State in Argentina, about to head off to Spanish class dressed like a seventeen-year-old prep-school senior. So absurd, in fact, that I almost miss the faint sensation, as I twist my key into the lock, that maybe, possibly, something wonderful is about to happen.

Getting on the subway is easy. Getting off is a little more difficult. The doors open on different sides for different stops. I'm not sure which side I need, and by the fourth stop, the car has filled to near capacity. (I'm sure there are dozens of interesting things to see if I were to look around, but I must concentrate on the stops.) I hover in the middle of two exits to hedge my bets, and when the doors open (on the right, I stash away in my memory), I let the flow of commuters carry me out, and up to the street.

In the sunlight, I give my eyes a moment to readjust, then sit on a park bench to get my bearings. I've made good time. My class doesn't start for another half hour. I examine my main map, take note of nearby landmarks to confirm my position, recheck the route, tracing the highlighted line with my finger. After I've done this several times, I attempt to repeat the route by foot. One block and one turn later, and I am already lost.

The maps all say the street I'm looking for, Reconquista, should be right here on this corner, where a wizened old man is selling what looks like candy-coated peanuts, but there is no Reconquista to be found. I could ask the man, I suppose, but I detest the idea of being one of those tourists who shout random words at locals as though verbs and prepositions are unnecessary bits of language. I remember my mother doing this on our family vacation in Mexico when I was twelve. Walking through the center of the old town, in desperate need of aspirin for yet another headache, she began shouting "Pharmacy? Pharmacy?" at every person who passed. They shrank from her voice, avoided eye contact, mumbled under their breath. Crazy woman, they must have been saying. *Loca americana.* I tried to make myself small against the side of a building, shrugged sympathetically at passersby. Finally, a young boy barely older than me answered, "*¿Farmacia?*" (one Spanish word I'll never forget) and pointed at the small white building across the street with a green cross in the window. I shiver at the memory. I'd rather roam around for hours than be that ridiculous.

And that's exactly what it feels like I'm doing. I have passed a dozen street corners and a dozen wizened old men selling candied nuts. Each time I get to an intersection, I locate it on the map before moving forward. I seem no farther from or closer to my final destination. The sidewalks are razor-thin and crowded. Suited Argentines swish past me at breakneck speed. They have no time for disoriented tourists, though I seem to be the only one. If I stop to read my map, they graze me with their elbows and bags, mumbling. I flatten myself against the sides of buildings, feeling twelve again, but this time embarrassed by my own actions. It's the hottest time of day, and somewhere the sun is shining, but downtown, under the canopy of concrete and glass, I am in the shade. Cold, confused, and, surprise, surprise, near tears.

After twenty minutes, I am both deflated and elated to find myself back at the subway entrance. This must be a sign. Forget the stupid class, get back on the stupid subway, and go back to the stupid apartment. I never should have strayed from The Plan. This is my punishment for doing so. Who needs Spanish, anyhow? So what if I end up shouting *farmacia* at frightened strangers? There are worse things I could do. Yes, Andrea will be disappointed. And what about smug Mateo? Well, maybe I'll get another apartment. One where people don't scorn you for speaking a different language or make you go downtown when you clearly aren't ready.

No, I remind myself, you can do this. You're already doing it, right? How is another question. I can't bear to look at the map. It's done me no favors this far. I might as well wing it. Listen to my gut. But it's been so long since I've followed anything resembling an instinct, I'm not sure how to do it. I search for a street sign. Florida. *If you don't like crowds, avoid Florida . . .*

I hold my breath and dart across the pedestrian street, ducking flyers left and right. "Leather coats! Leather bags!" one man yells at me. "Cashmere, twenty dollars!" shouts another. Five minutes ago I would have given anything to hear a little English, but now I just want back onto the relatively quiet streets beyond this hurricane of consumerism.

I don't stop until I come to a red light. Another intersection without street signs, another nut vendor. My shoulders sink and curl inward.

I am officially late. At this minute, a wonderful, beloved Spanish teacher is saying my name, shaking her head at the empty chair. I'll miss the first lesson, and then I'll never catch up. There isn't much I can do about that now. I've tried, haven't I? Wandered around this maze for over half an hour. Followed the map. Tracked back. Tried a different route. Then another. And another. Wound myself into disoriented circles. I'm tired, cold, and hungry. What more can I do?

I buy a bag of nuts for a peso. They're actually pretty good, caramelly sweet with a faint and not unpleasant burnt taste. I smile at the old man, who nods knowingly. Fortified by the promise of a sugar rush, I take a chance. What was it the little boy said to me on the street that day? *"Excúseme, señor."* I mumble to hide what is surely horrific pronunciation. "Do you know Reconquista? *Por favor."* He dips his forehead toward me. I hold a map out between us and point to my destination enthusiastically. "Reconquista?"

"Ahhh," he exhales more than says. *"Sí.* Reconquista." The rest are words I don't understand, but I don't need to. As he talks, he sweeps his hand left and right above the sidewalk and smiles. Carved into the concrete is the word "Reconquista."

The language school is housed in an old office building. The elevator, with its manual sliding wooden door and knobby black buttons, clunks to a stop at the fourth floor. I make my way down the tight corridor to suite 407, a glass door covered in brightly colored words, similar to the ones that ran like molding around my grade-five classroom. WELKOM! BIENVENUE! BOA VINDA! WELCOME! the door exclaims. *I can do this. I am already doing this.*

Inside, the school looks more like a doctor's office than an elementary classroom. The reception area is crowded with old mismatched office furniture. A long table to one side is cluttered with brochures. The building's white walls hold glossy posters of Italy, Spain, London, and France, the kind you see displayed in the windows of travel agencies. A woman speaks loudly into a phone in what sounds like French, her head bent low to examine a piece of paper on the desk.

Another woman pokes her head out from behind a corner at waist level. Leaning back in her chair, she is in serious danger of falling over. "*¿Hola?*" she says.

"*¿Hola?*" I say back.

"Cassandra?"

"Yes. It's Cassie, actually."

"Ah, wonderful!" she exclaims and snaps upright again, disappearing behind the wall. Her English is perfect. This must be Elena. A moment later, she rounds the corner, smiling warmly. "Welcome, welcome." I step forward with my hand extended, but she ignores it, planting a light kiss on my cheek instead. From her professional manner on the telephone, I didn't expect her to be so, uh, friendly. A disarmingly handsome man appears from Elena's office. "This is Andrea's friend Cassie. Cassie, this is my husband, Alessandro."

"Pleasure to meet you," he purrs. I offer my hand, but he ignores it, too. Another kiss. Am I blushing? They look at me and smile, clearly amused.

"You aren't used to the kissing yet?" Elena asks.

"Oh. No. I just . . . I didn't know."

"But you've been here for a week," she says, incredulous.

"I haven't really met a lot of people." I remember the yellow Post-it stuck to my knee this morning and cringe inside.

"You'll get used to it soon enough." If everyone looks like Alessandro, I'm sure I will.

Elena gives me some forms to fill out later and shows me to my classroom. I am ten minutes late. I take a deep breath and step inside.

"*¡Hola!*" shouts the slender woman in thick tortoiseshell glasses and a misbuttoned cardigan, standing at the blackboard. "Come in, come in!" Heads whip around, but there are only five students, and they all smile easily in my direction. Elena passes the teacher a piece of paper. She studies it briefly and looks up at me again.

"Welcome, Cassie!" Her English, even better than Elena's, is tinted with a slight British accent. "My name is Marcela."

"I'm sorry I'm late," I say quietly. "I got a bit lost." The story of my life lately. I was on my way to a corner office when I took a wrong turn and ended up in South America instead.

"Oh, no need to worry. We've been busy with forms, so the class is just getting started, really. You haven't missed a thing. Please, sit, sit!"

A small woman with a mass of curly dark hair who couldn't be over nineteen or twenty scoots to make room for me, patting the chair beside her.

"Well, then," Marcela begins. "Why don't we introduce ourselves."

We all look at one another, shyly, furtively, empathetically. One by one, starting with the guy on my left, my classmates say their names, where they're from, and why they've come to Buenos Aires. There is a smiley Irish couple who need to learn a bit of Spanish so they can travel around the country and teach English. Two young German guys think they will stay for a month before heading south to Patagonia to see the penguins. At least I think that's what the blond one said—he speaks some English, but it's thick. Grateful to be last, I use the few precious minutes formulating what I will say. I know my name and where I'm from, but what's a good reason to be here? "Running away from my rubble of a life" might not make for the best first impression. I must have done this same introduction bit at least twenty times in college, and I don't remember my palms ever sweating like this. I always knew exactly what to say, how any particular class would move me toward my business degree, which would propel me into my career as a high-powered executive. What great ambition is this class propelling me toward? I can't think of anything, and the curly-haired woman beside me is already beginning to speak.

"My name's Zoey," she says in a deep smoker's voice incongruous with her small frame. "I'm from New York, and yes, I'm older than I look. I'm here because my husband is a rotten lying cheating bastard. I'm going to spend lots of his money and forget I ever met him. And what the hell, I thought I might learn a little tango while I'm at it." She smiles at me, and I smile back. I have just met my new best friend.

CHAPTER SIX

Zoey's gravelly New York accent sounds like something straight out of an old gangster movie. Hearing it come out of her tiny, cherubic face makes me smile. She's like Little Orphan Annie if she'd never been adopted by Daddy Warbucks. And believe it or not, her Spanish pronunciation is worse than mine, but when everyone's watching her sputter out another conjugation, she doesn't go beet red like I do. Nothing seems to embarrass her. When Marcela tried to correct her R's, Zoey said, "I'm afraid the only way you're going to get me to roll my R's is by pushing me down a hill."

So you see why I couldn't help but adore her instantly. Who could? Except maybe M-the-perfect, who would think her another ridiculous tourist who can't speak his language. Did I mention that M snubbed me in the hallway yesterday? I fumbled through the front door, both hands full of grocery bags, and there he was, fixing a table leg or something. When he saw me, he looked startled, mumbled something in Spanish, and practically ran out of the room. I mean, I realize we don't like each other, but am I really that repulsive to him? Okay, enough about M. I might as well be wasting my time writing about J. I wonder if M and J would like each other. They could bond over their low opinions of me. What fun! Okay, okay, I'm stopping now. Back to Zoey.

There are so many things I love about the girl. She is as silly as my friend Sam, as sarcastic as my friend Trish, and occasionally, as wise as the Dalai Lama. "What's really so bad about having an American accent, anyway?" she said to me (the only other American) with grave sincerity at the end of class. "Americans are always going on and on about sexy Spanish accents. Maybe all this R rolling is actually detrimental to my chances of getting some hot Argentine action." Here I've been killing myself to get my R's into a perfect round trill, but you have to admit, the girl has a point. Not that I'm on the prowl for "hot Argentine action," but the thought of meeting someone who doesn't find me repulsive or "perfect"—or any other synonym for wrong—does have its charms. There I go again. Sorry.

Zoey's friendship proves to be a much needed distraction from thinking about things I don't want to think about, and by the third Spanish class, we are inseparable. We partner for dialogues, check each other's work, and giggle over Elena's smolderingly handsome husband during breaks. Whether we're helping or hindering each other's Spanish education remains to be seen, but at least I look forward to class. Over our lunch break, I discover that she's staying with an Argentine family in a neighborhood not far from mine, so we ride the subway seven short stops home together after class. Between downtown and the first stop along the grand and loud Avenida Santa Fe, we swap the basic plot points of our respective cheating-bastard stories. From there to her stop at Bulnes, she gives me what she refers to as an abbreviated list of her Argentine adventures to date. She is bursting with Argentina anecdotes, and despite the fact that she's been here for a week less than me, she's already been everywhere.

"Well, let's see. The MALBA is pretty spectacular. It's huge and really new and there are so many amazing Latin American artists. I met an art student there. He said he'd like to sketch me. Isn't that a great line? And you can walk right up to a Frida Kahlo self-portrait, nose to nose. It's funny. She clearly knew she was in possession of a serious unibrow but made the decision not to pluck. Do you think it was some sort of political statement? The cemetery in Recoleta has lots of beautifully carved tombs and cats everywhere. Some of the old tombs are a total mess, and you can reach right in through the gates and touch the coffin. It's gross. Too bad they close it at night—bet it's totally *Blair Witch* in the dark. Evita's there, but her crypt is actually really dull. On the weekends there's a big fair in the park right outside. It's the typical mix of music, food, and crafts, but it's huge, and there are all these artists selling their stuff. I met the cutest guy at a sandwich stand. What was his name? Sandy-blond hair and so cute. We had a little impromptu picnic, and then he had to get to work. I bought the most amazing drawing for, like, twenty-five dollars. The artist acted like I was some great benefactor, and here I felt like an art thief. Have you seen the Madres? Oh, God, they're amazing. There are all these old women, mothers and grandmothers of the people who were killed by the government in the seventies. Have you read that book *Imagining Argentina*? Don't bother. The ending's total bull. Anyway, the Madres march in protest every Thursday at this park downtown. It's the most heartbreaking sight. You have to go. I mean, these women are like a zillion years old. After that I ended up at the Teatro Colón. It's this totally over-the-top, ornate old theater, but it's kinda cool. You can take a tour or whatever, but I went to the cheap show. Opera for a couple of bucks. Not bad, if you like that kind of thing. I'd gotten it in my head that I could walk home from downtown, and my feet were starting to really ache because, of course, I'm wearing a pair of Keds that I love but are a size too small, when I walk by the theater and see all these people going inside, so I figure why not check it out and maybe have somewhere to sit for a minute. Oh, and San Telmo. Duh. There are these expensive tango shows all over the place—I haven't seen any—but if you go to San Telmo on the weekend, you can eat at an outdoor café and watch people dancing in the street. This adorable little man insisted he give me a personal demonstration, if you know what I mean." She smiles and winks. I laugh, nodding knowingly and generally pretending as though I'm not in complete and utter awe of her.

"But listen to me blather on. You've been here twice as long as me. You've probably done all this stuff and a ton more."

"Yeah, right." Here's the point where I would usually change the subject, but seeing how Zoey is my new best friend, I try honesty instead. "I am intimately acquainted with the inner workings of my apartment and can find my way around the local supermarket with relative ease. I saw the inside of an electronics store—mostly through tears, mind you, so I can't recall much about the decor or ambience. Oh, and I went on an accidental wildcat safari in a park. I'm practically a native."

"You mean you haven't gone anywhere?" Zoey looks at me in total disbelief. "You haven't done anything?"

"Well, there are tons of things I want to do. I just wasn't . . . ready."

Her face softens, her head tilting. "Oh, you poor thing. Of course not. I'm being so insensitive. I tend to get over an old boyfriend by getting under a new one, but that's just me—tough New York stock and all that bullshit. But losing your guy and your job in one day, it must be god-awful."

"Don't forget a place to live." I laugh, but it comes out like a little cough. She must think I'm a total loser. "But really, it's not like I've been lying in bed all day and crying." Not all day, anyway.

"Well, good."

"Mostly, I've been working on my plan."

"What do you mean?"

I take a deep breath and explain. As I speak, Zoey's face screws itself back into disbelief, then releases into a wide grin. She lets out a loud guffaw. The subway car is packed, but no one seems to notice.

"Cassie," she manages, catching her breath through lingering chuckles. "You are a kick. Really. But lady, it's time you got out of your room. This weekend we're doing something fun." The subway slows as we pull into the next stop. Zoey stands up and inches toward the exit.

"But I don't have anything fun scheduled for another week and a half." Only after I say it do I understand how ludicrous it must sound.

She furrows her brow at me and shakes her head. "I hope you're joking."

I fake a laugh.

"Cassie? That's short for Cassandra, right?"

I nod.

"The prophetess," she says, smiling to herself, then slips seamlessly into the stream of commuters and out the subway door.

As I watch the edge of her red sweater disappear from view, it occurs to me that while I'd assumed she was on her way back to her Argentine house, I really have no idea where she is headed. With someone like Zoey, someone who doesn't live according to a plan, you don't know where she's going when she slips out of a subway car in the middle of the afternoon. Maybe she'll wander down Santa Fe, letting herself be distracted by the seemingly endless line of shoe stores and clothing boutiques, spend all her money on leather goods, and have to go home to New York a few months early. She could duck into a café for a midday snack, flirt with the waiter-slash-student-sculptor and fall madly, instantly in love, get married, and live out her life as the exotic American muse. And that's when it strikes me cold and hard in the middle of my forehead: Zoey lives things I don't dare to daydream.

Is Zoey scared when she walks through a door, never knowing what it might open to? Is it thrilling for her, the not knowing? Does she give any of it a second thought? I can only imagine what it's like to be her, and even that I can't do very well. I don't walk to the grocery store without some sort of plan in my head before the front door locks behind me. My stepdad likes to tease me, telling stories about how I used to prepare itineraries for our summer vacations in my Hello Kitty notebook; how I came to him and my mother when I was nine and asked to be taken out of ballet because I realized that I had started too late to make anything out of it; how I broke up with my sixth-grade boyfriend, Steven Harris, because he still didn't know what he wanted to be when he grew up. Everyone always gets a good chuckle out of that one around the family dinner table. The first time Jeff had dinner at my parents' house, they were thrilled to regale him with these and countless other classic Cassie tales. Didn't he whisper in my ear, as I passed him the mashed potatoes, that I must have been the most adorable child? I was so happy to have found someone who really got me. Now, that's funny.

Adorable or not, for better or worse, I've been this way for as long as I remember. Well before I wrote down a plan, I always carried one in my head.

Saturday morning, Zoey calls to make sure we're still on for our "Argentine adventure," but she won't say where we're going or what we're doing. "Should I pack a suitcase?" I joke. Her long pause has me concerned. "Seriously?"

Zoey laughs. "Just bring a positive attitude," she says.

I shower, dry my hair, and then sit staring at the wardrobe full of my clothes. What does one wear to an Argentine adventure? Gaucho pants and combat boots? I choose a denim skirt and comfy tennis shoes and tie a light hooded sweater around my waist so I'm covered for at least a few different meteorological and sartorial requirements, tornadoes and red-carpet premieres notwithstanding. I've loaded my small canvas tote bag with maps, translation dictionary, bottled water, digital camera, an apple, and two protein bars.

At least tonight I'll have something interesting to write in my blog. I can only whine about Jeff for so long before I start to bore myself to tears. And it's not just myself I have to think of now. I checked my reader stats last night and discovered that four whole, real live people have visited my site. One of them actually added a comment!

> I've been through the same thing. Twice! Hang in there, sweetie. You're better off without him. You will look back one day and be grateful that you escaped the noose!!!
> hopefulromantic@excite.com

Not exactly insightful advice, and nothing that my best friends haven't said to me a hundred times, but for some reason, coming from a complete stranger, these kind words make me feel better.

And for that, I owe hopefulromantic@excite.com and any other people who may venture onto my blog something interesting to read about. Whatever surprises I'm in for this afternoon, no doubt they'll make for better reading than yet another treatise on how you can't trust anyone who has sex to symphony music.

Zoey is ten minutes late. Standing at the open front door but behind the locked gate, I grip the iron bars like a prisoner terrified by her impending freedom. Marcela's "five most important phrases" churn in my head: *¿Habla usted inglés? No hablo español.*

¿Cuánto cuesta? ¿Donde están los servicios? If I can just remember how to ask where the toilets are, everything will be okay. "*Estoy perdida,*" I whisper to myself. *I am lost.*

"You don't look lost." At the sound of Andrea's voice, I break instantly into a pleased grin despite my embarrassment. I'm glad Andrea's here to witness the start of my brave adventure. I know she's worried about me, thinks I spend too much time in my apartment. Yesterday she knocked on my door three times to invite me out on various errands under the pretense of needing my help. I finally relented and walked the three blocks to her beauty shop to assist her with the selection of a new cream rinse.

The truth is, I'm thankful for her gentle meddling. Her motherly instincts make her the closest thing I have to family on this side of the world, but I don't want her to worry about me.

"Your Spanish is sounding very good," she exclaims as she deftly pulls something surely lethal out of Jorge's mouth before it can be swallowed.

"Thank you. But I know my pronunciation is awful."

"Not at all! Even your R's are very good."

"Really?" Despite my protest, I can't deny the sense of satisfaction. The four-hour classes are headache-inducing, but at least they're paying off.

"*¡Sí! Sí!* Now when all the Argentine men whisper love poems in your ears, you will know what nonsense they are saying."

I can't keep a goofy grin from settling on my face. It's more praise than I've heard from my own mother in a long time. "*¿Donde están los servicios?*" I repeat for Andrea with what is quite likely the longest and silliest rolling R in the history of the Spanish language. She claps enthusiastically. Jorge claps, too, and doesn't stop even when he catches me smiling at him. The dogs come running, no doubt to see if the fuss involves some sort of meat being dropped on the floor. Finding none, they sniff my tennis shoes. I reach down and stroke the tall one on the head. His fur is soft and slightly damp. They must have had their baths this morning. He lifts his head and licks my hand. The other two try to get in on the action, but they're too short.

"You learn so fast!" Andrea beams with pride. "Say something else!"

"*¿Habla usted inglés?*" I fling a hand out as though I've just performed a great feat.

"*Sí, por supuesto.*" This time it isn't Andrea speaking. He's sneaked up on me again. Mateo. His tall frame slouches in the doorway, his hands shoved deep into the pockets of his paint-splattered overalls. He'd look almost sweetly shy, childlike, even, if not for the cocky angle of his head and that crooked smirk of a smile. A lone long black curl flops over one eye. I wonder if his hair is soft, too. No, probably not. Probably thick and coarse and wiry. "*Hola,*" he says.

I offer a small smile but don't say a word. I want to, acutely aware that I should be speaking, but no words come to me, Spanish, English, or otherwise. Except "water" (I'm suddenly very thirsty, my tongue all starchy), but I can hardly make clever banter out of that bon mot. Mateo dips his head, his hair falling across his face on one side. He looks up at me through those dark curls and grins. There's a bit of devil in that grin. I am not breathing.

"Oh, don't be shy," Andrea pleads. Her voice surprises me. I'd almost forgotten that she was here. "Say more Spanish for us."

"*¡Los pollos se han escapado!*" All heads, human and canine, turn to the space on my right. It's Zoey, grinning happily through the iron bars. I have no idea what she said, but it's clearly funny. Even Mateo chuckles a little, his white teeth shining, his eyes softening. And it doesn't stop there. Not only does he laugh at her joke, but he practically knocks me over trying to get the gate open to let her in. Suddenly, he's Mr. Manners. I look at him and then at her with bewilderment.

"The chickens have escaped," Zoey offers to me, and I recall the line from a story Marcela read in class. "I had a feeling that one would come in handy one day." But I barely hear her, preoccupied with the sight of back muscles twisting under Mateo's thin gray T-shirt. Zoey turns to Andrea and Mateo with a giant smile.

"*Hola. Me llamo Zoey,*" she says cheerfully, planting an enthusiastic kiss on Andrea, who is hugely pleased. A twinge of shame hits as I think of how reserved I was on that first night in the city.

"Welcome, welcome. I am Andrea. This is my son, Jorge, and my friend Mateo."

"*Hola.*" Zoey waves at Jorge, who quickly tucks behind his mother's leg. At least I know his distrust isn't personal. "*Hola,*" she says to Mateo, extending her cheek for a kiss. Mateo offers one gently. Not exactly the welcome I received from him. He clearly has manners, it's just a matter of whom he chooses to use them with. With Zoey, he's Hugh Grant. With me, Simon Cowell. Well, now I know for certain that it's me he finds distasteful, not all Americans. Great. That makes me feel so much better.

"*¿Hablas inglés?*" Zoey asks in her endearingly bad Spanish accent.

"Well, of course. Who doesn't?"

I'm sorry, but that sounded suspiciously like English. Not just English but really really really good English. Almost better than that of my Spanish teacher with the slight British accent.

"You speak English," I stammer out. "You speak English?"

"Yes," he says with the most aggravating grin. "And yes."

"Why didn't you say that before?" I feel my cheeks flush with anger.

He tilts his head again, his green eyes sparkling with what looks like genuine curiosity. "Why didn't you ask?"

We are ten minutes and seven blocks from Andrea's house, and I'm still so infuriated that I haven't even asked Zoey where we're going, just let her ramble on about her latest phone call to her mother, who, if possible, sounds even less supportive of her trip than mine. I nod and "mm-hm" a lot, wanting to demonstrate my empathy, but in my head I'm mostly thinking, He speaks English? HE SPEAKS ENGLISH! Which is probably a good thing, since when I do pay proper attention to my surroundings, I realize that we are far beyond my comfort zone—literally. Nothing looks even vaguely familiar. Which way is Andrea's yellow house? How many blocks are we from a main street? And most alarmingly, why haven't I seen Zoey holding a map at any point?

My new best friend is shaking her head and thrusting her empty hands to the sky. "How do you think you're gonna find a nice Jewish boy in Argentina?" she says, delivered in what I can only hope is an exaggeratedly high-pitched Long Island accent.

"Uh, right. Mothers. What can you do? Sooo . . . where exactly are we headed?"

"I dunno. Around. You know."

"Right. Cool." I try to sound nonchalant, remembering the look she gave me on the subway when I told her about The Plan. "Cool."

"I bet you didn't know you're staying in one of the city's hippest areas."

"I am?" Does that mean we're still in my neighborhood? It's a relief to know we haven't strayed too far, though I can't help but wonder how we'll know when we've strayed too far if we aren't using a map.

"Totally. Palermo Viejo is the Argentine SoHo."

"So, we'll be sticking nearby, then . . ."

She laughs. Hopefully with me, not at me. "Don't worry. I promise I won't take you anywhere that requires a visa." She laughs again, and this time so do I.

I watch Zoey's shoes as we move down the street. Her flip-flopped feet almost skip, turning this way and that, slowing when something interesting catches her eye. It's almost like dancing, the way children dance, not yet fully aware of the beat, just the feel of their own body swaying whichever way it wants to. I look down at my feet. Tennis-shoed and set firmly in the forward position, they move only to accommodate the occasional mass of dog poop. Left, right, left, right. My rhythm is military. Zoey's whole body is open to the world. Mine is locked, fortified, braced against— what? What exactly is the enemy in this analogy? I picture Zoey slipping through the subway doors and out of sight, off to another adventure or twelve. I picture myself leaving the house, one hand buried deep inside my bag and latched on to the safety of a map highlighted with yellow marker. I think of Jeff. *You're too perfect.* My ex-boss. *You don't take risks.* I think of my four-page (and growing) plan, the eleven tasks and three subtasks for the upcoming week alone, the thrill I got last night when looking back over it for the zillionth time that day. I realized that if I consistently tackled two things each day, I wouldn't have to deal with a single free day for the next six weeks.

"So what do you want to do first?" I say as lightheartedly as I can. *I can do this. I am already doing this.* Sheesh, spontaneity and self-affirmations don't really go together, do they?

"Hmmm, I don't know. Let's just see where this street takes us. Cool?"

"Cool." This time I almost sort of mean it.

"What do you think?" I pull the craziest-looking shaggy neon-pink hat down over my head. "Très chic?" Zoey tries on a silver top hat with a bend in the middle. We look at ourselves in a mirror. "It looks like a Muppet has taken up residence on my head," I say, laughing loudly.

"Hey, now." Zoey sizes me up. "You aren't actually having fun, are you?"

"You know, it's been so long, I'm not sure. What's fun again?"

"It's that feeling you get when you finally stop picturing your ex having sex with someone else and start picturing him lying at the bottom of the ocean."

"Ah, yes. That's right. Then yes, I believe I am." I know I'm having fun. In fact, I am acutely aware of this thrilling truth. Zoey and I have found so many delights to occupy our time that I haven't thought of Jeff since we left Andrea's. I am less successful in my attempts not to think about annoying but hot Argentine men with stunning green eyes and T-shirt muscles. Mateo's face pops into my head, and I toss it aside along with the furry hat.

I pull on a pair of funky sunglasses. I had no idea there were such amazing stores mere blocks from Andrea's house. All this time I've been living in a shoppers' paradise and I didn't have a clue. And with the exchange rate, I am beginning to feel like a bandit. Sam is going to love the hand-painted tank top I got her. No cheesy souvenir key chains and T-shirts for my friends and family. I didn't even put souvenir shopping in my plan. The thought of making a list of all the people I need to buy for and then checking them off one by one makes me exceedingly happy. But first, food. "I'm starving," I say.

"Me, too," says Zoey. "Let's get out of here and find some food. There's supposed to be a little plaza around here somewhere."

"Sure, whatever." Facing the mirror when I say it, I barely even recognize myself—and it's not just the sunglasses.

After we've looped around in circles a few times, our shopping bags are getting heavy. I make Zoey ask a woman for directions. She says something that sounds vaguely like "Marisa Tomei is cured of a key," but luckily, her gestures are simple. We thank her, then go left and right and straight.

We hear the plaza long before we see it. It's only two-thirty in the afternoon, but the place is vibrating with people, music, and cars. In the middle of all the activity, circled by restaurants and bars, sidewalk tables overflowing with coffee mugs and beer bottles, is a small oval-shaped park. This, I assume, is the plaza proper. The top of a rusty jungle gym is visible at one end, but from this angle, most of the park is hidden behind a tall fence covered almost entirely by paintings, drawings, and wood carvings. In front of the artwork, the artists smoke cigarettes and lounge with other vendors selling candles, crocheted hats, and jewelry along the sidewalk.

Zoey stops abruptly on the corner, her suede bag slapping against her hip. "Oooh," she says, crossing the street without even looking.

I, too, am distracted by something bright and shiny. Specifically, the bright and shiny smile of a gorgeous man sitting at a sidewalk café a few feet away. Light brown hair, dark brown eyes, skin the color of caramel, sharp jaw, pouty mouth, trim build. If I could sculpt the perfect man out of brown clay, this would be him. He looks up and catches me staring. I look away quickly and pretend to examine the contents of a store window. Why do beautiful men always make me feel like I'm eleven years old?

"I'll be right back," Zoey's voice calls to me from somewhere far away. "Find a table wherever."

"Mm-hmm." I turn in her direction and nod. It takes me a second to realize I'm nodding in his direction. He puts down his paper, gets up, and walks toward me. This time I can't look away. The closer he gets, the more striking he is. His eyes aren't piercing at all. They're like a little boy's, playful. His eyelashes stretch from here to Uruguay.

"Hello," he says in a buttery Argentine accent. "*¿Americana?*"

"Yes. *Sí*," I stumble. "Yes." He extends his hand to me. He is the first person here to offer me a handshake. When I take it, he pulls me in and plants a soft kiss on my cheek. The scratch of stubble catches me off guard. There is an undeniable rush of anticipation from regions beneath my denim skirt, and I am instantly aware of how long it's been since I've had sex. "Thirty-two days," I say out loud before I can stop myself. I look at my feet, blushing.

"*¿Perdón?*"

"The kiss," I say. "I'm not used to it."

"Is Argentine way," he says, noting my response with an undeniably mischievous grin.

"So I've been told."

"I am Antonio."

Of course you are. "I'm—"

"Beautiful." My American bullshit shield goes up automatically, and I can't help but laugh. "This is funny? I no mean to make joke."

"No, I know, I'm sorry. I'm just not used to hearing that."

"Now this is joke." And with that, all my defenses are gone. Shield down. Bullshit or not, it feels good. Antonio invites me to his table, says something about my hair and the sun. My hair is like the sun, maybe, or is my hair blocking his sun? Either way, I want to join him, but all I can think is, This is so not in my plan. It's one thing to wander aimlessly for an afternoon, buying silly gifts and making faces in a mirror at yourself. But this . . . this is way beyond me.

I look up and spot Zoey across the street, moving from one craft table to the next, tracing her fingers along the edge, stopping here and there to bend down and examine something she likes. It's as if she's floating, this tiny little thing, carried along by curiosity and desire. I wonder what would it be like to float like that. I took a camping trip the summer before grade seven with my best friend, Jenny Winter, and her family. We camped near a river, and Jenny begged me to go inner-tubing down it, but I wouldn't. From the campsite you could see only a few hundred yards down before the water, black and rushing, curved out of sight. "But you can swim good," she whined. "And it's not even taller than my head." Her dad assured me that the river was little more than a flat, slow creek that spilled out into a small lake about a mile away, where he'd be waiting to pick us up. But how could I be sure? I imagined it pulling me out to sea, lost forever. So I stayed put, and Jenny found a girl from a neighboring campsite to go with instead. I watched them float away, sitting back like lounging princesses on giant water lilies, their feet hooked together so they could share a bag of rippled potato chips. Two hours later, Mr. Winter drove up, and they jumped out of the truck, wet and laughing. When they saw me, they whispered unsubtly the way prepubescent girls do, having become instant best friends. From that point on, I was left out of everything. I knew they thought I was a baby for being scared of the water. How could I explain that I wasn't scared of the water but where the water might take me?

Antonio, gorgeous Antonio, looks at me sweetly, chair held out in expectation. What is there to fear, really? There is no cliff to avoid, no rapids to negotiate. The water isn't even over my head. All I have to do is sit back and float.

Apparently, I'm really good at this floating thing. My and Zoey's spontaneous lunch at a sidewalk café with a complete and utterly gorgeous stranger blends into a romantic dinner for two at an Italian restaurant, lingers into cocktails at a jazz bar, turns into slinking up the stairs to my apartment well after three in the morning, the two of us giggling at every floorboard creak and pawing each other through our clothes like teenagers. Inside my apartment, we fumble onto the giant, pristine bed (thank God I made it this morning), stripping each other down to nothing but skin. I have never had this kind of sex before, sex without consequence, sex without purpose, sex without the promise of anything but the twining of bodies. We are a drunken blur of kisses and strokes, fingers exploring, mouths wetting. This is so not in the plan, and I'm loving every minute of it. Even when he stops to put on a condom and I have that twenty-second grace period when I can think about what I'm doing, I choose not to, shut my brain down, focus on the caramel lines of his back instead, the salty taste of him still in my mouth. I can be impulsive. Antonio's tongue runs from nipple to nipple. I can go with the flow. His hand slips between my legs. I am a free spirit. He pushes inside me. All I have to do is float.

Only when we are lying still and spent, limbs curled through sheets and around each other, do I allow myself the pleasure of contemplation. I have had sex with an incredibly hot man who barely speaks English, who is (as far as I can tell in my drunken state) good in bed, who dresses impeccably, who looks like a movie star, who lives in Argentina, who thinks I'm beautiful . . . The pluses and minuses run through my head at lightning speed. None of this is in my plan, but maybe it should be. Have delicious affair with sexy Argentine. There's something so irresistibly romantic in that potential checkmark. Shouldn't every woman have one wild fling with a sexy foreigner? It could be one of those life-altering experiences, a time in my youth to savor when I'm surrounded by great-grandchildren. It could be meaningful, if temporary. It could be . . . delicious. I feel a warm hand slide across my stomach. My mind quiets, my body answers. Stop thinking so much, it tells me. I let the gentle current take me where it will.

CHAPTER SEVEN

Why didn't anybody tell me about Buenos Aires? It's fabulous! It's fantastic! It's fabutastic! It's so amazing it needs a new word. I don't know if it's all the shopping yesterday, the sex last night with A, or Sam and Trish's squeals of delight when I recounted every juicy detail over the phone this morning—or maybe I've just finally opened my eyes. But, my dear cyber friends, I now see that without a doubt Buenos Aires is the world's best-kept secret! Valium Lady wasn't kidding: The city is magic. And I plan on sucking out every last bit of that magic while I've got the chance. Even those disapproving looks from M, who seems to be lurking around every corner of the house at all hours these days, can't spoil the fun. Let him look down his perfectly shaped nose at me, for all I care. I am having a blast.

For the first time in my life, I am tall, exotic, and rich. Everywhere I go, I tower inches if not feet above most of the women and many of the men. In the midst of all these Penelope Cruz look-alikes, my blond hair is capable of producing whiplash in both sexes. Back home I would have balked at dating someone as empirically good-looking as A, would have plunged, inevitably, into immediate and debilitating insecurity. I'm attractive, sure, but hardly one of the beautiful people. Yet here in Buenos Aires, I am in a whole new beauty league. I constantly catch A staring at me with those wolf eyes of his, and he's not the only one. I can't seem to walk down the street without turning a few dark-haired heads. And since I haven't got a clue what they're saying, even the catcalls are charming here.

The contents of my wallet have gotten a makeover, too. Not only is the exchange rate far in my favor, but I can buy absolutely everything I could possibly want absolutely everywhere at just about any time. Shopping seems to be a national pastime, right behind plastic surgery and psychotherapy. What's not to love about this city? Plus, it turns out M was right about at least one thing. Practically everyone I encounter does speak some amount of English. Those who don't are admirably resourceful. Some point to my translation dictionary with me until we've managed to get through to each other. None talk slowly or loudly—is it only Americans who use this misguided tack? Zoey and I especially enjoyed the saleslady in the lingerie shop who mimed "B-cup" with surprising success. Zoey also wanted a new thong, but we thought we'd spare the poor woman that particular charade.

Of course, it's not all shopping. When I'm not roaming the streets with Zoey, I'm roaming the sheets with A. For those of you who haven't had a mindless fling in a while, I strongly recommend it. Let's just say the permanent flush on my face isn't from all the sun I'm getting.

*I*t's shameless, I know, but I can't help gushing about the city on my blog, in e-mails, to anyone from back home who will listen. My mother refuses to hear anything positive—I almost suspect she'd be happier if I called her from an Argentine hospital or prison in desperate need of rescue—but even her frosty disapproval can't spoil this first blush of love. I've fallen head over heels for the city, and I want to enjoy every second I've got here.

So it's with relative ease that I whittle away the warm Sunday afternoon in search of an irresistible outfit for my first official date with Antonio. Not that it would matter if everyone else were to suddenly begin speaking German. I am in my own little world, focused on the dialogues in my head. When I left him at the front gate early this morning, Antonio said he wanted to take me some-where really special this Thursday night. It's time to experience the glamorous side of the city. I can see the whole evening flowing out before me, shining and twinkling in the moonlight. A perfect meal. Heady red wine. Antonio's conspiratorial smile as he asks the waiter for the check. We can't keep our hands off each other. Our feet play under the table. We forgo pastries and espresso for dessert of a different kind. I will commit every word, glance, touch to vivid memory. There will be more scintillating tales for Sam and Trish. More fodder for my blog. More distance between me and the tangled naked mess of Jeff and Lauren. Strange how, in the matter of one day, that mess seems finally to be a world away, and receding farther and farther with each passing moment. Antonio is the ideal distraction. I am giddy just thinking about it, my Argentine love affair.

But I don't want to get ahead of myself. Or, more to the point, I don't want to get ahead of this moment. No second-guessing, no hedging. I've been blaming my quarter-life catastrophe on hav-ing the wrong plan. But sometime in the last twenty-four hours, a niggling question has burrowed its way into my brain.

What if it's having a plan that's wrong?

So an experiment: I left my apartment this morning without even a cursory glance at the plan, and I am determined for once to see where life takes me when left to its own devices. For now the only goal I allow myself is to find a drop-dead-gorgeous outfit for Thursday. Too dreamily distracted to worry about insignificant things like personal safety, I venture boldly into an unfamiliar neighborhood on Andrea's advice, in search of the perfect little black dress. (Yes, she has assured me, those are a date staple here, too.) Nothing can pop the shiny bubble that encircles me as I glide from store to store. Every shoe I try on tickles me pink. Every dress brings a blush to my cheeks. But it's a bright red dress that gets me at last. I shimmy into the slinky number with a flared skirt clearly made for dancing. It is completely unlike anything I would normally buy, and that clinches it. I take a twirl in front of the mirror, and the soft fabric swooshes against my bare thighs. It takes every ounce of my concentration not to imagine the way it will feel sliding off my hips and falling to the floor.

I meet Zoey for dinner on Tuesday night at the café where I first saw Antonio. Ostensibly, we're here to practice our Spanish. We do, proudly, manage to order coffee and ask for more sugar without a word of English, but aside from that, Antonio is all I can talk about. His face, his body, his voice, his gracious manners, his endless compliments, his insistence on calling me Cassandra, which makes me feel a bit like an Italian movie star. When I've exhausted all his attributes, I begin the comparisons to Jeff. I've known the man only half a day, but I find no dearth of material in this area. Zoey listens happily. It's nice, she says, to focus on someone else's love life for a change. She even joins in on the Jeff bashing, not letting a little thing like never having met him slow her down.

Two hours and four cafés con leche later, I realize that we haven't even cracked open our textbooks. We've been too busy amusing each other with our collective heartbreak—it feels so good to laugh about the misery. The waitress, her arms swathed in extensive tattoo work, doesn't seem to mind. She leaves us alone, mostly, sauntering by occasionally with a barely discernible nod in our direction. As she rounds the room, passing table after table with her nods, no patrons snap their fingers or wave to her, frantic for more coffee. Nobody hounds her for change.

"Did you notice how the people here are as fast as New Yorkers when they're on the move," Zoey observes, "but the second they set themselves down somewhere, it's like time stops?"

It's true. The rhythm of life here ebbs and flows. Inside this café, it virtually crawls. Seattleites are relatively relaxed. It's one of the reasons (right after seeing *Sleepless in Seattle* and drawing the conclusion that we all live in quaint million-dollar houseboats) that people migrate there from all over the country. But unless we're on vacation, we rarely come to a full and complete stop. The people in this café are savoring more than the amazing coffee. Everything from the stance of their bodies—elbows on tables, arms over chairs—to the way they set down their cups between sips, flaunts an enviable serenity. It reminds me that despite all the modern conveniences I am not on American soil. And for the first time, that fact doesn't leave me sad and wistful and longing for home.

Is it Antonio who's made that happen? I hate to think I'm so needy that a bit of attention from a man is all it takes to be happy. Is it my newly discovered buying power? I couldn't be that shallow, could I? No, it must be more than that. Maybe it's this café. I never had a place like this back home. Sure, Sam, Trish, and I have our favorite spots, but those places aren't so much restaurants and bars as concepts. There is always that unmistakable reality that you are the customer. *Like that coffee? Buy this music compilation. Enjoying that steak? Take home this barbecue sauce.* Somehow, in this place, I feel like I've stopped by a friend's house. A really, really cool friend.

I lean back in my chair and take it all in. El Taller. Zoey looks it up in her dictionary—that's almost like studying. It means "The Workshop." It does sort of have an industrial feeling, but it isn't cold at all. The walls are deep red, similar to my new dress, I note with a smile. The wooden tables are battered but gleaming, and giant rough beams run along the ceiling. In the middle, industrial-looking stairs hang suspended by some complicated system of chains and pulleys. And then there are the hauntingly beautiful abstract paintings. They remind me of the one in Andrea's foyer. Not the colors, so much, but their thick broad strokes and sheer size.

Plus, the location can't be beat: mere blocks from Andrea's house and with a prime view of the plaza's comings and goings. Antonio said it was fate that we met—he never comes here, this neighborhood being so far from his. He'll certainly make an exception now. We can stumble over in the morning for an omelet con queso. We can stumble home at night after too many beers. In between, we can sit for hours sipping enormous mugs of café con leche.

El Taller. The Workshop. Yes, I decide, this will do just fine. "I really do like this place," I say.

Zoey nods, inhales slowly as though breathing in the atmosphere. "Yeah. Me, too."

We both like it so much we make a plan to come back on Friday. We'll force ourselves to practice our Spanish then, we vow. But we both know the only thing we'll be practicing is the fine art of kiss-and-tell.

Wednesday is an eternity. Spanish class drags on and on and on. Back at the apartment, I try to busy myself with a new blog entry, but my mind wanders so often it takes me two hours to get a page out. A week ago I would have easily spent an entire evening fine-tuning my plan, but now that's the last thing I want to do. Since letting go of my rigid schedule, I've had nothing but fun, and, amazingly, I haven't lost a limb or landed in jail or anything. Instead I call home and let my stepdad blather on about his tulip bulbs. "I'm lining the whole front walk this year, and the packets say to plant them a couple of inches apart. That'll take about fifty-eight bulbs on each side. Imagine that!" My mom reads to me from the *Seattle Post-Intelligencer* classifieds. "Oh, look at this, they need someone to answer phones at Amazon.com. That sounds perfect for you, honey, with all your Internet experience." I send pointless e-mails to Sam and Trish. I clean my spotless bathroom. I hand-wash my bras. I dig out my traveling sewing kit and darn the small tear in my favorite cardigan.

Thursday morning is worse. After cooking an elaborate breakfast that I am too nervous to eat, there is absolutely nothing left to distract me. With Antonio coming by around nine P.M., I've got hours and hours to kill. It will surely be a slow and agonizing day.

I have to relax, I tell myself. The house being relatively quiet, I take my Spanish textbook and dictionary into the courtyard and stretch out on a lounge chair. Flipping ahead to the section called, cheerfully, "Making Friends," I manage to parse out a few good sentences I can use over dinner. There was so much I wanted to tell Antonio that first day we met but didn't have the words for. *"Trabajé para una compañía del Internet,"* I repeat over and over until I can say it without looking. *I worked for an Internet company.* Now, how does one say "They fired my ass"?

The house begins to rumble. Andrea must be back. I brace myself for the ensuing chaos of dogs and child, but it doesn't come. Finally, when all is still again and I can hear only the birds communicating in the trees behind me, Andrea enters the garden alone. Wordlessly, she shuffles over and slumps into one of the other lounge chairs.

"Busy morning?" I ask.

"Mmm. Many, many preparations."

"Jorge's asleep?"

"Mmm." Her eyes are closed, her arms folded across her chest.

Andrea's husband, Martin, is coming home this weekend. He'll be here for two weeks, and then it's back to Chile until Christmas.

She's been scrambling to "get the house ready," whatever that means. It always looks spotless to me, no jam fingerprints on the walls, no antique tabletops marred by felt pen. Except for the toys, you wouldn't even know Jorge lived here. Or three dogs, for that matter. Yet somehow she's managed to run herself ragged with preparations, carting in endless bags from the shops and boxes down from the spare room. But who am I to judge? I must have looked in two dozen shops before I settled on that red dress. I am already imagining how I will do my hair. I have been dreaming about Antonio's soft lips all morning. Am I falling for this beautiful Argentine man who looks at me like I am a goddess and can barely understand a word I say?

Andrea is preparing for the return of her husband, the father of her child, a man she has known and loved for nine years. I don't know Antonio from Adam. And my track record for judging men? Not so good at the moment.

I remind myself to be careful. Take it slow. Don't get caught up. After all, Jeff made quite a fuss over me in those first few months, and look where that got me. He was all stiffly pressed shirts and ties, elaborate home-cooked dinners and breakfasts in bed, flowers, sweet silly presents like the sour candies I'm addicted to, and that silver key chain with my initial. What do I make of these things now, these remnants of love? He's probably plying Lauren with the same gestures and trinkets at this very moment. Come to think of it, he probably already did that years ago. No doubt it was my experiences that were secondhand. How do you know when the gestures and trinkets are real? Perhaps you should assume they aren't.

My mom has always said it's best to expect the worst. That way you're rarely disappointed and often pleasantly surprised. "Better that than vice versa," I can still hear her saying to me through my bedroom door two days before junior prom. My first high school boyfriend, Tommy Hayes, had just unceremoniously dumped me by proxy. His buddy Cam called me, said, "Tommy doesn't want to go to the prom with you anymore. Sorry," and hung up. Determined not to miss my prom—I had spent three weeks looking for a dress in the exact soft pink to complement the beginnings of a spring tan—I third-wheeled it with my best friend, Monica, and her date. Then I spent the whole night sitting at a table, trying to pretend that I wasn't crying, while I watched Tommy ram his tongue down Angela Patterson's throat. Truthfully, I didn't much care whose throat Tommy rammed his tongue down (he was a sloppy kisser). It wasn't the loss of a boyfriend that bothered me, either—I had begun to realize that the conversational expertise of high school boys was limited to NBA scores and how much they could bench-press. It was the loss of the perfect junior prom night I'd been imagining since the eighth grade that had me in tears.

By the time Monica's dad dropped me back home, I was a mess of mascara. "What did I tell you?" my mom started in again with a misguided attempt to console me. "Expect the worst, and you'll rarely be disappointed." I looked up at her through my tears and, for the first time, saw her for the unhappy woman she was. She complained constantly, rarely smiled without the aid of a glass of wine. Had she always been this way? I had memories of her laughing, but they were few and far between. I promised myself right then and there that I would never be like her. If I couldn't expect the best from other people, I would manage my own actions, keep my own feelings in tight check, carefully control the few things I could. The Plan was not the only wall I built to protect myself from future disappointment, but it was a formidable one. Until Jeff came along with his Trojan horse of empty promises. And then Lauren with her wrecking ball hidden inside a cello case.

Still, I refuse to expect the worst. I won't become a miserable woman who forgets how to smile. No, this way is better. Not low expectations, but no expectations at all. Tear down the walls, put down the drawbridge, open the doors. Whatever happens, happens. This will be my new mantra.

When I open my eyes, Andrea's gone, and the garden is in shade. I dig my watch from my pocket. Eight o'clock! All that careful preparation, and now I'm going to be rushing to get ready.

I zip upstairs, jump in the shower—no time for my usual pre-date bubble bath—and forgo curling my hair in favor of a quick updo. All the rushing has my hand shaking while I put on eyeliner. A few sips of wine later, I'm feeling much calmer. It's almost nine. I slip into my new red dress and strappy black shoes and take a turn in the full-length mirror to make sure everything's in the right place. It's a bit cool outside, but I don't want to ruin the look with a jacket. Stud earrings and silver bracelet, and I'm as ready as ready gets.

By 9:10, my updo is starting to wilt. I fortify it with a couple more bobby pins and another sweep of hair spray. I fortify myself with more wine. By 9:20, I'm beginning to worry. Did he forget where I live? He's been here only once. Did he knock at the front door and get no answer? I could wait downstairs, but I don't want to look too eager. If I had his phone number . . . How is it that I don't have his phone number? Oh, God, I don't even know Antonio's last name. What in the world am I doing? In Seattle, I wouldn't have given a guy a second thought before I'd committed his entire résumé to memory. What happens, happens? Have I completely lost my mind?

I am saved from myself by a knock on my door. "Coming," I call out, taking one last look in the mirror. I have to admit, I look spectacular. The wine has clearly not hurt my self-confidence.

"Antonio!" I open the door, trying to pout adorably but unable to stop a wide, toothy smile from spreading across my face.

"Uh, hi." Not Antonio. Mateo. The timing couldn't be worse. He looks me up and down quickly. I can only imagine what judgment he's passing on this silly American woman now. My smile deflates instantly into a flat line, my confidence flying out the window. I sense the imminent return of the mumbling mess who answered this door on that first day in airplane clothes, smudged makeup, and bedhead. But before I can say a single inarticulate word, Mateo beats me to it.

"I, sorry, I just, well, Andrea, she wanted me to, she said there's something wrong with the uh . . ." He takes a step back and stares at his toolbox, shuffles his feet like a little boy. Once again I'm reminded of how charming and solicitous he was the day he met Zoey; with me, it's always awkward silences and avoiding eyes.

"Bathroom sink?"

He looks up at me again, his eyes huge green saucers, then looks away. Is it possible that I'm making him nervous?

"Right, bathroom sink."

"Well, it's dripping a bit, but it's no big deal."

"Oh." He looks at his toolbox again. We stand there not speaking, too long for comfort.

"But thanks," I add. "If you have time to fix it, I'd really appreciate it."

He looks at me again, this time with a small smile. "I don't want to interrupt you." His English is indeed flawless: only the slightest accent, just enough of the exotic to disarm a gal if she weren't being careful.

"You're not," I say as breezily as possible. "I'm on my way out." I hope, I pray. Please let me be on my way out.

"Oh. Sure. Of course you are."

"What is that supposed to mean?" My dress is beginning to feel too red, my heels too high. I cross my arms over my chest.

"Just that you look very . . . nice." This time when he looks at me, he smiles widely, that smile he gave Zoey. The smooth skin around his eyes crinkles softly when he smiles like this, I notice.

"Oh."

He picks up the toolbox, his arm flexing in a not unpleasing way, and I step aside to let him enter. He turns his body to pass, and for half a second, we are inches apart. I fix my gaze safely on his suntanned neck as he moves in front of me. His scent, spicy aftershave and soap and fresh sweat, trails behind him. Wasn't I waiting for someone?

After an extensive examination of my dripping pipes, Mateo spreads his tools on the bathroom floor and sets to work. I sit on the edge of my bed and pretend to read a magazine that I've read a dozen times. I've never dated anyone blue-collar—didn't exactly fit into the plan. Studying Mateo's hands wrench, twist, pull, and push the various parts in and out of place, I realize I may have been too hasty.

"How long have you been doing this?" I ask. He looks startled by my voice. "Fixing things, I mean."

"I don't, really. But I told Martin that I'd watch out for Andrea when he's not here. So . . ."

"Oh. Sorry. I just assumed you did this kind of thing for a living."

"You do a lot of assuming." A stab at me for assuming he didn't speak English. Somewhat earned, I suppose. But then he smiles— that devilish smile again—and all is forgiven.

"So what do you do? For a living."

Mateo looks down, shifts from one knee to another, twiddles with a short tool with multiple handles.

"I'm sorry. Is that too personal? The guidebooks say that Buenos Airians like to talk about themselves, so I didn't think—"

"*Porteños.*"

"Poor what?"

"*Porteños.* That's what people from Buenos Aires are called."

"Port town. I get it."

"That's right." Mateo smiles again warmly before turning to slot a new bit of pipe in place. He tightens it, runs the water, and checks for leaks. "Well, that should do it."

"Oh." Suddenly, I don't want him to go. Is it possible we're becoming friends? Or something? "Great. Thanks."

He packs up his tools and walks to the door. He looks me up and down again. "I hope I haven't kept you too long."

"No, not at all."

"It must be a fancy place."

"Where?"

"Wherever you're going in that dress." I look down at myself. Antonio. I'd forgotten all about him. But then he seems to have forgotten all about me, too. I open the door for Mateo. "I'm not sure I'm going anywhere."

"Oh?" Mateo's eyes go wide, his brows lift. He leans in toward me, one hand against the door frame. "Because if you're looking for something to do tonight—" He's cut off by loud knocking from below.

"Cassandra? *Hola,* Cassandra. This is Antonio."

"Antonio," I call down. "Just one minute. I'm sorry, what were you saying?" I need Mateo to finish that sentence.

"Not important. Have a nice night." Before I can say a word, Mateo squeezes past me and disappears down the stairs. I can hear the gate unlocking, muffled voices, and my heart pounding in my ears. What was he going to say? If I was looking for something to do tonight, *what*? And why does he care? Am I kidding myself? He was just being nice, right? He probably felt sorry for me. Poor clueless American, all dressed up and no place to go. Ugh. Please don't let it be that. Anything but that. I will die right now if he feels sorry for me.

"*Hola,* Cassandra. Where is my beautiful Cassandra?"

"Coming, Antonio," I call down the stairwell. I shake my head and smile to myself. Why am I wasting my energy on Mateo? Mateo who runs hot and cold. I have gorgeous, sweet Antonio waiting for me. So what if Romeo is a little late? Tonight I am Juliet.

CHAPTER EIGHT

People, it's like the whole world is spinning out of control—
and I love it! In Seattle, a wild night on the town meant
warm-up cocktails at home, dancing at a club, and maybe a
late-night snack before heading home around two A.M. Here,
they don't even go out until well past midnight. Last night A
met me and Zoey at the club with a couple of friends, and we
all danced for hours, stopping only to get a drink or bottle of
water. After, A walked me home, and along the way we found
a park bench and started making out like teenagers. (Before
you judge me, you should know that we weren't alone—in the
early hours, the streets of Buenos Aires fill up with young
couples who, as A explained, generally live with their parents
until they're married, so they have nowhere else to go.) Anyway, I was so tired by the time we reached the yellow house,
I insisted he go home. He gave me an adorable disappointed
puppy-dog look and left me at the door. I slipped inside quietly,
but there was Andrea already up and about, with Jorge under
one arm and a squirming dog under the other. M was right behind them, carrying his ubiquitous tool belt. (Is it wrong that
for a brief moment I wondered how exactly one gets a thing
like that off?)

My lips were still stung raw from kissing, my shirt unbut-
toned a bit more than it had been when I'd left the house.
I flushed with embarrassment, like a schoolgirl. I thought
Andrea would get all maternal and disapproving on me.

Instead it was M who mumbled something about it being dangerous to walk around alone at night. I wasn't alone, I told him. Not that it was any of his business, and why would he care, anyway? He shook his head and started to say something, but Andrea just laughed and shooed him out the door. Then, in typical Andrea fashion, she made me breakfast and kept me up for another hour talking about her old clubbing days in Brazil.

The whole time I sat there thinking, How did I get here? Who is this unknown woman who dances in a club until five in the morning and then makes out in the street until seven with a man who barely speaks English? Why, it's me!

Some days I don't recognize myself. Sam says I'm probably just going through a phase, responding to a bad situation or whatever. Trish says that new life experiences change a person, that we evolve through difficulty and pain. But I don't feel any pain anymore, and I don't think this is a phase that I'll pass through. At least I hope it's not. Maybe, when faced with crisis, most people either move forward or stand still. I like to think that I am shedding someone I never really was. Let M shake his head at me. For the first time in my life, I'm breathing.

*Y*ou go, girl!" The comment from elaine226@ myspot.uk seems to sum up the bulk of responses to my blog thus far. Not only has the daily visitor toll risen to over two hundred (notably, the numbers shot up right around the time I started writing about Antonio), but about thirty women and a dozen or so men from twelve different countries across the globe took the time to tell me that they fully support my Argentine fling. Which is nice, because while I'm in the process of being, um, flung, I'm not always clear on exactly what I'm doing or why or to what end (mostly, the doubt sets in when Antonio tries to explain something that is clearly important and I haven't got a clue what he's saying). Should I fear I'm sinking too far beyond reach, these encouraging words from faceless strangers buoy me up. There are, as is to be expected, a few naysayers who warn that I'm just rebounding. Of course I'm rebounding, I reply. And I am determined to relish every single bounce.

Not that it's all about Antonio. Far from it. I am squeezing as much fun as possible into my time here—these days, six months seems very, very short—doing things I never would have dreamed about back home: going to see local bands, strolling through tiny art galleries, walking everywhere during the day, dancing all night. I'm exhausted in the most fabulous way.

With so much going on, keeping up with my blogging isn't as easy as I thought it would be, but watching my readership grow has inspired me to make it a priority, particularly since so many of them are going through breakups of their own. For those just embarking on the seemingly endless journey to recovery, my silly adventures seem to give them hope that things will get better. Those ahead on the healing scale, like hopefulromantic@excite.com, do the same for me. It's like I have this tiny community of fragile souls living inside my laptop. When we huddle close together, you don't notice the cracks and fissures quite so much.

Here in Buenos Aires, another tiny community seems to be growing. Our nights at El Taller have expanded in membership, thanks to Zoey's irrepressible hospitality. "I found her crying outside the Teatro Colón," she explains as Julie from Toronto sits down at our regular table—near the windows, for an unobstructed view of the always fascinating plaza life. "I just keep meeting all these poor dears wandering the streets with broken hearts," Zoey says in her own defense when Maria, a pleasantly plump and pretty girl with long black hair and more metal poked into her face than I dare count, walks in the door and, seeing Zoey, gives an excited wave.

"Do you think we all give off some kind of odor, detectable only to our injured sisters?" I ask. "Like a sort of pheromone?"

"God, that's a depressing thought," says Julie. Everything is depressing to Julie, thin, pale, sad Julie, who left her husband because she'd woken up one morning and realized that they hadn't had sex in eleven months and neither of them had seemed to notice. Even when she's laughing at something, Julie's eyes don't seem to buy what her mouth is doing. But Canadians, she tells me, are in general a bleak and pessimistic people. Must be all the cold.

"I think it's a seventh sense," says Zoey as she stands up to give Maria a big hug. "Like gaydar but not."

Maria jumps right into the conversation: "What are we talking about?" The opposite of Julie, Maria is unfailingly upbeat. Her positive, don't-let-the-world-get-you-down attitude would be annoying if not for the fact that she is also undeniably funny. Her humor is mostly of the self-deprecating kind. Back home in Chicago, her three-year live-in boyfriend came out of the closet. ("It wouldn't have been so traumatic if he hadn't been wearing my best La Perla bra.") Two hours later, she has all of us—even Julie—doing café con leche spit takes as she recounts her attempts to get frisked at customs. "I must have had twenty keys in five different pockets, but I didn't get so much as a pat-down. What does it take for a girl to get a little heavy petting in an airport these days?" She fits in immediately, as though we were saving that fourth seat for her all along.

It's a good group, this foursome. After a few evenings together, it feels like we've known one another forever. Traveling is funny that way, I've come to realize. In the absence of a support group, you create one from readily available materials. You make best friends of virtual strangers, even if you know almost nothing about their life back home. You invest all your energy in getting to know them fast, because, like Julie, who's here for only a month, many will be gone from your life as soon as they've entered it. You don't think about details like past and future, only today. Today these three women make me feel rich with friendship.

Generally, being around them makes me miss Sam and Trish less. Sometimes it makes me miss my two best friends even more—I can't help but imagine how much fun it would be if they were here, too. I tell Sam and Trish this constantly, in part to prevent any feelings of jealousy but also to implant the idea of their coming to visit me here. They'd love to, they say, but they're pitching a new project at work, and things are crazy. So for now I make do with my Buenos Aires girls—not a bad deal at all. If I've found solace in a community of online friends, this is the live act. Between morning blog sessions, evenings at El Taller, all-night clubbing with the girls, and all-night loving with Antonio, life is full and sweet and wide open.

Maria stands up and raises a glass. "You are the most best people ever," she slurs. It's the end of the night, and there are six empty wine bottles for the four of us. "Here's to the ones we love. Here's to the ones who love us. Here's to the ones we love who don't love us. Hell, screw them all, here's to us!" She slugs back the remainder of her drink.

"Hear, hear!" we shout. Glasses clink, and wine is swallowed. The bill is paid. We peel ourselves from the table and venture out into the cool air. Anything is possible. For the first time in a long time, I feel like the luckiest girl in the world. I'm feeling so blessed, in fact, that when I get back to my apartment I issue an invite on my blog to the heartbroken masses in Buenos Aires. Why keep all the fun to ourselves?

> Calling all the brokenhearted in Buenos Aires. We meet once
> a week for an absurd amount of eating, drinking, laughing, and
> generally pretending life doesn't really suck all that bad. Bring
> your sob stories, bring your tantalizing tales, bring some money
> for beer! Come anytime after seven P.M. on Thursday. Look for
> the loud group near the window—you can't miss us.

Only after I post the entry do I stop to consider the odds that someone is getting over a relationship and traveling in Argentina and reading my blog and wants to meet a bunch of people he or she may never see again.

Apparently, the odds are good. On the following Thursday, not one new person shows up. Seven do. There are so many of us, we have to push two tables together. Four people squeeze onto a bench made for three. We borrow chairs from other tables. Amid the commotion, I catch what I could swear is a reflection of Mateo, his mass of dark curls appearing in the window behind Maria. Adrenaline buzzes annoyingly, hopefully, in my blood. But when I turn, I see only disinterested waitstaff. I've barely spoken to Mateo since he came to fix the sink, since he left so abruptly at the sound of Antonio's voice at the front gate. I swallow hard and try to think of something else.

"So exactly how many people have read this blog of yours?" asks Zoey.

I'm grateful for the new subject matter. "As of this morning, about three hundred and fifty a day," I say, barely believing it. When I saw those first few comments on my blog page, I couldn't fathom how total strangers in other countries could have any interest in my life; even less, why they kept coming back. Then readers started to tell friends about it, some posted links to my blog on their own sites, and it sort of snowballed. This morning I rechecked my stats page over and over again, but the numbers didn't change.

"Wow, three hundred and fifty. So basically, everyone here." She smiles at the chaos before us.

Throughout the night, three more people come, and we make room for them. I can't keep track of all the names, but it doesn't matter. I may never see any of them again, but that doesn't matter, either. On this night we swap sad stories, share too many bottles of cheap red wine, and celebrate that we have hearts to break.

There are six of us left at the end of the night, including the original group, a two-time divorcée named Sharon, and Dan. Dan came late, said little, and had half the women at the table smitten. I didn't notice him much during the evening, sitting way over on the far side of the table, but Julie and Maria began whispering conspiratorially when he got up to use the washroom. There was simply too much going on down at my end to pay much mind to the object of their attention. But now that the place has cleared out, I get it.

Dan is good-looking but not too good-looking. His teeth are white and braces-straight, his cheeks have that Ivy League flush. His jaw is strong but not chiseled. His mouth is not too small, his nose not too long. He doesn't have a hairstyle to speak of— his sandy-blond hair is just sort of there. He isn't overly built, but his shoulders are broad, and there appear to be nicely shaped pecs under his T-shirt. His khakis are lightly seamed, his suede loafers an inoffensive brown. On their own, these qualities don't scream "look at me," but together they are undeniably pleasing to the female eye. It's a biological alchemy we have little say over. In short, he has the look of a husband. He smiles in my direction. I smile back.

Dan returns the following Thursday, along with Sharon and her new German friend James. This time Dan and I speak to each other. He says, "So, how's the pizza here?" And I say, "You'd have to ask Julie. It's all she eats." Most of the time he is locked in deep conversation with Zoey.

"What's the deal with this Dan guy?" I ask later while I walk with Zoey to the bus stop near my place.

"Why? Don't you have your hands full with your Latin lover?" She draws it out for full effect. Latiiiin loveeeer. "Don't want to be greedy now."

"I'm not interested, just curious. Wondering what all the fuss is about."

"Besides the fact that he's adorable, let's see. He runs a hedge fund in Boston, but he hates his job. He saved tons of cash so he could hang out here for about three months and reassess his life. He's sweet, smart, rich . . . Yeah, you're right, can't see what all the fuss is about."

"Right."

"Mind you, he is as beige as his pants. I mean, he dumped his girlfriend because she wasn't ready to get married. Apparently, they 'didn't want the same things out of life.' " Zoey does air quotes to fully demonstrate her distaste for all things domestic. "Hearing that almost put me to sleep."

"Was that before or after you hand-fed him your french fries?"

"Fair enough. But in my defense, it's been days since I've had a really good flirt." We get to the bus stop, and Zoey rummages in her bag for change. "Besides, we spent half the night talking about you."

"You did not."

"Seriously. He asked me a zillion questions. What's her situation, where's she from, how long is she here, where's she staying, blah blah blah. Aha!" Finding the right coins, Zoey thrusts her fist into the air triumphantly. I've been here for almost two months, and I'm still too chicken to take the bus. There are a thousand different zigzagging routes, and deciphering the chaos of colored lines on my transit map is on par with cracking Cold War Russian spy code. Zoey doesn't even have a transit map, she just asks the driver in broken Spanish if his bus will take her wherever it is she wants to go. Sometimes, she tells me, she waits at a random stop and takes whatever bus comes along. Just to see where she'll end up.

"So what *does* he want out of life?" I ask.

"Who?"

"Dan."

"Oh, you know, marriage, kids, a nice house in a nice city, two vacations a year."

"So basically, he's perfect." And he's been asking about me. It occurs to me that someone like Dan would slide neatly into The Plan. It also occurs to me that when I wanted guys like Dan, nice, clean, beige guys, my life was beige, too. I didn't know it at the time—I wore Jimmy Choo boots, how could my life be beige!— but compared to the rainbow I'm riding now, it's impossible to pretend my old life was anything but. At its best moments, it might have ranked a nice, frothy cappuccino color. And the worst part is that I wanted it that way.

"Don't forget exceedingly dull," Zoey adds, as though she's reading my mind. It takes me a second to realize she's referring to Dan.

"Right."

"I really need to meet someone fun." The number 156 bus pulls to a stop in front of us. "You're so lucky you've got Antonio to entertain you."

"Sure—I can't understand eighty-five percent of what the guy says. For all I know, he could be rambling on about how he wants to get married and have kids, a house, and two vacations a year."

"Not likely." She looks at me slyly, and we both laugh. I've told Zoey way too much about Antonio's and my nocturnal activities. "And even if he was, who cares what's inside when the package is that pretty." We kiss each other on the cheek, and she climbs aboard the 156. The door slides closed between us, and the bus pulls away.

She's got a point. The truth is, not only do I not know all that much about Antonio, thanks to the language barrier, but (poor Marcela would be crushed) I kind of like that we don't understand each other. What was at first frustrating is now surprisingly liberating. When I started dating Jeff, I listened intently to every word he deigned to let fall from his lips, then I'd call Sam and Trish to dissect each precious morsel for deeper meaning. He might as well have been speaking a different language for all the time and energy I wasted interpreting him. How was I to know that "I'll love you forever" was Jeff-speak for "As soon as my ex comes back to town, I'm outta here"?

My Spanish is now on a level with Antonio's English—it would be better, I'm sure, if I hadn't skipped all those classes to meet him for lunch—but that still doesn't amount to a whole lot of deep, meaningful conversations. We stick to easy topics, like the weather, the meal, how much I am enjoying my trip. When he attempts more complicated fare that I can't understand, I fill in the blanks with my fantasy du jour. My new favorite: "You are the most beautiful, talented, smart, funny, amazing woman I have ever met in my entire life. When my father dies, I will inherit Argentina's largest cattle ranch. Marry me and be my cattle queen." I don't want to marry the man, of course, but the soap-opera element is too much fun to resist. It is a luxury not to care.

Besides, this is all about fun for both of us. Through the constant miscommunication, somehow we manage to make each other laugh, often because of yet another miscommunication. On our fifth date, while dear, sweet Antonio waxed poetic in his mother tongue, I imagined he was making plans to whisk me away to his private island on his hundred-foot yacht. What will I pack? I wondered. Then his voice rose excitedly, and his eyes widened. "Cassandra, do understand what I saying?"

A twinge of guilt. Could Antonio actually be pouring out

his heart to me? "I think so." He looked satisfied. "Well, no, not really."

He chuckled softly and touched my cheek. "You are wonderful, yes?"

"Yes," I answered. We both laughed. Then he leaned in across the table and kissed me.

No, no one is getting hurt here. You get hurt when you count on someone, plan for something, expect one outcome over another. You get hurt when you hope. The only thing I hope for when I hang out with Antonio is that the weather will hold out for our afternoon picnic or that I won't mispronounce a word too badly. It's fun. Casual. A fling.

Yes, just a fling. This is what I tell myself when I don't hear from him for three days straight. He usually checks in every couple of days, whether or not we have plans, so I'm not sure what to make of the phone silence. Maybe he got really busy at work—whatever that might be. It's probably no big deal. He'll call when he calls. Or he won't. Whatever.

I ask Andrea and Martin what they make of it.

"Girl to girl to girl. Argentine men are all like this. They only think of one thing," says Andrea, thrusting a long knife into the air for effect. She's carving an enormous slab of beef that her husband has carted in from the grill outside. "Tell her, Martin."

Martin is a tall, gentle man with a pleasant face and a welcoming disposition. He'd been in Chile for three months, yet on his first night back, he knocked on my door, with Jorge on his hip, to ask if my suite was warm enough. He can't seem to take his eyes off Jorge or his hands off Andrea for even a second. I've been trying to give them lots of privacy, but they keep inviting me to join them for meals. Tonight I am too upset to refuse. I'm glad I didn't. It's soothing to watch them all together.

"They are all like this," he agrees. "Even I was once." He smiles and leans in to kiss his wife, careful not to wake Jorge, who has fallen asleep in his lap.

"They're not bad," Andrea adds, smiling at her husband. "But very romantic. This is trouble."

My Buenos Aires hosts are the poster couple for romance. They adore each other with the intensity of high school sweethearts (they grope each other about as often, too). If Andrea drops a piece of food on the floor, Martin erects a velvet rope around it. When he hums along with the radio (endearingly off-key), she looks at him like he composed the song. So why the warning? Maybe something is getting lost in translation.

Or maybe A's and my relationship is the thing getting lost in translation. I keep reminding myself that A and I are not in a real relationship. He doesn't owe me a call—doesn't owe me anything, for that matter. But something more is bubbling below the surface. Is that panic or simple anxiety firing across synapses? Could I actually care, really care, about him? Despite the language thing, we do manage to have a lot of laughs together. I picture A's face, much the way I pictured M's that day in the cat park. Far from calming me, the outline of A's sharp jaw, deep brow, and puffy lips sets my pulse racing. I move down to his broad shoulders, his taut stomach muscles, and that delectable trail of dark hair from his belly button down to his . . . Okay, so what? I've fallen madly in lust?

The worst part is I feel like such a loser waiting by the phone, afraid to leave the house too long in case I miss A's call. And I'm so distracted. M caught me in the courtyard staring up at the balcony of my apartment. The magazine I'd started to read an hour before was still sitting open on my lap at the first page. He was here to drop off some toy he'd bought for Jorge— like that boy needs another toy—and he had to poke his nose

outside, where I was having a lovely time telepathically willing
the phone to ring. "Where is your boyfriend?" he said, smiling
wryly. "Shouldn't he be whisking you off to some five-star restaurant where the beautiful people congregate?" Did he know?
Did Andrea tell him?

I shrugged, pulled my sunglasses down from my forehead,
and pretended to read, but the very thought of M knowing
what's happening is driving me almost as crazy as A not calling. Also, did M just call me beautiful?

The advice my blog readers offer is heartfelt but unhelpful.
"Two more days and then you should definitely call him," says
heartsick@roamer.com. "Don't give him the satisfaction," counters
sexysamantha@orb.uk. "If you call him, he'll have all the power."
And there is the usual splinter group who refuse to discuss anything but Mateo. Some are convinced, insanely, that he is secretly
in love with me and vice versa. Others, like randysandy@bigtop.
net, want me to "do him 'cause he sounds d'lish." I've dubbed
them the Sado-Mateoists. Let the debate rage online.

On the third day *sin* Antonio, I decide to skip Spanish at the last
minute—I'm completely unprepared, anyway—and wander the
streets of downtown in a melancholy funk. An hour and two bags
of sugared peanuts later, I give my feet a rest on a park bench. The
skinny trees provide some much needed shade, and if I sit facing
the street, there's good people-watching to distract my mind. Unlike me, everyone seems to have somewhere important to go, and
this haste is not as comforting as it usually is.

My attention moves from the bustle of well-heeled business
types to a growing congregation of old women toward the end of
the park. They aren't rushing anywhere. Rather, they stroll slowly
around a small stone obelisk jutting up toward the sky. Many wear
kerchiefs over their gray hair. Most clutch some sort of poster
against their chest. I had thought there were twenty or so women,

but as they round the monument, their front blending into their tail, I can count at least forty. And it seems that more are joining all the time. Clearly, this is something important. Something is happening here.

"*Excúseme*," I ask a young man in a Che Guevera T-shirt. "*¿Qué pasa?*"

"*Son las madres*," he says impatiently, dragging hard on his cigarette. I nod slowly with exaggeration as if to say, Of course, the mothers. How stupid of me.

It does sound familiar, though. *Las madres*. Didn't Zoey mention something about this once? I rummage through my backpack for the sole mini-guidebook I now allow myself to carry. There they are, between sections on the city's famous cemetery and the choicest cuts of beef—Las Madres de Plaza de Mayo. *Over twenty years after the end of the Dirty War, during which over 30,000 Argentine dissidents "disappeared," Las Madres continue to march every Thursday afternoon, demanding information, justice, and closure.* This is Thursday. Their day.

I abandon my shady bench for one in the sun so I can get a little closer. From a few feet away, I can see that the signs they hold are photographs of people. Their beloved children and grandchildren, all missing. *Las Madres* walk and talk and hold their signs with such resignation. Hundreds of Thursdays they've gathered here, refusing to give up. Zoey was right. It is a truly heartbreaking sight. Yet also one pouring out hope and love.

I step into the shadow of a tree, feeling that I am somehow intruding on a private moment, a glimpse into their country's great grief not meant for my foreign eyes. But mostly, I am suddenly, deeply, to-the-core-of-my-bones ashamed of the way I've been acting about Antonio. Such self-indulgent behavior, and over someone I barely know. What is his disappearance compared to the loss they have suffered? I spot a nearby table with pamphlets and a collection jar. I take out all the paper money I have in my wallet and shove it into the jar. As I hurry, head down, toward the subway station entrance, I hear a woman calling after me: *"Gracias, chica. ¡Muchas gracias!"* But I don't look back. I don't want her gratitude, just absolution. Only when I reach the subway gate do I realize I've given away my fare. I rise into the sun again and start the long walk home.

CHAPTER NINE

You'll have to forgive me. I'm not feeling particularly entertaining today. It's been a week without any word from A, but I'm not sure that's what's bugging me. Since that day downtown, silently admonished by the presence of *Las Madres,* I have forced myself, rather successfully, not to think about him. He only popped into my head twice yesterday, and I chased him out quickly by singing an old Madonna song (thanks, Madge).

Still, there is an uneasy feeling brewing under the surface, a sense that things just aren't right. Something has shifted like a cloud eclipsing the sun, and my fabulous Buenos Aires self doesn't seem quite so fabulous lately. Shopping has lost its spark. I spend more time on the information highway than I do traipsing through the neighborhood streets. When I'm not reading the latest celebrity gossip, I'm updating my bookmark list—*mucho* exciting, let me tell you. The rest of the time I'm moping. Andrea has tried to lure me along with her to the grocery store, yoga class, even to one of Jorge's playdates, but I just can't find the energy. Even the animals are concerned. Chico, the smallest and oldest, keeps leaving his favorite chew toy at my door. Pity from a dog. I've got to snap out of this. Whatever it is. It's got to be A. Doesn't it?

*M*aybe you're ovulating," Zoey offers over the phone.

"Maybe I'm molting."

I drag myself downtown to Spanish class, but my mind is a churning, preoccupied mess. Every time I'm called on to read, I start on the wrong page, stammer over the most basic conjugations, mispronounce words. The ever positive, cheerful, supportive Marcela shakes her head at me several times. At the end of class she hands back our last pop quiz. I have failed another one. Zoey offers an encouraging smile and hides her own grade, which is, no doubt, near perfect. Everyone looks happy. They are all improving. If I want, Marcela offers kindly, I could start sitting in on the class after ours as a review. I decline politely. How important is it that I learn Spanish, anyway? I get around fine with the small amount I know. It's not as though I will ever be a *Porteño*. I am merely passing through this place, having fun, making a few memories to amuse myself when I'm old and settled. *Can I try these on? Another drink, please. Not tonight, I have to wake up early.* What else does an American gal need to know in this town?

After class, the friendly Irish couple invites the group for coffee. I beg off. I need to get home and check my messages. When I return home to find none, I sink back into my unmade bed and call Sam and Trish at work. They're working on their proposal for a new twentysomething-trends newsletter, which could mean a big promotion. I skip the usual updates and focus on the Antonio issue.

"Hold on a sec," Trish cuts me off before I can get out my full rant. "I thought you didn't actually care about this guy."

"So did I," chimes in Sam.

"I don't," I say firmly. "I really don't. It's just that—"

"Just what?" asks Sam.

"It's just that—" I stop. For the past week I've felt completely shaken, obsessing about why Antonio hasn't called, but have I even once wondered if he was okay? He could be lying in a field, trapped under a cow, for all I know. Have I been missing him or the predictability of him?

"Just that you hate not knowing what's coming next." Trish has this way of seeing through all the crap we pile on top of ourselves to avoid looking at the truth we're afraid to face. It's really annoying. "You can take the girl out of The Plan, but you can't take The Plan out of the girl."

"You're right," I sulk. "Forget everything I said. Let's talk about you guys."

As I listen to Sam's detailed description of her latest bartender crush, I make a decision: If I want to go with the flow, I've got to stop fighting the current. I will not care when or if Antonio ever calls again. What comes, comes, and that's that.

After we hang up, I walk over to El Taller to preoccupy myself with a gigantic mug of coffee, good food, and some midafternoon people-watching in the plaza. Instantly, I realize this was not the best decision. I seem to be the only person sitting alone in the café. There are happy groups, lovers, and BFFs all around me, enjoying the simple pleasure of another person's company. For the first time in weeks, I feel cavernously lonely. I should have gone out with everyone after class. I should be practicing my Spanish more. How much have I missed out on because I was going with the flow? Wasn't the point to stop missing out?

A waitress with short pink-streaked hair stops by and, determined to redeem myself in my own eyes, at least, I order completely in Spanish: café con leche and an omelet with lots of cheese. She nods confidently and returns five minutes later with the coffee and an enormous platter of olives. The sight of those tiny spheres skewered with toothpicks is too much. My eyes start to well.

"*¿Está bien?*" she asks, looking concerned.

"*Sí,*" I whimper. "*Sí. Gracias. Muchas gracias.*"

I take a deep breath. I will make the best of this day if it kills me. Staring out the window, nibbling at the olives, I indulge in a good dose of melancholy. As always, the plaza hums with activity. Do they all have a destination, or are they seeing where the wind takes them? A large, noisy family passes by. The man—the father, I suppose—has dark curly hair, Mateo's hair. How many Argentine men have this kind of hair? I wonder. Thousands? Hundreds of thousands? The man disappears from frame, yet I can still see Mateo's curls, shiny and reflected in the glass. I even imagine I see the outline of those paint-splattered overalls he seems to live in. I'm willing to accept that I'm capable of midafternoon hallucinations, but shouldn't it be Antonio I conjure? I shake my head, but the illusion won't go.

Someone clears his throat behind me. I turn slowly and see Mateo standing behind me.

"*Hola,*" he says, his hands shoved deep into the pockets of his overalls. I can't tell if he's smiling or squinting from the sharp beam of sun cutting across the room. "I thought that was you."

"It is."

"Are you by yourself?" he asks, scanning the table, my half-drunk mug of coffee, my closed notebook. Is that some kind of dig?

"Yeah. I had a sudden craving for olives."

A short, skinny guy with an overgrown mullet pats Mateo on the arm, providing a moment of relief. They kiss each other on the cheek and commence what I assume is Spanish small talk. I try to imagine my heterosexual guy friends back home greeting each other like this, but the image is all wrong. As I watch Mateo and his friend, I can see the reason it seems so natural here. Argentine men pull it off because, like women, they're more in touch with their sexuality. The way they walk, talk, dress, dance—it's all laced with sex. American men focus all their energy on female sexuality, ironically, but not much on their own. And they wonder why we think Latin men are so hot. Even the way they stand is sexier. American men work so hard to fill up space. Mateo holds his arms close to his sides, slouches a little, touches his stomach when he talks. A guy like Mateo doesn't try to fill up space, and that makes you want to fill up the space beside him. Theoretically speaking.

The friend walks off to join a table near the bar, leaving Mateo and me in awkward silence. Since that day he fixed the sink, things have reverted to their original state. The image of him rushing past me as Antonio called out from below is still between us. I think we might have been on the verge of near friendship until that moment. And now nothing. Mateo was supposed to come to dinner at Andrea's last week but canceled at the last minute. To avoid me, no doubt.

"Was that a good friend?"

"No, just a customer." Was that a smirk? He hates me, doesn't he?

"A customer?"

"Yeah, I work here." He frowns. Talking to me must be painful for him.

"You work here? I had no idea." Why didn't he tell me when I asked him that day? Why so secretive?

"I'm the manager. Technically." He looks out the window.

Manager? I don't like this at all. How will I ever relax here again, knowing he could be lurking about, waiting for me to do something stupid? "I've never seen you here before. I come here all the time."

"I know." He smiles slyly.

"Oh." What does that mean? *I know you come here every week, surround yourself with more loud Americans, get drunk, and carry on about your ex-fiancé?* I don't need to look in a mirror to know that I've gone beet red in his presence yet again. I fiddle with the menu. "Funny that I've never seen you here." Not funny at all, actually.

"I mostly work in the daytime. I've seen you here a couple of nights. I would have said something, but you're always with your friends, so . . ."

"Sure. Of course." I wonder if anyone would mind if we moved our nights to a new venue. "The sink's working great, by the way, so thanks."

"The what?"

"The sink. No more leaks."

"Good. So it's not giving you any more trouble?"

"Nope. No leaks at all." I'm sitting in a café in Argentina talking about sinks with a man who would probably rather be, well, doing anything other than standing in this café talking to me about sinks. I need to make this stop. Can I say I was about to leave? My mug of coffee is more than half full, and I've barely touched the olives I didn't want to begin with. Clearly bored, Mateo scratches his bicep, his rippling brown bicep, and looks past me out the window. Then he bites his lip. His soft pink lip . . .

If only the waitress would come over and rescue us from each other. If only a car would come crashing through the window and put us out of our misery.

"Yup," I say. "Everything's good as new."

"Good. I'm glad. How is your friend? That girl?"

"Zoey? She's great."

"Oh, good. Great." He scratches his other arm and looks at the door, no doubt developing his own exit strategy. The black curls shake when he turns his head. They must be soft, to move that easily. "And your other friend?"

"My other friend?" Mateo hasn't met anyone else in our little group. He's probably confused me with another American woman he doesn't like. There must be many. I tilt my head, semi-curious about his answer.

"The person who came to pick you up."

"Oh," I say. Antonio. A week, no phone call. Well, what should I say—I may or may not have been dumped? "We aren't really hanging out anymore."

He turns sharply and makes eye contact. "Oh. Well. That's too bad." Am I imagining things, or does he sound a lot happier? "I'm sure you're busy enough with all your sightseeing."

"Not really," I say, the truth being that I haven't done or seen much of anything, unless you count the insides of countless restaurants and nightclubs. My first week here, I listed more than twenty-five historical monuments, museums, outdoor markets, and buildings of architectural interest to be visited before I go home, all carefully culled from guidebooks, websites, and Zoey's recommendations. The last time I saw that list, it was buried under a pair of flip-flops and an old issue of *Marie Claire*. "I mean, I want to, but I've been so focused on my Spanish lessons." Sounds like a respectable excuse. It's even partly true.

"Toto trabaho ee no hwaygo . . ." Huh? I don't recognize a single word. Walked right into that one, I suppose. Way to go, Cassie. I picture Marcela shaking her head at me, disappointed in how far behind I've fallen. "All work and no play . . ." Mateo translates. Now I feel stupid and dull. He never seems to miss an opportunity to make me feel good about myself. Did I really think there was a possibility I could be friends with this person?

"That's true." I fake a self-deprecating laugh (the one I've honed over countless phone calls with my mother), then take a long sip from my lukewarm café con leche, hoping he'll get the hint and leave me alone to drown in my mug.

"But you're not studying right now," he says, grinning.

"That's true, too." No, right now I'm just a big fat loser.

"Well, I was on my way to the MALBA." He lifts his hands from his pockets and gestures toward the door. "If you want, you could come along. Unless you've already been."

"Oh. No. I haven't." At least I don't think I have. What the heck is a Malba? It sounds familiar . . . Better question: Why would I want to go there with Mateo? I look around. My waitress is slumped against the bar, deep in conversation with the bartender. No car crashes through the window. I mean, why wouldn't I want to hang out with a person I barely know who, in our rare moments of contact, has been alternately rude, aloof, and awkward around me? Though I must admit to a bit of curiosity. Why did he come over to my table when he could have easily hidden himself from view, as he's admitted to doing before? Why the spontaneous invite?

"So you'll come?" He looks at me, waiting for an answer. He's smiling. Sort of. He's sexy. Definitely.

"I guess I could . . . Sure. Yeah. Why not."

"Okay, then. Let's go." He signals to the waitress, who hurries over. I dig in my pocket for a five, but Mateo waves it away and says something to the girl.

As he speaks to her—too long to be merely settling up the bill, too quiet for me to even attempt to catch a word or two so I can guess the meaning—she turns my way, studying my face as though she has seen me for the first time and hasn't served me at this table by the window on countless occasions. A smile stretches across her face. Confusion flattens mine. She leans closer to Mateo, her eyes still on me, and whispers. He grins and shakes his head. She walks away, chuckling.

What did he say to her? That yes, this is in fact one of those obnoxious foreigners who gather here every week, talking loudly in English? That he's playing guide to this silly American girl as a favor to his friend? That he saw me sitting alone and felt sorry for me? That Argentine manners dictate he invite me along? A wave of hot indignation spreads out from my chest. I don't need anyone feeling sorry for me. I am no one's obligation.

I stand up quickly. "Mateo," I begin with as much cool as I can muster, "if you'd rather go alone, it's no problem. You aren't obliged to entertain me."

"Don't be ridiculous," he says, furrowing his brow at me. "I'm going to the MALBA, and you haven't been there. I don't mind if you come along." He walks to the door and holds it open. "Whether you're entertained or not is entirely up to you."

MALBA, it turns out, is a palatable acronym for the rather chewy Museo de Arte Latinoamericano de Buenos Aires. This wasn't one of the items on my old sightseeing list. The excitement of going somewhere that isn't on a list more than makes up for a five-minute cab ride during which the only words spoken were between Mateo and the cabdriver. For a moment I toyed with the idea of sexual tension until our thighs accidentally rubbed against each other in the backseat and Mateo's leg sprang away instantly, as though it had touched something scalding hot. All right, I thought, I get it. I'm hideous. We'll be friends. Or whatever it is we're being.

I follow Mateo to the museum's fourth floor, where the new exhibitions are kept. "I always start up here and work my way downstairs." It's the last thing he says for twenty minutes.

The current exhibition, I decipher from the plaque at the doorway, is a large collection of pieces by an abstract artist. Either the paintings were done between 1965 and 1985 or the artist died at the age of twenty. I'd ask for clarification, but Mateo seems to be in a kind of reverie the moment he enters the space. Moving slowly from picture to picture, nodding, frowning, leaning in, leaning back, he doesn't so much look at each one as look into it. I shuffle along and wait for him to explain something to me, a puppy waiting for a bit of praise or cookie, but I'm pretty sure he's forgotten I'm here. I sigh audibly but get no response. If I'd wanted the silent treatment, I could have sat at home and watched my phone not ring.

I give up on Mateo and focus on the art. Luckily, it provides some amusement. The large, labyrinthlike space must hold forty or fifty pieces, mostly paintings. I don't understand what any of them are supposed to mean, but I can't help liking them. Especially the ones that seem to depict strange childhood monsters, the kind of things you imagine in your closet after your mother has turned out the light, except these monsters look more sad than scary. When I come to the largest painting, which is easily ten feet across, I don't want to move away. You could spend hours tracing every brushstroke. The painting is home to dozens of sad monsters. I want to give them all a great big hug.

"Should we keep moving?" Mateo's voice startles me. I guess I can see how you could forget someone here. I nod, holding on to the bubble of quiet around me so I can digest the painting a second longer in my head.

"Did you see anything interesting?" he asks as we descend to the third floor via escalator.

Best not to say anything too specific, I tell myself. Wouldn't want to look foolish—again. But I can't help myself. I want to talk about what I've seen. I take a deep breath. "Well, I don't really know anything about art, but I really liked the ones with all the monsters or whatever they were supposed to be. They were more sad than scary, if that makes sense. Maybe even scared themselves. They reminded me of the things I used to imagine when I was a kid, and to see them scared like that made me feel, I don't know . . . safer." Mateo doesn't say a word, only looks at me with a slight frown. Then he shakes his head, and the frown dissolves into a bemused grin. I must have said something dumb. What was that I said, that the monsters were scared? Sheesh. "But I don't know what I'm talking about." Cue awkward, self-deprecating laugh.

"Are you sure?" he asks. "Because that was probably the most incisive critique I've heard of his work." I scan his face for sarcasm but can't find any, only a sweetly crooked smile and those gorgeous green eyes fixed on mine in a manner that makes me uncomfortable. Uncomfortable in a very, very good way.

The more comfortable Mateo gets with me, the more uncomfortable I become. We make our way down to the main floor, where the museum houses its permanent collection. Instead of wandering off to take in the floor at his own pace, he leads me around like a tour guide (make that an extremely hot tour guide). Twice his hand is on my elbow, leading me gently. When he lets go, I can still feel the light pressure of his fingers. He stops at his favorite pieces with a stream of excited praise. I blush ridiculously as though the compliments are meant for me.

Mateo pauses in front of an enormous wood and metal mélange. "Aren't they phenomenal? All these sculptures were transported from . . ." I lose track of what he's saying. It's very hot inside this museum, too hot to breathe, almost. I wipe my shirt-sleeve across my brow. Mateo leans to the side, cocking his head. His arm pushes against my shoulder. He doesn't move away. Neither do I. Silence. Did he ask me a question? I nod and try to look pensive. It seems to do the trick. We keep walking.

Mateo grins at the single Frida Kahlo painting and steps in to take a closer look. I step beside him, mere inches from the famous self-portrait. I stare into her eyes; she stares into mine. I wait for a skeptical crook in her monobrow, a sneer to form on her lip, but she gives none.

"Did you know that she was in a horrible accident and lived most of her life in pain?" He turns and looks at me. I keep my eyes on Frida. It is more than I can take, all this serious talk and touching and deep eye contact. "She had an amazing courage—as an artist and a woman. That's rare these days."

Rare. I get it. Hours ago, such a comment would have had every muscle in my body stiffening against the implied criticism. But with Frida's support, I am emboldened.

"What is that supposed to mean?" I thunder, with no regard to who can hear me or how far my voice carries in the wide-open space. Another crazy American woman talking too loudly. Add her to the pile. "You know, it might look like I'm just shopping and hanging out or whatever, but it took a lot of courage for me to come here." In truth, I was equally afraid of not coming and, consequently, looking like a complete idiot to everyone I know in Seattle, but that's neither here nor there.

"I wasn't implying—"

"I know exactly what you were implying." I cross my arms tightly over my chest, thrust my hip sharply to the right. I am American woman, hear me roar. "Besides today, you've probably said a total of fifty words to me. You don't know anything about me. You have no idea who I am or what I've been through."

"You're right, I don't. But you mis—"

"Spare me your criticism of American women," I spit. There's no stopping me. "I've had enough of your analysis for one day." It's a mean shot at what was, up until five seconds ago, a great afternoon. But he had it coming. Here I was thinking he might be a decent guy, maybe even someone I might want to get to know more. And then bam. Flat on my ass once again. "So thank you for the edification, but I'm out of here." I storm to the front door and down the steps, ignoring Mateo's voice behind me. But when I get to the street, I have no idea which way I'm supposed to go to get back.

There's a hand on my arm.

"Cassie," Mateo says plaintively. I don't turn around. I don't want him to see the tears welling in my eyes. "Cassie, please. You misunderstand. I wasn't trying to insult you. Far from it. I think it's incredibly courageous that you've come here by yourself."

"You do?"

"Yes, of course. I know how scary it is to travel to a strange place where you don't know anyone or speak the language. Trust me, I know."

"Oh, I thought . . ." Embarrassed by the scene I made, I turn and face him—well, I stare at his chest. Close enough. "I just assumed . . ."

"But why would you assume that?" He looks at me, so genuinely bewildered, his eyes crinkly and sad, that I don't feel angry or embarrassed anymore—I feel bad. I've hurt his feelings.

"We don't exactly have the best track record, do we? I mean, I get that you don't like me very much, and why would you? You're a sophisticated Argentine who speaks a hundred languages, and I'm an ignorant, loud American who wishes everyone would speak English. But it's totally fine. Just because I live in your friend's house doesn't mean we have to be friends." When I've hurt people's feelings, I tend to ramble.

"No, it doesn't."

"Right. Well. There you go." When my feelings have been hurt, I tend to shut up.

"But I'll be very disappointed if that's the case."

"You will?"

I look at the ground, and he lifts my chin with his fingers.

"Why don't you like me, Cassie?"

I gape, flabbergasted. "Why don't *I* like *you*?"

"Yes, why? Because *I* like *you*," he says, softly plaintive. What alternate universe have I just stepped into?

"You do?" I look up and see the cocky man who was at my door that first day, the sweet man who held out his hand to me in Andrea's dining room, the smiling man in those photographs, the gentle man before me now. His café-con-leche skin has been darkened slightly across his forehead and nose by the spring sun. His curly dark hair has been cut recently, the edges blunt. The long incisors that give that devilish edge to his smile sometimes, the soft pink lips, the thin white scar that peeks out from under his chin. Those impossibly green eyes are still rimmed by impossibly long lashes, but with the sun behind him, I can see my face reflected clearly in the irises. My heart races, my palms are undeniably sweaty, my throat is dry and sticky.

"Of course." Mateo chuckles and shakes his head. "You make me laugh." I look away quickly, disappointed and then disconcerted by my disappointment. Naturally, I make him laugh. I fall on my ass. I make scenes in museums. I'm freaking hilarious. What was I expecting him to say?

"Well, you're in luck, because I've got an endless supply of knock-knock jokes." Mateo doesn't say anything. Maybe he doesn't know what a knock-knock joke is. "Sorry about all that," I say, gesturing toward the museum. "I guess I ruined your afternoon."

"You didn't ruin anything." Again he gives me that look—amused and confused. "Do you always assume the worst?"

"No. Not at all." The words come as a reflex, but maybe it's true. Maybe there's more of my mother in me than I want to admit. Mateo smiles the sideways smile that I assumed was a smirk but doesn't seem quite so cynical now. In fact, it seems kind of adorable. "Sometimes," I add.

He grins and shakes his head again. "Then you're more Argentine than you think."

Mateo and I decide to walk back to Andrea's, enjoying the manicured streets of Recoleta, Buenos Aires' wealthiest neighborhood. He could suggest we walk to Canada right now and I'd happily oblige. The proximity of our bodies on the sidewalk is enough to make me ecstatic. His elbow rubs against mine as we walk, and neither of us moves farther apart. I've got goose bumps on my goose bumps. Mateo likes me.

Recoleta is a far cry from the young, hip, artfully decaying Palermo Viejo. Suited men climb into SUVs. Despite the heat, several women parade in fur. Wealth is alive and well in these few square miles. Where wealth has faltered, pride has taken its place. As we walk, Mateo points out historic homes and various architectural treasures, as well as things that have been lost over time in the name of progress. I remark that I can't imagine the area being more beautiful than it is right now. This sets Mateo on a rant against the fumblings of his country's ever shifting government. The things I have only read about in guidebooks and on websites, he makes alive and real. He speaks with such fiery eloquence, gesturing excitedly—the city's Italian influence, I imagine—to punctuate each point with jabbing fists, curling fingers, sweeping palms. He is passionate and utterly adorable.

Mateo is dissecting the last election and the misconduct of the IMF, and I am thinking this might be one of the most perfect afternoons I've ever spent. Then he stops abruptly and pulls me into a spare, brightly lit shop. "Where are we going?" I ask, but one look around and it's obvious. There is a pimply young guy behind the counter wearing a badly fitted blue polyester vest. There are buckets and buckets of ice cream everywhere.

"*Helado,*" he whispers in my ear. And *helado* to you, too, I think with a small smile.

The Argentine ice cream is sinfully creamy and intensely flavored. We sample flavors until the man waiting behind us sighs audibly. Minutes later, we are back on the street, deep into the IMF again, our hands dripping chocolate and pistachio. I am strolling historic streets in Buenos Aires, one of the largest cities in the world, with a brilliant, passionate, sexy Argentine who has green eyes and a devilish smile, discussing politics and eating ice cream. This is the most perfect afternoon ever. No contest.

The sky is easing into dusk as Mateo and I near Andrea's neighborhood. This has always been my favorite time of day. Every light glows gold against the deepest blue imaginable. In Palermo Viejo, dusk is sadly sweet. The daytime street life of focused shoppers, lazy college students, and playful children is replaced by the culture of night. Transvestite prostitutes have taken their places, leaning against homes locked up tight against the coming dark. In a few hours, the city's poorest will begin their nightly shift of rummaging through garbage bags for bits of metal, paper, and twine that can be redeemed at recycling depots. I recognize the half-pink, half-blue house up ahead.

"This house always makes me sad," I say in a near-whisper, as though to speak louder would wake the ghosts inside.

"Why do you say that?" Mateo asks in a similarly hushed voice.

"The unfinished paint, the untended garden. It's like life stopped here one day and never started again." It looks even sadder at night. All the lights are off, and the only sign of life is cats lounging in a lump on the stone walkway. "Even the cats seem depressed."

Strangely, as we pass by the gate's open door, one feline guard rises with a small cry and runs toward us. It slips through the gate and curls itself through Mateo's moving feet, nearly tripping him. He stops and frowns down at the little creature, shooing it away in soft Spanish. So he's not a cat lover. This I can live with.

He stops and checks his watch. "It's very late," he says. "I hope I haven't kept you from any plans."

"No," I say. "No plans at all."

We don't speak again for several blocks. It might be the dusk that's cast a spell on us. If we were on a date, this would be the point when the boy would reach out to hold my hand. But he doesn't, because we're not. Which is actually kind of a relief as we approach Andrea's great front door. There will be no tellingly uncomfortable silence, no clumsy hug, no panic over which way to turn my head for that awkward first kiss. Definitely a relief.

I dig for my keys, laughing when I see that Mateo already has his spare set out and is opening the gate and then the wooden door. "One of these days you'll have to explain how you and Andrea came to be such good friends," I say with a smile.

"One of these days I will," he says, looking very serious.

"Well, thanks again for letting me tag along today." I'm still smiling.

"You're welcome." He's still not.

"And sorry again for being such a spaz earlier."

"Again, apology accepted."

"Okay, well, good night." I turn toward the door.

"Aren't you going to kiss me goodbye?"

I freeze, hand on the latch, heart in my throat. "Oh" is all I can think to say. What I'm thinking is: Thank God, thank God, thank God! Praise tellingly uncomfortable silences, clumsy hugs, and panics over which way to turn my head for that awkward first kiss. I love tellingly uncomfortable silences, clumsy hugs, and panics over which way to turn my head for that awkward first kiss. I turn around slowly. Breathe, I tell myself, but it's no use.

Mateo leans in, tilting his head ever so slightly, passes my mouth, and touches his lips lightly to . . . my cheek.

My cheek. Of course. A goodbye kiss on the cheek. We're friends, and that's how friends say goodbye here. Realizing my near faux pas, I manage to lightly brush my lips against the hollow of his cheek before he pulls back. It's soft and warm. "Good night, Cassandra," he whispers into my ear.

"Good night," I say.

Safe inside the cool, sweet air of Andrea's yellow house, I raise my fingers to the small wet place where Mateo's lips met my cheek, then I touch my lips. They are still tingling from his stubble as I climb the stairs to my apartment.

How many times can I misread that man? First I think M is a total jerk. Then, in the span of a couple hours, I convince myself that he's totally into me. As if the sight of chocolate ice cream dribbling down my chin made him realize that he simply had to have me. As if my astute observations—what was that brilliant thing I said about war? Oh yes, that it's bad—pushed him over the edge of passion. But he was looking at me a certain way, wasn't he? I definitely didn't imagine that. And he kept touching my arm or my elbow or my shoulder. But then the chaste kiss on the cheek—there's no denying the lack of lust in that moment. It could have been my aunt Margaret, it was that steamy. How did I read M so wrong yet again?

Did I read J wrong, too? Did he leave clues that he didn't love me? Drop hints? Was there a trail of evidence that I stepped over or swept under the rug? Is it love that's blind, or am I the blind one? What if I'm doomed to fall for guys who don't want me?

Not that I'm falling for M. Those of you getting all excited about that crazy idea can just relax.

Okay, enough about men. Kiss or no kiss, I had a great day. I stood inches from a famous painting, had the best ice cream I've ever tasted, and realized that M doesn't hate me. *Because* I *like* you. He did say that, didn't he? I didn't imagine that. That's something. That's a lot, really.

Okay, then, M. Friends.

It takes me over an hour to get the retelling just right, but everything's in there, from the chance meeting at El Taller to the chaste kiss at my front door. Satisfied, I hit publish and get up to forage for food. I can't wait to see what they think of the day's events, especially the rather large contingent who's begun to pester me about the Argentine I call M. Postings like "Too bad M is such a jerk. He sounds hot!" and "Enough complaining—why don't you jump that M guy and get it over with?" pepper the comment boxes of completely unrelated blog entries.

Biting into an apple, I curl up on the love seat near the window and meander through the day's events once more, stopping the frame now and then to mull over a cryptic look on Mateo's face or admire the way he brushed his hair from his eyes while listening to me. The memories, pieces of moments, hold me in a delicious trance. Writing it all down in my blog is one thing. Running through it in my mind is another. Alone in my apartment with no audience but my own imagination, I am free to conjure alternate versions. Each one ends with a passionate kiss goodbye. Does it matter what actually happened? In the waning evening light, the entire day seems like a dream.

I get up to toss the apple core in the garbage and notice the voice mail alert on the phone base blinking at me from beside the bed. Oh yes, I think, Antonio. I realize with a grin that I haven't thought about him since . . . Mateo. All that fuss and then, poof, I forget all about the man. There could be a message from him on there right now, explaining everything in his sweet broken English, pledging his eternal devotion, begging me to come away with him to his private island. I'm curious to know if he's called, though I'm not sure I want to break this lingering feeling—whatever it is—just yet.

Eventually, with a might-as-well-get-it-over-with shrug, I relent and punch my code into the phone. There's a message from Sam. She's shouting yet barely audible over the din of what sounds like a party or bar. Trish chimes in at the end, but I replay the message and make out the words "new office," "all grown up," and "another round." It doesn't take a linguistic genius to figure out they got their promotion. A small twinge of envy pricks my stomach. But I won't give in to it. My best friends made their way up the ladder from lowly analyst assistants by working hard, taking risks, and carving out their own path. They deserve everything they have, and I am happy for them. Really, I am.

I fast-forward through a message from my mother reading aloud from the classifieds again. Database entry specialist? She's spending more on this international call than I'd make in a day. Computer store assistant manager? Because I look good in khaki? She must think I'll be desperate for work when I get home. Hell, if good jobs are that scarce in Seattle, I can always go to work for a couple of hotshot research analysts I know. I already know how they like their coffee. The voice mail system saves me, cutting my mom off halfway through a dubious ad for an Internet companion, whatever that means. Wait. I don't think I want to know.

The third message is Antonio.

"Cassandra, my beautiful girl," he begins, as usual, "*¿como estás?*" There are no heart flutters or sweaty palms at the sound of his voice, only a small smirk of satisfaction as he attempts to apologize. His explanation is lost on me. I think he is saying he has been busy at work but must see me soon or he will die from loneliness. At least I think *soledad* means loneliness. Or is he saying he sold his dad? Whatever, I think with a smile. The old Cassie would have spent a good half hour replaying the message over and over until she had analyzed every word for hidden meaning. Not the new Cassie. The new Cassie deletes the message with a bit of ceremony, holding the phone with an outstretched arm, and hangs up, immensely pleased with herself. It's exhilarating, this sense of complete freedom. I'll call him back tomorrow. Or maybe I won't. And now back to that lingering feeling . . .

CHAPTER TEN

*E*ven over the phone I can tell Zoey is pouting. Andrea is throwing an *asado*, a traditional Argentine barbecue, in honor of Martin, who leaves in two days, and I have to skip a night at El Taller for the first time. "I don't have a choice," I insist. "It would be totally rude not to go. They have friends coming all the way from Cordova. I live in the same house."

"Not to mention the fact that Mateo will be there."

"One more time, for the record, we're just friends." It doesn't matter how many times I tell Zoey this. She has much more fun imagining otherwise. Okay, yes, we've been hanging out a lot. It's not like we talk on the phone every day or even make plans together. And I do still see Antonio when I have a bit of spare time. It's just so easy with Mateo. He's always around the house or the café or the neighborhood. We seem to constantly bump into each other, and then we might as well grab a bite to eat or a cup of coffee or a drink together. But it's platonic. I mean, he's never so much as tried to hold my hand. Aside from the obligatory cheek kissing and the occasional accidental contact of clumsy limbs, there is no physical contact whatsoever. There was that one time at the jazz club when we sat side by side watching the band and he put his arm across the back of my chair, and it was almost like he had his arm around me—except not. "Just friends," I say again, more to myself than to Zoey.

"Right, right," she says and fakes an exaggerated yawn. "But seriously, half the people come because of your blog. What am I supposed to tell them? They'll be disappointed if the infamous Cassie isn't there."

"That's not true. They come for the company. I'm a . . . curiosity." All the poking and prodding about in my life that my blog readers do every day is beginning to make me feel like a bit of a freak. Most of the questions alternate between why am I friends with this M guy whom I've been slamming for so long to "When are you going to jump his bones already?" One reader even asked how I'd feel about "trading hot M for a balding guy from Tucson with some high school Spanish." Apparently, Zoey isn't the only one convinced that Mateo and I are an item.

"Well, Dan will be inconsolable." She laughs.

"Oh, God. Can we please not talk about that?" Poor sweet Dan. And poor me. His crush on me has become so obvious to everyone in the group that even some of the newcomers have made passing comments on the amusing drama. (Seems that no area of my life is private these days.) I don't understand the Dan thing, really. We've barely spoken to each other, yet apparently, he thinks I'm the cat's pajamas and will say as much to anyone in earshot. And while I can't prove it, I have a sneaking suspicion that he's behind the harsh comments from harvard155@hotmail.com about Antonio and Mateo. I'm partly flattered, mostly annoyed. "It's not funny."

"You're right. It's not. It's kind of sad. Even sadder is the fact that you've got three hot guys swooning over you, and I haven't even gotten laid yet."

"Antonio is hardly swooning, and once again, Mateo is my friend," I scold. Wasn't she the one who was bored of the topic?

"What a waste," she teases. "If I were hanging out with that man, friendship would be the last thing on my mind."

"I don't think of him that way." Yes, we've hung out almost every day for three weeks, and yes, he's sexy and smart and sort of funny and very sweet when he wants to be, but I don't have to want to jump every cute guy who pays me a little attention. It wouldn't exactly be awful if things moved beyond friendship, but then what? It doesn't matter, since Mateo clearly sees me only as a friend. Doesn't he? "Again, Zoey—friends."

My friend with impeccable timing knocks on my door. (Thank God I changed out of those raggedy sweatpants before Zoey called.) He's making a run to the supermarket—Andrea has gotten it into her head that she didn't buy enough wine—and he wants to know if I'll come and help him carry the bags. "I promise I'll take the heavy ones." Mateo winks at me from the doorway, and I swear the cartilage in my knees turns to Jell-O.

Since Martin's been back, Mateo has given his paint-splattered overalls a break. I thought the overalls were kind of cute, but I'm not going to complain about seeing him in well-fitted jeans, like the ones he has on right now. Like almost every other male in this city, he is obsessed with soccer and plays a pickup game in the park every Sunday, and even through the dark denim, I can tell he has strong thighs. Then I start thinking of other things hidden under those jeans. Bad friend.

"Zoey, I gotta go . . . get something."

"I bet you do." Zoey laughs. She's heard our conversation and isn't about to let me off the hook. "Just friends, huh? All right, *pal.* Go have fun with your *buddy.*" I can still hear her cackling as I hang up.

The air outside is soft and warm. Spring is here. I can't help but smile, thinking about everyone back home slogging through the endless autumn rains. Mateo and I are quiet as we walk the five blocks to the store. At one point he turns and gives me a smile from the corner of his mouth. I smile back. It's nice that we can be like this together, I think. It's a sign of a real friendship developing, a comfortable connection unsullied by all the nervous tension that comes when things are . . . more. What is he thinking about? I wonder. I almost ask but catch myself before the words can escape. That's girlfriend talk. When we reach the supermarket, Mateo steps back to let me through the automatic doors first, as always. I can't believe I ever thought he was rude or superior or stuck up. All the things I wrote about him in my blog, all those mean, juvenile things, make me cringe. Thank God he'll never see it.

We grab a cart and set to work. The wine aisle is a giant wall of burgundy. Mateo tells me about his last trip to Mendoza as he selects a bottle of Malbec from the famous Argentine wine region. "You'd love it. We should go," he says offhandedly as he runs a finger along a label. Did he just invite me to go away with him? Do friends go away together to wine regions? "We could get a group together. You could bring Zoey."

"Yeah, we could do that." See, Zoey, just friends. "Sounds fun."

"This'll do." Mateo pops the bottle of Malbec in the cart. Then another. And another. And another.

"How much wine do eight people need?" I ask as he fills the cart with over a dozen bottles.

"Eight?"

"That's what Andrea said yesterday. Eight, maybe nine."

He bursts into laughter. "As usual, she's invited a few extra people."

"How many extra?"

"Twenty, thirty, maybe. Who knows?" He shakes his head, his curls giggling at me, his lips stretching into a not displeased smile. It's the expression of bemusement that met me on our first encounter and one that I've grown familiar with—and fond of. "Andrea is the consummate hostess," he continues. "She can't say hello to someone on the street without inviting them. Last time she had an *asado,* half of us ate in the foyer."

Having grown up with Andrea, he has stockpiled funny stories about her, and he isn't shy about sharing them. As we select a few nice whites, he tells me how she went into labor with Jorge during

an *asado*. "She called from the hospital to remind me to put the olives out. Seriously." He makes a face, and I laugh so hard I almost
drop the bottle I'm holding. It feels good to laugh like this, full
and without restraint. I seem to do it a lot when Mateo's around.
I've even snorted once or twice without the complete humiliation
that usually entails. Strange to think that I was once so uncomfortable around him, this sweet, funny, charming man.

Mateo wasn't exaggerating about the number of people. By the
time meat hits the hot barbecue with a surrendering sizzle, there
are no fewer than thirty-five people squeezed into the courtyard.
Every few minutes the doorbell buzzes. Mateo and I are so busy
helping Andrea refill glasses, restock cheese platters, and corral the
dogs away from the tasty fingers of little children that I barely see
more than a blur of him for hours. The only times he seems to be
standing still are when yet another pretty girl is trying to hold his
attention. If we were more than friends, I would be beside myself
with jealousy. Instead, I leave him to his fan club and make faces at
him whenever our eyes meet accidentally across the room.

Only after everyone is happily focused on a plate of food does
he sidle over with two tumblers of red wine. "I wanted to make
sure you had a taste of my favorite."

"Are you sure you wouldn't rather be sharing it with one of
your groupies?" I try to sound teasing.

"Groupies?" His brow furrows.

I nod in the direction of three women in the corner who seem
to find our talk very interesting.

"Oh," he says, laughing softly. "That's nothing. Argentine
women are naturally . . ." He searches for the word. "Flirtatious.
It's generally harmless."

"Unlike Argentine men?" I sip gingerly from the large glass. It's
buttery and warm.

"You tell me."

I smile knowingly and take another sip of wine. "I don't know about flirting men. They usually skip right to buying me jewelry."

"I'm sure they do." I suspect that we are now the ones flirting. Nothing to get excited about, of course. Clearly, this is little more to Mateo than a way to pass the time. Which kind of makes it even more fun.

"But I'd take a free café con leche over a diamond any day."

"Good to know." Mateo looks me squarely in the eye. He isn't smiling. Have we gone too far with the flirting thing? I break his gaze, take a swig of wine, and look around the courtyard, searching for something new to talk about. Andrea is holding center court on a lounge chair. Her husband looks on, smiling, a sleepy Jorge in his arms. Two small girls chase the dogs around the legs of the buffet table—or maybe it's the other way around. Tails wagging, the dogs bark sharply. Mateo's groupies, craning their necks toward the French doors, seem to have identified their newest target.

"Everyone seems to be having a great time," I say.

"I know I am," he says. I don't have to turn around to know he is looking at me. I cross and uncross my arms, shift my weight from foot to foot, tuck my hair behind one ear, study the fascinating tile pattern under my feet. This flirting doesn't feel generally harmless.

Wasn't it just a few hours ago that we were so at ease together? Why am I so nervous? If this were Antonio beside me, I'd be making eyes right back at him, laughing inside at how much fun boys are when you don't care where it's all going to lead—as long as it leads to my big, fluffy bed. Wasn't I the brazen hussy who, only two days ago, interrupted Antonio in mid–incomprehensible sentence, pulled him into an alley, and shoved her tongue into his surprised but accommodating mouth? But this isn't Antonio. Far from playing fill-in-the-blanks when Mateo talks, I soak up every word he says to be replayed later as I fall asleep, one of the early warning signs that I could be falling for a guy. Even this stilted, awkward moment will be fodder for fantasy, no doubt with me recast as a grown woman who is unflappably witty and charming even when being stared down by a smart, funny, unbelievably sexy man. But here I am, irreparably stilted and awkward, a reprise of the disheveled, discomfited girl he first met. I might as well be sporting the same rumpled clothes, bedhead, and smeared makeup. I down the rest of my wine and excuse myself to get a refill. Maybe another drink will help. And if it doesn't, if I absolutely must be stilted and awkward, I'm sure as hell not going to do it in front of him. For the rest of the evening, I do a good job of being in any room that does not contain Mateo. Wherever he is, a group of women is always close at hand. Sometime after two, I can see his mop of black curls toward the back of the courtyard, where he's been talking to an elderly couple. Mateo looks up and scans the courtyard every few minutes. I hide in the salon under the pretense of gathering empty glasses. French doors and dozens of people safely separate us until Andrea's guests begin to leave. As they depart in twos and threes, they leave gaping holes in the crowd, clearing a path between us. He looks up again, and our eyes meet. I stick my tongue out at him, but he doesn't laugh, only says something to the man beside him and disappears.

When he reappears a few minutes later, he's holding a plate of food. "You've been working so hard, I was worried you didn't get enough to eat. It's a bit cold, I'm afraid."

"That's okay. I took a short dinner break," I joke.

"Did you like the food?"

"I loved it," I say with maybe too much enthusiasm. "Martin is a grilling genius. Though half the time, I had no idea what I was eating."

"Best not to ask," Mateo says in a hushed voice. "We Argentines make a point of eating the whole cow."

"Thanks for the tip," I say, smiling, and begin to clear glasses from the side table.

Suddenly, I feel the heat of him behind me. There can't be more than a few inches between us. His right arm reaches around me and . . . picks up an empty wineglass.

I exhale. Always reading too much into things, I scold myself. But then he leans in closer, so close I can feel his dress shirt against my bare shoulder blades. His chest is warm through the fabric. I'm so glad I wore my strappy-backed top.

"Why do I feel like you've been avoiding me?" he whispers in my ear, his lips tickling the sensitive skin there.

I drop a glass.

A dozen heads whip around in our direction. Mateo steps back as though recoiling from an electric shock. Andrea says something loudly in Spanish. Everyone laughs and returns to their drinks. I run to the kitchen to look for a broom. I find it in a closet near the stove, a closet just big enough for one person to hide in. After contemplating this option for a moment, I grab the broom and head back out into the salon.

When I return, the four remaining guests are gathering their coats from a chair in the corner. "*Buenas noches,*" they say to us, one of them patting Mateo on his shoulder. "*Buenas noches,*" I say with a large smile, waving my broom like an idiot.

Mateo looks at me intensely. We are alone in the room. I start to sweep. "You never answered my question," he says.

"Your question?" I bend to pick up a few large chunks of glass from under a chair. I sweep under the credenza, under the table, under the love seat. "You know, if you don't do this right the first time, you're stepping on glass for years to come."

"I think you're still doing it." I am vaguely aware of Andrea and her husband saying long goodbyes to their guests in the front hall. Mostly, I hear my heart thudding in my ears. What am I so afraid of?

"Doing what?" I begin collecting empty glasses again, trying to apply all my focus to the task. No matter how much I move, it is painfully clear that Mateo is remaining perfectly still.

"Avoiding me."

"What's the matter? Were you getting lonely?" I look at him with a teasing smirk. "Because you looked pretty entertained to me."

"Were you watching me?" He smiles that devilish smile and cocks his head to the right. It takes the length of a breath for the electricity to travel from my chest to my toes. I understand that flirting is a national sport in Argentina, but he's not playing fair.

"You wish."

I set the stack of glasses on the side table and turn to start on the bar, but my foot catches the carpet. Before I can hit the hardwood, Mateo grabs my elbow. I jerk against the grip, take a grounding step, and right myself again. His hand is still on my elbow, grip loosened but still there, warm and heavy.

My own hand to my chest, I take a deep breath. Then another. "Thanks. Yikes, that could have been ugly. Again." I push out a laugh.

"You're welcome. Though I kind of wish you fell."

"Gee, thanks."

"Only because this time, dogs or no dogs, I would have kissed you. Like I wanted to that first day." There is no smile or smirk or cocked head, just his eyes looking straight into mine. His fingers tighten around my arm. Electricity fires through my body in every direction, followed by a sobering jolt of fear. What am I so afraid of? I think of those women all over him tonight. I hear Andrea's voice in my head. *Girl to girl to girl.* But it's more than that. Antonio is hardly the monogamous type, and I couldn't care less. So what is it?

Mateo takes a step closer, and I know the answer: I could care about him.

And where would that get me?

You can take the girl out of The Plan, but you can't take The Plan out of the girl.

We are mere inches apart, our eyes still locked. He tilts his head down and parts his lips ever so slightly. I don't move. I don't breathe. Every cell in my body wants to kiss this man, but I can't. Please don't kiss me, I whisper in my head.

"Aha!" Martin bellows behind Mateo. "Andrea makes maté." He clasps his hands together happily, then stops and looks at us. "I interrupt?"

"No. *Está bien,*" I say.

"Good. Then you come, *sí?*"

"*Por supuesto,*" I answer with a big smile. "*Gracias.*"

"*Sí.*" Mateo drops his hand from my arm and looks at me. Before he can stop me, I follow Martin out into the courtyard.

I've watched Andrea drink yerba maté countless times. When she cleans, after a long day of running errands, in the evenings while she watches *Friends* reruns dubbed in Spanish, when she checks her e-mail in the small home office, before she goes to bed. Taking short sips from the silver straw, refilling the tiny pot with more hot water as it drains, she reminds me of an old man puffing on a pipe. When you are invited to take maté, my guidebooks say, you are being invited into the Argentine culture. It is a very rare experience for tourists, many of whom buy the pots and straws at local fairs as souvenirs but will never enjoy the hot herbal drink with a local. It is a small, yet powerful reminder that though I will be here only a few more months, I am not simply passing through.

Andrea always offers me some of her maté, and I take a few sips of the bitter tealike drink to be polite, but I know immediately that this moment in the courtyard, the dark sky a soothing blanket above us, is something different, something special. Mostly, I am honored to be in the company of these people, to be allowed inside the warm fold of their old friendship. The four of us take turns sipping the hot liquid from the silver straw. Andrea has added a bit of sugar against her husband's protests. At first it is strong, then mellows into something akin to green tea. While we sip, Andrea does most of the talking, entertaining us with stories from their collective past. Martin and Mateo jump in constantly to add details she's forgotten. Their rapport, the ease with which they tease one another, the eruptions of laughter, all make me long for Sam and Trish and the other friends I left back home. At the same time it makes me sad to think how soon I will be saying goodbye to these kind people. The thought, like the maté, is bittersweet.

"So how do you all know each other, anyway?" I interrupt, wanting to change the subject in my head to something more joyful.

The laughter stops, and everyone looks at one another furtively. Mateo stares at the table. Andrea sips long and hard at the maté straw, making a gurgling that signals the water is low. Martin busies himself with the task of refilling the pot for her. My question seems to have hit a nerve, but I haven't the slightest idea why.

"Well," Andrea starts slowly. "Mateo and I have been friends for so long, it's hard to say when . . ." Mateo gives her a quick sideways glance. Martin concentrates hard on refilling the tiny maté pot. There is a particular ritual to it, Andrea has explained, but he seems to be getting a bit carried away, patting the pot with his palm, assessing its insides, adding more maté. He mumbles something in Spanish that I can't make out.

"Martin, do you need help with that?" I ask teasingly.

"So now the American is going to show me how to make maté?" He chuckles and slaps his thigh lightly. Then he adds too much hot water from a thermos under the table. It spills over, and we all laugh.

"We are all friends from so long ago," Andrea says finally.

I nod and grin knowingly. "Friendships like that last forever."

"Not always," Mateo says, barely audible over Andrea, who coos lovingly to Martin in Spanish.

"Yes, well," Andrea interjects. "People come and people go."

"It's the one thing you can count on," Mateo adds flatly, sounding disconcertingly like my mother. He looks up and examines the star-filled sky.

"I hope that's not true," I say, my mouth curving into a coy smile. I am thinking of our moment in the salon, parted lips separated by mere inches, what might have happened if Martin hadn't burst in on us. Where could that have led? Now I'll never know. Why did I fight it? "There would be no such thing as family, or marriage, for that matter."

Mateo snorts out a snide chuckle. "I suppose you believe in true love and all that other Hollywood crap," he says with a snarl. I shift uncomfortably in my chair, thrown off balance by this inexplicable return of the old—and I thought gone—Mateo.

"I—I believe in the possibility of it," I stutter. "How can you not?"

"Have you found it?"

"Of course," I say, then check myself. Jeff and Lauren writhe naked and entwined in my mind. How long before these memories no longer come to me crystal-clear and sharp as an X-Acto blade? "Well, no. Not yet. But I—"

"Life isn't a Tom Hanks movie, Cassandra."

"I love Tom Hanks!" Andrea exclaims. "*Big* is very funny, no? And *Sleepless in Seattle*. Not *You Have Mail*. I did not like that at all. Her hair looked funny."

"I know life isn't a movie," I continue, determined to salvage my point. "But that doesn't mean those things don't exist. Millions of love stories have been written for a reason."

"Yes, to stop us from thinking about the reality that nothing is forever, that happily ever after is a fairy tale."

"Ah, the fairy tales. What happened to all the fairy tales?" asks Andrea jovially, snuggling into her husband's lap. "I had princesses and dragons, and Jorge has books about talking dogs. This is a shame, no?"

"*Sí, mi amore.* A shame." Martin passes her the freshened maté and wraps his arms around her small frame.

The subject is successfully changed, but the evening is unrecoverable. It isn't long before our little party breaks up, our goodbyes said with obvious awkwardness, a half-full maté pot abandoned in the courtyard, the kiss that wasn't a kiss dissipating into the cool morning air.

CHAPTER ELEVEN

So much of the night was wonderful. Beyond wonderful. Perfect, almost. But it's this tirade against true love that I can't let go of. Just when I start to think M is someone special, someone like no one I've ever met before, just when I begin to regret everything I've ever written about him in this blog, he does another 180 and turns back into the old M. Life isn't a Tom Hanks movie. What does he take me for? Some vapid, lovelorn, weak-minded woman, no doubt. What am I supposed to make of this return to the sarcastic, condescending man I could barely stand? Was I right all along? Is he really just a total snob? Or was he trying to tell me something about our ambiguous moment in the salon? Was he regretful and wanting to warn me away? Well, my Argentine friend, mission accomplished.

This latest entry, I think with no small amount of satisfaction, ought to get them going. No matter the subject matter, I always feel better when I blog. I'm averaging about four hundred hits a day, which seems like an awful lot. Knowing that so many people care, that I'm not completely alone even as I sit here plunking away on my laptop in this city so far from home, makes nights like this that much more bearable.

Sometimes I even get some good advice. Everyone has an opinion. The latest topic for hot debate: Is my infatuation with Mateo something new, or was I into him all along? "It makes sense," writes virgin@heart.com. "She criticized him way too harshly and way too often. It had to be an elaborate cover-up." Her comment stirs up a flurry of agreement. "I saw through it all along," claims kanders@biznet.com. Regardless of how off base this theory is, I enjoy the back-and-forth—not so much for the occasional pearls of wisdom but for the satisfaction of knowing that something I've created has brought all these disparate people together. Energized by their enthusiasm, I look forward to blogging at the end of every day—or at the start of the next, as the case may be.

It's 4:48 A.M., I note, sighing heavily at the clock. If I'm not asleep by now, I figure, I might as well skip it. I check my e-mail. It's been a couple of days—surely a sign of personal growth—and there are eleven new messages from the usual suspects. I know the content without even opening them, but the predictability doesn't make the ritual any less enjoyable. Sam and Trish filling me in on their office gossip—I don't know the players, but the drama is amusing all the same; job postings from my mom that have no relation to my degree or professional experience; Internet jokes, riddles, and goofy cartoons from my stepdad that have been around the World Wide Web a hundred times (I don't have the heart to tell him I've seen them already); a cryptic quotation by some obscure genius from C.J., the quirky but sweet programmer at my old job whom I've managed to stay in touch with; and two or three messages concerning online master's degrees, penis enlargement pills, and other very important, time-limited offers that I CAN'T MISS OUT ON!

And something from Jeff.

Just seeing his name (which even my mother has had the tact to avoid in our cross-continental communications) is enough to send me reeling. I brace myself against the chair, arms strapped behind me as in a straitjacket, and stare at the subject line. "Please read," it says simply, horribly, in bold black letters. Read? For the second time in twenty-four hours, I can't breathe. He might as well be standing in front of me, the words alone have such effect. Almost three months and no contact. It's an e-mail apparition, I tell myself. It isn't real. There must be another jkeller@bdfmlegal.com.

But I know it's him.

A world of possibilities ricochets through my mind. A thousand scenarios. He can't remember where he put the insurance papers. He's suing me for the engagement ring I sold on eBay. He's become a Buddhist monk and is coming to terms with past wrongs. And then the frightening, thrilling, unavoidable thought: He wants me back.

Could that be it? Do I want that to be it? The shape of him, of us, rises from the bold black letters. My perfect fiancé. Our enviable home. My ideal life. The Plan. It all knits together from fragments I haven't let myself think about for so many weeks, coming back into focus slowly, like a past life merging into the here and now.

The prospect of it is too much to take. I can't open the e-mail. I let go of the chair and fly across the room to my giant white bed. I burrow under the down duvet, find comfort under the weight of pillows.

In the quiet, downy undercover light, I assess. Do I want him back? No, no, I don't. I definitely don't. But I do want him to want me back. Yes, I want that more than anything. I savor the image of Jeff alone and crying, railing against his bad judgment, against his unpredictable, surprising, challenging, imperfect Lauren. I love the taste of him pining away for me, his perfect Cassie, always to be lost. If only, he's thinking, pounding his fists against his muted gray walls, Japanese knickknacks jiggling off the IKEA shelf and smashing against the hardwood floor. If only . . . And here I am having the time of my life, a new and exciting experience around every corner, hundreds of people online waiting to hear what's next, and there he is—dejected and alone.

I have to open that e-mail. I crawl out of my fluffy refuge and face the glowing screen again. I touch the mouse, hold my breath, and double-click.

> Cassie,
>
> I have some news that I want you to hear from me and not someone else. I know I've hurt you badly and I can't stand to hurt you again. But here goes . . .
>
> Lauren and I are getting married. It just happened. I asked one day and she said yes. It was a surprise to both of us, really. Anyway, I thought you should know. I don't expect you to be happy for me, but I hope you won't hate me.
>
> I hope you are okay.
>
> Jeff

Jeff is getting married. Jeff is getting married. To someone else. Lauren is marrying Jeff. My Jeff. He doesn't want me back. Nobody wants me back. Nobody is pining away for me, pounding his fists, wishing for what might have been. Other people are living my what-might-have-been without me. Jeff will get his wife. Lauren will get her perfect man, perfect home, perfect life. Meanwhile, I am flitting around with Antonio, almost letting myself fall for Mateo, who doesn't want marriage or love or anything real, widening the gaping hole in my résumé, and wasting my meager savings on useless trinkets. Almost three months and I can't even speak Spanish.

It feels like the blood is draining from my body, pooling in my hands and feet. They are so heavy. Everything is slipping away. I am tired. I close the e-mail. Summoning what is left of my waning energy, I retreat to my bed once more. There is much crying and then, finally, sleep.

Opening my eyes slowly, I let them process the room in the filtered light peeking through the trees outside my small balcony. It's 6:27 (A.M. or P.M., I'm not sure), and the house is quiet. The screensaver on my laptop swirls away. I rise, stretch like a bear awakened from a winter's hibernation, and open the curtains all the way. Pushing back the French windows, I step out onto the balcony. The air is still and thick and warm. My mind, clear and calm. That's enough, I say to myself, mentally wiping my hands of the last three months. It's time to get to work.

Someone knocks at my door. The phone rings several times. A child giggles in the hall. I am only vaguely aware of these things, like birds chirping from tall trees or cars honking on a distant stretch of freeway. My mp3 player provides a musical cocoon as I concentrate on the critical task at hand. I tell hours only by the end of albums and days by the end of my playlist. The sun comes and goes without much consequence. I get hungry and heat up some leftover pasta, get sleepy and lay my head down on the floor for a while.

But I don't stop until it's done. My new plan.

There it is in all its color-coded spreadsheet glory, page after page articulating in meticulous detail what, where, and with whom I will accomplish, how and when I will measure my success. It's all there, the real life of Cassie Moore, the life that counts—and it starts now. No more of this floating. No more coasting or sailing or any other silly metaphors for not making responsible decisions. Responsible decisions are what add up to a life. Floating along, clueless and out of control, never got anybody anywhere, ever. Whatever happened to my friend Monica, who thought I was a baby because I wouldn't tube down the river? She got knocked up by the quarterback and spent her senior year of high school "with an aunt in Ohio."

No, floating wastes time and opportunity. The shortest distance between two points is a straight line. Measure twice, cut once. The last few months were a hiccup, a small bump in the road. Everything will be fine now, I tell myself. Everything will be perfect. I toggle through the pages of my new plan one more time, highly pleased. Item 1: No more Argentine men.

I haven't answered the phone in two days, and I know there are probably a dozen messages on there from the El Taller gang, but my first call must be to Antonio. Before he can start into his usual Fabio shtick, I tell him plainly that I can't see him anymore, that I'm no longer interested in casual dating. "I like you very much, Cassandra," he says, cautiously. "Do you want I don't date other women?"

"No," I assure him. "I like you, too, but I don't think you and I would work that way."

"*No entiendo,*" he says quietly. *I don't understand.* At first I assume he's hurt but quickly catch myself. He actually doesn't understand.

"I can't see you anymore, Antonio. No more dates."

"Ah," he says, sounding a bit relieved. "Okay, Cassandra."

We exchange e-mail addresses, at his request, and I promise, out of politeness, to keep in touch. I know I will never talk to him again, and, I'm sure, so does he.

That done, I check my messages. Zoey's last one sounds somewhat panicked. "Are you coming to El Taller tonight? Tell me you're coming. Everybody was so disappointed you weren't there last time." Julie has called to say much the same thing. There's a message from Dan—it takes me a second to realize who that is. He's asking if I'm okay. If I'm sick, he adds sweetly, he could stop by with some food or something. Finally, I hear Mateo's voice, sheepish at first, and then it finds its usual confident tenor. The sound sends a nervous shiver through my body. "I've got to go to San Telmo on Saturday to bring something to a friend," he says. "It's an interesting old neighborhood. If you want to come along, I could pick you up around noon. You can bring your friend, if you'd like." No mention of the other night, the strangely tense conversation about true love, the way we left each other, brisk goodbyes and no eye contact, at the foot of the stairs to my apartment. And what's with all the references to friends? Could he be any more obvious? "I get it," I announce to the room. "We're just friends."

Thank God we cleared that up. I know some of you have been rooting for me and M, but let's face it, that was not going to happen in this lifetime. Things could have gotten way off track. Things already are—I don't need the distraction of M to make it worse. Looking back, I can't believe I even considered M and me a possibility. A fling is a fling, but what if M had wanted something more? That would have been a nightmare, not to mention awkward with Andrea and the house and everything.

pilotman@azflightschool.org, I should have listened to you when you said to "always trust your first instincts." Wise advice. My first instincts told me that I couldn't trust M, and so there you go. Well, glad that's settled. I've got to get back on track. No place for M in my new plan, that's for sure. No place for romance of any kind until I'm home again. Enough of these distractions. Yes, thank God. Now we can just go on as friends, simple and safe and no ambiguities to distract me. It's so much better this way. Better than better. Great.

This is the way I explain it to Zoey. We meet at El Taller early so I can catch her up on the last two days before everyone else descends. She shakes her head at me while I sip my beer. "You've been having a blast—didn't you tell me last week that this was the best time of your entire life?—and now you're going to give all that up because some asshole in Seattle is getting married to some other asshole? I don't get it. I just don't get it." She shakes her head at me again and looks at me like I'm an alien she's suddenly noticed.

"It's not about Jeff," I try to explain. "It's about the big picture. Yes, I'm having a good time, but what happens in three months when I have to go home? What will all this do for me then?"

"Who knows? At least you'll have fun finding out."

I can't expect Zoey to understand. In this way, we are from different planets—or solar systems. She lives in a world so far from mine, I'm sure the sky must be a different color, a beautiful shade of mauve, maybe. There is no tomorrow for Zoey, only *mañana*.

My blog readers don't get it, either. I try to explain The Plan and how important it is to me—posting it in all its color-coded glory to illustrate my point—but they side with Zoey. Like her, they blame it all on my broken heart or, more specifically, on the one who broke it. "Never let a man dictate the way you live your life," rails lovesucks@home.com. GeorgeK458@zing.be insists that if I don't do what makes me happy, I will have "a long, miserable future ahead—and no one wants to read that blog." Their intentions are good, I know, but they can't possibly understand. They don't really know me, not the whole Cassie, only Buenos Aires Cassie, blog Cassie. And they don't have to live my life, do they?

Still, their posts sting less than Trish's reaction on the phone this morning. "I knew it! I knew it!" she declared a bit too smugly. "It was just a matter of time before the old Cassie resurfaced."

I'm not sure if I was more bothered by Trish's lack of confidence in me or by the fact that, like her, I'd suspected all along that it was only a matter of time before I reverted to my old ways. Or, rather, came to my senses. Either way, the old Cassie has indeed resurfaced. If it isn't obvious from the amount of time

I spent choosing, ironing, and accessorizing my outfit this evening (denim skirt, white tee, leather sandals, gold hoop earrings and thin bangle) or the care I took in packing my handbag (map, passport copy, gum, sunscreen, sunglasses, Argentine pesos, and American dollars, just in case), or the obsessive checking of keys, locks, and aforementioned handbag contents before and after leaving the apartment, it is obvious in the way my leg jumps under the table at El Taller as I wait for everyone to arrive, my need to know what's next manifested in small jerking movements.

What is distinctly different is how this old tic makes me uneasy, the familiar nervous energy, so antithetical to the luxuriously slow pace of a Buenos Aires evening, which I have come to admire.

But I don't have to think about that right now. The gang streams in one by one, familiar and fresh faces brimming with anticipation of a unique and memorable evening. There are those brief moments of pseudocelebrity when newcomers ask, "Which one of you is Cassie?" and then we mix easily, like old friends meeting again after too much time.

I never cease to marvel at the instant bonding that occurs on these nights. There is rarely a trace of awkwardness as we fall quickly into what Maria calls "camaraderie of the road." Along with small bowls of peanuts and olives (I've grown to love them) and toothpicked cheese, bottles of wine and beer quickly fill the table's center. More than anything, we are thirsty for one another's stories. When we tell our stories, there is no turning back. We may never see one another again—many people come only once, stopping in the city for a few days on their way to Patagonia or Brazil or wherever—but once you've sat at this table, you are one of us forever.

Tonight, as always, all is simpatico under the tawny lights of El Taller. When all sixteen of us have found a seat, I raise my glass of beer for our customary toast, which feels particularly appropriate. "Here's to the ones we love. Here's to the ones who love us.

Here's to the ones we love who don't love us. Hell, screw them all, here's to us!" Half the table joins in, and everyone laughs, clinks glasses, cheers, claps hands. Another good night with my sisters and brothers of the broken heart has officially begun.

A woman named Beth stands up to say hello and tell us about herself, as all the newbies are asked to do. It breaks the ice and provides new material for the night's inevitable debates, jokes, and brilliant theories to be concocted. Beth is from Cleveland, and she's a lesbian. Her long-term girlfriend left her for a man she met at a carpet cleaners' convention. "And yes," she says with a self-deprecating grin, "I do see the irony." Everyone laughs. Someone squeezes her arm supportively. Next a Scottish guy named Ryan who's recovering from a six-year sexless marriage takes us on a hilarious journey through his many traveling conquests (none of which involve climbing mountains). I can't understand half of what he's saying, since his brogue thickens with each cheap beer, but Julie seems positively mesmerized by the pale, lanky redhead. Perhaps he reminds her of the Canadian boys back home, I think with a grin. Maria and I exchange hopeful glances across the row of tables. This is Julie's last week in Argentina, and she could use a bit of wild abandon before she goes home.

Zoey is at the far end of the table, near the windows. She's so tiny, I can see only the top of her wild mass of hair peeking out from behind the row of laughing people between us. Dan, bolder than usual, has squished himself between two women at my end of the table. He doesn't say much, but when I speak he watches me so intensely I feel myself blushing several times. He has the classic look of a boy with a crush—wide eyes, perpetual smile. I train my eyes on our Scottish storyteller. Don't want to give the poor boy false hope.

The Scot finishes his bawdy tale, and the table breaks into smaller conversations. That's my cue to do some mingling. Since I'm technically the host, I always feel obliged to talk to everybody.

It's also a good excuse to get Dan talking to the pretty blonde beside him. "Joan," I say, smiling warmly, "did you know that Dan here is from Boston?" Joan's face lights up. As she peppers Dan with excited questions about his hometown, I push back my chair and rise from the table.

I don't get far. Turning around, I come face-to-face with Mateo. I've never seen him here at night, and the sight of him stuns me. I had planned everything for tonight except how to deal with seeing him. Before I can think of something to say, he plants an enthusiastic kiss on my cheek. I fumble to return it before he pulls back.

"You never called me back," he says, offering the most incredible smile. I want to dive into that smile and swim around in it. "You're not avoiding me again, are you?"

"Oh, hello," I stammer. Of course I've been avoiding him, but suddenly I forget why. "Was I supposed to call you?" Be cool, Cassie. Remember The Plan. *No more Argentine men.*

"About this weekend. San Telmo?"

"Right. Sorry, I meant to. I just . . ." God, he's sexy. Crisp blue button-down and dark jeans. There is a ruby flush to his clean-shaven cheeks. He looks good. Too good.

"Don't tell me we're breaking up already?" He laughs. It doesn't matter that he's being facetious. The sentiment sends a shiver down my legs. Worse, he tilts his head and grins from one side of his mouth. That devil smile I love.

I laugh awkwardly and too long, like a thirteen-year-old on her first date. "Sorry. Really. I meant to call. I've just been really busy."

"I suppose I can forgive you." Mateo touches my arm and grins sweetly. I give that stupid laugh again. Only when I stop, and Mateo and I are standing in silence, do I realize that my end of the table has gotten very quiet, too. Dan's smile, I notice, has disappeared. I turn to our audience. "Oh, everybody, this is my friend Mateo." Too much emphasis on the word "friend," perhaps. Dan's mouth relaxes into a semi-smile.

"*Holas*" erupt from the table. Mateo nods and smiles, stuffing his hands in the pockets of his jeans. It's funny how obvious it is to me now, after knowing him for only a short time, that what I once mistook for smugness is actually shyness—especially endearing, since I can't imagine why anyone like Mateo would ever be shy.

"I don't want to interrupt," he says more to me than the group.

"You must be really busy," I say a bit too quickly. The words come out before I can check myself. Still, it doesn't matter how awkward I sound. There is nothing between us. This has no future. The Plan, Cassie, remember The Plan.

"Right." He furrows his brow and looks at me as if he's trying to place me, as if he doesn't recognize me. I hate that he's looking at me like that. It's all I can do not to reach out and touch his hand for reassurance.

Zoey, unwitting savior, springs to my side. "Mateo! ¡*Hola!*" She leans in, and he plants a hearty kiss on her cheek. "You must join us for a drink." So much for my savior.

He glances at me and then away. "I'd better not." Does he know I don't want him to stay? With him standing inches away from me, my eyes trained on his chest rising and falling under black fabric, I'm not even sure what I want. I wonder if he has black curls under there, too. I bet they're as soft as his hair. He adds, "We're really busy tonight."

A mixture of relief and disappointment washes over me. I do want him to go, but only because I don't know how to be around him. This is not the old Cassie. The old Cassie could turn off her feelings for a wrong guy in a heartbeat. I've done it dozens of times. And we haven't so much as kissed each other. I am not a thirteen-year-old girl. Snap out of it, Cassie.

"Yeah, of course." I look around the room as if to confirm that it's busy, though I know full well that it is—any excuse to avoid prolonged eye contact. "We totally understand."

"But I'll see you Saturday?" He looks at me, hopeful, insecure. It kills me.

"Saturday? Oh, right. I, uh . . . I don't think I can, actually." What I mean is I don't think I can be anywhere near you without wanting to jump you.

"Oh."

"I just have all this Spanish homework." I know it's a lame excuse the moment it comes out of my mouth, but it's all I can come up with. "We have our final exam next week."

"Since when do you care about Spanish class?" Zoey asks, laughing.

"Since always," I shoot back quickly, flaring my eyes at her.

"No, sure," Mateo says, looking around the room as though distracted by something. "I'm going there anyway, and I just thought you might want to tag along. No big deal."

"Thanks for the invitation," I say.

"Of course."

"Maybe another time."

"Maybe." Mateo checks his watch. "Have a good night."

"Thanks, Mateo," I say.

"Yeah, thanks, Mateo!" Zoey calls out loudly as he disappears into the back office. When he's fully out of sight, she turns and whispers, "You are certifiably insane."

I don't see Mateo again all night, though I watch for him from the corner of my eye. Emboldened, Dan attempts to engage me in various conversations over the course of the evening. Where did I grow up? What school did I go to? What is my family like? Do I miss Seattle? What's it like living with all that rain? Once upon a time I would have loved the attention from a cute guy like Dan. But I am no longer in the mood for flirting, or even socializing, for that matter. I simply nod, shake my head, or offer one-word answers. I've lost my appetite, too, thanks to this sinking feeling in the pit of my stomach. I switch from beer to coffee to water.

At midnight I excuse myself from the party, despite protests from my friends. They're planning to hit Pacha, a huge, internationally known club on the river. Thousands of *Porteños* grinding to electronic music as the sun comes up over the water. I've been wanting to go for weeks, Zoey reminds me. It was my idea in the first place.

I shake my head apologetically. I'm not in the mood for any more fun. When everyone is distracted with calculating the tip, I throw my share on the table and slip out the door into the black night, leaving the roar of their laughter and El Taller's warm glow behind me.

On the way home, somewhere after the Mexican restaurant with its cheerful patio lanterns and wide sidewalk seating, distracted, I take a wrong turn. I've walked this route so many times, I assumed I could do it in my sleep. But here I am, at least three blocks in the wrong direction, staring at the half-pink, half-blue house, illuminated on one side by an interior light. As always, there is no sign of life within. Even the cats have abandoned their post tonight. Under the cover of darkness, I stand at the gate and take in the whole heartbreaking sight. It's sadder tonight than ever, this home interrupted.

That's it, I decide. I will not waver. No one will keep me from having the life I want, no matter how sexy, cute, sweet, or charming he is. What will my new friends have to show for their time here? Lighter wallets? A few more notches on their headboards? Countless blurry memories?

When I get home, I go straight to my laptop and pull up The Plan. I read it over yet again, committing every item to memory, reminding myself where these checkmarks will take me. I find a new mantra as I climb into bed and fall asleep. I want more. It has to be more.

CHAPTER TWELVE

I don't need to finish my Spanish final to know that I've failed. As everyone writes furiously for an hour, I stare at the photocopied pages. Might as well be in Aramaic. Staring at the words really, really hard, I've discovered, does not make them magically register. Nor can I decipher the letters as if it's all some elaborate spy code that will eventually yield familiar English sentences, like "You have wasted three months" and "What the hell are you doing with your life?" Marcela knows a failing student when she sees one. She sends me glances of pity across the bent heads of my brilliant classmates.

I did study all week, like I told Mateo I would, but cramming for three months' worth of Spanish lessons in five days is a lot like trying to stuff a watermelon in your ear. I still have the jitters from the gallons of coffee and maté I consumed, but I can't say as much in Spanish.

At exactly 1:45, I stop torturing myself. I hand my paper in to Marcela with a Post-it note attached in humble blue ink: "I'm sorry I didn't do better." Zoey lifts her head from her test and looks at me with a generous smile, as though there is a possibility that I have finished early because I am that good. I shrug, defeated, and slip out the door.

It's early, and the late-September day is warm. Argentina's spring is in full bloom. Female office workers have traded their wool coats for slim cotton blazers. Not wanting to go back to Andrea's house and sulk, I consult my map and head to the famous

Porteño café that's featured in all my guidebooks as a must-see attraction—at least that's one thing I can cross off my list today. Three blocks to the east and a shortcut through the park should get me there in a few minutes. But I've forgotten it's Thursday, and a large crowd is forming around the obelisk. There are many onlookers today, so many I can't see the Madres. Only a single blue head kerchief, bobbing slowly to the right, is visible through the throng of people. My eyes trained on the other side of the park, I weave around amateur photographers, through gaggles of schoolchildren, under banners, and over picnic blankets. The crowd makes it hard to move quickly. I stop for a second to make sure I'm still headed in the right direction. A hand brushes against my arm. This park is known for pickpockets, my guidebook tells me. *Keep a close eye on your valuables. Cameras are especially vulnerable.* I passed a million cameras back there; why are they picking on me? They can have my Spanish textbook if they really want it. I don't have much use for it, apparently.

"Permiso," I say loudly, trying to break free from the crowd. "¡Permiso!"

A group of schoolchildren parts like the Red Sea. As I hurry through the temporary path, I hear a woman somewhere behind me shouting. "¡Chica, parada! ¡Por favor!" Good luck, sister.

I walk faster, one hand moving protectively to my backpack. Nearing a clear area at the edge of the grass, I check the zipper—still closed. I breathe deeply with relief. Ten more feet to the street, and I will disappear into the throng of commuter bodies. Another hand on my arm, but this time it doesn't let go. I laughed when my mother gave me that vial of pepper spray, threw it into the garbage at the airport when she wasn't looking, but now I'm thinking that might have been a naive thing to do. My heart pounding, I stop and turn sharply, ready to let some punk have an earful of vitriol, and see a small woman in a blue head kerchief smiling up at me. A photo of a young man is attached to the front of her dress with safety pins. GUERO SALAZAR, it reads. 1947–1969.

The hand on my arm, I see after collecting myself and unclenching my fists, belongs to another woman, about my age. "*Hola.* I am Augustina," she says in slow, careful English. "This is my grandmother Leonora. She wants to thank you. You were here many weeks ago, yes, and you give much money for the Madres."

"Oh, uh . . ." Augustina saves me from my embarrassed stumbling. "She says you are very . . . generous? Generous, yes? You give so much." I shake my head in protest. I couldn't have dumped more than sixty pesos in their collection jar. I suppose that's more than they're used to seeing at once, but still, I don't deserve such praise. What are a few pesos compared to their endless efforts? It was the beauty of the Madres that drew me out of my selfish haze that day. If not for them, I would have sat in this park and wallowed all afternoon. And about what? Antonio? I have thought of the Madres often since that day. When was the last time I thought about my Argentine fling? How embarrassingly childish it all looks in the light of their tremendous heartbreak and enduring strength.

"Thank you, but really it wasn't anything. I just wanted to help a little."

"Every bit helps," Augustina says kindly, looking down at her grandmother. "It is not just money. People forget, and this makes justice harder. She walks here for eighteen years. I came here a little girl and played in the park while she marched. I didn't understand then."

"Was he your father?" I ask cautiously, already feeling like an intruder. Maybe this is too intimate a question.

"My uncle," she says, looking at the grass. "I don't remember him much. He was tall, and he always brings Hershey's bars." She smiles at the memory.

"I'm sorry," I offer weakly. "I wish there was more I could do."

The women bend their heads together. There is translation. Then Leonora leans forward, blue-kerchiefed head bobbing gently toward me, and whispers throaty Spanish that I can't understand. She takes my hand and presses it to her breast. I nod and smile.

"She says you have a beautiful heart."

The words explode inside my chest like love itself. I am speechless. I want to throw my arms around this wrinkled lovely woman, around the photo of her Guero, around her granddaughter and whole family. I want so much to do more for them all. They are the generous ones.

"*Usted es demasiado abundante,*" I say slowly. *You are too generous.* I'm not sure I've got the words right, but the old woman smiles warmly and shakes her head. The tail of the blue kerchief flutters softly behind.

"Is there something more I can do to help? Anything at all?"

"You are American?" the granddaughter asks without the slightest hint of disdain.

"*Sí.*"

"You tell people?" She pushes a pamphlet, the worn paper soft as cloth, into my hands. On the cover is a montage of photos of the disappeared. "The world cannot forget. Memory honors them."

Who can I tell? Sam, Trish, a handful of other friends, a few dozen acquaintances? Then it hits me: the blog. I have access to hundreds of people every day. That's something, isn't it? Maybe I can't solve the world's problems—or even my own—but I can do this. *Memory honors them.*

I squeeze Leonara's hands and look at Augustina. "Tell your grandmother I will tell people."

Back in Palermo Viejo, I throw open my apartment door, invigorated with purpose, and fire up my computer. Instead of my usual blog, I write about the Madres.

> I whine daily about men and love and my poor broken heart on this blog, but the Madres de Plaza de Mayo know true heartbreak. These women have lost more than you or I can even begin to imagine. They have had their children, husbands, brothers taken from them wordlessly, darkly. "Disappeared." The word is terrifying. There was no warning, no recourse, and no closure to this horrible chapter in Argentine history, this unbearable hole in these women's lives. And yet here they are, week after week, marching so the perpetrators can't forget, so the world will remember. I hope you will remember them with me.

On the top right corner of my home page, I create a permanent banner that links to the Madres' website. "They need money," I write, "but also to be remembered." I hope their story has the same effect on my little community as it has had on me. After all, these virtual friends and the Madres are not so different. Reach out for help, even to strangers, and hands will reach back to you. The Madres have one another and their children and grandchildren and countrymen and, hopefully now, some of my blog readers, too.

As for me, it feels good to focus on someone other than myself, to think of something infinitely more important than where I'm going to live when I go back to Seattle in two months, how I'm going to pay the rent, or if I'll ever be able to step outside my front door without fear of running into Jeff and his soon-to-be bride. It feels so good that when I do think of these things, as I do constantly and unavoidably, they don't seem so wholly insurmountable. Today I dive into my scheduled daily Internet job hunt with unprecedented optimism. Surely, when you put good things out into the world, the world will bring good things back to you.

Unless folding sweaters at the Gap and running a hot dog stand are good things, my new theory doesn't hold much water. The only job in Seattle that looks even remotely related to my qualifications requires, ironically, fluency in Spanish. Two hours, seven job sites, six cover letters, and four versions of my résumé later, I am no closer to gainful employment. A quick e-mail check reveals no responses from yesterday's applications, either. Don't these people see what a great catch they're passing on? Cassie Moore, ex–Web producer, ex-fiancée, expat. How does one go about un-exing herself if no one wants her? My optimism gives way to sulking. Oh well, my old bedroom in my parents' house is always waiting for me. Why, just imagine all the eligible men who will be beating down the door to date me.

I curl up on the love seat, the cool evening air easing in through the French doors, and indulge my self-pity by contemplating throwing myself off the Juliet balcony. *Don't be ridiculous,* I hear Trish's mocking voice say. *It isn't in The Plan.*

A gust of warm, wet wind pushes across the darkening courtyard and into my room. The trees rattle. The French doors shudder. The air calms again. Did Andrea mention something about a storm coming today? Or tomorrow? Nervous about my final, repeating verb conjugations in my head, I was only half listening. "You know it's spring when the storms begin," she said. That must be it. There wasn't a cloud in the sky all day, and now this urgent humidity.

It reminds me of home. There was nothing better than falling asleep to the sound of heavy rain thumping against a window. I could use a good Seattle rain. I grab my purse and my cardigan from the back of the chair and head out into the dusk.

Beyond Andrea's courtyard, things are stormier than I expected. No rain yet, but the wind throws a tantrum against trees, screen doors, and garbage bags left on the sidewalk. My hair flies in every direction, settles, then flies out again. Old women latch shutters. Small children peer through upstairs windows. Transvestite hookers run for cover, holding their hair and skirts. The night is warm and wild and I love it. I button my cardigan to the top, wrap my arms tightly around my rib cage, and try not to think about how nice it would be to have someone walking beside me. For a moment I feel Jeff's long fingers lace through mine, the phantom limb of our severed relationship. I shake it out and hold tighter on to myself.

Not in the mood to be alone and surrounded by couples and groups, I head south toward the smaller, less popular plaza a few blocks west. I'm not sure what I'll do when I get there—have a coffee somewhere or maybe cry into a slice of pizza. Along the way, the universe, perhaps feeling bad about the whole job situation, offers up an ice cream parlor. The glowing pink HELADO sign hanging over the door is a welcoming beacon. Inside the startlingly fluorescent-lit room, empty except for the teenage boy behind the counter (the Buenos Aires equivalent of the Starbucks barista), I decide on four scoops of the chocolate almond—my favorite—and a huge fudge-dipped cone.

The boy raises his eyebrows. "*¿Cuatro?*" he asks.

"*Sí,*" I say, tempted to make it *cinco.* With my discount on Gap sweaters, hiding a few extra pounds should be no problem.

Out in the humid night again, it doesn't take long before the chocolate is oozing toward the cuff of my cardigan. I am mid-wrist-lick, tongue coiling around the back of my hand, when my eyes meet Mateo's. Three things stampede through my brain: I didn't return his message yesterday, wishing me luck on my Spanish test; he looks adorable with his hair twirling around in the wind; and who the hell is the woman with her elbow locked through his?

"*Hola,* Cassie," he says with a smile. What happened to Cassandra?

He leans in to kiss my cheek (letting go, I note, of the woman's arm) but stops short and laughs lightly. He rubs a thumb gently across my jawline and licks it. "Chocolate almond?"

"Of course." I return the laugh and pat my face with a napkin. Is it wrong that, for just a second, I wish I could rub the ice cream all over my body? "Thanks."

I look from him to the woman. She watches us expectantly, eyebrows raised. Everything about her is refined and lovely. Even her long straight brown locks seem to dance playfully in the wind. My hair sticks to my mouth, fingers, and ice cream cone in long, wet chunks.

"This is Anna." Mateo mumbles something to the woman in Spanish. She nods and smiles broadly. What did he say? *This is my friend's tenant. No one of importance. Just smile and we'll be on our way.*

"Hola," I say a bit too loudly. "*Me llamo* Cassie."

"*Encantada,*" she replies softly with a fragile smile and leans in for the obligatory kiss. This must be the kind of Argentine woman people talk about when they talk about Argentine women.

"So how did you do?" Mateo asks jovially. If I look as awkward as I feel, he doesn't seem to notice.

"With what?"

"Your test."

"Oh. I don't know. Okay, I guess." Before I am forced to elaborate, wind kicks up a bale of street detritus—leaves, plastic bags, shopping receipts, dirt—into the air around us. Sheltered by Mateo's height, the beautiful Anna is spared. With slim, manicured fingers, she removes a small leaf that made its way down her ample caramel-colored cleavage while Mateo and I brush debris from our arms and shake things from our hair, laughing.

"*Felicitaciónes.*"

"What?"

"Congratulations. On the test."

"Oh, right. Duh." I laugh at the irony of my ineptitude. What can only be called a snort erupts from my mouth. Anna grimaces, looking terribly embarrassed for me. Mateo laughs and pulls a piece of blue string from my hair.

"Well, it was good to see you, Cassie. I'm glad to hear your test went well. I really should get Anna home before this storm gets worse."

Why the formality? I wonder. For Anna's sake, no doubt. *I really should get Anna home.* That stings more than it should. You're the one who stopped returning his calls, I remind myself.

"You're on your way home, too, I hope." He looks at me with concern and presses his hand to my elbow when he says this. I almost drop my ice cream cone. There he goes again, acting all sweet and thoughtful and . . . Mateo threads his arm through Anna's. No, forget it, I'm not getting sucked into that fantasy again. Still, I can't help imagining what it would be like if I were the one on his arm tonight, his broad shoulders shielding me from the coming storm. In all the commotion, I've forgotten about my ice cream cone, which, besides the recently acquired topping of street grit, is seriously in jeopardy of collapsing into a pool of goo on the sidewalk. I know exactly how it feels.

"Yeah, I should get going, too," I squawk, trying to sound peppy, breezy. "Great to see you, too. *Buenas noches.*"

"*Buenas noches,*" he says softly.

Anna smiles cordially, and they move past me into the dark and muddled night.

The air is getting thicker by the second. I toss the cone into a garbage can and double my pace back to the yellow house. Every few feet, tiny tornadoes whip themselves and everything around them into frenzies. With no way to avoid it, I dip my head down and soldier on, continuously brushing bits of branches from my hair, images of Mateo and Anna from my head.

The streets are empty; not even the crazy motorcyclists have ventured out, Argentines all having the good sense to get inside when a storm is brewing. I seem to be the only one left in Palermo Viejo, the only one left in the world. But the solitude matches my mood perfectly. As long as I make it home before the rain starts.

Two blocks from the house, the air gets eerily, suspiciously still. And hot. Very, very hot.

Something hits my cheek gently. Then my collarbone. My knee. Forehead. Stomach. Thigh. Cheek. The hits come faster and faster. What it is or where it's coming from, I have no idea. It feels like I'm being pelted with small nuts from every direction. Something hits the sidewalk and windows and car hoods, making snapping sounds. Hail? I remember an afternoon in Seattle when I was four or five, chunks of ice the size of walnuts crashing down for mere minutes, my arms covered in tiny bruises, to my mother's dismay. Only when I pass a large brick house, security lights blaring, do I see that it isn't hail. Dozens of cockroaches the size of my thumb thrash through the fluorescent beam. They're flying! Those are giant flying cockroaches! I look down, and they are everywhere. Not dozens, hundreds. One hits my ear, and I can hear it fighting to free itself from my hair. I scream and shake my head, then clamp a hand over my scream. If one of these things gets in my mouth, I will die, I swear, right here on this empty Buenos Aires street. Now, there's a scenario I didn't think of.

My lips locked, my flip-flopped feet crunching down on grounded roaches, I run like I've never run before.

The swarm thins about a block from Andrea's, but I keep running until I'm safely behind the door. Inside the dark entrance hall, I hold my breath and shake my head, torso, and limbs furiously until I'm convinced all is clear. Nothing flapping in my hair, nothing clinging to my sweater, nothing thwacking against the walls. One hand over my thumping heart, the other feeling for the long bench that runs along the wall, I stretch my mouth and gulp at the air.

Small clicks on a wood floor announce Andrea before she appears. The lights flood on. Before she can get a word out, I fly across the hall and throw my arms around her.

"*¿Que pasa, chica?*" she asks with a smile in her voice, leaning back to get a good look at me.

"Bugs . . . big bugs," I manage to spurt out between deep breaths. "Cockroaches . . . huge . . . flying."

"Ah, *sí, sí, sí.*" Andrea nods knowingly. "Storm comes, they come." Okay, that's something she might have mentioned earlier.

As Andrea recounts the damage the last summer storm wreaked, I see something moving on the wall behind her.

"Oh, God." I point to the crawling brown spot. "There's one right there. Behind you. Oh, jeez, it's moving. Oh, God."

Andrea turns slowly. The roach scurries toward a crack in the stucco, but before it can reach its destination, a demure blue slingback does it in. The crumpled insect drops to the floor, leaving a smudge of blood on the white wall. "Ha!" Andrea exclaims proudly and continues with her story.

It takes two refills of maté and three non-bug-related stories for me to get the courage to go up to my apartment alone. They rarely find their way upstairs, she assures me. Unless I left the balcony window open. Did I leave the window open? I can't remember. Shit, shit, shit.

Does she want me to go up with her? she offers kindly.

"No, *gracias.*" I do want her to come upstairs with me, but I don't want her to think I am one of those women who fall apart at the sight of a tiny spider. Worse, I don't want her telling Mateo this later on. Anna is probably one of those women—and she probably looks lovely when she shrieks. But I am not one of those women. I am in Argentina, for God's sake! On the other side of the world! All alone! And I haven't been kidnapped or killed or anything! I will not let a bug send me into hiding!

Then again, those weren't tiny Seattle spiders out there. Those were huge flying Argentine cockroaches.

I move toward the stairs and think of the Madres, the shrunken Leonora and her sisters marching against all fear and doubt. I think of Andrea and her little blue shoe. My whole body shivers when I pass the smudge on the wall, but I keep going.

Thank God I remembered to close the window. Exhausted, I fall onto the bed with all the weight of the day. The air inside my suite is warm, but I can breathe easy. I slowly suck in air and let it out in a soothing gush. The next breath turns into a chuckle. The chuckle morphs into full belly laughter. Cassie Moore, ex–Web producer, ex-fiancée, expat, and brave survivor of flying cockroach attack. If Mateo could see me now, he'd surely push aside his lovely Anna for the chance to be with such a strong, fearless woman. I picture it in my head, giggling, and then shake off the silly thought.

Enough already. When will this crush go away? If I can (almost) get over Jeff in four months, I can stop thinking about Mateo—now. But then I remember the softness of his hand against my elbow, the concern in his eyes. God, I hope this is only a crush. Either way, I'll be back in Seattle soon enough. If I'm still set on messing up The Plan and ruining my life once I'm back, I'm sure I'll be able to find plenty of underemployed garage-band musicians to waste my time on.

It can't be all that late, and I am still fully clothed and covered in a thin layer of dirt and debris, but sleep comes, and who am I to argue with it. A Seattle version of Mateo—his hair is long and tied into a ponytail, his shirt plaid and untucked—is making me an extra-foam sugar-free vanilla cappuccino and telling me he likes my spunk when a loud buzzing sound blasts over the PA system. PA system? I come to and realize it's the phone ringing.

Mateo? My hands stumble over books, clock, hairbrush on the nightstand until they find the phone.

"Hello?" I say hopefully.

"*Hola, chica,*" says the peppy voice on the other end. Definitely not Mateo.

"Who is this?"

"It's Dan." Oh. Dan. "*¿Como estás?*" He pronounces every syllable so clearly, so Americanly. I was wrong: Spanish spoken with an American accent isn't sexy.

"Hi, Dan. I'm good, thanks. Just sort of . . ." I check the clock. 8:48 P.M. Jeez. "Napping."

"Oh, well, I don't want to bug you." *Bug.* The word gives me the heebie-jeebies. "I just wanted to see if you wanted to, I don't know, maybe get a bite to eat or something."

"Now?"

"If you're not busy."

I knew this was coming, and yet I am totally unprepared. He's so nice, and the stories about his ex-girlfriend are so awful. He rarely mentions her to me, but I've heard all the stories through Zoey and Julie. The poor guy has suffered enough. I can't bear to hurt his feelings.

"Well, there's a storm on its way." The French doors rattle ominously, as if to prove my point.

"Right, right. Best to stay put, then."

"Yeah."

"What about tomorrow?"

"Tomorrow's El Taller." There's a crash outside. Hopefully not one of Andrea's beloved sculptures.

"Course. Duh."

"But thanks for the—"

"The day after that?"

"Oh, well, maybe. I don't know." The French doors swing open violently and bash against the walls. "Oh, shit. Shit shit shit."

"What happened?"

"Shit." The balcony doors pop against the walls in a fit, glass panes warbling. I pull them closed and lock them this time. And put a chair in front of the latch. And sit on the chair.

"Are you okay?"

"No, not really."

"Should I come over?"

"No!" I say a little too emphatically. "No, I'm fine. Dan, can I get back to you?"

"Okay. Yeah, sure. You're a busy girl. No worries. As long as you're okay . . ."

He's talking so fast. Nerves, I guess. In the month or so that I've known him, I've never seen him with a girl outside the group or even heard him talk about one, except his ex. The last thing he needs is more rejection. I know that better than anyone. But will a pity date only make things worse in the long run? What if his crush turns into something real? We're supposed to be helping each other get over heartbreak, not cause more. Then again, he is kind of cute. And nice. And successful. Trish would say, *Don't waste your time. If you don't feel it, you don't feel it.* Sam would say, *What the hell, you never know.* Zoey would wait until after she'd had sex with him to make a final decision. The thought of having sex with Dan makes me uncomfortable. He's too . . . what? Maybe I don't feel a spark because I've been deluding myself about someone so completely unavailable. What if I give him a chance now that I've got all that Mateo nonsense behind me? Because it is behind me, right? Yes, behind me.

"Why don't I give you a call tomorrow?" he's saying. "You can let me know then."

He sounds so insecure, so fragile. I don't want to lead him on if I'm not sure. Best to nip this in the bud.

"Dan, I appreciate the offer. Really. It's just that I—"

"I'll call tomorrow, okay?" He hangs up before I can respond. Oh well, I'll deal with it tomorrow.

Tired, hungry, and still frazzled from my near-death-by-flying-cockroach experience, all I want to do is watch some bad TV. But The Plan doesn't allow for slacking. So I make a grilled cheese sandwich and rework my résumé while I eat. Trish, confidence bolstered by her recent career advancement, has sagely suggested that I add a list of achievements under each job. It seemed like a great idea at the time, but my "achievements" are looking pretty scant. How many different ways can I say "created a master spreadsheet" and "was a scheduling genius"?

Forty minutes and four million undos later, I realize with great pain that my boss was right. I did my job well, but I never did anything exceptional. No wonder she fired me. The realization is like an anvil falling on my head and setting off a series of land mines buried underneath. Does that mean Jeff was right to dump me, too? Was I as dull in our relationship as I was at work? All that time I spent being a perfect fiancée, doing all the perfect things a perfect fiancée does—should I have been different?

Andrea says Argentine women are famous for keeping their men guessing. They alternate affection and aloofness until the poor guy doesn't know whether he's coming or going. It's a point of pride, a game that keeps the passion alive. She's not like this with Martin, quite the opposite, actually, but maybe that's because they're separated all the time—the game of withholding is built into the relationship already. Anna, with her sweet smile and long dark hair, is probably a master at the game. And she's going home with Mateo while I'm sitting on my bed, hunched over my laptop, a hardening cheese sandwich balanced on one knee.

But games aren't in my nature. I am who I am. Straight talker. Plan maker. Creator of spreadsheets. I don't take risks. I don't run with scissors. I don't disappoint people. So why do I feel so disappointed in myself?

I'm roused from my thoughts by small scratching sounds, like nails on wood. *"Basta,"* I say toward the door, assuming it's little Chico looking for a fetch partner as usual. The scratching doesn't stop. I go to the door, but there's no dog behind it. The house is quiet down below. The sound is coming from inside the apartment. The wind is strong, and the house is old and, no doubt, full of drafts, loose boards, and other charmingly noisy quirks. I walk around the room, trying to locate the sound, but just when I think I've found it—beside the desk, under the table—it stops and starts up somewhere else.

As though it's moving.

I'm not sure I want to know what the noise is anymore, as long as it stops.

It doesn't stop, but it does park itself behind the headboard. The bed is heavy. I manage to pull it half a foot away from the wall and peek my head around slowly, eyes squinting protectively. There, looking up at me—if those are its eyes—is an enormous cockroach.

I jump back and hear it scurry down the wall and then, oh, dear God, under the bed. I grab the closest shoe and scramble onto the mattress. All is quiet for a moment. Then the scratching starts again. It's moving, I scream inside my head, it's moving! I lean over the edge of the bed, armed with the tennis shoe. A shiny brown head, antennae twitching, pokes out of the shadows into the light. The body follows. I take a deep breath. Oh, God, I pray, please don't move. Just stay right there. I raise the tennis shoe slowly, trying not to think about the sound of Andrea's roach crunching against the wall downstairs, like squishing a grape and a peanut M&M at the same time. Another deep breath. Steady, Cassie. Steady.

But it hears me (or maybe it smells my fear) and scuttles away, toward the armoire. I've got to kill it now or it'll be in there with my clothes, and that means there's a good chance I'll be wearing this cardigan and these capri pants for the next eight weeks. But it's too fast. Scared to get off the bed, I throw the shoe. It hits the floor three inches too far to the right, and the huge shiny brown flying cockroach slips safely under the armoire.

I reach gingerly for the other tennis shoe, careful not to touch the floor. I perch on the foot of the bed, armed with the second tennis shoe, and watch the floor near the armoire for signs of movement.

"Please stay there," I whisper to my new roommate. "I'll stay here if you'll stay there." I sit like this until there is a crack in the sky and the courtyard beyond the French doors floods with light. The rain comes down hard. The sound is a relief. It drowns out everything else.

I reach for the phone and dial.

"*¿Hola?*"

"Okay. Dinner. I'll go out with you. If you still want to."

"Of course I still want to," Dan says with a chuckle. "I'll pick you up Friday at nine."

We say good night. Dan hangs up. I fall asleep in a ball at the end of the bed, still clutching the phone in one hand and the tennis shoe in the other.

CHAPTER THIRTEEN

*O*ur Spanish course over, Zoey is going home, and I am already missing my smart, funny, stylish friend. I'd known that she wasn't here forever—none of us is—but her imminent absence has still come as a shock to me. At our last meal together, surrounded by a dozen new and old friends, we fail miserably at our promise not to cry. As Rick from Calgary rounds the table, refilling everyone's glasses with red wine, and Gina from Texas recounts the calamitous tale of her first post-divorce date with a taxidermist who gave her a stuffed chipmunk in lieu of flowers, Zoey and I huddle antisocially in the corner and play the "remember when" game.

"Remember when you first met Antonio?" she says. "Your face went bright red, and you could barely talk to him all through lunch."

"Remember when that guy grabbed your arm and pulled you onto the dance floor?" I giggle. "I've never seen somebody flail his arms with such talent."

These things may have happened only months or weeks ago, but it is our only history, so we hold on to every memory with both hands. It's all we have. At the end of Gina's story, we are wet-faced and hysterical. "It wasn't that funny," the Texan insists. We both burst into laughter.

Zoey and I promise to visit each other back home and to e-mail constantly, but behind these promises we harbor the unspoken truth that the friendship we embraced so voraciously here—for travelers, I have learned, must be voracious with their friend-ships—won't be easily re-created on a Seattle pier or a New York subway.

"This was the best time, you know," she whispers to me the next morning as we wait for her taxi to the airport to arrive. "Nothing will be the same as Buenos Aires."

She didn't tell me that Buenos Aires wouldn't be the same, either. Without my new best friend, the sheen has been stripped from everything, and the city seems a little grayer, a little duller, a little less Zoey. Just when I thought I was getting to know Buenos Aires so well, the city turns on her beautifully crafted leather heels and disappears. When I stroll the streets of Palermo Viejo, I see only cracked foundations, loose stones, piles of dog crap crumbling in the South American sun. The history, the beauty, has evaporated in the fierce heat. The late-spring sun beats down on the sagging city, and the endless blue sky is a heavy blanket I can't shake.

Not to sound like a weathergirl, but the heat in Buenos Aires has gotten positively oppressive. Or maybe it just feels hot in comparison to M's chilly treatment these days. If any of you has any lingering doubts about my reasons for backing away—because I like to flatter myself with thinking there was something between us to back away from—he has made them moot. Aside from the concern he displayed on the street that night of the storm, he has become distant, almost unfriendly. Right back where we started.

Okay, I probably should have called him the next day to say I'd made it home alive, like he asked me to, but I'd have had to ask about Anna, out of politeness, and I'd rather shave my head than listen to M going on about his great new relationship. So hiding in my stuffy apartment all afternoon the following day was maybe a bit juvenile, but when I heard M downstairs, helping install a new security system, I panicked. And yes, sitting slumped down in my seat to avoid making eye contact with him the other night at El Taller wasn't my finest hour, either, but it seems easier to avoid him altogether.

Besides, not having to think about M and what he's feeling has freed up an unbelievable amount of time that is better spent on getting my new plan going. I really think things are turning around.

I don't tell my blog readers that I miss Mateo—our talks, his quick wit, his devilish smile, his passionate cynicism. I hardly like to admit it to myself. What's the point? Whatever my reasons for avoiding him, Mateo seems to have given in to them easily enough. He has stopped calling, stopped knocking on my door in the middle of the day to see if I want to go for coffee. That night at El Taller, he knew my group was there but never came over to say hello. I was relieved and disappointed.

And now I've gone and made things worse. I was heading out for a cup of coffee this morning, suffering through a massive caffeine craving because I'd run desperately low on groceries, and there he was, looking far too good in a tight T-shirt and jeans, oiling the hinges of the French doors in Andrea's great hall. I was surprised to see him—couldn't Martin take care of something that simple now that he was home?

"*Hola,*" I said weakly.

"*Hola,*" he returned abruptly. Then, his face softening into something resembling a smile, he asked if I might want to go for a cup of coffee. "It's been awhile."

I offered the lame but conveniently true excuse about needing groceries.

"I'll come with you," he offered, but I insisted I was fine by myself.

"No need for both of us to go out in this heat."

He nodded slowly and turned back to his work. I watched him fiddle with his tools for a second or two, then caught myself and slipped out the front door.

I walked for over a mile, finally settling on a café where I have sat for almost three hours nursing one giant café con leche after another. How things have changed, I muse. When I first arrived I couldn't get over how rude and unwelcoming Mateo was, picking over each new injury he seemed to throw my way. Now I am the one shunning his friendship. Every week I befriend a tableful of strangers, but with Mateo, this simple thing seems too risky. Dangerous.

And yet the time I spend with Dan doesn't scare me in the least. Isn't that how you know when someone is right for you? When he makes you feel perfectly at ease all the time?

We've spent several days together, and while I'd be hard-pressed to find a single thing wrong with Dan, something isn't right. He's great. Really, really great. Smart, fun, toothachingly sweet, ambitious but not obsessively so, and clearly into me. But I don't feel it. And though I might not know exactly what "it" is, I sure as hell know when it's missing. When Mateo's eyes landed on mine from across the hall this morning, it was like a lightning bolt had shot straight through me. My mouth went dry, my palms damp. When he gave up on me and turned back to his toolbox, I felt as though all that energy had instantly drained out and onto the floor. Okay, so Mateo isn't the guy for me, so I'm crushing on him like a teenage girl—does that mean I should settle for less than that feeling with someone else?

Can't I have at least a little Mateo with my Dan?

Everything is backward here, is my theory. On the other side of the world, you can't trust your impulses. How else to explain my temporary insanity those first months here, or why Dan—a sort of Jeff 2.0 but with all the bugs removed—doesn't quite do it for me? If I'd met Dan in Seattle instead of Buenos Aires, as Trish has suggested, I might feel differently. Maybe after the sexual whirlwind of Antonio and the emotional confusion of Mateo, a decent, earnest, available guy like Dan doesn't stand a chance. Then again, aren't you supposed to fall faster in foreign places? Isn't that the whole idea of the travel fling? Yet when I'm with Dan, there's no denying it: I don't want to be flung.

I take a final sip of coffee and start the trek back to the yellow house.

Reaching Andrea's, I listen for sounds of tinkering but don't hear anything. Just in case, I slink through the great iron gate as quietly as one can after consuming the yearly coffee export of Colombia. Only inside do I hear Mateo in the foyer, wrestling with the wires of the old chandelier that burns through bulbs every few weeks. The iron door latch thuds into place behind me, and he looks up from his work. He eyes my suspiciously empty hands. I realize that I don't have any grocery bags with me. "Get lost?"

"Oh, yeah. Ha!" I look around the room, vying for time. "Actually, I forgot my wallet."

"You've been gone for three hours," he points out.

"I went for a walk." His strong, accusatory gaze makes me squirm. "Lost track of time."

Mateo doesn't say a word, only nods curtly and turns back to his work. I climb the stairs to my apartment quickly, exaggerating my steps to drown out the sound of tools clanking in his toolbox.

I sit on my bed and kick off my shoes. What must Mateo be thinking? He's probably happy that he's free of the crazy American. I sigh. Oh, well. That's the way you wanted it, right?

Head buzzing with coffee, I wake up my laptop and see an e-mail waiting from acucher@hotmail.com. "Thank You! Thank You! Thank You!" she shouts at me from the subject line. I don't realize who it's from until I've read a ways.

Dearest Cassie,

What you have done is a wonderful thing. By telling people about our cause on your website you make us known and this is very important. Some people have sent money to help. Many people write with good thoughts. A reporter is going to tell everyone about us in a newspaper! Thank you for caring about the Madres. Please come and visit us again soon. We all love you.

Augustina

I stare at the screen for a long while, taking it in. I never expected much to come of that quiet plea on my little blog. An hour or so of time, a few square inches on a Web page. Nothing, really. But I'm glad to have helped, if only in some small way. I'm trying to express this in the simplest terms to Augustina in my reply when there's a knock at my door.

Mateo calls my name softly.

Maybe it's all the coffee, but my heart jumps into my throat at the sound. Between leaping from my bed and wrapping my shaking hand around the doorknob, the next few minutes spin out wildly before me. Screw The Plan! I will apologize for avoiding him, will throw my arms around him and beg him to forgive me for being so stupid. He will tell me it doesn't matter, that everything is going to be okay. We will kiss a kiss to put every romantic kiss to shame, and he will lift me up and take me back to the rumpled bed. Grinning madly, I open the door and there he stands, an Argentine god, a slash of black grease on his forehead, his beautiful green eyes locked on mine. I can almost taste his lips on my lips, smell his skin against my skin.

"Mateo." I inhale and hold the letters on my tongue, expectant, readying myself. For a moment, a long moment, he doesn't speak, just stares at me, unreadable.

Finally, he says, "There's someone here to see you."

I exhale, deflated.

"Oh." And then I remember—Dan insisting on the phone this morning that he would pick me up and walk with me to El Taller. "That must be my friend Dan." I'm not sure why I feel the need to explain, but the explanation has little effect on Mateo anyway. He doesn't say another word, just slips away down the dark stairs.

First Antonio, now Dan. I can only imagine what Mateo thinks of me. Or worse, that maybe he doesn't think of me at all.

I check myself in the mirror. My face is flushed, my chest splotchy. I look away quickly, embarrassed once again at this man's ability to turn me into a silly schoolgirl, at how ready I am to throw everything away. And for what? A man who lives on the other side of the world. A man who doesn't believe in happily ever after. A man who will forget about me the moment I step on that plane in December. You'd think I would have learned from Antonio. Am I really willing to set myself back to where I started—with nothing and no one—for another fling with a man I can have no future with?

It's the coffee, I tell myself. The stuff's like crack here. It's got me all jittery and jumpy and confused. Gotta watch that. I pat back a loose lock of hair, grab my purse, and slip into my sandals. Dan is waiting. He might not be my dream man, I tell myself, but there could be potential. At the very least, he won't get in the way of the dream. I repeat this in my head on my way down the stairs.

As we walk to the café, Dan talks and I nod. He could be confessing he's Seattle's Green River Killer, and I wouldn't have a clue. Inside my head, I am doing battle with the image of Mateo at my door. I conjure up Jeff's face, a sort of aversion therapy. There will be no more time wasted on inappropriate men. There will be no more time wasted, period.

Dan says something that sounds like a question, so I say, "Sure." Then his hand, warm and dry, is lacing itself through mine. What did I just agree to? I look at him for some clue. He looks straight ahead, grinning widely. Not knowing how to extricate my hand without hurting his feelings, I leave it there.

By the time we reach El Taller, Dan is positively beaming. But I can't possibly walk into the café like this. Everyone will think we are a couple. Are we a couple? No, that's silly. This is just a distraction. I mean, we haven't even kissed yet.

But Dan is smiling an awful lot.

I break free from his hand at the café entrance, making a show of opening the door with two hands. Dan puts an arm around my shoulders. I break free again and make an even bigger show of saying hello to all the regulars and welcoming all the newcomers. Dan, unflappable, doesn't seem to mind that I plant myself at the opposite end of the table—he simply gets up, asks Jeremy from Alaska to shift over one, and plants himself beside me. I promised myself I wouldn't lead Dan on, but I wasn't prepared for him to lead himself.

But my concerns about Dan are quickly replaced by something far more perturbing. As we make our toast, I sense someone behind me. I turn quickly, nearly spilling my beer on Mateo, who stands inches from my elbow. He is grinning that devilish grin, but tonight it looks more sinister than playful.

"Well, well," he says loudly. "If it isn't the Buenos Aires Broken Hearts Club."

The group bursts into approving laughter.

"It appears that some of you are less heartbroken than others." With that, he looks at me sharply, then at Dan, his smile flattening into a tight line. A few people snicker, catching the joke. Dan, beaming at the acknowledgment, seems to grow three inches taller in his seat. I want to crawl under the table and stay there until everyone leaves. Instead I sit perfectly still, my beer frozen in the air, a wholly unbelievable smile stretched across my face.

Mateo smiles warmly at the group. "Can I get anyone another

drink?" Drink orders erupt from around the table. Mateo laughs and puts his hand on our waitress's arm as she passes by, signaling her to take over. Jamie, a fun, busty woman from Vancouver with a booming voice, tries to get him to stay. He declines politely. Too much paperwork to do tonight. Yeah, right.

"Buenos Aires Broken Hearts Club," says Tony, laughing. He rarely laughs. "That's hilarious."

"Fucking brilliant!" declares Jamie above the din of chitchat and beer pouring. "I love it!" I had considered making Jamie my new Buenos Aires best friend, but I am seriously rethinking that.

Mike from Arizona proposes a new toast. "To the Buenos Aires Broken Hearts Club."

"That's not the toast," I whine, but no one hears me.

"To the Buenos Aires Broken Hearts Club," replies a chorus of voices. All around me, glasses clink.

I'm not in the mood for a crazy night out, not that anyone even asks me along anymore. *We know it's not in The Plan.* When the others get organized to check out the infamous drag show at a local nightclub, I head out the door.

Outside, I feel a hand on my shoulder. Dan. Sweet, well-intentioned, hand-holding, perma-smiling Dan. On the walk home, with Dan as my chaperone, I keep my hands jammed as far as they'll go into the shallow pockets of my pants. Seemingly oblivious, he chats happily about the tourist sights he wants to visit before he leaves. It gives me time to dissect the scene from earlier. What did Mateo mean by that Buenos Aires Broken Hearts Club crack, anyway? Was it supposed to be clever or mean? "Who does he think he is to judge me like that?"

"Who does *who* think he is?"

"Oh, sorry. Nothing. Just thinking out loud."

"Are you talking about that Matthew guy?"

"Mateo."

"Whatever."

"I was thinking about what he called us. It seemed sort of like an insult, didn't it?"

"Buenos Aires Broken Hearts Club?"

"Yeah."

"Kind of funny, I guess. He's your friend, isn't he? I'm sure he didn't mean anything by it. Things get lost in translation."

"No. No, it was definitely an insult. And he's not my friend. Not anymore. Clearly."

"Oh." Dan's voice lifts a notch, and his face brightens visibly. "Well, then, who cares what he calls us?"

"You're right, Dan. Absolutely right. He can think whatever he wants. I couldn't care less, to tell you the truth."

"I'm glad to hear it," he says, looking down at me, earnest and hopeful. I change the subject to my fruitless job hunt. Nothing romantic about that.

A block later, Dan stops abruptly and wraps his hands around my biceps. Those earnest, hopeful eyes again. "Cassie, I—I like you a lot. I'm sure that's completely obvious to you, but—"

I have to stop him before he goes any further, for his sake and mine. If he says too much, he won't be able to stand the sight of me again.

"Dan," I begin gently. "You're a great guy. I just don't think of you that way." Even as it comes out of my mouth, it sounds so trite, I wish I could take it back and start again. I shuffle, search the ground for better words, but they aren't to be found. "I go back to Seattle in seven weeks. You go back to Boston in five. We shouldn't get attached."

"Oh," he says and lets go of my arms. "I thought maybe—"

"I'm sorry if I've given you the wrong impression." It's too hard to look him in the eyes. Those earnest, hopeful eyes. They're kind of nice, a soft brown with bits of gold. Still, I catch myself wondering what he'd look like if they were green.

"No, you haven't. Not really. But I was hoping." He stares intently at a spot on the sidewalk to my right.

"I do like spending time with you." Ugh. Trite again. "But if you have other expectations, maybe we shouldn't hang out anymore." I feel like I'm reciting from the Brush-off Manual. "Chapter 1: How to Crush His Spirit in 3 Easy Steps."

"No, it's fine. I get it. Hey, I gave it a shot. You never know how these things are going to turn out. That's half the fun, right?" His eyes dart from sidewalk to tree to hooker on the corner to my elbow to sidewalk. I know it's bullshit, but I take it gladly. He's obviously read "Chapter 2: How to Play It Cool When You've Just Been Crushed."

"Sure, I guess."

"Don't give it another thought. Anyway, I was thinking we should check out the Teatro Colón this week. There's all these levels, and you can go backstage and see how everything's made. What do you think?"

"That sounds like fun." I encourage his ramblings on medieval costume making for the remaining two blocks, thanking God for the fragile but resilient male ego.

At my door, I can relax. Home free. I turn to say good night and realize midpivot that I have no idea what the appropriate form of salutation is in this situation. Do I kiss his cheek and risk his taking that the wrong way? Do I shake his hand and make him feel like a complete jerk? I settle on a quick one-armed hug. But when I pull back, Dan doesn't. We stay locked like that, my chest curled away from his, an awkward gap between us, for too long. If I could will myself to want his touch, I would, for his sake. He releases me and steps back. "Is it that guy at the café?"

"Is what the guy at the café?"

"Is that why you . . . Are you and he . . ."

"No, not at all. I told you, we're just friends." Why am I always having to convince people of this fact? I see Mateo poised above me, his lip curling smugly as he releases his barb. "Well, we *were* just friends."

"Is there someone back home?"

I think of Jeff, picture him with Lauren. They're naked and on my old bed. She plays the cello, her long white legs wrapped around it, Jeff's long tan legs wrapped around her. There's a veil on her head. He wears a black bow tie. I wonder briefly if they're married yet. I let the image slip into the dark night. Goodbye, Jeff.

"Nope," I say. "No one back home."

"So there's no one here and there's no one there."

"There's no one." I breathe deeply, involuntarily, sucking in the suckiness of my far-from-stellar future. I want to be one of the transvestite prostitutes cackling under the streetlamp at the end of the block. I want to curl up in a ball on the sidewalk and fall asleep there forever. And at this moment, just a little, I want Dan's arm around me again. "No one at all, really."

"Then can I ask you something?" Dan inches closer, almost un-detectably. Those few cautious inches wouldn't amount to much if I weren't, against my better judgment, doing the same.

"Sure. Shoot."

"Will you at least consider it?"

"Consider what?" I know exactly what he means, but I want to hear him say it. I want someone to want me.

"Consider us. Don't take it completely off the table? Because I think there could be something really good here. I think you might be the most amazing person I've ever met."

I start to laugh at the idea, but Dan isn't laughing. Gone are the puppy-dog eyes. He stares at me, focused, intent. He's rather handsome when he's serious like this, I note. But it's not his classic bone structure so much as his resolve. What does he see that I don't? Am I so blinded by my infatuation with the wrong guy, I wonder, that I can't see something truly great in front of me?

"Cassie," Dan says, his voice low and deep. "I think I could really fall for you."

The words floor me. There it is, right in front of me: the possibility of being loved again.

Dan steps closer, so close we are almost touching. His hands cup my face and draw it up to his. He leans in, slow and tentative, until our lips are touching. It's not a long kiss or the best kiss—a bit dry from too much wine—but it is earnest and hopeful, and now, right now, I find earnestness and hope utterly irresistible. Without a word, I open the great iron door, lead Dan inside, up the stairs, into my apartment and my bed.

It's nothing like my nights with Antonio, nothing like how I've imagined a night with Mateo might be. Every move, both his and mine, is urgent and hurried, as though he is afraid I will change my mind. As though I am afraid of the same thing.

CHAPTER FOURTEEN

Did you know that most employers get more than a hundred applications for every job opening? This is just one of the many daunting stats I've come across in my job-hunting research. But wait, it gets worse: Even if you're lucky enough that someone actually notices your résumé in the slush pile, chances are he or she will read only the very top bit and the very last bit. I was thinking maybe I should send out a résumé with the complete lyrics to Gloria Gaynor's "I Will Survive" buried in the middle section of my employment history and see if anyone notices. I might not get a job, but at least I'll grow strong, and I'll learn how to carry on.

No wonder my blog readers have lost all interest in me, with subject matter like this. I've tried to add some spice to my detailed descriptions of job hunting or how I've decided to spend my first month back in Seattle, but there's no way to make life under The Plan anything more than it is. No wonder mylife@bluestudio.uk, blondie261@earthvibe.com, and the rest of my former fan club are vastly more content to entertain one another via the comment function of my website. At first they used my less than titillating tales as a jumping-off point to splay open their own (generally unrelated) experiences for public consumption and commentary. Now they don't even bother with the formality of polite illusion. They simply disregard what I've written and start in on their own infinitely more interesting lives. They're discussing heartbreak and healing, and I'm debating the merits of various résumé formats and font sizes. Jeez, even I don't want to read my blog anymore.

I'd stop altogether, but with almost a thousand hits and hundreds of comments made each day, the site serves a purpose greater than anything I could have imagined when I first put fingers to laptop. This growing family of broken hearts might not need my story to bring them together, but they still need one another.

C.J., my code-writing genius friend back home, has volunteered to build me a fancy new site, one with a designated place where readers can chat with one another. I'll still keep the blog, I've decided—I'm not quite ready to lose all evidence of my time here—but it won't be the main focus anymore. Like so many other things in my life, my website has outgrown me.

Which means I'll have more time to plan my return home. Which gives me more dull things to write about. So really, everyone wins.

It did occur to me on a few occasions (like when one of the less sensitive readers wondered why I got "so freaking lame all of a sudden," provoking a flurry of theories about parental coddling, sexual frustrations, and serotonin levels that I'd sooner forget) that I might catch the attention of my wayward audience with a few titillating tidbits about Dan and me. It also occurred to me that I'd have to embellish a great deal to get those tales to the level of interesting, never mind titillating. Why that is, I can't quite put my finger on. It's not that I don't enjoy Dan's company. We do have a nice time together, and I generally look forward to our excursions to museums, parks, and other must-see places on our blended lists. He's a great guy, really great. In a lot of ways, the perfect man. He has direction, good values, goals that are similar to mine. The couple of times we had sex, it wasn't all that bad. For a broker from Boston, he can be rather frisky. I don't ache to touch him, though. You should ache to touch someone you're sleeping with, shouldn't you?

But then maybe this is what a husband is supposed to be like. Solid. Dependable. Beige.

"Do you want a husband or Jude Law?" Zoey asked over instant messaging the other day. "Wait, dumb question."

My mother, who thinks Jude Law has something to do with the penal code, would be gaga for Dan. He is everything she holds dear in the world: stability, reliability, security, and every other synonym for "not going to leave my daughter for his secretary." I should have known better than to tell her about him during my last phone call home. She went from excited to anxious in sixty seconds flat. "Men like this come along once in a lifetime, Cassie!" And then: "For God's sake, please tell me you're not wearing that ratty blue sweater around him." I almost remind her that it's three thousand degrees here, but why ruin her favorite pastime: imagining how I'm screwing up my life even worse than it already is.

Funny thing is, I think as she swings into the story of how the neighbor's daughter snagged herself a nice optometrist with a house in Capitol Hill, Dan is sort of like my ratty blue sweater: comfortable, easy, safe. Being with him is like being at home. We speak the same language—that of suburb commutes and CNN, Starbucks, and 401(k)s. Plus, Dan totally gets The Plan.

"I think your plan is terrific," he said as we waited in line for movie tickets one night. "If you don't know what your goals are, how do you know when you've reached them?"

"He likes The Plan because he thinks he's part of it," wrote Zoey in a recent e-mail.

"He hasn't said anything to even suggest that he thinks this is going anywhere," I protested.

"Oh, he will. That boy fell hard before you even knew his name."

"We're just having fun together," I shot back. "He's got a life back home. And I've got to get one."

"And I'm telling you he's gonna drop the L-bomb any day now."

"You are so wrong," I wrote.

"And you are so in DENIAL."

I didn't tell Zoey about the CD he made for me. Nor did I mention the morning he got up early, bought groceries, and made me breakfast in bed. But no, Zoey's just being dramatic. Maybe Dan has fallen for me a little, but it's only an innocent, I'm-getting-over-my-ex-and-need-someone-to-distract-me kind of crush. Everyone who meets at El Taller is looking for distraction. Besides, how deep can feelings grow when they obviously aren't returned?

I try not to think about it while I get ready for our afternoon trip to the Teatro Colón, but I find myself dressing even more conservatively than usual, and there's no denying why. The loose ponytail and boatneck T-shirt are a message to Dan that if I were really into him, I'd be trying harder. The tennis sneakers scream, "Just friends!" My preference for clear gloss over lipstick apologizes, "I'm sorry, but I don't feel that way about you."

I've done everything I can to keep things as light as possible with Dan. I constantly talk about what I'll do when I'm home in Seattle. He talks about Boston. No, there will be no soulful gazing into each other's eyes nor furtive hand-holding nor long, awkward goodbyes at my door late at night. Which I suppose means there will be no more of that for me at all while I'm here. That's fine, I tell myself. There'll be plenty of time for romance once I've got things sorted out back in the real world.

I offer one last sigh to the mirror and head downstairs to wait for Dan outside. When I open the front door, I can barely see him for the humongous bouquet of roses he's holding. There must be at least thirty of the small bunches that are sold everywhere on the street. He must have bought out an entire flower stand.

"I couldn't resist," he says, grinning like a little boy. "They were so beautiful, I immediately thought of you."

It is precisely the kind of thing that I've always dreamed of a guy doing for me, yet I can feel my face pulling down instead of up, the way I know it should be. I should be thrilled or at least pleased, but I feel mildly annoyed, as though Dan has broken some unspoken pact, pushed me into a corner. Something is wrong with me. I cover my irritation with a brief kiss. I don't want to hurt his feelings.

"You're such a sweetheart," I say, hoping it doesn't sound as patronizing as I think it does. "Thank you so much. Let me put these in some water."

I run the flowers upstairs to find a vase. The closest thing I can find that's big enough to hold them is a giant salad bowl. I shake my head at the sad sight of Dan's beautiful roses bobbing helplessly in the wooden bowl. I can't help feeling a twinge of guilt. Dan is a dear, sweet guy. Why am I being so careless with something so precious? So I'm not head over heels. It's not every day that a guy as great as Dan comes along. *Men like this come along once in a lifetime.* And occasionally, romantic feelings take time to bloom, don't they? I'm not sure how I feel about the roses—or Dan—but I pull out my ponytail, give my hair a good shake, and swipe on a quick coat of red lip gloss. Just in case.

Aside from the supersize flowers, my day with Dan is, predictably, predictable. We tour the inner workings of the great Buenos Aires opera theater with a group of Germans, Swedes, and other Americans. I play along, the dutiful tourist, listening closely to the guide, consulting the program we were handed at the entrance, nodding and oohing and aahing at this costume dummy or that giant sewing machine. It's like faking an orgasm.

Halfway through the tour, I remember Zoey's excitement months ago at happening upon a cheap performance here. Puccini for three dollars. She skipped the tour. Or, more likely, the idea of a tour never occurred to her. The tour always occurs to me.

The theater is certainly impressive, with floor after floor opening onto a world of production, from the massive set design area to rows of sewing machines where meticulous costumes are crafted to make every performance spectacular. It's a beautiful old building from any angle, and I know I should be more captivated, more thrilled, by it all, snapping continuous photos like the others in the tour group, but it all seems a little empty, a little—pardon the pun—staged.

"Aren't you enjoying this?" Dan asks, concerned. I lie and say I am, snapping a photo to prove it. He smiles approvingly and turns his attention back to the guide. We might be getting an insiders' look, but we are still outsiders, viewing it from the outside. It doesn't come near the way I once felt wandering the streets of Buenos Aires, each turn unfolding something new, something unexpected. The simplest things filled me up. Mateo would point out an interesting architectural feature or maybe a home of someone he's known forever, and I'd ask a zillion questions about what it was like to grow up in Argentina. Even lazing about at random cafés, listening to Mateo's stories, meeting his friends on the street, soaking up the city at its own pace, I experienced a cultural immersion you can't stand in line for or take pictures of.

I begin to explain this to Andrea when I get home from the theater. She nods with understanding.

"Me, I never did any of these tourist things when I come here," she says, shaking her head emphatically and fanning herself at the same time. I pour a glass of iced tea for her. "But I still don't do them. That's not the real Buenos Aires."

She takes a sip and smacks the table between us, smiling wide. Jorge, napping on the lounge chair beside her, flicks his fist at the air in protest. "I have the best idea for you. You must take a tango class!" Jorge opens an eye. The dogs come running.

"Tango? Oh, no, I couldn't." Chico jumps up and nuzzles my hand. He was Andrea's baby before Jorge came along. I scratch his chin. He loves this. His stub of a tail twitches happily. If only all men were this easy. "I'm a horrible dancer. Three left feet. The doctors tell me it's incurable."

Andr .] ighs and shakes her head. "No, I don't believe you. You must go. You must! Don't you think so, Jorge?" Still sleepy, and mildly accosted by two licking dogs, he crawls over to his mother and up into her lap. He eyes me quizzically, as though we've just met. "And there is a class tonight, very close to here. Oh, yes, you must go!"

I want to remind her that the last time she insisted on my taking a class, it didn't work out so well. Though it's hardly Andrea's fault that my inability to dance is surpassed only by my inability to learn Spanish. Reluctantly, I agree to tango, hoping this will absolve me of at least the latter.

But I'm not going alone. No, sir. I call Dan so I have an instant dance partner, warning him to wear steel-toed shoes. I call Jamie, too. She might be a bit brash, but she's fun. She's been wanting to meet more locals, so she's thrilled by the idea. "What does one wear to tango?" she ponders on the phone.

"A rose in your teeth?" I offer.

What does one wear to tango? I pull on a flippy little skirt, a black shell, and strappy high-heeled sandals and twist my hair back into a tight bun. I'll need a complete field of vision tonight.

Dan and Jamie both show up in jeans. Jamie's are topped with a revealing black camisole and a pair of swishy earrings. I tell them to wait while I change, but they won't hear of it.

"You look amazing," Dan gushes. "Really, really amazing."

Jamie agrees enthusiastically. "*Mucho* Argentina." Her compliment makes me smile. She moves up a level on the friend-o-meter.

"Yeah, she's right." Dan looks at me as though for the first time, tilting his head, puzzled. "You do sort of look like you belong here."

That settles it. I don't change. At the class—held, curiously, in the basement of an Armenian community center a few blocks away—almost everyone is wearing jeans. Only the instructor, a striking older woman who's had too much plastic surgery—Dan calls it the Tango Special—is wearing a dress and heels. When she spots me, tucked in behind Dan and another tall guy in a blue T-shirt, she looks me up and down and nods approvingly, saying something in Spanish that I can't understand. Let's hope she remembers that she once liked the look of me after she sees me dance.

Luckily, it's easy to hide my footwork in the massive group of beginners on our side of the hall. It's so crowded, Dan actually thinks I'm good, blaming other couples for the constant assault on his feet. But then Dan's not exactly Fred Astaire. "If we had a little more room, you could really show them your stuff," he says. I smile and step on his foot. He grins proudly.

A few rounds of the dance floor, and I've mastered the first two steps. For the other fourteen, I kind of wing it. I suspect a step or two from high school square dancing has made it in there somewhere (nothing wrong with a little cross-cultural exchange). Meanwhile, Jamie, in the hands of a cute young Argentine with a scruffy mullet, is shuffling, turning, and heel-toeing in perfect sync with him. She talks to her partner while she dances. She doesn't count to herself, scrunch her forehead, or bite her lip. The instructor passes Jamie and nods approvingly. When the instructor sees me plodding along, she smiles weakly and moves on to someone she can help improve: an octogenarian with a limp. Ah, it was nice while it lasted.

The music stops and we all switch partners. Jamie gets another cute Argentine. "Isn't this a blast?" she shouts to me over the teacher's introductions. I get the impression that Jamie would have fun whatever she was doing. Brash or not, it's hard not to like her. Dan, glancing apologetically in my direction, has landed in the arms of a giggly teenager. I have no one. There are too many women in the class. I turn to join the wallflowers along the edge of the dance floor—grade-ten high school dance all over again—when I feel someone's hand on my wrist. Please, I pray, don't let it be that greasy-looking guy with the unbuttoned shirt and chest hair who was eying me earlier. Please, oh, please.

It's not the greasy guy. It's Mateo. He's dressed sharply in black, his hair smoothed back from his face, which wears a subtle stubble. For a second I think I must be dreaming. His voice snaps me out of it.

"Cassie. I wasn't sure that was you."

"Well, it is."

"What are you doing here?"

"Am I not allowed to be here?"

"I didn't mean—"

"Of course." I look over his shoulder and see Anna watching us intently. I find Dan in the crowd and wave, but he is too busy watching his footwork to see me.

"It's just . . ." His eyes move down my outfit and back up to my eyes, looking almost pleased. He smiles wickedly. His hand, I realize, is still on my arm. Oh, no. I'm not falling for that again.

Anna's eyes are still trained on us, yet she looks more amused than jealous. I guess I wouldn't be much of a threat to her, would I? Mateo leans in as though to whisper a secret. I can feel his breath against my bare neck. "I see you don't have a partner," he says.

Rub it in, I think. "I'm fine," I say, looking for Dan. The music has started again, and I can see his head across the room, bent in deep concentration. His poor partner. "I was getting tired, anyway." I'm not going to be his charity case. That, and there's no way Mateo is going to see me dance. Oh, God, I think, maybe he already has. I reprimand myself once more. So what if he has? Good. Great. Perfect.

"Scared of me?" That devil's smile again, unnervingly sexy and slightly infuriating.

"Yeah, right." I chortle. "Sure. Okay. Why not?"

"Why not," he repeats.

On the dance floor, Mateo draws me in close to him, much closer than demonstrated by the instructor, his hand pressing against the arch in my back. He starts to move, falling effortlessly into the music, and I attempt to follow. I can tell he is very good, far beyond our beginner group, and I hope he can't tell that I am very bad. The crowd is my only salvation. We trip over other couples, they trip over us.

Mateo never falters. He holds his head tilted up, his neck elongated, jaw firm. There's no denying it: Tango looks good on him. Women young and old misstep, craning their necks to get a good look. Men clumsily sweep their partners away from the distracting view. He is oblivious to the attention—oblivious, it seems, to everything but our small sphere of dance floor—until a large man's protruding bum almost knocks him to the ground.

Mateo recovers with a laugh and suggests we move to the outside of the circle. I hesitate, thinking of my embarrassing feet, and of Dan, who is buried somewhere on the other side of the room, but Mateo doesn't wait for an answer. He pulls me after him, his arm warm around my waist. The women around us sigh visibly with disappointment.

Finding a clear spot on the floor, Mateo waits for the right point to enter the music, looks at me intently, and steps forward. Right on my foot.

"Sorry," I offer weakly.

"No, my fault. You weren't ready. Here we go." He steps forward again, and this time I step back with him. The next few steps, I'm okay, but then we get to the side-shuffle thing and I'm lost. No matter how hard I stare at my feet, I can't will them to get it right.

"What are you looking at down there?" Mateo asks jokingly. "Did you lose something?"

"Yeah, my dignity." I stop and drop his hand from mine. "I'm sorry, Mateo, I should have warned you. I can't dance. At all. Unless they start playing the Funky Chicken, you might as well give up on me as a partner." Just saying the words is a huge relief. My name's Cassie, and I'm a bad dancer. Hi, Cassie.

"What's the Funky Chicken?" he asks, his smile so soft and sweet.

"Never mind," I say. "Thanks for trying." Thanks for taking pity on me.

"Come, Cassandra." He holds out his hand. "Everyone can dance."

"That's like saying everyone can do brain surgery. Nice thought but not true."

"Well, *you* can dance. I'm sure of it. I've seen you."

"You've seen me?"

"At Andrea's, when there's music on that you like, and you think no one's watching, you do this little step." He demonstrates, his feet gliding front and back in a slow salsa waltz.

"I do not." I shake my head, laughing.

"You do." He laughs back.

"So you've been watching me, have you?" I cock my head and smile. Mateo blushes. He's blushing! I scream in my head. I've actually made Mateo blush!

"Well, when you're dancing, it's hard not to look."

"Because it's so funny."

"No, not funny. Not funny at all." He looks down at the floor for a second and then straight into my eyes. We stand there looking at each other until the music stops. Everyone is switching partners again. I see the greasy, unbuttoned guy coming my way.

"Oh, well, I guess we're supposed to—"

"How about one more try," Mateo says, taking my hand again and wrapping his other arm around my waist. The music starts and my body goes rigid in anticipation. I look down at my feet to prepare. Back, front, side, side, I think. "No watching the feet this time," Mateo says, lifting my chin so we are eye-to-eye.

"Then how will I know if I'm doing it right?"

He laughs. "Don't think so hard. You can't anticipate the steps with your head. Trust your body. It knows what to do." He sweeps me even closer, too close for me to see my feet, and I can feel my heart pounding in my chest. Or is that his heart? I look up at him. He blushes again and pulls back an inch.

And then we dance.

With our bodies this close, I can feel his every movement. There is nothing to think about, nothing to anticipate or analyze or complicate. The shift in his hips tells me when to glide to the side. The pressure of his thigh on mine means it's time to step back. The weight of his hand against the small of my back brings me forward again.

"Perfect." He beams. "You've got it." I don't step on his foot once.

"Ready for something more?" he whispers into my ear. I pull back enough to look at him. "I can teach you another step."

"Yeah. Why not?"

But the music stops, and this time Dan has found me.

"Having fun?" he asks, not quite smiling, not looking at Mateo.

"Yes, lots." We stand in silence for a few seconds. "Dan, have you met Mateo?"

"Not officially." He turns ceremoniously and holds out his hand. They shake. "Well, shall we?" I take Dan's arm.

Over his shoulder, he says, "Nice meeting you, Matthew." I look back, apologetic, but Mateo, surrounded by a flock of women, is already walking toward Anna on the other side of the hall.

Dan and Jamie are full of energy and want to go for drinks. Tired, I head home and leave them to find their way to large bottles of cheap beer.

"Are you sure you trust me alone with your man?" Jamie says with a huge smile. Dan blushes.

"I'll take my chances," I say with a smile, playing along.

It's only ten-thirty, but the house is dark and still. Andrea and Jorge must be out—no one goes to sleep before midnight around here. It isn't until I'm ready for bed that I realize I'm not that tired after all. It's cool enough to make a cup of tea. I turn on the radio and curl up on the couch by the window with my steaming mug. With all the lights off, the courtyard flora sparkles in the moonlight.

Someone's knocking on my door. It must be Andrea wanting to hear about my tango adventures. She hits her stride after dark. Some nights she keeps me up until the sun rises, talking and drinking maté.

I open the door, the sliver of hall light stretching across my feet, and see Mateo.

Did I fall asleep on the couch? I must be dreaming.

"What are you doing here?" I whisper.

"We didn't get to finish our dance," he says and steps toward me.

Before I can put down my mug of tea, his hands are on my face, his lips against mine. His tongue pushes softly into my mouth and finds mine. I taste red wine, I taste tango. I throw my arms around him. Warm tea sloshes out of the cup and against his back, but he doesn't stop. A slow song comes on the radio, and Mateo pulls me to him, his hips pushing against mine. I step back and to the side. His right hand moves down my cheek, throat, breast. My left hand strums the side of his torso. I am vaguely aware of music in the background. Mostly, I hear the sound of us breathing into each other, our hearts beating out their own rhythm against our chests. There is no thought, no anticipation, no plan. Every part of us, feet, hands, fingers, lips, tongues, breath, just dances. It's everything and nothing like I'd imagined it would be. I don't want this to stop.

"I could kiss you forever," he whispers.

Forever. From him, the word rocks me out of reverie. Does he mean it? I remember that night after the party. *Life isn't a Tom Hanks movie. Happily ever after is a fairy tale.* I'm reluctant to let anything ruin this moment, but now this is the only thing running through my mind, trampling all in its path. Everything I want— things I didn't even know I wanted—pushes to the surface. There is no stopping it.

"I don't understand you," I whisper back, frightened of the words as they come out of my mouth, frightened of what I want them to convey, frightened of their potential to end this moment, this kiss, this dance.

"What don't you understand?" He kisses my shoulder.

"What do you want from me?"

"Isn't it obvious?" He laughs lightly, nuzzling my neck.

I pull back. "Is that all?"

"No, no, that isn't all." He pulls back enough to look me in the eye. "Of course that isn't all." He shakes his head. "Is that what you think of me?"

"How would I know what to think?"

"I let you stomp all over my feet for half an hour. That should tell you something." He laughs but stops when he sees I don't get the joke. "And I'm here right now, aren't I?"

"And what about tomorrow?" Even as I say it, I know I've ruined everything, but I can't stop myself. "What happens tomorrow, Mateo?" I can see in his eyes, in the disappointment pooling there, that the moment is over.

I've looked at my feet again. For good or bad, it's the only way I know how to dance.

"I don't know, Cassie. I don't know what happens tomorrow," he says quietly, cautiously, adding, "I know you've been hurt . . ."

He's right. I have been. Which is why I've got to stick to The Plan. Spontaneous decision-making isn't my strong point. "Look, I'm going home soon, and I just don't see the point of us . . . I don't see the point of us wasting our time pretending."

"I didn't realize this was wasting your time," he says sharply, straightening up.

"Well, it is," I force myself to respond. "Maybe you should go find Anna." I don't even recognize my own voice.

"Anna?" He looks at me with a question mark. "Maybe I should leave," he says at last. We stand apart, arms rigid at our sides. Our swollen lips are all that remain of our kiss.

"Maybe you should."

As I shut the door after him, it makes a sucking sound, and I feel that sound inside of me, that sucking of air until there's nothing left to breathe. I open my mouth wide, placing my shaking hands against the door to steady myself, and catch my breath. When I can breathe again, I have nowhere to go but mad. Any residual passion from that one kiss twists into a rage. How dare he! How dare he come up here and kiss me like that! How dare he walk out on me! Mostly, I'm angry that he can get to me like this. So I am determined not to let him. He is of no consequence in my life. Mateo de la Vega can take his "forever" and stick it where the sun don't shine.

Wide awake with anger, I notice that my apartment is a mess. While I stomp around picking up papers, tossing food wrappers, and slamming cupboard doors, "You May Be Right" comes on the radio. I used to love Billy Joel. Before my father left us, he played this song all the time. He'd turn it up loud, and he and I would boogie around the living room, limbs flailing, not caring how stupid we looked or that we didn't know the right moves. Once my mother came in from the kitchen, yellow dish gloves dripping with suds, and started singing along into the spatula she'd been scrubbing. Even her. Even me. I walk over to the radio and turn it off.

I give up on cleaning and try to sleep, but after tossing, turning, and watching the clock for far too long, I give up and check my e-mail. How could I waste time stewing over Mateo when a stellar job offer might be sitting there waiting for me to come to my senses?

Three form e-mails notifying me that my résumé has been received, a joke from my stepdad that I read about two years ago, a lengthy update from Sam and Trish on everyone we know in Seattle, and a message from C.J.—the new website is ready to go live.

I click on the link to his work in progress. C.J. has outdone himself. I can't believe this is my website. It's better than I ever imagined. He's added tons of new bells and whistles and redone all the graphics. The main color used, as I requested, is a deep red. It's the color of my apartment walls, the color of my un-Cassie dress, the color of a painting that hangs in El Taller, the color Mateo's cheeks blush when he's embarrassed. It is the color of Buenos Aires.

"All it needs is a new domain name!" C.J. proclaims in his e-mail. For some reason, he is enthusiastic about this new home for my silly scribblings. He thinks my website is brilliant.

Could he be right? Maybe the website is brilliant. Maybe Jeff and my old boss were wrong. Maybe I'm fantastic. Maybe Mateo is missing out on the best thing that ever happened to him. Not that I care. I am strong and determined. I am Cassie Moore, and I have a plan.

I also have my website's new name. I type those five words— Buenos Aires Broken Hearts Club—and hit send.

CHAPTER FIFTEEN

*T*he next morning, over a plate of sweet mini-croissants drizzled with honey, the way I love them, Andrea asks how the dance class went. I tell her, as offhandedly as I can manage, about running into Mateo at the community center.

"Oh, yes," she says, turning away to fuss with Jorge's jumper. "I forget he goes there sometimes." She passes me the platter of *medialunas* again, even though my plate is still full. "So you liked the class?"

"Yeah," I say casually. "It was fun."

"Just fun?"

"It wasn't quite what I expected, but I learned a lot."

Andrea peers at me over the rim of her teacup, sizing up my response. I don't expand. We sit in uncharacteristic silence for a while. Jorge reaches for a *medialuna* and attempts to shove the whole thing in his mouth. Half of the pastry sticks out, like a crusty tongue. The tallest dog, Maradona, named for a famed Argentine soccer—that is, football—player, helps himself with one lick, setting off a fit of little-boy giggles. Andrea shoos Maradona away and wipes Jorge's face with the corner of a napkin dipped in water. I scan the morning newspaper that's spread across the kitchen table as a makeshift tablecloth. The president is campaigning up north, where support is waning. The local government is trying to get an injunction against a group of workers who have taken over an abandoned factory in the city. La Boca won its last football game. I am halfway through the front page before I realize I actually understand most of what I'm reading.

"Would you do it again?" Andrea asks as she hands Jorge an orange slice.

"What?" Have I been found out? Did she see Mateo let himself in and climb the stairs to my apartment last night?

"Tango?"

"Oh. I don't think so," I say, rising to clear the table. "Tango's a beautiful dance, but maybe too complicated. I don't think I'm cut out for it."

"Ah," she exhales, like a wise sage divining truth, and takes a sip of coffee. "*Entiendo. Entiendo.*"

Jamie, on the other hand, doesn't understand at all. "I don't get it," she says, lifting a pleather miniskirt from the rack. We're on our eighth store. With the power of the U.S. dollar sinking in, Jamie has gone into serious, and inevitable, shopping mode. She holds the skirt against her waist and does a little *America's Next Top Model* for me. I laugh so hard, I snort.

"What don't you get?"

"You say you don't want to waste your time with something that can't go anywhere, right? Something that isn't in your plan, or whatever."

"Yeah?"

"But in a month you and Dan will be on opposite ends of the U.S." She slips on a pair of white Elton John sunglasses and makes a face at herself in the mirror. "You know that isn't leading anywhere. So why is it okay to hang out with him and not Mateo?"

I think of Dan, sweet, stable, safe Dan, with his humongous bouquet of roses, his fumbling hands in the night, his silly jokes that make me giggle against my better judgment. And then Mateo.

Mateo doesn't come to me as a series of qualities or memories or other essentials that make up normal human relationships. There is no Idealmatch.com profile that ticks through my head. No, when I think of Mateo, it's not even about thinking. It's just feeling. That feeling fills me up. There's no other way to put it.

"I don't know. It just is."

"Uh-huh." Jamie puts the skirt back on the rack, watching me from the corner of her eye. "Care to elaborate?" Jamie, I've recently discovered, is one dissertation away from her master's in psychology. She'd planned her wedding date to coincide with her graduation, but a few chapters from finishing, she realized she didn't want to be a psychologist or a wife or anything else she had planned on.

"Not really." She stares at me hard until I give in. "Okay, maybe it could go somewhere with Dan. He could move. I could move. People do those kinds of things when they find the right person."

Jamie takes a pile of clothes into the dressing room, but she isn't about to drop the interrogation. "And you think Dan might be your Mr. Right?"

"I don't know. Maybe. He's pretty much exactly the kind of guy I've always seen myself with. He fits."

"Fits what?"

"The Plan." I cringe when I say it, though I don't know why.

"And why is that so important to you?"

"Well, Doctor . . . I think it all began when I didn't get a bike for my eighth birthday."

The dressing room door swings open abruptly. "Classic avoidance," she says seriously. "Though if you want to talk about the bike, I'm all ears."

"I'm not avoiding. I just don't see the point in agonizing over something that's simply not an option."

"Agonizing—that's an interesting word. Does thinking about your plan feel like pain?"

"No. It usually makes me feel really good." Good and happy

and safe, but sometimes lonely—kind of like eating an entire To-blerone bar all by myself. But I'm not about to tell Jamie that.

"Usually?" Holding up a sheer blue blouse for inspection, she watches me through it, and I'm reminded of my cryptic conversation with Andrea just a few hours before. Only this time I haven't got the slightest clue what's really being said. "Your parents are divorced, right?"

"What does that have to do with anything?"

"Your mom's kind of controlling?"

"Whose isn't?"

"What you'd really like to do is pretend nothing's wrong, and when you get back to Seattle, every piece of the puzzle that is your life will fall magically into place?"

"Yes, please." I take a big breath.

"And Mateo doesn't fit into that puzzle."

"Exactly."

"Good thing you're going home soon, huh?"

"Yeah," I say, puffing my cheeks, and letting out the air in a car-toonlike whoosh. "Good thing."

Once the hunting, gathering, and analyzing is done, Jamie heads back downtown to her hostel with her bags of booty. It's been a fun afternoon, but I am left alone with my thoughts again, and that's no fun at all.

Going home. There's something I have no choice but to think about. Somehow, amid all my preparations for going home, be-neath the comfort of list making and box checking, going home has become a reality. I knew the day was coming, but I didn't expect it to come so fast. Now here it is, hurtling toward me at breakneck speed. And I'm glad. Thrilled, really. It's just so soon. Under five weeks to go, and nothing's in order. I haven't made any headway in the job department, my savings are running out, I don't have a solid plan for where I'm going to live once I'm back in

Seattle, let alone any idea what I'm going to do with my life when I get there.

What I do have is a lot of e-mail, mostly messages from old blog readers raving about the new site. People love the new chat pages that C.J. designed—many seem to be using them as a makeshift dating service—and there is a daily stream of praise in my in-box. Unfortunately, their praise isn't going to help pay my rent back in Seattle. Or could it? There is a message from a woman who wants to buy space on the website for a personal ad. If she's willing to pay me, how many others might be, too? I could definitely use a few bucks in the bank once I'm back in Seattle. Mostly, I like the thought of helping some of these broken hearts fall in love again. I forward her e-mail to C.J., asking if there's some simple way to automate ad purchase and posting for site visitors. If it works, I tell him, I'll cut him in for half. Within minutes, there's an e-mail from him. "Great idea! I'm on it, boss!" I smile at his enthusiasm, then shake my head, worried that I'm wasting more time—mine and his—on some silly website for complete strangers, something that isn't in The Plan.

When I tell Sam and Trish about the website in our next weekly phone call, they don't seem to think it's silly at all.

"Cassie, this is fantastic!" declares Sam, who wastes no time keying in the URL. "You did this by yourself?"

"I've had some help from a friend on the technical bits, but basically, yeah."

"Why didn't you tell us about it before?"

"There wasn't much to it until now," I say, though I'm not sure that's the real reason. Part of me might also have felt stupid showing my little blog to my career-fast-tracking friends.

"What a great name," says Trish. "And it looks so professional."

"Yeah, C.J.'s the best," I say, trying to sound casual. In truth, I'm thrilled that they like it.

"I love that color red," Sam pipes in.

"Me, too." I consider explaining its inspiration but decide to keep that just for me. "It's the color of that old velvet jacket I had," I say instead.

"Ooh, yeah. I loved that jacket," says Sam. "What ever happened to it?"

"I think I might have stashed it at my parents' place."

"If I may interrupt this very important discussion," Trish bursts in, "Cassie, how many hits are you getting?" She is always one for the hard facts.

"I don't know, exactly." I think for a second. "I guess it was about two thousand when I last checked."

"Two thousand hits a month is pretty good."

"No, I mean two thousand a day."

"Holy shit! That's huge for a personal blog,"

"It's not really a blog anymore. They mostly chat with each other. Some of them have actually started dating."

"Really . . ." Even over the phone, thousands of miles away, I can tell that the wheels are turning in Trish's head.

"Oh, yeah, they're hooking up left, right, and center. I should have called the site Wheretofindyourreboundrelationship.com."

"That would have saved me a lot of hangovers after my breakup with Joe," Sam says, chuckling.

"Have you thought about looking for advertisers?" asks Trish.

"Well I hadn't planned on making money off it. But one of the readers asked to post a personal ad, so my technical guy is working on a way to let people do it."

"Really . . ."

"What?"

"Crazy idea: How would you feel if we covered the site in our newsletter?" asks Trish.

"Brilliant!" shouts Sam.

"Why would your readers care about my blog?"

"We're supposed to keep them informed on what's hot with the twentysomething crowd, especially high-tech stuff. I'd say this definitely qualifies."

The idea of my blog being featured next to articles on the hottest jeans trends and Apple's new teeny-tiny whatever makes me feel good. Almost proud, even. And that's what friends do, isn't it? Make you feel good about small, meaningless accomplishments like starting a blog or getting your hair highlighted in the perfect shade of blonde. "Okay. Sure. Why not," I say. Sam and Trish squeal with joy. On this end of the line, I am positively beaming.

Once we hang up, I am filled with a restless energy. I throw on my sneakers and head out for a long walk. I round a couple of plazas, then make my way to the cat park. The cats are lazy from the heat, lolling about under the trees, sleeping in the shadows along the iron fence. Worried that their inactivity will be contagious, I move on to the next park. There are miles and miles of green in this part of the city. Not far from Andrea's house, the parks are more urban—sparse grass, decrepit wooden benches, ponds filled with questionable water. To the west, flora and fauna gather sophistication. Forty-five minutes into my walk and the grasses are thick and soft, the benches are wrought iron, and the small, man-made lakes picturesque. Walk this far and you exchange the hum of city life for the sounds of birds singing, children laughing, and the occasional oar lapping at water. I've read that if you go even farther east, there's a stunning rose garden, so farther I go.

I wind through the garden, over emerald mounds, under iron arbors painted an optimistic white, between rosebushes. There are dozens and dozens of them, each labeled with its Latin name. It's a bit late in the season, though, and most hold only remnants of flowers, a drying petal here and there. I try to imagine how glorious they must have looked a few months before, when I first read about the garden. Back then I was too busy fooling around with Antonio. This annoying thought leads to even more annoy-ing thoughts of time wasted on Mateo, and those I do not need. I notice a small white building on the edge of the garden. This must be the Japanese greenhouse I heard about from someone at El Taller. They're supposed to have great sushi. I haven't had sushi in forever. I duck inside.

But the building, it turns out, is home to a contemporary art gallery. The last thing I need is a trip down Mateo-memory lane. However, the woman at the desk looks so excited to see a visitor, I don't have the heart to walk out. I pay the three-peso admission and step into the bright white exhibit space.

A large sign announces a new exhibit featuring local artists from the second half of the twentieth century. Some of these artists, the sign explains, have gone on to international recogni-tion. Others have faded into relative obscurity. All, it asserts, have played an important role in the story of Argentine art.

There are so many beautiful pieces, each as different, I imag-ine, as the person who created it. Some artists have a whole wall devoted to their work. For others, there is only one painting. How sad, I think, that this might be all the world knows of this person's talent. I rush through the watercolors—they've never held much appeal for me, too delicate and wistful for my tastes—and laze through the acrylics and oils. It's just me and an older British cou-ple happily snapping their digital camera at everything, so I can take my time winding through the mazelike building, discover-ing each artist slowly, quietly introducing myself with the respect they each deserve.

When I turn into a room lined with three enormous abstracts, I slow to a near-stop. I could look at these for hours. I'm held cap-tive by every brushstroke, the thickest licks of paint wrenching themselves away from the canvas as if they could almost leap free. It takes guts to paint this big, to blow yourself wide open like that.

My favorite is a massive city scene done in brilliant oranges, yellows, and reds. It should be angry, but it's sad, instead. The short buildings twist and lean in to one another. A lone face, square and gray, peers out of a window. It reminds me of something I can't put my finger on, stays with me as I move between the sculptures in the next room.

I am outside again, sunlight on my face, before I remember the red paintings in El Taller. Wasn't there one with a square gray face? It can't be a coincidence. It can't. Ignoring the woman at the front, I run back into the gallery, to the room with the enormous paintings. There it is, printed on a small white card beneath the giant canvas: MATEO DE LA VEGA, 1995.

A few blocks from El Taller, I start to run. The speed of my legs matches the speed of questions storming through my head. How is that Mateo's name on that painting? How is that painting in that gallery? Why were there only three? Why so long ago? What happened between then and now? There are too many things I need to know, and if I don't know them soon, there's a good chance I'll spontaneously combust right here on the streets of Buenos Aires. There's also the question of why I need to know these things so desperately, but I push that one away and run.

Bursting through the door into the half-full café, I head straight for the back wall, bumping into three chairs along the way and almost knocking over a waiter's tray. There they are, all four enormous paintings, nearly identical to the one in the gallery. The small square gray face looks out at me again and again. At the bottom right of each canvas, written in thick black paint, is a large M.

The waitress with the tribal tattoos down one arm approaches and asks if I'm okay. I nod, unable to take my eyes off the paintings. My chest still heaving, beads of sweat above my lip, I ask if Mateo is here.

"*No entiendo*," she says.

Right, I remember, she doesn't speak English. I try again in Spanish. This is no time to be shy about my language skills.

She shakes her head. "*No trabaja hoy.*" He's not working today. She turns her attention back to the refilling of salt shakers.

Does she know where I can find him? I continue in Spanish, surprising myself no small amount. As if I'm speaking a foreign language in a dream, the words flow easily and without thought or second-guessing. Suddenly, I am a Spanish-speaking savant. If only Marcela were here to give me a gold star. I have to talk to him, I tell the waitress. I have to.

She looks me up and down, skeptical, then nods with recognition. Am I one of those Buenos Aires Broken Hearts Club people? she asks.

"*Sí*," I say, embarrassed until I see that she is smiling warmly. "*Sí, yo soy. Me llamo* Cassie."

"Ah, *sí.*" She turns to the painting closest to her, tipping her head toward it with reverence. "*El es muy talentoso*," she whispers as though sharing a secret.

"*Sí*," I agree. "*Muy talentoso.*"

"*Y muy hermoso.*" And very handsome. Where this is going, I have no idea.

"*¿Sí?*" I draw the short word out into a question, expecting her to finish the thought.

"*Entiendo*," she says with Andrea-esque confidence, nodding sagely as though she knows something I don't. As though she knows something I should. "*Sí, sí, sí. Entiendo.*" What is it that everyone thinks they understand? I just want to know where Mateo is.

I press her for his whereabouts again. She holds up a finger and disappears into the kitchen. A few minutes go by, and that anxiety creeps into my skin again. My Spanish might be better than I thought, but it's still shaky. I probably asked her for a turkey sandwich. She reappears with Mateo's address. I recognize the street.

It's nearby? I ask.

"*Sí, muy cerca.*" She gives me directions.

"*Muchas gracias,*" I call over my shoulder. Out on the sidewalk again, I start running.

I go into autopilot, flying past block after block of homes and stores, so familiar they barely register. The street signs need only a glance to confirm I'm not there yet. Finally, I come to the street written on the torn piece of paper and only then realize I don't know which way to turn. Did the waitress say *izquierda* or *derecha*? Guess I should have listened better to those directions. I fumble for my map, hands shaking, and locate the street. "Left!" I shout. A woman cradles her small daughter against her chest as she passes, moving to the outside of the sidewalk, but I don't care. "Left!" I shout again. "Left!"

2245. 2249. 2257. When I see it, I double-check the paper, then the address plate. There's no mistake. She wrote 2257, and this is 2257. I don't know what I was expecting, but I wasn't expecting this. The pink and blue house.

I stand there behind the rusting bars of the iron fence for a long time. At last I see him. The house is dark inside, but there's no mistaking those paint-splattered overalls or the way he walks with his hands shoved deep in his pockets. He crosses the gap of half-raised blinds on a second-floor window, and they fall shut. He hovers between the gauzy curtains of another set for a second, and they snap together. Like a ghost, he drifts from room to room closing out the light. His presence in that house is so ethereal, I don't even think to hide myself. How is this where he lives? Why didn't he say anything that day we walked by here together? Andrea was just as mute, though I specifically asked her about the house's story. Unsure how to process what I see, unsure what this means—or if it means anything at all—I stand there behind the iron bars and watch.

Back at my apartment, I Google Mateo. I can't believe I didn't do this before. In Seattle, this was as much a part of my dating ritual as buying new stilettos. The oracle of search engines offers me twenty-seven pages of Mateo miscellany, from his name on a list of 1994 fine-arts graduates to an old advertisement for a cooking job at El Taller. Clicking on entry nineteen, I land on a short article on an art website that mentions an exhibit in 1998. I make my way through it slowly, with help from a translation site. The new pieces are full of promise, the critic proclaims. This is an artist to watch. Three other Web pages mention Mateo in passing. On another is a photo of him participating in a neighborhood rejuvenation project in 1996. The young Mateo, one hand holding a bag of trash, the other squeezing the shoulder of a pretty girl leaning on a rake, smiles widely at the camera. It's the Mateo from Andrea's photos, a Mateo at ease with the world. There isn't a trace of cynicism in that face. He looks happy. Really, really happy. What could have happened to change that?

Beside the photo, someone has included a caption: *Local artist Mateo de la Vega and fiancée Silvana Diaz.* A slim girl with long dark hair stands behind them in the photo. She's younger but unmistakable: Anna.

Downstairs in the kitchen, Jorge is helping Andrea make cookies. Her balls of dough are uniform and evenly spaced on the baking sheet. His, to the delight of the dogs, are mostly on the floor.

"Looks like you have a budding baker in the family," I say, laughing. Jorge eyes me suspiciously. Over four months and I'm still the outsider, the interloper, the party crasher.

"Oh, Jorge is going to be great chef someday." Andrea tweaks her son's nose, leaving a splotch of cookie dough. He giggles softly. "Or maybe world-famous dog trainer. We haven't decided, have we, *hijo?*"

"Can I help?"

"No, no. Just sit. Relax. Have some tea."

I pour myself a cup and add a bit of milk. "So I saw something interesting at the rose garden today."

"Oh, are the roses still there?"

"No, they're long gone. But there was an exhibit at the little art museum. Do you know it?"

She rubs her jaw the way she does when she's thinking hard. Bits of cookie dough fall on her T-shirt. "*Ah, sí. En la casa blanca. Sí,* I know it."

"There was an exhibition on Buenos Aires artists."

"Mmm?" She pops the baking sheet into the oven.

"And there was a painting by Mateo. Our—your Mateo."

"Mm-hm . . ." She shoos away the dogs, who are licking dough from Jorge's sticky fingers.

"It was dated 1995."

"Mmm." She holds Jorge over the sink while he plunges his hands into the stream of water.

"He was a painter," I say.

"*Sí.*"

"And engaged."

"Ah." Andrea sets Jorge in his high chair, pours herself another cup of tea, and sits down. She's smiling, but it's a sad smile. "It is many years ago," she begins. "Much things have happened."

Andrea takes her time with the telling, each turn of events something to mull over and examine carefully before articulating. I appreciate the pace. It gives me time to digest. I sit, literally, on the edge of my seat, washing down her words with hot tea. Jorge squirms, bored and cranky, on the floor between us.

Andrea moved here from Brazil when she was nine, she says. Mateo and Silvana were her best friends. They went to the same school and lived a few blocks from each other. As children, they played together on the streets of Palermo Viejo, these streets I stroll each day. Mateo's and Silvana's parents were good friends. There were Sunday *asados* that rotated from backyard to backyard and legendary Christmas parties at the de la Vega house. Then Mateo moved to the U.S. with his family.

"He wrote letters sometimes, and we sent him pictures so we wouldn't forget each other. We did, of course. We were thirteen, fourteen. But then he came home again." Andrea laughs gently, shakes her head at the ceiling as though remembering a secret joke. "He was changed. A man now. Not so easy to forget anymore."

I nod in understanding. I seem to have the same problem.

With his family still in the U.S., she continues, Mateo moved back into his empty childhood house and enrolled in the university's fine-arts program. Silvana was in the psychology department. "Every girl in school wanted his attentions, but he only saw Silvana. She was beautiful. Long hair, huge black eyes. And a kind heart, you know? Even as a small girl, she was gentle and caring. Would catch spiders in a jar and put it outside." It was no surprise to anyone, she tells me, when they fell in love.

"It was perfect," she says, wistful. "They planned to be married when they graduated. The families were very happy. Everyone was happy. It was like a . . ." She looks at me for help.

"A fairy tale?"

"*Sí,* a fairy tale. *Sí, sí.*" Andrea pauses to take a long sip of tea. For her last year of school, she tells me, Silvana wanted to go to New York to study there, like Mateo had done. She wanted to see it, too, wanted to know the things that he had known. He didn't want her to go, but he understood. So she went and he stayed behind, getting things ready for his bride-to-be. He arranged a date at their families' church for the wedding. He bought Siamese kittens like the ones she'd had when she was a little girl. He started to paint his house pink, her favorite color. Andrea stops and looks down at Jorge, who has fallen asleep against her feet. His small chest rises and falls. The peace of a sleeping child fills the room. "He wanted everything perfect for when she came home."

"What happened?" I ask, though I already know. It's all crystal-clear now. Andrea doesn't even need to speak the words. While his childhood sweetheart was away, he fell for a bewitching girl named Anna. Poor Silvana. Mateo is the Argentine equivalent of Jeff, I realize. Thank God I didn't let myself fall for him, I think. Thank God. Thank God.

Andrea lets out a breath, like a balloon deflating. "She didn't come home," she whispers.

That can't be right.

"Because he hurt her?"

"No, no. She say she is in love with another student there."

The puzzle shifts. Nothing fits.

My eyes open wide, I encourage her to continue. Mateo went to New York, she says. He thought that Silvana had cold feet. He would forgive her and everything would be like they'd planned. "I don't know what happened there," she says. "She stopped writing to me—but she never came home again."

The puzzle shifts again.

"And he stopped painting." I am the one whispering now.

"He couldn't anymore." Andrea rests her chin against her hand. Under the curl of her fingers, I can see her lips tremble slightly. "I wish you had known him before, Cassie. He was different before. Always laughing, always joking. He saw good things in everyone. You know that painting there?" She points in the direction of the foyer. "This is Mateo."

"Really?" I should have known, I suppose, but it looks so different from the others, lighter and more hopeful somehow. "It's beautiful."

"*Sí, sí.*" Andrea pets Jorge's brow, smoothing hair from his eyes.

She shakes her head. "I loved Silvana, too. She was like a sister to me. But she broke him inside of his heart. *Entiendes?*"

"She broke his heart," I say. "Yes, I understand." And suddenly, I really do.

I try to read but can't concentrate. What am I to do with this new information that's turned my stomach into a pit of butterflies? I would blog, but this is one thing I wouldn't dare share. Sleep comes, begrudgingly, fitfully. I dream I am back in my old apartment, pale gray walls, spare, sharp ebony furniture. There's no music, just the sound of eggs sizzling in a pan, popping and crackling in the hot oil. I'm wearing an apron, the goofy kind my stepdad wears when he's barbecuing, and my hair is in rollers. I call out to Jeff. Does he want eggs? The eggs are done. He doesn't want any, he calls back, but I want him to try the eggs, so I take the pan and move through the apartment. Except it isn't the apartment anymore. There's a long staircase and shag carpeting, wallpaper and Pledged furniture. I enter the dining room, formal and set for dinner, and see them naked and writhing on the Persian area rug—that much doesn't change. Jeff and Lauren, limbs entwined so intricately I can't separate one from the other. Jeff, I scream. Jeff, what are you doing? Stop, Jeff, please stop. I stomp my feet and shake my arms at him like a child. The eggs slide from the pan onto the floor. I notice a dirty shovel in the corner beside the buffet and think how curiously out of place that seems. The room begins to swirl around the naked bodies. I can see them from every angle. Jeff looks up at me and then Lauren. Except it isn't Lauren anymore, it's Silvana. Jeff and Silvana, her long black hair trailing down her bare back, over his feet, and out the door.

I wake up sweating, the sheet twisted around my arms and legs like a rope. I rip the bedclothes off, lie there panting until I catch my breath. The dream comes back to me in small gray pieces. They bring with them a sleepy, fuzz-headed clarity. We are the same, Mateo and I. The only difference is that I know how to carry on, how to rebuild from the rubble, how to stop the wrecking ball from striking again. He needs me to show him how, I understand abruptly, brilliantly. This is why we've found each other. He needs my help. The clock flashes 2:14 A.M. I wrap a long sweater around my nightgown, slide into my flip-flops, and walk quickly to the pink and blue house.

Outside, the air has been cooled slightly by a weak breeze from the river. Yet another streetlight has burnt out and only the lights from windows illuminate Mateo's block. There are no cars on the road. A neighbor is listening to classical music. A violin crescendo lifts up through the hushed street and into the night, a trail of sweet notes chirping behind it.

The dim blue of a TV glows through the large window on the main floor. Otherwise, the house is dark. I push open the iron gate, walk slowly to the door, and knock. There's no answer. I knock again, long and loud. I hear footsteps, and then the great black door swings open. I step back protectively. We aren't on the best of terms at the moment. After the scene at El Taller that night, I think it's likely that he's written me off completely. But he doesn't look mad when he opens the door, just surprised and then, dare I think it, maybe a little bit pleased.

"Cassie." He's wiping his hands on something. A painter's rag, I think, excited that I might understand something, know something real and important about his life, until I realize that it's only a dish towel.

"Hi." Never in the history of the world has this word sounded so stupid, so trite. This is no way to begin such an important conversation, one that will . . . I realize with a jolt of fear that I have no idea what I'm going to say next. Why didn't I practice something on the way over here? I plan every tiny detail in my life, but not this?

"What are you doing here?"

"I, uh . . ." What am I doing here, pounding on his door in the middle of the night? I look at Mateo's sweet green eyes, crinkling at the corners with curiosity. The night we kissed seems like forever ago and only yesterday. I want it again, want it so bad I ache.

I take a long breath and, standing there at his doorstep in my nightgown and sweater, let it all come pouring out, the museum, the paintings, the talk with Andrea. These are loose fragments and unclaimed remainders tenuously held together by my perhaps wishful arithmetic, but somehow it adds up to something in my head.

Mateo looks at me hard, as if I'm speaking another language—one he doesn't understand. A fat Siamese cat coils around his leg, mewing gently for attention. He doesn't seem to notice.

"What I'm trying to say"—I take a gulp of air—"is that I know you're scared. I get it. When someone breaks your heart, you feel like . . . like you won't ever breathe right again. But you do. You will. You have to. You can't just give up. You're so talented and smart and funny and amazing. I understand why you're scared to love someone . . ." These last words surprise me, leave me breathless. I hadn't planned on using that word. It's slippery, that word. But there's no going back. I stand in front of this man vulnerable, exposed. I suck in my breath and wait for him to reciprocate and reveal himself to me.

He doesn't say anything. Why doesn't he say anything? Please say something.

"Thank you for your concern," he says finally, dragging out the last word scornfully. The sardonic tone jolts me off my cloud. There is no curious crinkle in the corners of his eyes, only a stern crease between his brows. "But you really don't know anything about me. I'm not one of your broken hearts that you can fix with a bottle of wine and a few good cries."

"I know you're not. That's not what I meant." I don't know

what I meant. I don't know what I'm doing here in the middle of the night, half naked. "I didn't—"

"You can save the love advice for your circle of admirers, online and off."

"What do you mean?"

Mateo reaches behind the door and tugs at something on the wall. He pushes it at me—a page from the *Clarín*, Buenos Aires' biggest newspaper, folded into a small square with a pinhole in the corner. It's a half-page article in Spanish. Other than the word "blog" peppered through the article, I have no idea what it says.

"I can't read this." I try to hand it back to him, but he won't take it.

"It's about a travel blog based on one woman's adventures in Argentina. An American woman." My eyes widen in disbelief. It couldn't be. I scan the article again for more familiar words. I find *americana, compasión, anónimo, gratitud*. And there, near the end, my old URL.

Augustina mentioned something about a reporter, I remember, but I figured he was from some small neighborhood paper. And when she said that he wanted to write about "us," I assumed she meant the Madres. I never dreamed of including myself in that "us." I never dreamed any of this could come from my little blog.

"Apparently, you've inspired newfound interest in an old, forgotten cause. The Madres attribute over sixteen thousand dollars in new donations to you. Some guy from Michigan even started an online letter-writing campaign to U.S. politicians."

"Wow" is all that comes to me. Wow. I did this. I did this? I did. I did this. I am seconds from bursting into song and dance when I glance up and see Mateo looking nowhere near as pleased as I'm feeling. This is no time for self-congratulation. *Your circle of admirers, online and off.* Has he read my blog? He's read my blog.

"You read my blog."

"Yes," he says flatly. "Catchy new name, by the way."

My heart pounds against my chest, in my ears. It all sinks in, the whole big fat ugly truth. Oh, God, I am shouting inside. Oh, God! Oh, God! He knows about my blog!

He. Knows. Everything.

Adrenaline buzzes through my veins, a fight-or-flight response. I vote for flight, but my feet won't move. All those entries about the haughty, superior, sexy M. The rantings about his rudeness and, later, the rapturous retelling of every word exchanged, every glance, every accidental touch. Please, oh please, don't let him know all that. Why did I write those things? What was I thinking? I pull my sweater tight around me, around this stark nakedness. I am all exposed skin, nerve endings, and organs.

"Mateo, I'm sorry if I've said or done anything to offend you or embarrass you." He doesn't speak, forcing me to fill the space between us. I struggle to remember why I'm standing here on his doorstep in the middle of the night. The paintings. "But that's beside the point."

"And what is the point?"

"I understand why you stopped painting. I really do. But it's been years. You shouldn't give up on everything because of what one—"

"Give up? And what are *you* doing, Cassie?" he asks, his voice growing louder and angrier. "You're too scared to let anything happen to you that you can't control, anything that doesn't fit neatly into your plan for this imaginary perfect life. You shut out everything and everyone that isn't on some spreadsheet. That's just a fancy form of giving up."

Perfect. Once again the word is hurled against me. Just like Jeff.

Who is Mateo to judge me? I think, my anger rising. Living in this half-painted house, living this half-painted life, who is he to judge anyone?

"At least I'm trying to make a future for myself. It's like you

stopped living. You don't paint. You work in a bar. You won't . . .
And this house." I throw up my arms and shake my head. "At least
I'm not afraid to try."

"Aren't you?"

"No, I'm not. Not by a long shot."

"Maybe I'm wrong." His face is softening, but his voice sounds
so cold, so far away. I want to reach across the space between us,
to touch his arm, his cheek, to pull us together through this awful
moment. "But it doesn't matter, does it?" he says. "You're going
home soon. You can go back to your perfect life, and what I do
here won't matter."

"You're right," I say, straightening. "It doesn't matter." I step
back from the doorway, ready to flee. But I don't really want to
go. "Sorry I bothered you," I say. As I make my way down the
tiled walk, all I can think is: *Stop me. Stop yourself. Don't leave it like
this.*

But he doesn't try to stop me, and I keep walking. From across
the street, I glance back in the dark. Mateo lifts the cat to his chest
and shuts the door, taking with him all the light from within.

CHAPTER SIXTEEN

*A*fter two and a half days of unplanned sulking, marathon Spanish-sitcom watching, and a self-imposed moratorium on all communication devices, I give myself a good talking-to: You can torture yourself, or you can put this whole Mateo thing to rest once and for all and get on with things.

I meet Jamie at her favorite *helado* shop for a double scoop of sensibleness. I don't know if it's her expression when we talk, her right eyebrow rising into a comically Freudian point, or the fact that we have so little history together, but I feel like I can tell her things I barely dare tell myself. Naturally, I leave out all the ridiculous stuff Mateo said about me.

"So he stopped painting and now he just works at that bar?"

"Yep. Andrea said his uncle owns it. It was supposed to be a part-time job while he was in art school." I look at my ice cream cone. There's too much of it. Why did I get dulce de leche? I never get this flavor. It's too sweet. These damn Argentines and their sugar cravings. It must be contagious. I almost never ate sweet things at home. My feet are sticky from the heat. It's too hot for tennis shoes. I should stick with flip-flops from now on, I decide. I turn my gaze out the window. A fat cat strolls by the open door with all the swagger of an L.A. pimp.

"Jeez. Poor guy. That's some serious damage that woman did to him. He sounds really screwed up."

"I know. It's positively tragic." It feels good to get Jamie's confirmation that it is indeed Mateo who's the screwed-up one. I take a long lick of ice cream. Not such a bad flavor, actually. It kind of grows on you.

"Anyway, I was thinking I might want to do a bit of traveling." The idea has just come to me. How's that for doing things that aren't on a spreadsheet?

Jamie's eyebrow arches skeptically. "Why now?"

"Well, Doctor, I've been thinking about that bike I never got . . ."

"Okay, smart-ass." She makes a face.

"I just want to see more of Argentina before I go home," I say seriously. "Which is pretty soon. So do you want to come with me?"

I wait for the litany of reasons why I shouldn't run away from my problems.

"Okay," she says, dabbing the gooey mess with her napkin, her eyebrow sinking into calm repose. "Where shall we go?"

Jamie will be here within the hour, and there are still a few loose ends to tie up. C.J. has researched a few options for letting people post personal ads on the website. We confer via instant messaging and decide to go with the simplest solution. I've already put together a pricing scale—with photo, without photo, etc.—and created an ad for the service to go on the home page. Once the back end is ready, we'll be set to go.

C.J. is psyched. "This could be huge," he writes.

I am slightly less enthusiastic. "Move over, Idealmatch.com," I write, wondering if the sarcasm translates.

I send a mass e-mail to family and friends, letting them know I'll be incommunicado for a week. My paranoid parents have requested my itinerary, so I send that, too. I do, however, ignore my mother's question about my preference in bedding. The great quilt-versus-duvet debate of 2005 will have to wait until I'm back.

I make a quick call to Dan to say goodbye.

"I'd be lying if I said I hope you have fun," he says. Yesterday he offered to come with me. When I said it was going to be a girls' trip, he went online and researched a bunch of "girl" places Jamie and I could go to for fun, like good shopping areas and spas to hit. He really is such a great guy, cute, sweet, considerate—a total catch. He's even hinted at his openness to leaving Boston for the right person. If only I felt . . . more. Everything would be so easy. "The truth is, I hope you have a miserable time and miss me terribly. I miss you already."

"Me, too," I lie kindly. I'm looking forward to getting a break from his sometimes overly enthusiastic wooing. Before I can feel too guilty, I remind myself that this trip might just be the best thing for us. I've taken Dan for granted, but maybe I really will miss him and realize that I am actually madly in love.

Finally, I post a brief "gone fishing" blog, just in case anyone's still reading my personal page. I try to sound as upbeat as possible, though I realize the chance is pretty slim that Mateo will be visiting my blog anymore.

I close my laptop and grab my newly purchased backpack. There's a small twinge of sadness as I shut the lights and close the door behind me. Better get used to that, I tell myself.

Andrea, Jorge, and the dogs are waiting for me downstairs. "We'll miss you," she says, handing me a freezer bag full of home-made muffins for the flight.

"Me, too," I say, meaning it fully.

"But you'll love Mendoza."

"So I've heard."

"All the wine and sunshine you want." She waves her arms around with a Brazilian flourish that tells me she's working her way up to something.

"Mmm," I say.

"Did you say goodbye to all your new friends?" she asks. I don't have to be a brain surgeon to know who she's talking about. He obviously hasn't told her about our fight.

"Everyone but Mateo. I haven't seen him around." I omit the fact that I've done everything in my power to steer clear of him for the past three days.

Andrea smiles thinly and gives me a big hug. For a split second, I could swear I feel two little arms wrap themselves around my leg, but when I look down, Jorge is safely tucked behind his mother's leg.

A car honks outside. I wave to Jamie through the iron gate. One final look at my packing list: passport, wallet, guidebooks, thinly disguised last-minute trip to avoid dealing with . . . things. Check, check, check, check.

Everyone from everywhere who comes to Buenos Aires eventually heads south to Patagonia, with its breathtaking snow-dusted mountains and whales frolicking in the ocean. But there'll be mountains and whales enough for me when I'm home in a month—not to mention plenty of cold. So I've convinced Jamie to come north with me to the deserts of Salta. I've never been to a desert. They say there's snow-white sand as far as the eye can see, and I like the sound of that.

We have to fly into Mendoza, the famous wine region that Mateo once raved about, and rent a car from there. I don't know much about wine, except that I like to drink it, but Jamie is excited to see this popular Argentine vacation spot.

"There are vineyards that date back hundreds and hundreds of years," she says enthusiastically, scanning my guidebook's section on the area. "Just think of how fantastically drunk we can get!"

The last thing I want to do is sit around getting drunk every day and thinking about the kind of things I'll no doubt think about if I sit around and get drunk every day. "I read that there are white-water rafting tours," I counter.

Jamie sticks out her tongue and turns back to the book. "You'll love it," she says.

"Yeah," I say. "So I've heard."

Driving in from the airport, we ask the cab to stop at an ATM. "Lie loose," he tells us, pointing at the ceiling and shaking his head. I ask again, thinking he didn't understand my Spanish. "Lie loose," he repeats. "Lie loose."

"Do I seem particularly uptight, or do they say this to all the tourists?" I whisper.

Jamie laughs and shakes her head.

"What's so funny?" I ask, frowning. She points to a page in her Spanish dictionary. *La luz* means "the light," a slang term for a blackout. The cabbie isn't telling me to lie loose. He's telling me there's a power outage.

I'm not in a very lie-loose kind of mood when we roll up to the hotel I booked online—I'm worried about how we'll register without computer access—but the lovely old converted house puts a smile on my face. Inside, Jamie flits from wallpaper to rug to banister, oohing and aahing at things. Luckily, the power outage doesn't faze the proprietors, who use good old-fashioned paper. No need to worry, they tell us. The power will come back soon.

We take a short power nap—seems fitting—then take turns showering. I put on a cotton dress and flip-flops and try to get in the spirit.

It doesn't take long. Mendoza is an oasis created for the sole intent of its citizens' enjoyment. What else should one expect from winemakers? This must be the most restful place on earth that isn't beside an ocean. Outside the hotel doors, the world is in calm repose. Other travelers are difficult to spot, for everyone seems to take on a slow pace here, strolling the streets, it seems, with no other purpose. The weather is sunny and warm and pleasant. The trees, lush and plentiful, bend happily over the wide tiled sidewalks to offer much-needed shade. At some point in the falling dusk, the power comes back on, but there are no sudden noises or glaring lights to mark its return, nor is there the familiar collective cheer that accompanies the end of a power outage in Seattle or anywhere else in America. As Jamie wisely points out, "You don't need electricity to open a wine bottle."

I give in. We spend the next few days touring vineyards and the next few nights getting drunk on Malbec. (The key, I've discovered, is to drink so much that thinking about anything becomes virtually impossible.) We meet locals and dance until the vine-loving sun comes up and we can start all over again. Consulting Dan's list, we indulge in a spa day at a luxury American hotel where all the products are made from grapes. We eat more than we need, sleep longer than we should, and stay two days longer than intended. By Tuesday, we are plump, polished, and dangerously close to never leaving. I am doing such a good job of forgetting what it is I came all this way to forget that when it comes back to me, it comes back so hard it nearly knocks me to the ground.

Jamie is ordering clams in white-wine sauce in very poor Spanish when a table is seated behind us on the sidewalk. They are a young raucous bunch, and if my language skills were better, I would be glad to listen in on what sounds like a fun conversation. As it is, I pick up only snippets, such as "They're too hungover to come out tonight again" and "I don't want too much cheese on mine." While Jamie goes to survey the salad bar, I piece a silly conversation together in my head, filling in the gaps between their jumbled words.

Do you think the octopus is good here?

Well, I haven't seen it sing, but I hear the dance number is spectacular.

Good. I'm bored of beef.

Yes, he really should have retired years ago.

I am thus amusing myself when several of them look up and exclaim, "Mateo!"

I swear, my heart stops for a second. It's not him, of course. Turning around slowly, I see a short young man with long shaggy hair approach the table. I shake my head and laugh at myself. What did I think? That he found out I had run off and flew across the country to track me down?

I don't want to think about it, but the table makes that difficult. The next few minutes of their conversation go something like this: Blah blah blah Mateo blah blah blah blah Mateo blah blah Mateo blah. The memory of him standing in his doorway that night, so angry and cold, floods my mind. *You shut out everything and everyone that isn't on some spreadsheet.* It isn't true, is it? I don't shut people out. I tried to be his friend, didn't I? I wanted to let him in. Just because I take control of my life doesn't mean I have control issues. I'm a strong woman, and I guess Mateo doesn't know how to deal with that. If he'd rather hide away in his house, lock up his feelings, who's stopping him?

"Oh, Mateo!" a pretty young woman with long dark hair squeals, throwing her arms around her shaggy-haired friend. *"Te quiero,"* she coos.

"Te quiero," he says back with a big smile. He takes a thin gold chain out of a small box in her hand, and she lifts up her hair while he threads it around her neck. They lean in and kiss. Their friends clap enthusiastically.

Jamie returns with an empty plate. "I was about to get a massive salad when I saw this woman chowing down on a huge plate of pasta," she says. "Suddenly, it's all I can think about."

"Must be nice," I mumble.

"What?"

"I need to go somewhere else." I stand up, looking around for my cardigan. I need to get away from here. Really, really far away.

"Okay, I think I saw another nice-looking restaurant at the end of the block."

"No, I mean I think we should leave tomorrow."

She looks at me for a moment. I don't blink. "All right," she says, grabbing a piece of bread from our table and tossing down a couple of pesos. "There's only so much fun one person can stand, anyway."

The next morning we rise early for the first time in days. I rent us a Jeep and buy a detailed map book of the region that's as thick as an atlas. Later, Jamie will have a good laugh at the fact that there's only one road all the way from here to there. Still, we manage to get lost. Twice.

The first time we end up in a town that, except for a modern bank and a billboard advertising a new Wal-Mart being built in Mendoza, looks like part of a Hollywood set for an old Mexican town. As I think this, a man rides by on a cart pulled by a real, live donkey. "We're straddling two centuries here," I say to Jamie, who's captivated by the tiled sidewalk.

"Do they tile everything in this country?" she asks rhetorically. She's traded a pair of rubber flip-flops for a gas station attendant's straw cowboy hat. It sits low on the back of her head, poised to fall off. Out here near the desert, we're easing comfortably into our Thelma and Louise personas.

"Only if it's standing still."

"Then let's keep moving."

Half an hour later, we meet a withering old man with no front teeth who tells us in thick Chilean Spanish that we have missed our exit by twenty kilometers. After assuring us that we haven't landed in Chile, he offers to rent us the floor of his kitchen for the night. There's also the snake that tries to hitch a ride when we stop for lunch at a nearby roadside diner. We decline both proposals as politely as possible.

"Drive that way until you hit sand," advises a tall Englishman who tells us he's been living in Argentina since the mid-1970s. He waits at an imaginary bus stop outside the second town—if you can call a diner, gas station, and church a town—in blistering heat, wearing a Peruvian poncho and a pair of red bell-bottoms. "Can't miss it."

"Bet he wishes he could say the same for the past two decades," Jamie whispers as we drive away, waving over our shoulders.

Our British guide was right about the desert, though. When we find it, it makes itself obvious. Brown earth abruptly gives way to nothing but white. A line drawn with sand.

We stop in the middle of the road, wordless, understanding that some things need no saying.

Before long, sand is everywhere. Here, there, behind you, beside you, in your hair, between your toes, under your tongue. It coats the world like a dusting of sugar. The whiteness is stunning. Stunning and breathtaking and startlingly quiet.

I didn't plan on so much quiet. And I didn't plan on how disquieting quiet could be. No longer drowned out by winery guides or raucous partyers or the din of restaurants, that last conversation with Mateo, running on a loop in the back of my mind, grows louder and louder, demanding to be heard. I talk endlessly to Jamie about the desert's beauty, read aloud from the guidebook about the different rock formations in the distance and the impossible alien plants that speckle the white plains. Inside, I am saying to Mateo and Jeff and anyone else who's ever doubted me, Look at me doing something wild and unplanned and uncontrolled. Look at me living my life without fear.

As the sun dips, the air cools sharply. Our romantic vision of sleeping under a desert sky gets revised. We spend our night at a motel that looks constructed from cardboard.

After a meal of barbecued mystery meat at the only restaurant in town, we sit poolside, sweaters tugged around our torsos, sipping cold sodas. Our sneakered feet hang over the edge. There's no water, only drifts of sand at the bottom. I am crafting a catalog of the pleasures of the desert: sand, dryness, lack of wetness, sand . . .

"What are we doing here?" Jamie interrupts.

"We're drinking sodas?"

"What are *you* doing here?" Jamie cocks her hat to the side and looks at me squarely. She's trying to hone her cowboy look, but it's the look of psychic mothers and seasoned high school principals.

"I don't know, Thelma. Seeing the desert, realigning my aura. What do you think I'm doing here?"

"I think you're running away." The eyebrow again. As silly as it looks arching up like that under the straw hat, that damn eyebrow sees right down through me.

"From what, exactly?"

"You tell me."

"Nothing to tell."

"Bullshit."

"You know, you should really work on your bedside manner."

"Avoiding," she says.

"Annoying," I sing.

"Suit yourself." She throws her head back and sucks down the rest of her Coke. "I'm going to bed."

At night the desert is so quiet it's deafening. Bundled under the extra blankets brought by the small dark silent woman who runs the motel, Jamie falls asleep almost immediately: I can tell from the snore that's become so familiar on this short trip, a soft puh-puh-puh as though she's stuttering in her sleep. What might she be trying to say? I wonder. Possibilities? Persephone? Peanut butter?

I wish I could sleep that easy, but my head is buzzing with questions. What *am* I doing here? Am I running away? Of course I am. But from what? Mateo's harsh comments? Dan's unwanted affection? An in-box devoid of job offers? All of the above? And what has this accomplished? How will things be any different when I go back? This debris of failure that seems to coat everything I touch now will still be waiting for me.

Why did Mateo's words cut so deeply? It was nothing I haven't heard before. And his opinion is inconsequential, isn't it? I mean, who is he to me? He doesn't know me or understand me at all, has no idea who I am or why I've made the choices I have. So what if he's gorgeous and smart and talented and funny? A lot of good all that does him, hiding away in that house. Where does he get off making judgments about how other people live their lives? Following a life plan isn't giving up. It's just good sense. It keeps me from making bad decisions, like falling for emotionally unavailable foreign men. So what if I sometimes have a tight feeling in my chest when he's around? That doesn't mean anything. That's just physical attraction, right? So what if I always look for him in the neighborhood, if I feel slightly disappointed when we go to El Taller and he isn't working, if I get a little excited when I hear a squeaky hinge in Andrea's house because that means he might be by to fix it soon. That's a little crush, isn't it? And so what if I wish he were here right now, talking me down off this mental ledge, wrapping his long arms around me, kissing the back of my neck, whispering my name in my ear, rocking me to sleep so I can dream about things as harmless as peanut butter. That's just, that's just . . .

"Jamie?" I whisper. Then louder: "Jamie."

She throws an arm violently over her chest. It makes a smacking sound

"Jamie?"

She shifts and snorts. "Hmph?"

"Jamie, are you awake?" I feel bad, but I can't stop now.

"I am now."

"Sorry."

"What's up?"

"I *am* running away from something." Funny how it's so much easier to say things in the dark. It's almost like I'm not saying them at all, like tomorrow they won't have been said. "I'm running away from Mateo."

"Why?"

"We sort of had a fight before I left."

"Must have been some fight."

I flick on the bedside lamp and reach down to the floor for my backpack. I retrieve the folded newspaper clipping from inside my passport and hand it to her. She rubs one eye and squints into the bright light.

"Hey, that's your website!"

"Yeah."

"What is this?" She unfolds the page. "The *Clarín*? You're in the *Clarín*. Holy shit. That's great."

"I know."

"But what does this have to do with Mateo?"

I bring her up to speed. She listens without adding a single psychotherapy sound bite.

"So what do you think? Any way to recover from this one, or should I give up?"

Jamie looks at the clipping intently and hands it back to me. She shifts onto her back again, shielding her eyes from the light. I watch her carefully but can't decipher the body language. I think I like the quips and wisecracks better.

"Give up, right?" I say. "That's what you're saying. Right, you're right. He probably hates me now."

"Did you notice that article is from October?" she says.

"No. Why?"

"I don't know. I thought it might interest you that he's kept the thing so long, that's all."

"Oh. Oh . . ." He kept the article. Why did he keep the article? It was pinned to something behind his door, a bulletin board, I assume. Does that mean anything? Or perhaps the right question is, *did* it mean anything?

I turn off the light and lean back against the hard foam pillow.

"Cassie?"

"Yeah."

"You do realize that you love this guy?"

I cross my arms over my chest, as if this will protect me from what's coming next. "Oh, fuck, Jamie. I do, don't I? I love him."

The words explode inside me, sting my stomach, ears, eyes. Saying those words is everything good and bad and scary and wonderful and awful. Really awful. Saying them is no good to anyone. I'm not just veering off The Plan here, I'm leaping off a cliff into the crashing waves and sharp rocks below. I want to suck those words back inside, but it's too late. They won't come back. It's true. I love Mateo. I do. I love him. Love everything about him, from the bounce in his curly black hair to the devilish curl of his lips when he's teasing me. Even that horrible fight, standing in the doorway of his house, each word between us was a stinging barb, but still I hated to end it, so thrilled was I to be near him. Even now, thousands of miles away, I ache. I've never felt like this before, never hurt, hoped, wanted like this before. I can't love him, but I do. Four weeks before I go home, and look what I've gone and done. I can't seem to get anything right anymore.

I shake my head, a vain gesture in the desert dark. "I fucking love him, Jamie. Fuck, fuck, fuck."

CHAPTER SEVENTEEN

*E*verything seems different. The city is alight with the coming Christmas season, colored bulbs and plastic holly strung over doorways, under awnings, around trees and lampposts. The days are longer and hotter than ever. Coal briquettes in the *asados* seem redundant at this point. And I am in love with Mateo.

An impossible, irresponsible, unrelenting love. I'm tangled in it. It stops sleep and clouds waking. It seeps into my conversations, and I lose track of what I mean to say. I lose track of where I am. I stare into space. I alternately stalk and avoid all places where Mateo might be, skulking around corners and ducking behind shrubbery every time I see a mass of curly black hair.

Two days into my cloak-and-dagger routine, I discover it's all in vain. Jamie says Mateo hasn't been at El Taller all week—a waiter said he's on vacation—so I can start coming to club nights anytime. Andrea hasn't said a word, but it must be true. I stalk the pink and blue house much of Tuesday and part of Wednesday but see only the cats lolling about in the sun.

Angry, I log on to Buenosairesbrokenheartsclub.com under a pseudonym and interrupt someone's lament on her failed relationship: "Why are we all sitting around our computers complaining about some guy or girl who treated us bad and whining about how we wish we had some new guy or girl who would treat us just as badly? What's so great about love, anyway?"

My comment gets twenty-two responses in two hours, most of them gushing sentimental schlock that I could have picked up in a card shop. But one reply gets to me a little. "The great thing about love," writes YeatsFan32@globalnet.com, "is that it makes you feel like you can do anything."

I stop reading the comments after that.

I am not thinking about it.

There are nineteen days left until I go home.

I am not thinking about that, either.

Which is difficult, as my mother calls constantly to arrange the plans for my homecoming. My childhood bedroom has recently been taken over by her stair climber and craft station, so she's making space for me in the downstairs guest room. She wants to know if I prefer a firm mattress, how many dresser drawers I'll need, whether I'll mind if the dog sleeps in there with me—he thinks of it as his room.

"It doesn't matter," I always say, not to be difficult, but simply because it doesn't.

I have sent e-mails to almost every person I know in Seattle in hopes of unearthing a job lead. So far, two people have invited me to join their pyramid scheme, and a guy I dated briefly in college has offered me a gig as his personal assistant, nudity optional. "Gee, thanks," I write back, "but didn't I already have that job? I seem to recall late hours and subpar benefits."

I try to muster a tad more excitement for C.J., who is thrilled that after launching our new personal ad service on the website, we already have eighteen ads bought and paid for. At five dollars an ad per month, divided between the two of us, it's not quite enough to retire on, but I could buy myself a nice umbrella when I get back to Seattle. I'm surprised to find I'm disappointed. What did I expect? That my site could be the next Idealmatch.com? It wasn't about the money, I remind myself. I wanted to help people fall in love. And there's always hope that BigBoy@usamail.com will find the "chronic cuddler" he's looking for. Good thing I didn't add multimedia empire to the plan. I don't need another thing on there to remind me of how little I've managed to get right.

"Give it some time to catch on," C.J. writes over MSN. I tell him not to quit his day job. It's bad enough that Sam and Trish's latest trend newsletter is touting Buenosairesbrokenheartsclub.com as "a new organic approach to online dating" and "a Web trend to watch." Letting myself down may be getting to be old hat, but letting my friends down is not something I want to get used to.

It's all very depressing, in a daytime-talk-show sort of way. I throw myself into anything that will offer the relief of distraction. I return to El Taller with gusto, the life of the party again with exaggerated tales of Jamie's and my adventures in the wild Argentine desert. I make detailed lists of souvenirs left to buy. I help Andrea get ready for Martin's holiday homecoming. I bake my famous shortbread cookies. I bathe the dogs, soaking myself in the process, much to Jorge's delight. I loop the banister with garlands and string greeting cards above the fireplace—something Andrea learned from Mateo's tales of Christmas in Chicago, she tells me cautiously. "My family did that, too," I say merrily and change the subject to popcorn garlands. When I'm not helping around the house, I go for long walks with my digital camera and take pictures of absolutely everything.

I even let Dan drag me all over the city for a few days, checking off things from his must-see list. I've been making excuses not to see him since I got back—feeling like a complete and total fraud around him—but it's his last week in Buenos Aires. Besides, I tell myself, a few daytime outings can't do any harm.

Monday we subway to Puerto Madero, the city's docks. Recently refurbished, the area is new and white and clean. Once you've surveyed the water in either direction, there isn't much else to see, so we drink cold beers at a stand on the boardwalk and shield ourselves from the sun with laminated menus. I make a point of using the word "friend" a lot, as in "Well, friend, that's enough beer for me," and punch him in the arm a couple of times like I've seen Trish's brother do to her.

Tuesday we visit Evita's grave. Zoey was right—the famed tomb is rather unremarkable, with its sober black marble and simple engraved lettering. But the cemetery in general doesn't disappoint. Grand sloping trees, Gothic angels, and—like Zoey said—rotting caskets so close you could touch them if you wanted. It all makes for an eerie walk, despite the noon sun overhead and the mews of grave cats sprawling in the heat. I snap a couple dozen digital photos. Dan with Evita. Dan with cats. Dan pretending to touch a casket.

"I missed you when you were gone," he says while I fiddle with the light settings.

"Well you better get used to it," I say as jovially as possible, punching him in the arm again. "Word has it Boston is pretty far from Seattle." I feel like a jerk, but Dan just smiles and strikes a goofy pose in front of an ornate cross. "Hurry up, woman. You're wasting my light."

Wednesday we spend an afternoon window-shopping in the posh neighborhood of Recoleta, eating *helado* and talking about the heat. The shops are beautiful, each display holding an immaculate collection of merchandise I can't afford. One small outdoor mall has run its sidewalk with red carpet.

"I feel underdressed," I say.

"You look lovely," he says with all sincerity. "As always."

Dan is the one who looks lovely, dressed in cream-colored linen pants and a white shirt that shows off his not offensively large muscles. His hair is perfectly coiffed into waves. He's gotten a bit of a tan these last few weeks, I notice. Other women notice, too. Wherever we go, female eyes seem to follow. And they don't even know how good he is on paper, I remind myself. If I hadn't been derailed by pointless feelings for Mateo, I surely would have fallen for Dan a long time ago. We always have fun together. We have tons in common. The few times we had sex, it was nice. Happy unions have been formed on less. And it would be so easy. Dan is plug-and-play, ready-to-wear. There are no deep secrets, no trolleys full of baggage to stumble over in the dark. He never talks about his ex anymore. He chose to move on and that's exactly what he did. These are the qualities I'm looking for. These are the qualities I've written down in The Plan.

"Aw, shucks," I say and make a face. I'd punch his arm, but he's too far away.

Dan walks ahead, then stops at a jewelry store to admire a row of men's watches.

"See something you like?" I ask.

He turns to face me. "I certainly do."

I blush, feeling instantly embarrassed and awkward. How sad that statements like this don't fill me with glee. I look through the glass at the selection. "That red croc band is pretty sharp. Or the brown one—more classic."

"Everything's nice," he says. "If you could pick one thing from this window, what would it be?" Dan is always asking me questions like this, as though we are speed-dating. In the past three months, I've discovered that I would live in Italy first, then France; would rather be a rock star than a movie star; and want to come back as a horse. It's best, I've learned, to go along with the game.

"Hmmm. Just one, huh? I know what I definitely wouldn't pick." I point to the large diamond set in yellow gold near the front.

"Too big?"

"Too Jeff. My engagement ring was almost identical."

Dan nods, understanding. Dan always understands.

"It's funny," I say with a sardonic chuckle. "Half my life, I wanted a ring like that. I saw a picture of one like it in a catalog that came to our house, you know, one of those fancy Christmas flyers. My mom and I picked it out." We'd torn the page out of the catalog and put it in my jewelry box, like a wish. "Seems kind of strange now. I was only fifteen. I hadn't even had a real boyfriend yet, but I knew I would get that ring someday."

"And you did."

"Yeah." I smile, thinking of how I paid for this trip. "I sure did."

"So if not that ring, which one?"

The question surprises me. The kind of ring I got was so important to me all those years, was one of the first things I wrote in the original plan, and yet I haven't even thought about such things since I've been here. Too busy sorting out the more pressing questions, I guess. "I don't know. Haven't thought about it. Maybe . . . that one." I tap the glass near the middle of the display. A demure square diamond, simple white-gold band. The opposite of what I've always wanted.

"Excellent choice, madam," he says in a bad English accent, and we move on to mock a display of bejeweled pet accessories. "For the dog who has everything," Dan jokes.

"When kibble isn't good enough." I chuckle. See, I am genuinely having fun.

Thursday's activities are my choice. I take Dan to the old café downtown, where elderly waiters in black vests and red bow ties serve strong coffee with delicate cookies. He marvels at the memorabilia on the walls. Every inch of wall is covered with old posters announcing the jazz and tango bands that played here decades ago, yellowing soda ads encased behind glass, and trumpets and trombones strung about. The Christmas decorations are nothing compared to the gleaming attraction of these ancient treasures.

We have four cafés con leche, a chicken sandwich, lima bean soup, and three chocolate *medialunas* between us. Dan talks about Boston, its historic neighborhoods, his friends, the nightlife, the Red Sox. I'd love it there, he says. Everybody does. I'm jealous of his excitement. I try to conjure this enthusiasm for Seattle, to tell

Dan about the things I love back home, but I sound like I'm reading from a tourist brochure.

"You miss it," he says, nodding with empathy.

"What's not to miss?" I say, shivering slightly.

"Are you cold?" he asks. "Those fans are doing too good a job."

"Yeah," I say and wrap my hands around the hot cup in front of me for comfort.

When lunch is done and I can't possibly eat another bite, I offer to take Dan to the English bookstore I found a few months back so he can buy something to read on the marathon plane ride home. After we've wandered in circles for twenty minutes and I've relived the first day of my Spanish lessons, I reluctantly admit that I've forgotten where it is. I ask at a newspaper stand, but the man has no idea.

"That's okay," Dan says cheerily. "As long as I can sit down for a minute, I'm happy." And he is. Thinking back over the months, I can't remember Dan ever getting upset or bothered about anything. Dan pulls at his sideburns, which means he's thinking. "We passed a park a couple of blocks back, didn't we?"

I nod and follow him back the way we came. As he passes a group of women eating their lunch on a bench, all heads swivel his way.

"You know, you're going to make some lucky girl very happy one day," I say.

He looks over at me, grins, and shakes his head. He points across the street. "There it is."

I stop abruptly. Plaza de Mayo. The Madres. I can see the top of the small obelisk that they circle every Thursday afternoon. I think of those old women taking slow, arthritic steps around the monument, Augustina and her grandmother Leonora gushing over me the last time I was here, the numerous e-mails they've sent thanking me for my help. The newspaper article. Mateo. So much for distraction.

"Let's go somewhere else," I say. I want to stay and see the Madres, but I can't.

"Where?"

I try to remember the list of places that I absolutely had to see, but I draw a blank. "How about there?" I point to a sketchy-looking restaurant across the street. "I'm kind of hungry."

"Already?"

I shrug.

"Come on." Dan grabs my hand and pulls me in the direction of the park. "I'll buy you a bag of those candy peanuts you love so much."

"No, really, let's go somewhere else."

"What's going on?" Dan steps back and gives me a good look.

"Nothing." He's not buying it, but he drops it. He's so easygoing that way. Oh, why can't I like him more? He's perfect for me. There is something seriously wrong with me. I must be a masochist, falling only for guys with the potential to break my heart. Like him, I tell myself, for God's sake, like him. Like him like him like him. If only it were that simple.

"Okay," he says. He threads his fingers through mine, and I let him. "Whatever your heart desires."

What my heart desires. I'm thinking of this as I help Jamie pack. Like Dan, she's almost giddy, talking about home. "This is gonna be perfect for New Year's," she says, holding up a sequined halter dress we found at the craft fair near the cemetery. "Did I tell you about the massive party my friend is organizing? Vancouver isn't known for its wild nightlife, but there's this restaurant with a courtyard and they put all those little lights up in the trees. Very glam. You know, I've never been single on New Year's Eve before. Not ever. I can't wait. Just me, my friends, and all those cute boys in suits . . . Do you think this purse goes?" She holds a black satin clutch against the dress. I nod encouragement. "But you know what I'm really looking forward to? My bed. God, I miss it. That's one relationship I can't live without."

Although I smile at the joke, when she turns to tuck the purse into a suitcase, my smile folds. As our last afternoon ticks away, I should be getting sad; instead I'm jealous. Leaving is easy for her. She had a great time here, and she's excited to go home. She's been here only a month, I remind myself. It would never occur to her to think any differently. Buenos Aires is another place she can check off her list. She can pack it all up and take it with her—dresses to wear, photos and stories to share, souvenirs to display, and nothing left behind but unwanted guilt about leaving her fiancé.

Jamie catches my sour face. "Thinking about him again?"

"No." Still, in a way, she's right. I am thinking about Mateo because I am always thinking about Mateo. He's always there, on my brain, under my tongue, in the pit of my stomach. But I might never see him again, and I've got to come to terms with that. It wasn't meant to be. It was three galaxies over from meant to be. "I told you, I'm going home in three weeks. Period. End of story."

"Okay . . ." She looks around at the pile of clothes on the bed and grabs a pair of short red boots. "Then let's talk about how fabulous I'm going to look in these."

Her taxi comes sooner than expected. While the driver risks dislocating a disk trying to get her giant suitcase into the trunk, Jamie gives me a big squeeze at the curb. I am accosted by shopping bags dangling from every shoulder and elbow. "Ouch," I say, and we laugh. She shimmies into the backseat, and I shut the door for her.

"We'll always have Buenos Aires," she says through the window and blows me a kiss. The taxi pulls away, and I hold back my tears until I'm certain Jamie won't be able to see me crying. *We'll always have Buenos Aires.* It's normal to be sad, I tell myself. It didn't turn out to be quite so awful here. There are things I'll miss. Places. People. All perfectly normal.

I walk to the closest busy street and hail my own ride home. A few blocks from the yellow house, I reach into my purse for my wallet. Tucked in between the bills is a note, scribbled on the back of a sales receipt in Jamie's barely legible pseudo-doctor script:

A good psychotherapist never gives advice. But screw it. I'm no therapist. So here goes . . . You are an amazing person, Cassie Moore, and you deserve everything you want from life. But love doesn't come on schedule. Or in the right place or the right time, the right size or the right color. It just comes. Take it from someone who knows. If you wait around for what you think you need, you might miss out on what you really want. Be brave, chica. XOXO Jamie

Romantic poison, my mother would call it, the kind of Hallmark sentiment that sucks the reality out of a woman. I leave the note on the seat beside me, retrieve five pesos from my wallet, and thank the driver. And then, hand on the car door, I reach back and grab the scrap of paper, stuffing it into my purse and swearing under my breath.

Right about now Jamie is waking up in her own bed in her own bedroom in her own apartment to what is, no doubt, a perfect moment of pure bliss. Thousands of miles away, I am standing in front of a mirror that doesn't belong to me in an apartment full of someone else's things, getting ready for the wrong man.

I'm wearing the Antonio dress again, but tonight it's for Dan. He's called four times to confirm our plans for his last night. He won't tell me what we're doing, but I'm supposed to dress up. I twist my hair into an unsuccessful bun. The crown is bumpy and there's a big chunk of hair at the front that refuses to stay back. I take charge with a comb and a liberal dusting of hair spray. How is it that Argentine women always manage to look simultaneously flawless and effortless? Anna probably doesn't even use hair spray.

No doubt she wakes up every morning looking like she stepped out of a hair salon.

Dan arrives at exactly seven o'clock, looking quite handsome in a pale gray suit and blue tie. "You look beautiful," he says.

"So do you. I can't believe you brought a suit all the way from Boston."

"I didn't," he says.

Dan ushers me into the waiting taxi. He still won't say where we're going, even insists on covering my eyes for the last minute of the ride. My eyes open to bright marquee lights. A poster in front of the theater advertises tonight's tango show. It might as well have the words "tourist trap" written across it.

"Oh," I say. "How wonderful."

"Is this okay?" He looks concerned. I smile brightly. "You told me once that seeing one of these shows was near the top of your list."

"My list? Of course." Seems like a million years ago that I made that list. "No, this is great, really. I'm just so surprised."

"That was the idea." Dan's chest puffs with pleasure. "Well, then." He offers an elbow. "Shall we?"

The room is packed with tourists, easily identified by their un-kempt blond hair, slogan T-shirts, and menu squinting. No one is as dressed up as we are. We make the best of it, eating too much and drinking even more. The lights dim to signal the start of the show. Dan's hand squeezes mine in the dark and I squeeze back. It doesn't spark so much as a tingle. She doesn't know it yet, but one day some lucky woman in Boston is going to be thankful for that fact.

Touristy or not, the show is spectacular. Men in tight black pants and shirts and shiny patent-leather shoes move with smooth confidence. Women with red lipstick and hair slicked into tight buns float across the stage, their ruffled dresses fluttering bird-like. The choreography and music are raw, sexual, dangerous, but the dancers' faces remain stoic, their bodies impossibly graceful. I can't help smiling at my own efforts to learn tango—the two things bear little resemblance. Though with the right partner, the dance didn't seem so daunting. There's no point in thinking about that now, I remind myself. I push away the rest of that evening and focus on this one.

I don't know if it's the tango or the hot summer night or the sweet champagne, but I'm buzzing when we leave the theater. I try to mimic the dancers' steps and almost twist my ankle. I hum those last bars of music that won't leave my head. Da-da-ta-da-da. I feel like skipping. Things aren't looking so bad anymore. I don't protest when Dan suggests we go back to the grungy one-bedroom apartment he shares with an American student he met online. It is his last night, after all.

The apartment is pitch-black and dead quiet. "Like the desert," I whisper.

"What's that?" asks Dan.

"Nothing," I say and stumble over the suitcases lined up in the hall, cursing loudly, then clamping my hand over my mouth. "Sorry," I say, giggling through my fingers.

"It's okay." Dan laughs. "Be as loud as you want. John's gone rock climbing for the weekend."

"You mean we don't have a chaperone?" I ask jokingly.

"No lifeguard on duty," he says into the dark, finding my shoulders.

"Which way to the couch?"

Dan spins me around and gives me a nudge. I grope my way over to the gray outline of the couch and flop down. I sit and wait in the dark. Dan moves down the hall, flicking on a light as he goes. A slice of white carves across the living room's hardwood floor in the shape of a question mark. I hear him fumbling with kitchen things. Sharp metal noises and soft cursing. Finally, he walks in carrying champagne in one hand, glasses in the other. He sets them on the small table in front of me and leans forward to light a couple of candles. Vanilla. The gold light glows and flickers and jumps.

The rest happens too fast. One second Dan is pouring the champagne and talking about how happy he is that he met me, the next he's down on one knee and proffering a small pink box. Before I can process it, there's an enormous square-cut diamond on my hand. I study it in the candlelight. It sits like an alien thing on my finger, big and sparkly and strange.

"It's not the real thing," Dan says quickly. "I went back to that store in Recoleta, but the one you wanted had been sold. This one's the closest thing I could find, but it's not a diamond. We can pick out the real one together when we're back in the States." *Real one. Together. We.* I hear the words, but they aren't adding up into anything I understand. "You can come to Boston, or I can go to Seattle," I hear him say, his voice small, as though from a distance.

"What." It isn't a question, just the only word that comes to mind. It hangs in the air between us for a moment.

"Sorry?" Dan squints at me, trying to decipher.

"What are you saying?"

"Cassie." He grabs my hand. "I'm asking you to marry me."

The details of the scene come into focus. Wax slowly tracking down the candlesticks and oozing onto the tile tabletop. Bubbles rising and bursting inside the two full glasses. Dan perched shakily on one knee. Coldplay warbling sincerely in the background. The scent of vanilla cloying in the hot night. Then something even clearer pulls into view. Dan at my parents' front door, stepping inside, shaking my stepdad's hand, complimenting the spread my mother has put out for us. She's set out the good dishes, the expensive nut mix with no peanuts. She beams at Dan with approval, thrilled at this catch of a man her daughter has landed, all her hard work paying off in one spectacular parental moment.

My stepdad looks on supportively. I see Dan meeting my friends, who adore him instantly, Dan working in the garage on weekends when he's not playing golf, Dan on a beach in Puerto Vallarta. It looks so perfect. Everything is the way I've always thought it would be.

This is it, I tell myself. The drama and confusion of the last few months have been leading me to this moment. It all seems so obvious that this is the way it was supposed to be. Yes, I shout in my head. Yes! Yes! Yes!

The word leaps into my throat.

I choke it back down.

I look at Dan waiting for an answer. He watches me calmly. Why is Dan so calm? I see him again in my parents' house, at backyard barbecues, on the beach. He looks calm there, too. Happy. But how do I look? Am I happy? Content? I can't see myself. Where am I in all those moments? Inside this brilliant plan I've made, where am I?

I need a second to catch my breath. I hold up a finger, but my breath slips away. The buzzing starts in my ears; it's soft, but I can hear it. My chest contracts slightly. I press my hand to my breastbone. A tingling in my shoulder. Panic is coming.

"Where am I?" I whisper, the words snagging in my throat. Dan leans in toward me. "Where am I?"

"You're here with me." He crinkles his brow. "Are you okay, sweetie? Too much bubbly, I think."

I look at him and realize that he's right, though not about the champagne. I am here. He is there in Seattle or Boston or wherever, and I am right here in Buenos Aires, watching this other life unfold as though it's happening to someone else. Part of me wants so badly to say yes, to take the easy way out. But I can't. I'm looking at Dan—perfect Dan—and knowing in every cell and corpuscle that the wrong man is kneeling beside me. I force the words out.

"I can't marry you, Dan." The buzzing recedes. Breath comes. I inhale long and deep. It feels like this is the first breath I have ever taken.

"Why not?" His voice is unsure, his eyes pleading and hopeful.

"You're a great guy. A really, really, really great guy. Any woman would be lucky to have you. But I don't . . . I don't love you." I shake my head at myself, both astounded and incredibly proud. I am rejecting the perfect man. I haven't found a job. I will go home broke and alone, with nothing to show for my six months here. None of this has gone the way I expected, but I'll be okay. I came to Buenos Aires all by myself, didn't I? I had no job, no friends, no Spanish. But I found ways to be productive, I made friends, I even learned a bit of the language, to my surprise. I didn't fall apart or run home. I didn't get kidnapped. Someone once told me I am brave, and I'm beginning to think he was right.

"Oh." Dan contemplates this for a minute, still balanced precariously on one knee. I'm thanking my lucky stars for getting off so easily when he stands up and paces the floor. Then he stops and holds up his hand.

"Hold on. Wait. Why can't this work? We want all the same things. Your plan, the whole thing, it could have been me who wrote that stuff. And I can give you all of it, every single thing. Home, family, everything you want."

My plan. The thought of it makes me weary. I think of the note in my purse on the floor near the door. *Love doesn't come on schedule. Or in the right place or the right time, the right size or the right color.* I look down at my fidgeting hands, at the water-stained floor, at the chipped polish on my left big toe. These imperfect things are real, not some spreadsheet on a computer. I didn't plan to be sitting here on this couch saying no to a marriage proposal to a dear, sweet man, but these are the moments that make up a life, for better or worse. "I was wrong," I say. "It's not enough. It's not everything."

Dan slumps onto the couch beside me, nearly knocking over one of the candlesticks. He takes my hand. The fake ring digs into my skin. Our faces are inches apart; I can feel his breath on my forehead. Every part of me is trembling. It's not just Dan I'm letting go of here. I'm letting go of an idea of myself. It feels terrifying and crazy and really, really, really good. "I don't get it," he says, shaking his head. "We're perfect for each other."

"Maybe you're right," I say. "But I think I'm done with perfect."

The second I get back to my apartment, I fire up my laptop. I haven't decided if I'm having a breakthrough or a breakdown. Either way, there's no time to lose. I locate ThePlan2.xls on my hard drive and highlight it. I do the same to ThePlan1.xls, ThePlan1b.xls, and ThePlan1bBackup.xls, to make sure. With my hand, my arm, my entire body shaking, my finger hovers over the delete button. I can do this, I tell myself. I am already doing it.

CHAPTER EIGHTEEN

*T*hree mornings in a row, I wake up and tell myself, This is the day I talk to Mateo. The time left until I go home is ticking down fast, and I hate the thought of leaving things the way they are between us. Even Dan and I have promised to keep in contact as friends, although I half suspect the first (and perhaps only) correspondence from him will be a wedding announcement in the not too distant future. It's not that I expect to get birthday cards from Mateo, but it would make me feel a lot better if I knew there wasn't someone on the other side of the world who hated me. It doesn't matter who was right or who was wrong, I tell myself. I can be the bigger person. I'll apologize for what I said, for what I wrote, for sticking my nose in where it doesn't belong. Who doesn't like to hear that he's right? My courage bolstered, I get dressed, head outside, and start walking in the direction of the pink and blue house. A few blocks from my destination, the doubt starts. What if Mateo refuses to listen? What if he won't talk to me? Or worse, what if he doesn't care one way or another? So every day I wake up and tell myself, This is the day I talk to Mateo, and every morning I lose my nerve.

Thankfully, Andrea's house is full of distractions. Christmas is still two weeks away, but Martin is home again, so there is no shortage of reasons to celebrate. Each day is filled with music and laughter and the scent of lavish meals. The five pounds I lost over the last six months by walking everywhere are put back on easily, thanks to the endless spreads of baked goods, roast meats, and red wine. "You live only once," Andrea scolds when I refuse yet another plate of cookies.

"You're right," I say, taking the biggest cookie on the plate. The soft, buttery shortbread melts in my mouth. I decide then and there to give up on talking to Mateo. I've got better things to do with the time I've got left here.

Today, with me as her sous chef, Andrea is preparing a Brazilian feast, while Martin and Jorge put the final touches on the giant tree in the salon. After dinner, with one tired little boy tucked into his bed upstairs, we sip maté around the tree. The lights twinkle gold against homemade paper decorations. Argentine holiday music plays gently. The happy reunited couple snuggles on the love seat. They hold hands, kiss each other on the forehead. I stretch out on the chaise with Lola at my feet, her soft fur tickling my bare toes. Andrea tells stories about Brazil at Christmastime. Martin fills me in on local customs. No one mentions our absent fourth party or the fact that I leave in six days.

The holiday music follows as I climb the stairs to my apartment. While I undress for bed, I can hear Andrea and Martin through the open courtyard doors, cooing sweetly to each other. Life isn't perfect—they hardly see each other—but they are a couple in love.

Tucking under the covers, I catch the glint from Dan's ring on the nightstand. "A souvenir," he had said, pushing it into my hand before I stepped into the waiting cab that night. I didn't want to keep it, but now I'm glad I did. It is a souvenir, though not of Dan and me. This ring, I've decided, will be my talisman against bad decisions, my icon of imperfection and all its joys.

I toss and turn in bed thanks to too much maté. When I finally fall asleep, I dream I'm at the Buenos Aires airport, checking in for my flight. Are those your bags? the lady asks. I shake my head.

I don't recognize them. They're the wrong size and the wrong color. There are too many. Dozens and dozens of tiny red bags. The people in line behind me are getting irate, shouting things in Spanish. I open the bags one by one, as fast as I can, but can't find anything that looks remotely familiar. The airline lady tells me I can't take them with me if they aren't mine. Just as the security men are carting me off, I see a big blue suitcase. My suitcase. That one's mine, I try to explain. That one right there on top. But no one is listening.

I open my eyes, and they go instantly to the corner of the apartment, where I've lined up my suitcases. Two large blue bags, already packed, and one empty small black carry-on. I shake my head. It's the third time I've had this dream, and it's starting to make me feel more neurotic than usual. When I looked it up on three new-age dream sites, I learned that luggage in a dream suggests the start of a journey. No freaking kidding.

The sound of giggling in the hall is a welcome disruption of my morning self-analysis session. Andrea and Martin at it again, I assume. But when I throw on a robe and open the door, I find Jorge and the dogs. He wraps his hand around two of my fingers and pulls me toward the stairs. Andrea and Martin are in the kitchen feeding each other breakfast. I hesitate at the door, but Jorge pulls me down into a chair and crawls up on my lap, a warm, live squirming teddy bear.

Andrea claps her hands and laughs. "Somebody's made a friend."

"And it only took six months," I say, laughing. Andrea shakes her head and squeezes his fat forearm affectionately. I want to squeeze the whole of him, but am worried this might scare him off. Jorge ignores us all, focusing his attention on the sugared *medialunas* set out on the table beyond his reach.

"He knows you are one of us," says Andrea. How bittersweet to finally belong now that I'm leaving. "Did you sleep okay?"

"*Más o menos,*" I say. Martin raises an appreciative eyebrow at my Spanish.

"Are you hungry?" Andrea pushes the plate of pastries toward me. I pop a piece of *medialuna* in my mouth, then tear off half for Jorge. I pour myself a cup of coffee from the carafe. Martin passes me the milk. Andrea passes me the sugar. Jorge smiles up at me, his lips coated with sugar. If you didn't know any better, you might think we were family.

"So, Cassie, what you will do on this beautiful Thursday?" Martin asks.

"Is it Thursday?" I ask offhandedly, as though I'm not counting down the days on my Outlook calendar. My last Thursday. *El jueves final.* I don't need a plan to tell me I've got something left to do. "I think I'll take a walk." Jorge chews on his chunk of the *medialuna* and smiles up at me approvingly.

I arrive at the Plaza de Mayo in the late afternoon. The Madres have already begun their slow, steady march around the monument. The older women shuffle along, some supported at their elbows by younger versions of themselves. Mothers, wives, and sisters linked arm in arm. As on the first day I saw them here, they chat, laugh, gesture, shake their heads as they walk. Even for these stubborn women who won't give up, life goes on.

A few young student types recline on the grass and watch the strange, marvelous spectacle. I inch my way forward and settle on a nearby bench. From this distance, I can see the faces on the placards the women carry. In some cases, I can read the names and ages of the disappeared. Augustina rounds the obelisk with her grandmother. She looks my way, and I wave. She waves back and turns to her grandmother. Offering the old woman's arm to another marcher, Augustina heads my way.

"I didn't want to interrupt," I say as she approaches, startled that she would break from the circle of women for my sake.

"No, please, I am happy to see you. You didn't answer my last e-mail."

"I'm sorry. I've been busy. I'm going home soon."

"Home?" She tilts her head and looks at me as though this idea of "home" is nonsensical.

"America?" I say.

"This is too bad." She tilts her head the other way, then shrugs. "But you are here now."

"Yes. I wanted to say goodbye."

She waves the idea away with both hands. "Okay, okay, there is time after for goodbye. Now you come walk with us." Augustina stretches her hand out to me.

"What? Oh, no. Really, I couldn't. But thank you."

"Are all Americans this much shy?" She laughs and grabs me by the wrist, pulling me toward the obelisk and the marching women. My body is yanked forward. This small Argentine woman is stronger than she looks. *"Vayamos."*

As we get closer to the Madres, I bow my head, more from embarrassment than deference. I'm hoping we will slip quietly into a gap in the crowd and attract little attention. But no such luck. The circle breaks slightly where we enter. All heads turn to make sense of me, this blond American woman, this intruder.

"I don't belong here," I whisper. Augustina shakes her head and squeezes my arm.

"Madres," she announces loudly, *"ella es* Cassie Moore." A murmur of excitement percolates. I hear my name said over and over, mutating slightly while it goes around the monument, as in some surreal game of telephone. An ancient woman, even older than Augustina's grandmother, locks her arm through mine. "Well come," she says slowly, tapping her fingers on mine, smiling a gap-toothed smile. "Well come Cassie Moore." The women nod in approval, and the circle of warm bodies closes back in around us.

Augustina bumps her shoulder against mine and smiles. "They think you belong."

The subway rocks its way through the city. I let my body be loose, let it rock along, and think of those women opening their arms to me, enfolding me in their sacred circle. I feel blessed. There's no other word for it. I enjoy the feeling, let the tears come warm and fast without the usual self-reproach. A teenage girl sitting alone and reading a book asks if I am okay. I nod to reassure her, but this only makes me cry harder, which in turn makes me laugh. She smiles gently and goes back to her book.

When I open the door to the yellow house, I see a figure in the entrance wearing overalls and balancing on a ladder. My heart sinks when the man turns his head and I see that it is just Martin replacing a chandelier lightbulb in the foyer.

"*Hola,* Cassie."

"*Hola,*" I say, trying to sound cheerful. "*Hola, chicos,*" I call out to the dogs, who are nestled against one another in a corner like puppies. Lola lazily slaps her tail against the floor tiles, but no one comes up to greet me with the usual sloppy kisses and soft head butts.

"Don't take this personally," Martin says, smiling from the top of the stepladder. "Jorge runs them all day. We went to the plaza."

"Sounds like fun."

"Oh, yes." He unscrews the offending bulb and holds it out at arm's length, patting his various pockets with his free hand. "Always. And how was your walk?"

"Wonderful." I peer into the giant toolbox under the ladder and locate the package of new bulbs. I pass him one, smiling to myself. "Best walk I've ever taken."

The moment I step into the apartment, I can hear the IM going wild. Exhausted, I don't feel like talking to anyone, virtually or otherwise. I lie down for a quick nap, but the pinging sound continues. I rise again, snorting my displeasure. The blue icon jumps excitedly in the corner of the screen. It's C.J., and judging from the trail of IM messages, he's been trying to get ahold of me for a while.

I type. "I'm here. What's up?"

"Swedish company. Big VP. Sponsorship! Call now!" He messages as if he's out of breath.

"Easy, tiger. Can you expand a bit?"

"Check your e-mail."

I find his forwarded message in my jammed in-box.

Subject: Website Sponsor Proposal

Dear Website Operator or Owner,

Please be advised that the SVadko Company of Stockholm, Sweden, has interest in being a sponsor of your website: www.buenosairesbrokenheartsclub.com. We take several opportunities such as this in a year and would today be happy to talk to you about this exciting proposal. We believe that your website would be an ideal match for our company and its objectives. Would you please discuss this opportunity with us at the below number?

Sincerely,
Johan Karlsson
Director, Global Marketing

Isn't SVadko that premium vodka company? I think. This has to be a joke, a crank e-mail, some sort of hoax. I look up the company's website, and the domain name does match the one in the e-mail sender's address. I check the contact page. There's a Johan Karlsson listed, and the phone number is the same as the one at the bottom of the message.

Okay, so it's not a joke, but it must be some mistake. What would they want with my little website? I put together a few sponsorship deals for Idealmatch.com, and they were huge. Not we-can-all-cash-our-stock-options-and-retire-in-the-Bahamas huge, but definitely I-can-finally-buy-the-fully-loaded-BMW huge. I read the e-mail again, vaguely aware of the IM pinging in the background and the icon hopping up and down impatiently.

"Hello? Are you there? Have you fainted?"

"I'm here," I write. "I'm definitely here."

"This is huge!"

I tell C.J. not to get too excited until I figure out what's what. But my hands are shaking as I dial the SVadko number. When a receptionist answers in Swedish, I nearly pee my pants.

Thankfully, she speaks English and transfers me to Mr. Karlsson. While holding, I tap my foot nervously to a Muzak version of ABBA's "Dancing Queen." My hands are shaking. This could mean my own apartment in Seattle. No parents, no guest room, no senile dog for a roommate. This could mean my own business. C.J. and I taking the online dating world by storm, turning it on its head. My old boss coming to me for a job. This could mean Jeff having to eat everything he ever said about me. Predictable? Structured? Unchallenging? I don't think so.

This could mean staying in Buenos Aires.

I sit back in the chair and let the thought sink in. Staying in Buenos Aires. Staying in Buenos Aires? Where did that come from? The idea has never crossed my mind, not really, not seriously. The second my plane took off from Seattle, I instantly missed everything about home. My family, Sam and Trish, happy hour at Jimmy's, the wharf, the market, four-dollar coffees, my own pillow, the rain. I ached for all of it. But what about Andrea and Jorge, El Taller, the cat park, one-dollar coffees, the sun? A thousand blue suitcases couldn't hold these things. I still miss Seattle, but the missing has a sort of sweetness to it now, like remembering an old friend you've lost touch with but know you'll see again. And then there's this place, this Buenos Aires, this magical city on the wrong side of the world. I love this city. Despite everything that's happened—and not happened—with Mateo, I love Buenos Aires. I barely know it and I love it. I want to know it better. I want to be old friends.

Could I stay? Could I do it?

This is usually the point where I'd start making a pro-and-con list, but this time I don't have to. I want to stay. I do. Oh, jeez, I want to stay in Buenos Aires. I want to stay. Of course I want to stay. There is no internal debate, only a series of questions whose answers get me more and more excited about the idea. What will I do? Whatever I want. Where will I live? Here if I can, somewhere else if I can't. Is this about Mateo? I'd be an idiot if it were. Is this forever? I don't know about forever, don't even want to think about forever. But today. Yes, definitely, today.

"Miss Moore?" a man's voice cracks through the receiver.

"I can stay!" I shout. "I am going to stay!"

"How wonderful for you," the man says in a posh Swedish accent. "But stay where?"

Turns out I am not too predictable or perfect or a control freak or unadventurous or boring or dull. I am not an ex-fiancée, ex-employee, ex-anything. I am not a disappointment, not a big fat failure. I am a website entrepreneur genius and, according to the marketing department at SVadko, the creator of "a distinct niche online product with deep branding potential." I am Cassie Moore, American, world citizen, and global heart-mender. All this time, I'd been waiting for the wrong kind of proposal.

Contracts are being written up at this moment. Europe's third largest producer of premium vodka will soon become the exclusive sponsor of Buenosairesbrokenheartsclub.com, with an option to renew after six months.

And that's what I've got, too—an option to renew.

I need to tell someone before I burst. Andrea is napping. Sam and Trish will still be in bed at this hour. I'm not ready to spring it on my parents. I suppose I could try Zoey or Jamie online, but there's really only one person I want to talk to. Okay, so the thought of knocking on his door and talking to him in person still makes my heart race, and not in a good way, but that's what phones are for.

I dial Mateo's number, holding my breath while it rings. No answer, only a beep. "Mateo, it's Cassie." I say this part calmly, but the rest bursts out. "I know it's been awhile since we've talked, and maybe you don't want to talk to me anymore, I don't even know if you're in the country, but if you are in the country and you haven't written our friendship off completely, I've got great news and I . . . I need to tell you."

An hour passes and Mateo hasn't called back. Two hours. Three. I eat the slightly crunchy remnants of day-old pasta, send e-mail announcements of the good news to friends, and confer with C.J., who is not quite quitting his day job but is picking out a new car on the Jetta website. I call my parents and decide as the phone is ringing not to tell them the news yet. I mean, what am I supposed to say? *Hi, guys, I'm not coming home for a while. Staying here indefinitely, as a matter of fact. Merry Christmas!* No, best to let my mother have a few more unspoiled days of redecorating the guest room and making homemade holiday wrapping paper. When my stepdad gets on the phone, I ask if he's heard any good jokes lately and laugh loudly when he tells me two I've heard from him a dozen times before.

The apartment is stiflingly hot today. I cope by stripping down to my T-shirt and underwear. Hungry again, I make a salad out of some browning iceberg and half a tomato. I'm stuffing a wad of it into my mouth when the phone rings. My heart pole-vaults into my throat, and I nearly choke on a leaf of lettuce. I wipe my mouth as I look for the phone. I can't find it. It rings a second time. How can I not find it! I've been waiting for it to ring for hours, and I don't know where the stupid thing is? I rifle through papers on my desk. Nothing. It rings a third time, my last chance before voice mail. The ring is muffled slightly. The bed! I extract it from the folds of fluffy duvet. "Hello!" I gasp into the receiver. "I'm here!"

"And apparently that's where you're staying." It's Trish, sounding a bit sleepy. "I just checked my e-mail. What the heck is going on?"

Disappointed it's not Mateo but still happy to hear her voice, I get comfy on the sofa and tell her about Dan's proposal, the sponsorship, walking with the Madres, deleting The Plan. The call must be costing her a small fortune, but she lets me lay out every detail. "Mhm," she says now and then, or "Aha."

At the end, I ask the question I'm afraid to have answered. "Do you think I'm crazy?" She's silent on the other end. "Come on, Trish. You're killing me. What do you think?"

"What do I think? I think I'm gonna miss you like hell. I also think it's about time. Hallefuckinglujah."

After I hang up, I check voice mail. No messages. Another hour passes, and no more calls come. But I can't think about that. I have other things to think about—like finding a place to live.

Jorge's day care is closed for the holidays, so Andrea has hauled out a chest of arts-and-crafts supplies to keep him busy. I offer to help, drawing on my vast knowledge gleaned from working at a day care for a summer in college. We are cutting snowflakes from folded paper when I ask how she'd feel about extending my lease on the apartment.

Andrea throws up her arms, scissors flailing dangerously, and shrieks, "Oh, Cassie! You stay!" Seconds later, I am sandwiched between her and Jorge, and we are all jumping up and down. "Cassie stays!" she shouts. "Cassie stays!"

When the hugging and jumping and shouting have subsided, we talk about my decision while stringing paper snowflakes around the courtyard. They flap gracefully in the breeze. As I help Jorge string twine through the delicate holes in a snowflake, Andrea reaches over and pats my hand. "I didn't say anything before, but I didn't want you to go," she says. "It is like having my sister here, *¿entiende?* You are our family."

"*Sí,*" I say, filling to the brim with love. "*Entiendo.*"

Still, it doesn't really hit me until I go upstairs to make some dinner.

I am home.

I look in the fridge. My fridge, I think with a smile. My fridge is empty. I walk to the grocery store. My grocery store, I think. I see the security gate pulled across the glass doors. My grocery store is closed.

I turn and head for the bigger store a few blocks south. Practically sprinting, I reach it with a full fifteen minutes to spare. I grab a basket and hit the pasta aisle. Rounding the corner at full speed, I nearly collide with another woman who's just as rushed to fill her cart before closing. We say our apologies, laughing loudly, and I move aside to let her pass. That's when I see him standing there looking at me.

The sight of him stuns my system. Dark hair, brown skin, pink lips, green eyes. I'd forgotten how beautiful he is. But it's more than that. When I look at him, I see everything we were and everything we could be. Talking, laughing, debating, telling jokes, eating ice cream, carrying grocery bags, gazing, touching, kissing, wanting—it's all there written on the surface of his skin. I don't want to be his friend. I want him in every way possible but that.

"Cassie." He looks a bit stunned himself. "*Hola.*"

"*Hola,*" I say, barely above a whisper.

We move toward each other cautiously. It's been a long time, and harsh words were spoken, but all I want to do is throw my arms around him.

"I called you," I say.

"Yes," he says. "I heard your message."

"Oh. Okay. Right." God, I'm an idiot. He doesn't want to talk to me. Doesn't want to be my friend. Doesn't want to be my anything. "Well, then, good to see you." I turn to walk away.

"Is everything okay?"

"What?" He cares! Thank God he cares! "Yes—more than okay. Mateo, the most amazing thing has happened."

He listens to the sponsorship story without a word. "That's wonderful," he says when I finally stop for a breath. He smiles softly and shakes his head. "Really wonderful. I'm so happy for you, Cassie."

"That's not all." I hold my breath for a few seconds. "I've decided not to go home. I'm going to stay in Buenos Aires."

He looks up, clearly surprised. "What?"

"I'm staying here."

"For how long?"

"I don't know." I smile at him broadly. "I've decided to wing it."

"But your plan?"

"I've given it up."

Mateo turns his head, and eyes me skeptically. Every romantic movie I've ever seen flashes through my mind. There is always that scene where something is revealed—some mistake, some fear, some easily surmountable problem—and that revelation removes all barriers to true love. And I've done it. I've fixed the problem, let go of The Plan, let go of everything. There are no barriers to us, no more obstacles. I am ready to be swept up.

"A good friend once told me I was a brave woman."

He smiles at me warmly but doesn't speak, doesn't move forward, doesn't sweep me up in his arms. Why doesn't he sweep me up in his arms? Is he still angry? His expression isn't one of anger, but if that isn't it, what is it? God, I'm such an idiot. I haven't seen him in weeks, and what's the first thing I do? Jump into my fabulous news. He probably hates me, and here I am going on and on about myself. I should be apologizing for all the presumptuous things I said at his door that night, the awful things he had to read on my blog.

"Mateo, I'm sorry. That night, everything I said. I had no business telling you how to—"

"No," he cuts me off, shaking his head, holding up his hand. "No, I don't want your apology." His voice is gentle, but the words sting nonetheless. My heart sinks into my socks. I don't know what to say to make him forgive me. If only I could explain. Standing here in the pasta aisle, with Argentine Muzak playing in the background, and a gangly teenager noisily restocking jars of sauce a few feet away, I want to tell Mateo everything I've been scared to say because it isn't scary anymore. I want to say I love him. I want to ask if he loves me, too.

"Mateo, I—"

"Mateo?" someone calls before I can finish. "Mateo?" Anna appears behind him. There you are, she says in Spanish. She looks at me with a pleasant smile of recognition. "*Hola*, Cassie."

"*Hola*, Anna," I say, forcing a smile.

Anna puts her hand on Mateo's arm and tugs gently. "*Se está cerrado pronto*," she says. The store is closing.

"I've got to go," he says sheepishly, his eyes to the floor. It doesn't matter that I'm staying, it doesn't matter that I've given up The Plan. I'm too late.

"Sure," I say. "Me, too."

I don't go anywhere, just stand there staring at the empty space where Mateo was. The aisles clear. The ringing and chirping of cash registers stop. There's a rumble behind me, the gangly teenager yanking at the metal security gate.

"*Lo siento, chica.*" A tall man in a polyester vest taps me softly on the shoulder. "*Se está cerrado.*"

I look down at my basket. There's no way I'm leaving here empty-handed. I grab the closest package of ravioli from the refrigerated case, shove five pesos into the manager's hand, and walk out the door.

CHAPTER NINETEEN

I allow myself one good cry over my plate of cheese ravioli, and that's it. The old Cassie might have indulged in a weeklong pity party, but the Buenos Aires Cassie has too much going for her to let a little heartbreak slow her down. Come morning, I throw open the French doors to a beautiful December day, step onto my Juliet balcony into the sunlight, and greet the morning with a smile. At first I fake it, but within a few seconds I am surprised to find it happening naturally. The fact that I am smiling makes me smile even more.

Sure, it might seem on first glance that I shouldn't have anything to smile about, that I am right back where I started. Heartbroken and alone in a foreign country. Yet, strangely, I'm not scared. Sad, yes, that things didn't work out with Mateo, but not scared. I am a Web genius, entrepreneur, virtual matchmaker. And tan, I think, examining the lovely golden sheen of my forearm.

This feeling of satisfaction seems to be sticking around, so after a bit of breakfast, I phone my parents and wait until they're both on the phone to deliver the news. I haven't even gotten to the part about how, if the website takes off, we might create versions for a bunch of different countries when my mother interrupts.

"What about all our plans?" I know she's talking about more than Christmas dinner, more than redecorating the guest room.

"I'm sorry, Mom. I didn't expect any of this. But for the first time in forever, I'm really, really excited about something."

"Is there a man? Are you staying in that god-awful country for some Hispanic gigolo?"

"No, I can honestly say that I'm not staying because of a man."

"Then I don't understand you."

I can't help but laugh. My mother is not impressed.

"This is ridiculous," she snaps. "You're coming home in three days. It says right here in your itinerary—flight four-five-seven, arriving December eighteenth at six-forty-five P.M. Period. End of story."

"No, Mom," I reply with as much composure as possible. I know this is the last thing she expected to hear today. "Not end of story." Beginning of story, in fact. "I'm staying here."

"I can't talk to you if you're going to be ridiculous. Call me when you're thinking straight." She hangs up. My stepdad is still on the line but doesn't say a word.

"I'm sorry," I say. I've upset her, and he's the one who has to live with her. "I hope I haven't ruined Christmas for you."

"I'll talk to her," he says, calm as always. It's hard to tell what he's thinking. Nothing ever seems to faze him. "It'll be fine."

"Thanks," I say, knowing he's right. It will be fine. "So . . . got any good jokes?"

"I'd be lying if I said I wasn't worried about you, kiddo," he says instead. "But I'm proud of you. I want you to know that."

"Thanks, Dad," I say, choking back the beginning of tears. "I'm proud of me, too."

With everything settled one way or the other, I can concentrate my energy on the website. Getting the sponsorship deal meant agreeing to create a new home page that would accommodate the SVadko logo, but there are also a few enhancements that C.J. and I can now justify spending time on, including a search engine for personal ads and, more exciting, our very own instant-messaging system so members can connect to one another in real time.

I've even hired one of those cyber cowboys (aka freelance design-ers) from back home to give the overall look a bit more polish.

C.J. and I work like crazy for a week straight, but it's worth it. The site looks amazing, SVadko is thrilled, and the fan e-mail is al-ready pouring in from our members. When everything's done, we send out a joint press release to every relevant media outlet, from *Cosmopolitan* to Webweekly.com. An editor from *Seattle* magazine responds almost instantly. They love the local angle and want to interview me by phone after the holidays. As I fire off a reply, I can't help wondering what my old boss at Idealmatch.com would say if she saw me now. Then again, who cares?

When there's no work left to do, I reward myself with a cold drink at El Taller. If I don't show my face there soon, I've decided, I'll never be able to again, and that simply won't do. Instead of taking my usual spot near the window, I tuck into an armchair in the back corner. From here I have an unobstructed view of the entire café. The room is decked out in kitschy Christmas deco-rations, furry garlands, foil bells, and colored lights everywhere. Most tables are filled, and the waitstaff moves around the room with more hustle than usual. One wears a Santa hat. There is a new waitress I've never seen before. There is no Mateo.

The new waitress brings me a bottle of beer and a cheese om-elet. I sip the beer slowly, closing my eyes to fully enjoy the sen-sation of cold liquid sliding down my throat. Sensing someone nearby, I open my eyes. The waitress with the tattooed arm is wiping down the table beside mine and looking at me.

"*Lo siento,*" she says. "*¿Te llama Cassie, sí?*"

"*Sí,*" I say.

"*¿Y está interesado en las pinturas de Mateo, sí?*"

Yes, I say, I was interested in his paintings.

Do I like the new one? she asks, pointing at the wall behind and above me.

I turn and see what she's talking about, a new painting completely different from the others in the room but similar to the one in Andrea's house. The colors are mostly bold blues and bright yellows, with a dark punch of green here and there. It is spectacular, full of life and energy, full of hope. I was so worried about running into Mateo that I didn't even notice it.

"*Es maravilloso,*" I say. It truly is marvelous. He's painting again. Maybe something I said got through to him after all. I guess Anna can thank me for that someday.

The tattooed waitress smiles and nods and moves on to clear the next table. When her back is to me, I reach up and touch the canvas. The paint is still tacky to the touch; it leaves a bit of green on my fingertips and a small smile across my lips.

The morning before Christmas Eve, I help Andrea get a head start on dinner. We need to eat early (meaning before eleven P.M.), she says, if we're going to make the neighborhood street party tonight. There's already a huge pot of stuffing bubbling away on the stove.

"Why so much?" I ask.

"We will be twelve this year," she says, adding chopped onions to melted butter in a saucepan. "The neighbors on that side, Martin's parents, Mateo . . ." She doesn't look at me, just takes my hand and places it on a spoon and says, "Keep stirring."

"Oh, is he coming?" I ask casually, stirring as directed. "That's nice. I assume he will be bringing Anna?"

Andrea adds a handful of chopped apple to the onion and butter. "Anna? I don't think so. His sister takes Christmas with her husband's family in Uruguay."

"His sister?"

"*Sí.*"

His sister! His sister! Of course his sister. She came back from the States a few years ago. She married an architect from Montevideo. Her name is Anna. He'd told me about her months ago. How did I not make the connection? All this time and it was his sister. I'd feel like a complete ass if I weren't so happy. Anna is Mateo's sister! I want to scream it from the roof. I want to do cartwheels.

My mind crashes to a stop. If Anna is his sister, why is he avoiding me? Why didn't he return my phone call? I don't know, but I'm not making the same mistake twice. This time I'll ask.

"Keep stirring, please, or it burns," Andrea says. I look down at the spitting saucepan. Bits of apple and onion stick to everything, including my T-shirt.

"Andrea, I'm so sorry, but I've really got to go."

She turns to face me, smiling her all-knowing smile. "Go, *chica*," she says, laughing. "Go! Go!"

I throw my arms around her and squeeze tight. Her great Brazilian laugh follows me out the door.

I run all the way to his house, so fast I miss it. I stop at the end of his block, turn, and walk back to 2257. Am I seeing things? There's no pink and blue house anymore. It's been painted green, like the painting but lighter. I step through the creaky iron gate and walk down the tile path and up to the wall. I reach out and touch the wall. It leaves green paint on my fingertips.

"It was my hardest piece." The front door opens, and Mateo leans against the frame, smiling. His overalls are covered in every kind of green. "It took me over twelve years to finish."

"I saw the one in El Taller. It's wonderful, really wonderful. I'm so happy for you."

"Did you come to critique my work?"

"No, I came to . . ." Tell you I know about Anna. Tell you I've been an idiot. Tell you I love you. "I needed to tell you . . ."

"Come inside," he says, holding out his hand to me. "There's something I want you to see."

I step inside the green house and follow him into a dark room. Mateo pulls back the curtains, and light floods in. Except for a simple wood chair in one corner, there is no furniture, only easels and paints and canvases. Dozens of paintings in various sizes and in varying states of completion line the perimeter of the room.

"There are more," he says, taking my hand and leading me into the kitchen. The sink is full of dirty dishes, the floor littered with take-out boxes. And the counter is covered in canvases.

"Wait," he says. "There are more." He pulls me to the second floor. We pass canvases in the hall, up the stairs, into a bedroom.

"There must be a hundred of them," I whisper.

"One hundred and three," he says.

"What happened?"

"You happened." Mateo takes my other hand and turns me toward him. The intensity of his green eyes sends a shiver through my body.

"I inspired you?"

"Not exactly," he says, laughing. I blush. "When you came here that night, I was furious. I needed to do something with all that anger. The first one wasn't a very good piece, but I couldn't stop. A lot of it was bad, but I needed to do it so I could get back to something good again."

"Then I guess I'm glad I made you hate me." I try to look away, but he won't let me, holds my face in his hands.

"No, Cassie, no. I hated . . ." His voice catches. I look up, and his eyes are heavy with tears. "I hated myself. I hated what you saw in me."

Tears roll from his deep green eyes. He tries to look away, but I won't let him. I hold his face close to mine, so close we are almost kissing.

"Ever since I came to your door that first morning, you have amazed me over and over again."

"I have?"

Mateo laughs softly and shakes his head. "You must have noticed how I was always trying so hard to impress you. Always talking about important things and taking you to important places. But when I found your website, I knew I would never be enough for you the way I was."

"*You* were trying to impress *me*?" I think of all the time we spent together, from our trip to the MALBA to the tango lesson, me always saying and doing the exact wrong thing.

"Of course," he says. "But it was always you who was impressing me."

"Why didn't you tell me all this when I saw you at the supermarket?"

"I wasn't ready," he says. "I was so proud of you, I wanted you to be proud of me, too."

That's it. I draw him to me. His dark curls fall into my eyes. I run my green-tipped fingers across his cheek.

Our mouths open, eyes close. Heart beats against heart. Lips meet lips. Tongue touches tongue. It is our second kiss, our first kiss, every kiss. It is the kiss to begin all kisses. It is a kiss brimming with the promise of something I've yet to dream of. I've deleted the future that haunted me, and he's erased the past that haunted him. There is no plan, no past, and no future. Just these two people, this moment, this kiss.

I look down at a stack of canvases beside us and whisper, "I really hope there's a bed under there."

He laughs and lifts the canvases off the mattress. Then he sweeps me off my feet and lays me on the bed. Every part of me quivers. It is nothing I've ever known before, this feeling. It is impossible, irresponsible, imperfect, and unrelenting.

"Mateo," I whisper. "Would it be horrible of me to say that I love you?"

The word is too small to contain what I feel for this man in this place at this moment in time, but it's all I have.

"I love you, too," he whispers back.

And when he says the word, when we've both spoken it out

loud, it swells to contain us. I don't want him to make things perfect, I only want him.

I hold out my arms to him. He stops at the end of the bed and looks at me gravely. "But," he says, "I still don't know what comes next."

"Anything we want," I say, taking his hand and pulling him down beside me. "Anything at all."

It's been almost two months since a club night at El Taller. With the holidays behind us, I figure it's about time to start again. I post an invite on the website to all the Broken Hearts in the area. The following Friday night, twenty-seven people pour into the café, the biggest group ever. They are all strangers.

I give everyone the chance to order and introduce themselves to the people sitting beside them. When all the glasses are full, I stand up and wait until I catch everyone's attention. A hush falls around the table. Every eye is on me. Some of these people will become friends; most I'll never see again after tonight. I am in a country thousands of miles from where I started. I take a deep breath and begin.

"Welcome to the Buenos Aires Broken Hearts Club," I say. The table erupts into cheering. "My name is Cassie." More cheering. "But I guess you already know that."

When the laughter dies down, I raise my glass. From behind the bar, where he's training the new manager, Mateo raises a glass of water and smiles. I smile back at him, a founding if silent member, and begin.

"Here's to the ones we love." To my surprise, a chorus of voices joins in. "Here's to the ones who love us. Here's to the ones we love who don't love us. Hell, screw them all, here's to us!"

The table bursts into laughter and cheering and glass clinking against glass.

I let out a slow breath. I have come a long way. Thousands of miles, six months, one marriage proposal, countless good friends, an old plan, a new plan, no plan, a new business, a surrogate family, a man who loves me and believes in me, a man I love and believe in. I am unsure and unsteady and occasionally convinced I've gone insane because I don't know what the future holds—and I like that more and more. Whatever comes, I'll be okay. I have learned that even a life shattered into a million pieces can be put back together, better than new. I have discovered that I am brave.

As I sit down, a pretty brunette beside me leans in.

"I'm Kate," she says abruptly. "Is that your boyfriend?" She points to the bar.

"I guess he is," I say, smiling.

"Let me get this straight. You live here, run your own website, *and* have a gorgeous Argentine boyfriend?"

I nod.

"So, basically"—she leans in closer, her eyes lighting up—"your life is perfect."

"Oh, Kate." I burst into laughter. "What an awful thing to say."

Like my main character, Cassie, I spent several, shall I say enlightening, months in Buenos Aires. Unlike Cassie, I never had much of a plan before, during, or after that time—unless you consider tearing pages out of a guidebook and shoving them into my pocket planning. This characteristic lack of foresight might explain why I got married at twenty-two and divorced at twenty-eight (the only true casualty being my parents' hope that I would ever settle down); why I got my Master's in English Literature (anything to prolong entry into the real world); and why I've changed hair color more often than Sarah Jessica Parker (will switching to Carmel Golden Blond No. 63 actually change my life? I think so!).

Yet somehow, despite or perhaps because of the zigs and zags my path has taken, I've managed to end up at a fairly good place. Indeed, had I the foresight to make a plan I might very well have planned for this exact life. Okay, I'm unmarried, I still rent, and I don't have a nine-to-five job. But on the upside, I'm unmarried, I still rent, and I don't have a nine-to-five job. Which is to say, also like Cassie, I've found happiness in unexpected places. So here's my hard-earned advice for those of you tottering along your own winding road: Be true to yourself whether you follow a plan, follow your dreams, or follow the cute cowboy in the red pickup. And always, always, do a strand test first.

J Morrison

TOP 5 TIPS
FOR *Female Travelers*

1 Do not assume people in foreign countries don't understand English. They will assume you are an idiot, and by
shouting things like "Internet? Internet?" you only confirm
their suspicion.

2 Do assume people in foreign countries will instantly dislike
you for being a loud, brash American who shouts things
like "Internet? Internet?" You can either prove them wrong
or pretend you are from Uzbekistan or Canada or some
other fake-sounding place.

3 Accept that you will forget your toothbrush, run out of
tampons, and break the strap on your only pair of leather
sandals; be grateful that these will likely be your worst ca-
tastrophes; and take a credit card with lots of room on it.

4 Say yes to the chicken bus. Say no to the street meat. A stay
in the local hospital is not the adventure your travel agent
was talking about.

5 There will be nights when you find yourself hungry or
lonely or both. Keep a bar of very good chocolate on hand
for just such emergencies.

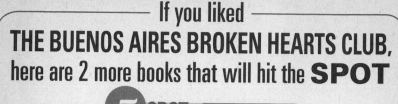